The Visitor

C000155951

Angela McKenna

ISBN: 9798568395997

PUBLISHNATION
www.publishnation.co.uk

Thank you to Christine Aitchison, Deborah Best and Nicola "Wee Nickie" Craig, for all their support and suggestions.

Chapter One

Secrets and Lies

Ingrid stared into the bathroom mirror and bit hard on her bottom lip as she ran a critical eye over the old woman peering at her from the other side of the glass. She told herself the woman was a fake and she tilted her head to the left and then pulled it back to the right, hoping a quick shift in position would trick the impostor, but it didn't. The old woman staring back at her was clever and she was quick, matching every manoeuvre without effort and leaving Ingrid with no alternative but to accept she was indeed, transforming into her own mother. Brushing a hand over the extra lines which gathered in tight formation and in ever increasing numbers around her eyes, she allowed her fingers to count the passing years and she drifted, thinking once more about mamma and her awful loss.

Pain was something Ingrid always believed she could bear, more so after giving birth to three children, one of them weighing in at over thirteen pounds and with a head the size of a football. From that day, and she would never forget it for as long as she lived, she was convinced she could cope with anything life threw at her but life, as it so often does, found a way to prove her not just wrong, but spectacularly so. It was just over two years since mamma passed but the burning loss still felt fresh and memories of nursing her ravaged body remained potent enough to disturb even the most settled sleep. Towards the end, and it had been a long, wretched end, Ingrid had finally understood the meaning of true pain as she watched mamma fade before her eyes. In better times she had been like a shining star who could illuminate a room with just the twinkle in her eyes and a few, kind words but in the tight space between one shallow breath and the loud silence which followed it, her light slipped away. What remained to fill the gaping hole she left behind, was miserable agony and with it, realisation that the torment would not be an ephemeral thing.

Stepping over the loose bundle of her nightdress, Ingrid stretched into the shower cubicle and flicked the steel control bar before snatching her hand back from the freezing torrent of unheated water. She waited for a few moments before inserting an outstretched hand back into the flow, hoping for the best but prepared as always to find not a degree of difference. Any genuine expectations of the ancient boiler's prowess had long been abandoned and today, like every day, it had not by some quirk or by dark magic become more efficient overnight because the water, as she expected, remained stone cold. Experience had established it was likely to stay that way just long enough for prickles of goose flesh to appear although not for so long that it would be worth trekking into the bedroom to seek out the comfort of a robe. So, she waited, arms about herself for warmth and lost, cold settling around the outside of her much as it had settled around the inside of her when mamma died. She had just started to convince herself that the boiler had finally given up the ghost when she heard a loud thump from the pipes, three times in quick succession, and the shower head announced a change in pressure by squealing at her, before the water settled back into its hypnotic thrum. Ingrid smiled, pleased, and relieved, to see steam spreading over the glass and before the boiler had time to change its mind, she stepped inside and sighed again, this time in pleasure as the warm water cascaded over her darkening blond hair. This was another loss; once golden hair reduced by time to a muddy shade of nothing special. She could have it coloured of course, but things being what they were she didn't believe it would make her feel any better and in truth, she hadn't found much joy in anything since long before her mother died. Playing with these thoughts she finished her shower without lingering and rubbed herself dry with a faded, grey towel, its condition synonymous with much else in the house in need of attention. Like everything else, it would have to wait for now. She wrapped the towel around her torso and headed for her bedroom to dress.

***

Throwing the wet towel on the stool next to the wardrobe, Ingrid pulled on a pair of plain, black knickers then turned her

2

focus to the day ahead, delighted that it was laundry day, the highlight of her week and one which gave her another opportunity to get hot, uncomfortable and damp and to risk injury by venturing into Oskar's room to change his bedding. She could hardly contain her excitement at the thought but she cautioned herself to be serious and to dress in a manner appropriate for the labour ahead because Oskar's space wasn't somewhere you ventured without the protection of thick-soled footwear, not if you had any sense anyway. Trying not to think about what her feet had encountered in previous unprotected excursions, she began rummaging through a bundle of T-shirts and after a few false positives she found what she was looking for, a black, cotton V-neck that would help her cope with the persistent hot flashes still plaguing her despite the internet, and her doctor, giving assurances they would long since have disappeared. Shaking her head, she nudged the drawer closed with her hip then slipped the shirt on and headed across to the bed to get her jeans. As she slid into them, she looked back over her shoulder towards the chest of drawers, her eyes creasing as her mind toyed with the incongruity it had encountered just moments ago. The confusion, such as it was, didn't last long and even as she began to retrace her steps, a smile was tugging at the corners of her mouth because she knew what she would find when she yanked the drawer open and pulled back the concealing layers of black and white cotton. It would be a photograph, an old one, taken on a...now, what did they call it again? The name threatened to elude her and for a few seconds she stood with eyes closed and her hands steepled, as though praying for the return of the errant memory. Then, from nowhere, and with what felt like an almost audible snap, it was there; *Instamatic*. The photograph was taken on an Instamatic camera. She opened her eyes and slid the middle drawer open, revealing the treasure within, a frisson of excitement running through her at the sight of the small rectangle of faded colour churned up from its hiding place when she was fishing for something suitable to wear. As she stared at it, not yet daring to touch it, she imagined a fishing boat fighting against heavy seas, the nets straining not only with the weight of the day's catch but also with the weight of something dangerous, perhaps, an unexploded bomb left over from a long-forgotten war. The image came to her unbidden, or so it appeared, but it wasn't as far removed from reality as it at first seemed. As she stooped to pluck the photograph from its nest, she considered how damaging it could still be if it found its way into the wrong hands, its explosive nature one factor in its long-term concealment. She should have destroyed it many years ago and had been on the verge of doing so more than once but somehow, she always pulled back from taking the final, irrevocable step, perhaps convinced the casual eye would make very little of the three ordinary looking people frozen in time together. Her eyes drank in the scene, a tall blond man hugging a smaller, dark haired woman, and Ingrid herself, all of them holding up champagne glasses and laughing. She remembered the photograph being taken and then, the moment when everything changed. It was supposed to be a silly thing, a dance to make everyone laugh and there was no doubting its success on that score, but for the dancers themselves, they discovered the hint of a spark between them and took the first step towards a joyous intoxication that led both to the brink of destruction. Ingrid ran her finger over the photo, almost able to taste the champagne, almost hearing the laughter of the unseen crowd of friends hidden from the eye of the camera, the little Instamatic. She smiled, basking for a second in the glow of the past but the smile began to fade almost as soon as it formed and she found her lips pressed into a tight line as she refused to allow herself to keep to her train of thought. If she did that, she knew where it would lead and in the end, it was all just a memory, fed by nostalgia and romanticised by a broken heart. It no longer mattered; nothing much did. With a deep breath she bent and slid the photo back into its hiding place, taking care to wedge it face down before covering it with a T-shirt and nudging the drawer closed, shutting off the past once more.

Time was marching and the day was at risk of getting away from her so Ingrid grabbed a hairband from the bedside cabinet and wound her way across the room to stand before the wall mirror, tying her hair back in a loose ponytail and applying some light moisturiser to her face in what she accepted was a futile attempt to hold back the tides of time. She looked tired and old, and she knew Gary thought so too because he was very fond of telling her. Glancing at the photo of the two of them which sat to her left on the dresser, she reached to pick it up but hesitated, her hand resting on top of the frame. She stared at Gary's smiling face for a few moments, her jaw clenched, bristling at the memory of the last conversation they'd had before he left again for work. It hadn't taken too many years of marriage for her to realise Gary's face rarely matched his words and the photo in front of her was a good example, taken less than a year ago and no more than a few hours after they had fought their way through another afternoon. And yet, there he was, smiling like a champion. At this thought, Ingrid yanked the frame from the dresser, leaned over and threw it with force into the nearby bin, enjoying the satisfying sound of breaking glass. Then she gave herself a final look over in the mirror before deciding she looked as good as she could and that it would have to be enough because laundry wouldn't do itself. With that, she headed downstairs.

***

"Hey Oskar, what's got you so busy down there?" Sophie stood, hands in pockets, looking down at the huge frame of her baby brother squatting beside the fridge. She forced a smile onto her face, in no way unhappy to see him, but careful nonetheless to ensure he saw what she wanted him to see.

"Mmm... Mum thinks we might have mice so I'm on mousetrap duty. Dirty job, but as the man of the house it's down to me." He grinned up at her and flexed his muscles then ran a hand over the light stubble fighting its way along his jawline. "Go on, Sophe, admit it, I am rather manly."

"You are an idiot," said Sophie, the smile spreading over her face now one of genuine warmth, "do you know that?"

"Of course I know," Oskar's grin broadened and he winked at her, "but I'm a useful idiot so be a sweet sister and pull me up." He brushed away a flop of blond hair from his eyes and thrust a shovel-like hand towards Sophie, who grabbed it and yanked hard, easing him to his feet.

"Good God Oskar, you weigh a ton, what's mum feeding you?"

"Meat, of course," he replied, "I'm a man, so I eat nothing but meat." He flexed

his biceps again. "I drink beer these days too though, when I

5

have the money of course, which isn't often."

"Well, it's lucky for you I brought enough beer for two then." Sophie ran her eyes over her little brother and held her arms out, feeling the need for an embrace but not quite sure why as it hadn't been part of her plan. "Come here and give me a hug, you daft ape."

"I think I can manage that," said Oskar, at once dropping his rugged man look, "but be warned, these lips aren't for family use so don't go all soppy and try for a kiss."

Sophie pretended to hold back the urge to vomit as she stepped towards him. "As if I would kiss your ugly mug," she said, "it's grotesque." She scrunched up her face for effect as he leaned over and pulled her close, then they both stepped apart and laughed.

"It's been a while, Sophe," said Oskar, stuffing his hands deep into the pockets of his

jeans, "mum was on the verge of taking me into town for a new suit to make sure I was presentable at your funeral. Is everything all right?" There was a hint of a smile on his lips.

"Of course it is, why would something be wrong?" Although stung by the barbed comment about her lack of presence, Sophie pushed it to the back of her mind and forced the smile back onto her face, hoping it didn't look fake.

"Well," Oskar's eyes flicked beyond his sister for a second and then back again to meet her gaze, "it's twelve-thirty on a Wednesday and you should be in class. You've got a suitcase with you too." He gestured to the black, wheeled suitcase blocking the kitchen door. "I'm not Sherlock Holmes but..."

"Where's mamma?" Sophie winced at the sharpness of her tone but held steady, determined not to be side-tracked by Oskar's hurt expression and thus be unseated at the first hurdle. She needed all her strength to clear a far more daunting barrier lying in wait for her, quite literally, it was the mother of all fences. "I said, where's mamma?"

"You didn't answer my question which means it's fuck off Oskar time." Oskar's deep voice cracked as he spoke but he straightened his shoulders and didn't look away.

"I didn't tell you to do any such thing, I just..."

"Forget it." Oskar shrugged his shoulders and turned towards

6

the direction of the hallway. "Mum's in the utility," he paused for a second, shaking his head, "Wednesday's laundry day again after a brief flirtation with Friday nights. It was quite exciting around here then; you might have enjoyed it if you'd bothered to turn up." With that, he turned on his heel and bolted from the kitchen, his long legs carrying him into the hallway and upstairs before Sophie had any time to react.

"Well that went well." From the empty space where Oskar had stood just moments before, Sophie's words bounced back at her and she bit her bottom lip, toying with going after him but holding herself back to avoid the inevitable furtherance of a conversation she wasn't yet prepared to have. Although her brother would make a good ally when things began to unwind, for now she felt it best to keep him in the dark, as much for his own sake as for her own. She affirmed her chosen course of action by nodding to herself but her shoulders slumped as she made the short walk to the kitchen table and as she pulled out a scuffed, white chair and sat down, appreciation of the magnitude of her task began to sink in and she felt her resolve begin to falter for the first time since she had set the plan in motion. Oskar was an easy, if rather unexpected, diversion but the real test was ahead of her; mamma was no fool and it would take more than well practised sad eyes and a trembling lip to slip anything past her. Once again Sophie felt herself sigh and she was just about to let her head rest on the table and indulge in a bout of reflective gloom, when a voice from the doorway startled her, and she snapped to attention.

"A penny for those thoughts."

"Hey mamma." Sophie gave a brief smile, not trusting her ability to pull off anything more dramatic, and she stood up, pleased to see her mother entering the kitchen wielding a full basket of bedding as it gave her somewhere to take the conversation. "It's not like you to bring laundry into the kitchen mamma, your standards are slipping." Again, a brief smile, this time with the addition of one raised eyebrow for added authenticity.

Ingrid snorted as she heaved the full basket onto the counter top. "This is what happens when other places have already been filled. I think Oskar wears something once and then puts it in the basket for washing. Does Michael do that?" She glanced at Sophie for a second before turning her attention back to the washing basket.

At the mention of Michael, Sophie's other eyebrow shot up of its own accord and she felt a hitch in her breath as she spoke. "I don't get too involved with laundry these days apart from dropping off a load to get washed and ironed. I suppose you could say I outsource it." Despite trying to suck it back in, a laugh escaped her and she heard the nervousness within it and felt she had to add something. "I suppose that's what gives a lady like me, time to lunch."

Ingrid stopped pulling at the laundry and turned to Sophie, her eyes crinkled and drawn downwards. "Lunch? Surely you have not found time to grace us with your presence for lunch today? Are all your friends busy?"

"That's not fair." Sophie heard the childish whine in her voice and could have kicked herself for being drawn into a discussion that even at this early stage, was being conducted on her mother's terms. "I have a busy life, mamma, you know the job brings a lot of pressure."

"Oskar and I thought you might be dead," Ingrid seemed not to have heard Sophie's plea for understanding, "we even considered getting him a new suit to make sure he would not shame me at your funeral." She smiled, but it wasn't a happy smile at all. "In the end we chose to wait as we had not seen any deaths reported in the newspapers where the deceased matched your description although," she snorted again, "we were working from memory so..."

"You've made your point." Sophie scowled, her cheeks burning red. On any other day she would have said more, far more, but today, she needed her mother on her side so she capped off the anger welling up inside her and opted instead for acceptance of her failure as a daughter, and an apology. "Look, I know you're annoyed at me..."

"Do you think so?" Ingrid folded her arms as she interrupted Sophie's flow. "What makes you think I could ever be annoyed at you?"

"Oh for God's sake mum, it's obvious!"

"Actually, I was not sure whether to be annoyed or not,"

Ingrid unfolded her arms and turned back to the washing basket, her mouth twitching into a half smile, "because I failed to recognise you at first and it would be unfair to be annoyed at a stranger."

Sophie stood in silence and stared at her mother's back. It was all going wrong before it had begun and she couldn't think of a way to bring it back. To make matters worse she felt a tremble in her bottom lip and she bit down on it, desperate to prevent it becoming more pronounced or worse still, be the harbinger of tears that would serve a better purpose if they arrived just a little later. In the end she could only squeeze out a few words. "Mamma, I'm sorry."

Ingrid turned to face Sophie again, her face set and her lips tight. "One phone call, Sophie, it would have taken a few minutes of your time. I do not ask for much but to have nothing at all, that is not fair."

"I know, mamma." Sophie nodded her agreement, detecting the subtle thickening of her mother's Swedish accent and realising it was time to tread carefully because when the accent came out, it signalled trouble for whoever was hearing it. There was nothing else for it; she had to make herself think about the one thing she most dreaded because she needed tears and she needed them now. As she cast her mind back and pushed guilty feelings to the side, she felt her throat tighten and began to speak. "It's just...it's just.." Her bottom lip trembled again but this time she didn't interfere with it, instead, letting nature take its course and sure enough, seconds later, the first tear rolled down her left cheek.

"Oh Sophie, why are you crying?" Ingrid marched across the space dividing them and pulled Sophie's hands into her own. "Tell me what is wrong. What has been happening?"

Sophie felt another tear trickle down towards her chin and her nose began to run in concert with it, a pleasing addition which added an extra layer of realism to proceedings and which prompted her mother to release one hand and fish a tissue out from the pocket of her jeans. "I'm fine, mamma...it's nothing." She allowed her head to drop.

"For goodness sake, I am not stupid, do not tell me this is nothing." Ingrid's face was tight with concern as she used the tissue she had taken from her pocket to tackle the confusion of tears and snot on Sophie's crumpled face. "Come on, we will find a comfortable seat and you can tell me what is the matter."

Sophie nodded her agreement, as there was nothing else to do. This was mamma in full blown mother mode, capable of fixing anything from a splinter in your finger to the trauma of a marriage breakdown and it was just where Sophie needed her to be although she didn't plan to tell her what was wrong, at least, not today. There would be time enough for a confession later once the next hurdle was cleared, the thought of which, as Sophie sniffed and wiped at her nose with her free hand, encouraged her insides to jump and ripple. She sniffed again and flicked her eyes upwards, giving a wan smile before allowing herself to be led to the sitting room, holding hands all the way like she used to do when she was a child.

**

The sitting room was as expected, neat and tidy as always. It was a well-proportioned space, decorated in an unmistakable Scandi style which made Sophie smile because mamma wasn't one for following trends yet here she was, her taste bang in fashion. She thought about mentioning it but decided at once it would be wise to leave it unsaid rather than risk raising suspicions that her tearful episode a moment ago was in any way manufactured.

"Come on Sophie, sit down, please."

Sophie nodded and took a deep breath just as an inner voice told her she could forget the whole enterprise and that there need be no drama. She hushed it. Things were now in motion and would be what they would be so there would be no backing out.

"Sit here." Ingrid patted the adjacent space on the sofa, her eyes fixed on Sophie who was still hovering near the door, her face etched with indecision. "Please, will you come and sit down?"

"I'm coming, mamma." Sophie removed her coat and threw it over a chair near the door then walked over and flopped down onto the soft, thick cushions of the sofa. The moment was at hand, so, as she brushed a curl of auburn hair from her face, she set her expression to pained, and launched into the first part of her story. "I've left Michael." She let the words hang in the air for a moment, taking in her mother's less than shocked expression before continuing. "We had a huge fight over a ridiculous thing…a stupid thing, but he won't listen to reason, so I left." She sniffed and dropped her gaze, judging she had confessed just enough by concentrating on what had happened and not why it happened. Best of all, she hadn't told a lie because she had indeed left her husband.

"I see," was all Ingrid said. She looked Sophie up and down. "What ridiculous thing did Michael say to make you leave him?"

Sophie didn't answer.

"If I had abandoned your father for uttering ridiculous things then it is likely you would be my only child." Ingrid reached out a hand, placing it on Sophie's and giving it a squeeze. "How ridiculous could it be that you had to leave?"

"This is serious." Sophie risked a quick glance and was surprised to catch her mother in a wistful half smile. "I don't see what's funny, mamma, I've left my husband and you think it's funny!"

Ingrid shrugged her shoulders, but held her smile. "How am I to know it is serious when you will not tell me about it?"

Sophie pulled her hand away and stood, making a concerted effort to appear hurt before walking over to the window with small, deliberate steps. When she stopped, she looked back at her mother and shook her head. "I can't tell you mamma, not now and it doesn't matter anyway because it's done and I can't go back." She rubbed at her eyes for effect then dropped her gaze, hoping she looked sad and upset enough to forestall further questioning. "I was hoping to stay here for a bit, if it's ok."

"Darling, I cannot help you if you will not speak to me." Ingrid's tone had a sharp edge to it. "Why did we come through here to talk if you will not talk? Tell me why."

"I thought I could tell you, that's why, but I can't…can't face going over it all just now." Sophie indulged herself in a long, heavy sigh. "Can I stay here, please?"

Ingrid pulled herself up from the sofa and stood, hands on hips. "I do not intend to sit here all day trying to drag this from you. You will tell me when you are ready, I suppose, it is always the same." She gave a thin smile. "And the answer is yes, you are welcome to stay here for as long as you need to, but I thought you would know that anyway."

"Thanks mamma." Sophie aimed a smile of gratitude at her mother, knowing the worst was yet to come. "I will tell you about it I promise, but not now, I'm all over the place."

"Come on," said Ingrid, nodding, "we should sort your room and get your suitcase

unpacked." She gestured to the door and began to walk towards it.

"I didn't think you'd seen it."

"Of course I saw it," Ingrid stopped walking and smiled, "I do have eyes in my head or did you forget that?" She stood waiting, her head tilted and her hand poised to open the sitting room door.

Sophie took a sharp breath; it was now or never. "We need to sort out Anna's room too." The words spilled out in a breathless rush which wasn't her plan. During mental rehearsals for this moment she always imagined herself throwing it casually into the conversation like it was nothing to be concerned about, just another ordinary occurrence. She realised at once practice hadn't made perfect.

Ingrid's eyes widened and she took a step backwards. "Anna is coming? Please, tell me your sister has not also left her husband."

"Oh God no, but it's a bit awkward and I'm so sorry to land it on you like this. Do you remember I told you about Dr Miller, the professor from UCLA?" Sophie paused to search her mother's face for a hint of recollection, but she saw nothing and so continued with her pitch. "She's in Economics like me and she was supposed to be staying at my place for a few weeks. It's a joint university project, I'm sure I told you." She saw her mother's lips tighten as the penny dropped.

"Sophie..."

"It would only be for a few weeks mamma, I promise." Sophie heard the pleading tone creep into her voice again. "I wouldn't ask but she's flying in tomorrow and it's too late to make other arrangements. Can she stay here, please?"

"No, she cannot." Ingrid's voice was firm.

"Mamma, I'm serious, she won't have anywhere to stay if you

say no."

"I have *already* said no and you know as well as I do she will be able to find a nice hotel somewhere." Ingrid folded her arms and glared at Sophie, her expression one of horror combined with determination.

"Mamma please, I stayed with her when I was in America and I can hardly throw her into a hotel for a month just because Michael's being an arse."

"Oh, now it is a month." Ingrid's voice rose to a high peak. "It has gone up from three weeks in an instant." She glared at Sophie and shook her head again. "I am very sorry, but the answer is still, no."

Sophie dropped her chin and fell silent for a moment. She had expected the first answer to be an outright refusal and so hadn't been disappointed, but she had no intention of giving up and already, she had spotted the first beam of hope when mamma apologised for her refusal. Things were going well. "It's fine, really, it's all right. I suppose I'll have to phone Cassandra and ask for her help. She'll love something like this to hold against me."

"Why would anyone hold this against you?"

"Mamma, it's all politics and points scoring, you wouldn't understand that sort of thing." Sophie sighed then shook her head for added drama, anxious for a blistering response and knowing if she got it, she was almost home and dry.

"Oh, of course, I am just a stupid housewife who could not possibly understand anything so complicated." Ingrid threw her hands in the air and snorted, her cheeks acquiring tiny pinpoints of red. "No, I am useless and suited only to cooking and cleaning and daytime television. You have such a low opinion of me Sophie, so low."

"I didn't mean it like that." Sophie made a dash towards her mother and when she arrived, she took both hands in her own and looked her in the eye. "I'm sorry it came out that way and I don't think you're any of those things. It's just...Cassandra got promoted last year ahead of me and she's made my life a misery ever since." Once again, Sophie dropped her gaze for a few seconds, allowing her admission to sink in. "So, I volunteered to be a one-woman welcoming committee for Dr Miller and I went above Cassandra's head to do it. She was furious, but it was a done deal and there was nothing she could do. Now, of course..." Sophie let her words trail off and she sighed.

"You went above your boss's head." Ingrid tilted her head.

"Yes."

"And you are surprised she was angry with you."

"No, not really." Sophie sensed an easing in the tension and although she kept her head down, she lifted her eyes as she spoke. "This joint project, it's a big thing for us and I thought if I could get myself involved then it would help me get promoted. It's stupid but... it's not enough to be good at the day job any more mamma, you need extras and this was my extra." She saw her mother's eyes soften and she smiled at her. "I'm sorry."

Ingrid nodded. "Do you realise how much you are asking of me?"

As she heard the words, Sophie felt herself relax for the first time that day. She knew it was all going to be fine. "Of course I do. I know it's not ideal but I'm desperate."

"You know how I feel around people I do not know, and it is much worse to have that in my own house. You must know this, Sophie."

"Mamma I know, but I'm in a bind and I don't know what else to do." Sophie held her breath; this was it.

"All right, she can stay for one week, until you can make other arrangements." "Thank you, mamma." Sophie smiled, this time not having to force it.

"I will prepare Anna's room, but after I do, you will deal with this woman for anything she needs, I will not be running after her."

Sophie nodded. "Of course," she said. "I love you, mamma."

"I know you do, and I love you too."

Sophie stood with eyes closed as her mother left the room. It had gone better than expected but she wasn't a fool; it was all going to be a nightmare.

Chapter Two

The Visitor

Ingrid glanced at her watch and felt her jaw tighten; within a couple of hours they would be here and for one interminable week, she would be trapped within the walls of her own house and forced to tolerate endless pleasantries and awkward conversations. To make an already disastrous situation worse, she would have to endure all of that with an ignorant, flag waving, garrulous American! As she sat at the kitchen table, hacking at the corpse of a cabbage, she made valiant attempts to keep her train of thought fixed on reconciling Sophie with Michael, but it was hopeless. Every time she thought she might be getting somewhere, her deliberations were derailed by an intrusive mental picture of a strange woman striding into her house, probably to the sound of a marching band playing the Star-Spangled Banner. For Sophie's sake, she had agreed to take the woman in, reassuring herself it would be for a brief period and that, like all things, it would pass. This was of course true but she now regretted her hurried acquiescence to the plaintive appeals for help because in the cold light of day, she realised she would not be able to cope. Adjusting her glasses, she put the knife down and glanced again at the coleslaw recipe in her magazine; *four cups of thinly sliced cabbage.* Her eyes flicked to the mangled remains in front of her and she pursed her lips in annoyance. It was all a mess.

After dinner the previous night Sophie had been in a talkative mood, delivering a retrospective narrative of her time in America to a thrilled Oskar and although Ingrid had immersed herself in a book and indulged in a form of defensive deafness, enough information broke through to leave her filled with dread. Sophie described the woman as buoyant, talkative and bold and it was at this point when Ingrid excused herself for the night and rushed to the sanctuary of her bedroom because she knew what those words were masking; the American woman would be brash and loud.

Ingrid rose from her seat, fighting against a languorous weariness that had settled upon her and as she began to throw cabbage into the bowl beside the other ingredients, she heard muted laughter coming from the direction of the front door and the unmistakable racket of Oskar thumping down the stairs. He blasted into the kitchen with a huge smile plastered on his face.

"Mum, they're here," he shouted, then bolted back out of the kitchen and down the short hallway to the front door which by this point was open, allowing the muted laughter to spill into the house.

Ingrid launched a handful of cabbage back onto the chopping board in panic and ran over to the sink, yanking her apron off as she went before splashing some water on her hands and wiping them on the apron before it was hurled into a nearby cupboard. Just as she was smoothing back her hair and straightening her sweater, the voices got louder and when she looked up, Sophie was already standing in the doorway.

"Hi mamma, I'm back." Sophie's face shone like a well-polished diamond and she wore a broad smile. "We're a bit early though."

"So I see," Ingrid replied, feeling flustered and unprepared, but realising it was too late to do anything about it.

"I'm sorry," said Sophie, giggling, and glancing over her shoulder, "I got confused about the flight time and she was already through Customs when I got there. I know I should have called."

"Yes, you should have and..." The words perished on Ingrid's lips as Oskar appeared behind his sister, followed by the visitor.

"Mamma, this is Dr Miller," Sophie gestured towards Ingrid, "and this is my mother."

"I'm very pleased to meet you Mrs. Martin."

The accent was American, but rather soft, and Ingrid thought she detected hints of another voice lurking beneath it as the tall, dark-haired woman stepped forward with her right hand extended. Ingrid did likewise and as they shook hands, she glimpsed a look of puzzlement on the woman's face but it was fleeting and insubstantial and there was no time to give it any in-depth consideration as formalities had yet to be concluded. "I am happy to meet you too but please, do not call me Mrs. Martin, I am Ingrid."

"All right, I'll call you Ingrid if you forget the Dr Miller thing. I'm Helen." She smiled, displaying a row of perfect, white teeth but her bright look dimmed as she turned to Sophie. "Since when did you introduce me as Dr Miller? Seriously, did you forget your mom has a name as well?" She glanced at Ingrid and shook her head as if apologising for the lack of manners on display but Ingrid didn't speak.

Sophie laughed at Helen's admonishment but didn't comment on it, instead, giving Oskar a nudge, awakening him from his thrall. "Be a sweetheart and take Helen's bags to her room."

"Sure thing," said Oskar, grinning like a fool, "if you need anything else Helen just ask, I'm the man of the house."

'No, he isn't,' said Sophie, rolling her eyes, "dad just works away a lot."

"Which means," said Oskar, broadening his grin, "I'm the man of the house."

"The bags." Sophie exaggerated her impatience with an overly dramatic sigh.

"Right away Miss." Oskar saluted his sister before lifting the luggage. "I'll be in my room if you need me," he said to Helen, then he turned away and bounded upstairs at speed, blond hair streaming behind him.

"Thanks Oskar," Helen shouted after him, before turning to Ingrid and Sophie. "He's very nice," she smiled at both of them in turn, "and he looks very Swedish, if you know what I mean."

"I am afraid I do not know what you mean," said Ingrid, thinking it was the oddest thing for anyone to say, "how on earth can someone *look* Swedish?" Her eyes met Helen's for a second and she saw in them a look of surprise, perhaps even panic, and it was obvious the visitor hadn't expected to be asked to expand on her rather crude generalisations.

"Yes, do tell," added Sophie, a mischievous smile beginning to curl at the corners of her mouth as she cast a conspiratorial sideways glance at her mother. "How can someone look Swedish?"

17

Helen seemed unprepared for the twist in the conversation and she said nothing, instead, licking her lips several times as her eyes darted between Ingrid and Sophie, the ensuing silence becoming louder as each second passed. Just as the pause began to reach the uncomfortable stage, a huge grin spread over her face and she pointed the index fingers of both hands at mother and daughter, then blew out a breath. "I've got it, I remember what I meant." She nodded at them before continuing. "He's very tall, then there's the blond hair and he's got lovely teeth, very nice teeth." She looked relieved. "He also looks great in knitwear. I love his sweater." She turned and looked directly into Ingrid's eyes, appearing pleased with her answer. "He's very like you," there was a moment's pause, "and you look... very Swedish and I like your sweater too."

Ingrid felt her face flush and pulled her gaze away, but despite feeling a creeping tingle of embarrassment, she laughed, unsure what to make of the woman smiling at her and certain she had never encountered anyone like her before. The peculiar comments demanded a reply but Ingrid was at a loss as to how she could respond to something she believed was meant as a compliment but which was so off the wall. Relief arrived when Sophie spoke.

"Helen, that's your worst one yet, where do you get all that from?" Sophie laughed and walked further into the kitchen. "Mamma, I'm starved, what's for lunch?"

"I am making chicken salad," said Ingrid, feeling herself relax, and grateful to be back on familiar ground after the rather odd exchange she had just experienced, "I was making the coleslaw when you arrived." She motioned to Helen to go into the kitchen, allowing her to enter first, and they both then made their way over to Sophie who was standing at the table, picking at shredded carrot from a large, stoneware bowl.

"Careful," said Helen in a hushed tone, pointing to the mangled, green mass covering the abandoned chopping board, "I think that might be dead but I'm not sure." She laughed, a rich, warm laugh and Sophie giggled in return.

"My chopping skills are lacking do you think?" Ingrid raised an eyebrow and looked at Helen and then at Sophie. "Perhaps one of you would like to take over if I am so bad."

"No way," said Sophie, grabbing another pile of grated carrot and shoving it in her mouth, "that's your department mamma, you're the best."

"I'll have a go if you like," Helen took the knife which lay discarded beside the cabbage, "but, can I check, are your first aid skills up to date?" She looked directly at Ingrid, eyes shining but with the hint of a frown shadowing her brow. "It's just, the last time I used a knife like this one I cut my hand and I ended up in the emergency room getting it stitched and that was an experience I'd rather not repeat if I can help it. I have a scar, would you like to see it?" She thrust her left hand towards Ingrid, motioning with her eyes for her to examine it which she did, although without moving any closer. "They said I was lucky not to sever a tendon. Told me to be careful in future if I was chopping things but I didn't bother saying I was only trying to get the last of the peanut butter from the jar though. That would have been horrific, severing a tendon I mean. Don't you think?"

"Yes, that would have been dreadful," Ingrid replied, studying the solemn look on Helen's face and marvelling at her verbosity and at the sincerity with which she related her story, particularly the part where she offered a view of the offending scar. This woman was like a whirlwind and although she had been dreading having an over-confident, talkative American in her house, she found herself thinking Helen was rather sweet. "Perhaps it is better if I do the chopping. It might be safer."

"You could be right." Helen smiled and handed over the knife. "Can I do anything else to help? I like to be useful."

"I do not know, what things can you do?" Ingrid glanced at Sophie, wondering what she was making of the conversation but she seemed absorbed in looking at her fingernails from different angles so Ingrid brought her attention back to Helen.

"Well," Helen shrugged her shoulders, "I could maybe put the green stuff in the bowl," she gestured to the remains of the cabbage, "not much could go wrong doing that I don't think."

"That would be a great help." Ingrid smiled, trying to hide how underwhelmed the offer left her but it was in keeping with the rest of the odd exchange so she went along with it. "If you need assistance, you must let me know."

"I will, don't worry," said Helen, "if it all starts slipping through my fingers, I'll give you a shout but I'll wash my hands first though, excuse me please." She grinned at Ingrid again, giving another flash of perfect, white teeth before sauntering over to the sink, nudging Sophie on the way. "Will you be helping today or will you just stand there looking as pretty as you always do?"

"Mamma," said Sophie, rolling her eyes, "what would you like me to do?" She didn't look at Helen who was now busy lathering up her hands under a torrent of water.

"You?" Ingrid took off her glasses and put them on the table, staring at Sophie in surprise and wondering if this was the Sophie she knew, the one who never offered help with anything in the house but who was now, it seemed, volunteering to do just that.

"Of course, me," Sophie replied, sounding indignant, "what needs done?"

"Well, this is quite something." Ingrid heard a quiet laugh coming from the direction of the sink and glanced towards Helen, but she didn't turn around. "Sophie has me at a disadvantage I'm afraid Helen because I do not know what she can do and I have nothing prepared for such an unexpected moment." She watched as Helen pulled a small, red towel from its hook and began to dry her hands and she also saw the knowing look on her face as she glanced at Sophie and then looked back at Ingrid.

"Yeah, I can see this is a shock for you, it is for me too." Helen finished drying her hands then replaced the towel on the hook before striding back towards the table. "You're busted, Sophie." She began to lift handfuls of cabbage into the bowl. "When I met Sophie, she told me she was a domestic goddess but I wasn't fooled, Ingrid, I knew." She looked at Sophie again. "I bet you a hundred bucks she doesn't help wash up after meals. I *know* she doesn't make up her own bed in the morning."

Sophie stared at her nails and said nothing, the haughty look on her face suggesting she felt the conversation to be beneath her.

"You are correct," said Ingrid, glancing at her daughter, "many times I have tried to teach her these skills but all have ended in failure."

"I'm not listening you know." Sophie didn't raise her head.

"Ah yes," Ingrid smiled and nodded," this is another thing she does not do."

Helen put the last of the cabbage into the bowl and waved at Sophie to catch her attention. "Hey pretty face, how about we give your mother some downtime and we fix lunch?"

"If you like." The reply was short and Sophie looked up, giving what appeared to be a forced smile. "How hard can it be?"

"Looks like you've been relieved of lunch duty," said Helen, nodding to Ingrid and then plunging her hands into the bowl, mixing everything together. "Sophie, find something resembling chicken. Check the refrigerator first, you know, the big white thing in the corner. Shout if you need help."

"Very funny," said Sophie, stomping over to the fridge and yanking its door open. She reached in and grabbed a pack of pre-cooked chicken then slammed the door shut and walked back to the table. "Chicken," she said, and dropped it next to Helen.

"Hey, you learn quick," Helen said, laughing, "do you think you could risk going back in there and finding tomatoes? Red things, small and kinda squishy." She glanced at Ingrid as Sophie flounced off towards the fridge. "You're a free woman Ingrid, make the best of it before Sophie's enthusiasm runs out." She eyed Sophie who was standing in front of the open fridge, arms folded and with a frown lodged on her face. "I'd go now, doesn't look like you have a big window."

"Yes," said Ingrid, "you might have a point." She nodded towards Sophie who was now wrist deep in the salad drawer and not looking happy about it. "I do not know how you did that but perhaps you could teach me." She turned back to Helen, pleased to see the twinkle in her eye which confirmed that, when it came to her daughter, they were both on the same page.

Helen chuckled and her eyes crinkled. "I could try but Sophie would be hard to operate even if you had a manual. I think I just got lucky."

"I heard that," shouted Sophie as she continued her rummage through the fridge.

"I will be in the sitting room if you need anything," said Ingrid, turning away away from the scene and heading towards the hallway. On reaching the kitchen door, although she wasn't sure why, she looked back and was surprised to see Helen had finished what she was doing and was watching her, head tilted and hands laid flat on the table in front of her. The expression on her face was difficult to categorise but Ingrid was certain it contained hints of the puzzled look she wore when they were first introduced, and it seemed odd. She felt she should say something, anything, given she was the one who stopped and glanced back but before she could, a burst of heat surged up her neck and, to her horror, spread across her face.

"Keep going, you're almost free." Helen used an exaggerated stage whisper and nodded towards the exit.

Ingrid turned her flushed face away at double speed and rushed into the hall without responding, pulling the kitchen door half closed behind her and feeling the familiar, cold rush of panic and the tightening in her chest, both of which prompted her to move away from the door and lean against the wall with her eyes closed. Hanging there, almost limp, for a few minutes, she slowed her breathing by focussing on the rising and falling motion of her chest and although she heard laughter from the kitchen through the part-opened door, it was a faraway sound like the dull echoes she often heard when swimming underwater in the local pool. Another few minutes passed before she pulled herself upright and ran a hand over her cheeks, relieved that although they still radiated heat, it was less ferocious than before. She walked over to the small oak table which filled an awkward corner just before the downstairs toilet, and she stared into the mirror hanging above it, taking in the blotchy red islands on her neck and face, the blotchiness being a recognisable sign that the worst was over. Pink cheeks puffed outwards as she sighed, her greatest wish now being for just one thing; solitude. Time alone after anxious moments wasn't just something she wanted, it was a necessity and it provided a gap where she could collect her thoughts and gather her wits about her before re-entering the world, in most cases, looking only a little the worse for wear. With another sigh she pushed herself away from the table, intending to head for the sanctuary of her bedroom but before she was able to retrace her steps and head for the stairs, the voices from the kitchen became louder and clearer and what she heard stopped her in her tracks. The first sound to reach her was Sophie giggling, the pitch of it high and girlish which brought with it a feeling of deep discomfort although the reason for this wasn't clear. Ingrid crept towards the conversation, no longer overheated but chilled, and as she arrived at the kitchen she heard Helen's voice.

"What would your mom think if she saw where you just put your hand?" There was a challenge in the tone but also, Ingrid thought, an element of playfulness. She leaned against the wall, and listened.

"I thought you liked it." Sophie's reply dripped with suggestiveness, and in her mind's eye Ingrid pictured the look on her daughter's face, and she shuddered.

"I'll ignore your last remark Mrs Reid because I have a question, which is, if your sister is the good looking one, will she be in my new bedroom when I get there later?" It was Helen's voice and Ingrid heard the smile in her tone.

"Oh, so it's my sister you've got your eye on?" it was Sophie, her voice deeper than before and no longer girlish, "did I mention Anna's room is the one next to mine?"

"Are you saying it's two for the price of one? That's a new one for me but when I go to bed tonight, I might need help to relax and if there are two of you then..."

Sophie's giggle made another appearance and at the sound of it, Ingrid pressed her hand to the door, ready to ease it open and erase the minimal doubt she felt about what was going on. The urge to take a step back and walk away was powerful and she almost did, but even as she played with the thought she felt herself give the door a sharp push, watching as it swung open to reveal the scene within.

"What is going on here?" Ingrid's exclamation began as a shout but shock seized it almost at once, transforming it into a hoarse whisper as her eyes widened at the sight of Sophie, leaning against Helen her arms draped around her neck. "What do you think you are doing, Sophie?"

"It's not what it seems." Helen broke the embrace and pushed Sophie away before striding towards Ingrid, laughing, and gesturing to Sophie and to herself. "This isn't what you think, it's just a joke." She reached out to grasp Ingrid's arms as if to soothe her but she drew back when Ingrid shook her head and raised both hands to push her away.

"Do not touch me," Ingrid retreated one step, her eyes blazing and fixed on Helen, "do *not* touch me." She could feel the coldness growing again as panic began to settle around her and she dragged in several deep breaths, fighting to keep control.

"I'm sorry," said Helen, dropping her arms to her side as she took a step back of her own, "no touching is fine, I didn't mean to do any touching."

"Oh mamma," Sophie flounced over to the door and stopped beside Helen, "it's just a bit of fun, it's a joke thing between us."

"I do not think so," Ingrid shook her head, recognising Sophie's lie for what it was, "do you both think I am stupid?" Her eyes flicked to Helen's and caught a look of sadness there which was so unexpected, it robbed her of further comment and all she could do then was stand motionless and stare as the coldness crept into her again.

"I promise, you didn't see what you thought you saw." Helen's face flushed and she moved as if to reach for Ingrid again but jerked her hand back before it had travelled any distance. "There really isn't..."

"I am going," Ingrid interrupted and held up both hands, "I will not listen to this." She looked between Sophie and Helen again before turning on her heel and marching off down the hallway, aware of Sophie calling to her, but with no intention of listening. She had to get away.

"Mamma," Sophie shouted, "it was a joke, for God's sake, where has your sense of humour gone?" She puffed out her cheeks and folded her arms, looking at Helen and rolling her eyes. "It's always the same with her these days."

"Leave it." Helen gave Sophie a light tap on the arm, her brows knitted together and her eyes unfocussed, tension evident in the tautness of the skin on her face.

"But she's being ridiculous, Helen, I won't leave it."

"That's always your problem, isn't it, you can't let things be. What the fuck did you think you were doing back there anyway?" Helen's words had a flint-like edge and her eyes narrowed as she stared at Sophie, who blinked several times before finding her own voice.

"You can't be serious. I didn't hear you complaining, did I?"

"That's not the point," Helen said, "and your mother..."

"My mother, "shouted Sophie, barging into Helen's flow, "is over the top as usual and she needs to be told."

24

"Let it go, Sophie, please," Helen's eyes lost their focus again, "I'll fix this."

"Really, well, bloody good luck with that," said Sophie throwing her hands up, "I give up, I really do." She strode out of the kitchen then ran up the stairs, and moments later the sound of a slamming door reverberated through the house.

***

Ingrid stood at the window of the sitting room, her eyes puffy and red-rimmed, a perfect match for the deep-red hue of her tear-stained cheeks. She caught movement outside on the street and craned her neck to see beyond the tumult of the overgrown rhododendron hugging the boundary of the front garden, but it was only a cat meandering along the wall so she looked away and allowed it to go about its business unwatched, wishing she had truncated her earlier observations in the kitchen in similar fashion. Had she had the foresight to do so, she would still be ignorant about her daughter's hitherto undisclosed Sapphic tendencies and as things stood, ignorance would indeed have been bliss. Ingrid felt her stomach lurch as she contemplated the possible fallout from Sophie's liaison despite believing she would find a way to cope with it, as distasteful as it was. Why though, did it have to be with...

"That didn't go too well, did it?"

Ingrid jumped, startled by the interruption, turning around to face the speaker and feeling herself stiffen when she saw the American heading for the sofa. "Please do not sit." The words emerged as little more than a croak and they faded to nothing as Ingrid twisted around and fixed her gaze back on the garden.

"Sorry, it's too late, I've kinda done it."

Ingrid took a slow, deep breath and forced herself to face Helen again. "I asked you not to sit." This time her voice was stronger although she realised it sounded cold and flat which wasn't at all how she felt; inside she was like a hot water spring, bubbling away under the surface and preparing to erupt at any moment. She would have to be careful.

"Yeah, I heard you," replied Helen, maintaining eye contact, "but come on, can't we sit and talk about this and maybe dial back the tension?" She tilted her head to one side and smiled. "I'm sorry you saw our demonstration of extreme stupidity back

25

there but it's just something we do as a joke," she leaned forward, resting her elbows on her knees and clasping her hands, "and I promise, there's nothing going on between me and your daughter, despite what you think you saw."

"Who are *you* to come into my house and tell me what I think?" Ingrid's words, steeped in contempt, escaped before she could restrain them and Helen's face fell, her head dropping as she gazed at her feet, which then shuffled and tapped in apparent discomfort. Ingrid swallowed hard, fighting against the dryness in her throat and dismayed at how she had spoken for, despite her anger at the impertinence of the American, the harshness with which she rebuked her was unintentional and she tried at once to soften it although without offering an apology. "I know what you were attempting to say but please, you cannot tell me what I think about this." Helen raised her head then sat further back on the sofa, from where she gave an almost imperceptible nod to confirm she understood the point just made. Feeling on more solid ground, Ingrid then asked what she considered to be the obvious question.

"You say this is all a joke so please, what is the joke? Explain it to me."

"All right," Helen met Ingrid's gaze and although she appeared to be uncomfortable, she continued, "I'll tell you, but I don't think you'll appreciate the punchline." She gestured again to the sofa. "Please come and sit down."

After a moment's indecision, Ingrid took a deep breath and walked over to the sofa, hesitating when she reached it and moving beyond Helen to sit at the far end, leaving a large gap between them.

"Thank you, I think," said Helen, her shoulders slumping as she sighed.

Ingrid heard the rebuke in her tone but chose to ignore it, preferring to remain steady, and determined to have the conversation despite dreading what she might hear. She settled herself before holding her palm out as an indication she was ready to listen.

"Okay, here's the thing." Helen lifted her eyes to meet Ingrid's. "Sophie and I worked together on a couple of joint projects and we clicked. For some reason and I don't know what it was, we just got along and it was a lot of fun. However," she paused, "Sophie got it into her head I had a thing for her, you know, she thought I fancied her."

Ingrid shifted in her seat and folded her arms.

"You're not comfortable with where this is going, are you?" Helen rubbed at her mouth and grimaced. "Look, you said you wanted to know but..." She cut herself short and looked away, shaking her head.

"Please, just tell me why my daughter would think such a thing Helen."

Helen's eyes widened in surprise as she turned back to Ingrid and smiled. "You called me Helen."

"That is your name, is it not?"

"You used my name," Helen smiled again, "and I thought maybe a little détente had broken out there, which would be nice." She made a back and forth gesture with her hand as she spoke. "Am I right?"

Ingrid bit at her bottom lip and shook her head, resisting the attempt to derail her from her original purpose and pull her instead into exchanging pleasantries. "Please, go on."

With just a fleeting hesitation, Helen nodded and continued. "Sophie knew I was gay because I told her not long after we met. I don't pretend otherwise because I'm not ashamed." She stretched and leaned back on the sofa, giving Ingrid a lop-side smile. "Do you know, you and Sophie both do the bitey lip thing?" She gestured to Ingrid and then touched her own mouth.

Ingrid felt her face redden, the heat spreading down to her neck, and she looked away, not knowing where to focus but certain it had to be on anything but the woman opposite her.

"Anyway," Helen said, appearing oblivious to Ingrid's obvious embarrassment, "ultimately, that's what led Sophie to believe I had a thing for her." She laced her long fingers together behind her head. "We sorted it though and we sometimes play a game to let us both know it's not a problem. You saw the game."

"No," Ingrid shook her head and looked Helen in the eye despite her embarrassment and discomfort, "I do not think so." Although her face was burning and she needed the discussion to end, her anger at Helen and Sophie for lying and treating her like a fool aroused a determination in her to see it to an end and hear the truth.

"What don't you think?" There was puzzlement in Helen's tone and on her face.

Ingrid's head snapped up and her eyes narrowed. "Do not treat me like an imbecile. I am supposed to believe Sophie makes a mistake because she *knows* you are gay. That is absurd."

"Well this is something different," said Helen, smiling, "makes a change from people thinking I'm chasing every woman *because* I'm gay."

"So, are you telling me you did nothing to confuse my daughter?"

"No, I'm not," said Helen, "I kissed her."

Ingrid gasped. "Why?"

"Pretty much why I always do things; it seemed like a good idea at the time so I didn't fight it." Helen shrugged and an awkward smile grew on her face. "I accept it sounds dreadful but there's more to it than..."

"I do not want to hear more of this." Ingrid slapped the palms of her hands hard against her knees, using them for leverage as she began to rise to her feet, all the while regretting her own eagerness to unearth the truth behind the scene she had stumbled upon.

"Wait, please let me explain." Helen darted from the sofa and threw herself to the floor, kneeling in supplication and holding both hands up in a pacifying gesture, her proximity trapping Ingrid's feet and preventing her from doing anything other than retreating into her seat. "We both had too much to drink and I reacted to some harmless flirting by doing something ridiculous. We didn't have sex, I promise, and that's the truth."

Ingrid felt herself shrinking back, every inch of her skin recoiling as if in a desperate race to unpeel itself from something malignant and when she spoke, her voice trembled. "You will move, please, you will move."

Helen at once shuffled backwards. "I'm sorry, I was trying to explain and help you understand and I didn't intend to make you uncomfortable. See, I'm on full retreat here."

As Helen backed away, Ingrid watched wide-eyed, the rising panic losing its grip and sliding back down, replaced instead by a sense of infuriation at the audacity of the woman before her who, it seemed, lied with impunity, blind to the fact her audience was more informed than she thought. "Tell me," Ingrid said, her voice rising as the denouement arrived, "if there is no sexual relationship between you, why did Sophie leave her husband?" She licked her lips, intent on seeing Helen's reaction and to establish the truth from her face and not from her words.

"She did *what*?" Helen's mouth dropped open as she pushed herself further back, clambering out of her submissive position to sit fully on the floor, her gaze fixed on Ingrid.

"Come now," said Ingrid, anger rising, "you cannot expect me to believe you do not know." She folded her arms and stared back at Helen, determined that, no matter how uncomfortable it made her feel, there was not a chance she would let this one wriggle out of things unchallenged.

"I didn't know." Helen shook her head, astonishment writ large across her face, curtailing her reaction to only a few words.

Although Helen's shocked expression was unexpected, Ingrid held fast to her quest to find the truth, wavering in her certainty about the facts, but unwilling to concede quite yet. "Why do you think you are staying here and not in Sophie's house?"

"She told me they had builders in." Helen gave a dismissive wave of her hand then launched herself upright from her prone position. "Before you say anything, I'm not omniscient so yes, I accepted the explanation without question." She stood, hands on hips, waiting for a response.

Ingrid said nothing and rubbed her eyes, in one sense satisfied part of the truth had been established, but overall, no further forward. She now felt more bewildered than ever, lost for words but with an overwhelming need to say something to placate the angry woman before her who, in fairness, had accepted the accusations levelled at her with more than a little good grace. Some form of contrition was required but exhaustion got the better of her so she embraced the easier option of a compressed explanation of events. "Sophie left Michael yesterday and arrived here asking to stay and for you to stay also."

"You have got to be fucking kidding me," Helen shouted, spinning around with her arms wide and head raised skywards like a revival preacher swept up in a new, Great Awakening. "She never breathed a fucking word all the way here from the airport."

"Please, there is no need for such language." Ingrid winced, her abhorrence of foul language trumping the weariness now hanging over her.

"*Really*?" Helen's face flushed and contorted in anger "Your daughter lied to me and you're accusing me of breaking up her marriage. Don't you think that deserves a fuck or two?"

Ingrid felt tears spring into her eyes and she rushed a hand towards her face in a futile attempt to hide them. Everything was in turmoil and despite her efforts to unearth the truth, it remained opaque, the only certainty being that Sophie had lied, although what she had lied about was unclear.

"Look, Ingrid, I'm sorry, I didn't mean to shout at you," Helen's voice was soft, "I had no right to speak to you that way, that was awful of me." She brought both hands up to her face and rubbed at her forehead and eyes, letting out a breath through puffed cheeks.

Ingrid nodded but didn't look up, unwilling to allow her tears to elicit sympathy, or worse, pity.

"I think Sophie owes us both an explanation," said Helen, "and I'm going upstairs to bring her down here so we can clear up this whole thing."

Ingrid gave another nod and risked a glance in Helen's direction without allowing her gaze to linger, seeing enough in one glimpse to know she was upset and that the bold confidence she exuded earlier, had vanished.

Helen sighed, shuffling her feet and kneading her hands together. "Can I presume you'll be here when I bring her down?"

Ingrid forced herself to nod again, surprised Helen realised she was a flight risk but resolved anyway to head straight to her room the moment the coast was clear and in no mood to tackle Sophie that day. She waited in silence until she heard Helen leave the room, then she prised herself from the sofa and did the same. Discovering the truth would have to wait until tomorrow.

Chapter Three

Partners in Crime

Helen had always been a fixer. No matter what the problem was she could always smooth things over and find a path through the angst towards resolution but this time she wasn't sure it was possible, because for the first time ever, she felt out of her depth. She sat alone, halfway up the stairs, staring dead ahead and trying to make sense of what had just happened, certain of only one thing, Sophie had lied to everyone. Although it was lying by omission, it was no less damaging for its indirectness and Helen almost detested it more than a bare faced fabrication because the fabricator was taking the extra step of building themselves an escape route, a loophole through which they could jump to declare their innocence. Somehow that made it feel worse although ostensibly, it all came to the same thing in the end, it was still a deception, and it was still trouble she had to address.

Then, of course, there was Ingrid, a woman the likes of whom Helen had never encountered in all her many travels, a perplexing combination of aloofness and warmth, whose sparkling blue eyes shone at you one minute then burned a hole in your soul the next. It had been rather intoxicating when they were both evaluating each other over the dissected cabbage, and Helen smiled as she remembered how a simple compliment about Ingrid's sweater brought out an endearing blush. She wondered now, from her spot on the stairs, whether Ingrid had noticed the colour of her eyes when she had gazed into them at their initial introduction or when she had fixed her Medusa-like stare on them when they were fighting in the sitting room. Either way, Helen couldn't help feeling intrigued by her but she knew any further beguilement would have to wait until her lodgings here in the house were secure which required a satisfactory resolution of the Sophie situation. This wouldn't be easy.

Finally, and she grinned at the thought, there was the man-child called Oskar who seemed quite functional for someone with excess testosterone coursing through his body. The second he appeared at the door that afternoon, Helen had called it and she knew she was right. He was all goofy smiles and attentiveness which was flattering apart from the fact, in his current state of hyper-adolescence, he would have acted that way with any woman who had a pulse.

This left only the mystery sister Anna and the husband who worked away a lot, who, if they were anything like the rest of the family...Helen let the thought trail off and she stood up, taking in her surroundings in earnest for the first time and making a snap judgement that it was a nice house. It wasn't huge by any standard, but it was large enough, with the décor consisting of pale greys and whites with snatches of colour here and there to pull it in the direction of stylishness and away from blandness. She noticed it was a tired in parts and perhaps overdue for an update, but despite that, she rather liked it because it had a pleasant and comforting vibe.

Her critique of Ingrid's house over, Helen knew she could delay the confrontation with Sophie no longer and she began to climb the remaining stairs to hunt her down for a fight. She managed two steps before halting at the sound of one of the bedroom doors above opening and closing and she saw Oskar striding towards her. At first, he seemed not to notice her, absorbed as he was in whatever was on his phone but just as he reached the top of the stairs, he glanced up and juddered to a halt with a look on his face somewhere between delight and embarrassment.

"Hey, Helen," he said, flashing a grin and stuffing his phone into the pocket of his jeans.

"Hey Oskar," Helen replied, "fancy joining me for a seat?" She pointed towards the stair on which she had been sitting just moments previously, conscious she was indulging in another delaying tactic but doing it anyway.

Oskar nodded and clumped down towards her before easing himself onto the

stair with all the elegance of a baby giraffe, pulling his knees up and wrapping his arms around them as if wrestling for control of his lower body. "What's happening?" He glanced at Helen for a second before averting his gaze, his downcast eyes signalling he perhaps wasn't ignorant of that afternoon's events.

"Oh, I think you know what's been happening, am I right?" Helen smiled, and nudged him with her elbow, trying to cajole him into revealing what he knew to ensure she didn't make a bad situation worse by divulging too much information herself, something she tended to do in fraught situations.

"Are you and Sophie," he hesitated for a moment, "are you and Sophie lovers?"

Helen was delighted at his direct line of questioning, and she laughed, wondering for a moment why his mother hadn't done the same and saved herself a lot of heartache in the process. "No, we are not lovers and we never have been," she jabbed him again, "come on, how much did you hear?"

Oskar shrugged his huge shoulders and unfolded his legs in a languorous stretch before coiling them back in tight again. "I'm not sure really," he said, "enough to know Sophie's bombed out on Michael again, you and her had a thing going at one point and mum's upset." His eyes flicked to Helen and then away.

"Sophie and I have never been together in that way." Helen sighed. "I kissed her when I was drunk, ridiculousness on my part and a misunderstanding on hers. That's a long way from having a thing going together, I can assure you."

"Okay," said Oskar, "why has she arrived here with her suitcase, without Michael?"

"Well, it appears she's separated from him, I imagine on her terms but she seems reluctant to go into detail." Helen shook her head. "That'll be because she hasn't got her story straight but I'll drag it out of her and when I do, I'll bring you up to speed." She glanced over her shoulder in the general direction of Sophie's bedroom. "I presume the lady in question has retreated to her boudoir."

"Yes, she's hiding in her room." Oskar twisted around and pointed to the first door on the right-hand side of a long, narrow hallway on the first landing. "I knocked, but she told me to fuck off so I don't think she's accepting visitors at the moment, not without an appointment anyway."

"Yeah, she'll be sulking, it's her forte." Helen smiled at Oskar, taking in his deep blue eyes and the shape of his lips which formed a perfect bow, just like Sophie's. She wondered if his capacity for sulking was also similar but discounted the notion almost at once given how unlikely it would be for anyone on the planet to be able to match her in that regard. The first major tantrum Helen witnessed was when Sophie disconnected a row of computers in the data lab, using the free power bank to charge her phone. The techs went crazy but their furious reaction only made Sophie apoplectic and the argument was epic, bordering on enjoyable. Thereafter, Helen hadn't seen her until morning and the more they got to know each other, the clearer the sulking pattern was. Despite this, Helen liked her and as she had told Ingrid already, they just seemed to click.

"I heard you shouting at mum." Oskar looked directly at Helen, his gaze accusatory, one glance conveying more than a hundred words ever could.

"I'm embarrassed about that and I promise, I'm not proud of myself." Helen pushed her hair back from her face then forced herself to meet Oskar's troubled eyes, reluctant to relive the experience but simultaneously, desperate for someone to listen to her side of things. "I explained she was mistaken about me and Sophie but she refused to accept the explanation and then she blamed me for breaking up your sister's marriage, which is when I lost my temper. I got frustrated and your mom got both barrels but I wasn't really upset at her, I was angry because Sophie had lied."

"So, mum got a rollocking because Sophie's a liar, that's not fair Helen, it's not even close to being reasonable." Oskar pressed his lips into a thin line. "You should apologise."

Helen hung her head, shamed by Oskar's condemnation of her in defence of his mother, his earnest excoriation penetrating the defensive hard shell she always carried with her. "I did offer an apology but she was agitated and seemed disinclined to accept, which is reasonable, considering my behaviour."

"Mum's a bit troubled at the moment," said Oskar, his voice subdued, "she has...difficulties."

"What difficulties, what's wrong?" Something in Oskar's tone suggested matters were serious and Helen looked him in the eye, parking her shamefacedness for the moment, content to torment herself with it another time.

"It's quite personal so I probably shouldn't tell you." He looked straight ahead and

unfolded his legs again, on this occasion resting them a few steps below where they were sitting. "What's your impression of her personality?"

The question hung in the air for a few seconds as Helen gathered her thoughts, believing it prudent to give a thoughtful, serious answer to help re-establish the rapport she had shattered just moments ago. "Let me see now," she said, keeping her eyes fixed on him, "so far we've bonded over some cabbage, shared the story of my escapade with a jar of peanut butter, argued about marital infidelity, discussed you sister's latent lesbian tendencies and," she paused for a second as she remembered Ingrid's tearful face, "then I made her cry. On that basis," she gave him a rueful smile, "I don't believe I've seen the best of her to make a fair judgement."

"You've dodged the question," said Oskar, scratching at his chin then half turning his body to bring them face to face.

Helen turned away from him then leaned forward and rested her arms on her legs, hands clasped as though in prayer. Impressed as she was with Oskar's skill in recognising her monologue as the solid gold bullshit it was, it meant he wasn't admitting defeat which also meant she would have to give him something tangible, all without disclosing too much. She closed her eyes and thought for a moment, indulging herself in remembering all the parts of Ingrid's character so far encountered, and smiling when she recalled the shy backwards glance from the kitchen door, her flushed face betraying what Helen recognised from her own reaction, as inner turmoil. Of course, she could mention nothing of this so she elected to hitch her wagon to chicanery and decided to side-track him. "I guess she's younger than I expected, the way Sophie told it you'd think she was about ninety." On the drive from the airport, Sophie painted a picture of her mother so far removed from reality that Helen now suspected it to be a deliberate distortion and a foolish one too, given that the truth would be evident at first introductions. However, as Oskar seemed to perk up at this observation, she dropped any further consideration of what Sophie's motivations could be and she gave him her best smile.

"She's sixty-three next month," he said, responding at once to her smile with a matching one of his own, and looking more than a little proud.

"Seriously?" Helen summoned up a mental picture of Ingrid without difficulty and imagined herself looking over her as she had earlier that afternoon, finding no evidence to suggest she had managed to get close to breaking the sixty barrier. "Jeez, she looks much younger than that, how old are you?"

Oskar laughed. "You mean how old was she when she delivered the little blond bundle of joy that was me?"

Helen nodded. "Yes."

"She was forty-five, I was her surprise baby."

"I bet you were," said Helen, doubting there had been anything small about Oskar when he was born and calculating that he must now be eighteen and the age gap between him and Sophie, sixteen years. She already knew Oskar was the baby of the family, but she hadn't thought the difference in age would be so huge. "What about your other sister, Anna?"

"Four years younger than Sophe and twelve older than me."

"You really would have been a shock to the system." Helen laughed, reminding herself to quiz Ingrid about her menopause baby and hoping she could stay in the house long enough to enable her to do so. She took a sharp breath at the thought, remembering she still had to navigate her way through perilous waters and uncertain whether her ship was seaworthy or if she would need to launch the lifeboats. Oskar's cheery voice interrupted her train of thought.

"I was a rather large surprise to be honest but mum says she has no regrets because I keep her young."

"Yeah, I bet you do." Helen remembered all the things an eighteen-year-old adolescent could bring to a parent's door and she smiled, her anxieties about forcible removal from the gang, diminishing.

Oskar reached for his pocket and brought out his phone, holding it up for Helen to inspect." I have loads of pictures, would you like to have a look?"

"Pictures of what exactly?" Helen's face contorted in mock horror and she drew back from him in a theatrical manner.

"Family pictures." He laughed and then started swiping

through screens on his phone without giving Helen an option to refuse his offer. "That's us last year at Christmas." He clicked onto a thumbnail which opened into a traditional family photo, and pointed to a pretty looking blond girl wearing a short, black dress. "That's my sister Anna."

"She's rather lovely," said Helen, smiling, "who's that, is it your dad?" She gestured to a wiry looking, red-haired man standing beside Sophie and a little apart from the others.

"Yes."

The one-word answer said more than Oskar realised but as much as it intrigued her, she decided to move on, not wanting to delve deeper and cause further upset. "Your mom looks beautiful in that picture." The words slipped out before she could stop them but Oskar didn't seem to notice and his eyes sparkled.

"Yes, I know." The compliment for his mother appeared to vanquish whatever demons his father had earmarked for him and Oskar's face lit up as he burst with boyish enthusiasm. "She made a massive effort last year you know, she even got her hair coloured again and bought a new outfit. She looked amazing and...it was like she was alive again, if that makes sense."

Helen re-examined the picture and nodded. The Ingrid captured by the camera looked vibrant and it was clear she had a spark of life in her that was missing from the woman with whom she'd crossed swords earlier. She sighed and placed a hand on Oskar's arm, squeezing it as advance reassurance that what she was about to suggest, was beneficial. "Why don't you explain what's wrong with your mom?"

Oskar shifted on the stair and began fiddling with his phone, his discomfort obvious. "You can't tell anyone I've told you."

"Don't worry, I'll dummy up I promise." Helen squeezed his arm again, hoping it would give him encouragement to divulge what the problem was because she could see he needed to get something off his chest.

"Because I'm not supposed to know." Oskar's face tightened and he coughed and rubbed at his chin again, the pressure bringing out tiny spots of red under his nascent beard.

"Okay." Helen knew he was going to spill it, and she was pleased for him as his body language had all the hallmarks of someone eaten up from the inside by an unpurged, terrible

37

poison. Despite that, she felt nervous for herself, aware of her well-developed loquaciousness, a trait with previous convictions for getting her into trouble and which made her cautious now about becoming Oskar's lay confessor although she realised it had to be done.

"It started several years ago when gran wasn't well and mum and I were over in Sweden most of the time, well, I went with her if it wasn't during school term." Oskar rubbed at his mouth as though trying to erase what he had just said.

"What was wrong with your gran?" asked Helen, shifting on the stair as she tried to get comfortable, but failing in miserable fashion.

"Lung cancer. She had it for a long time before she died and she'd have remissions and it would come back and start over again and just before she died, mum wouldn't let me go with her anymore but nobody else wanted to go, so she was on her own."

Helen felt herself stiffen. "Are you serious, nobody *wanted* to go? Nobody *wants* to do stuff like that but Jesus, you can't be telling me nobody here had the common decency to support your mother and comfort a dying woman."

Oskar nodded, his bright blue eyes now clouded with sadness. "I was frightened to go at first, I mean, I'd never seen a dying person and it was worse because it was gran but then I discovered dad wasn't interested and the rest of them had bombed out so I volunteered because I couldn't let mum face it alone. She said no to begin with but I kept insisting until one day, she caved."

Helen took a deep breath and looked at Oskar in admiration, proud he stepped up to the plate when the rest of them exposed their own selfish, spinless dispositions in Ingrid's hour of need.

"Sophie was especially reluctant," Oskar went on, "she couldn't handle it, said she couldn't stomach it and preferred to remember gran the way she was before the cancer."

Now, to Helen, it was hardly news that Sophie wasn't the most reliable person in a crisis, but in leaving Ingrid to soldier on alone as her own mother died, she revealed a streak of self-preoccupation deeper than anything Helen had thought possible. She shook her head in despair and placed a consoling hand back on Oskar's arm, squeezing it tighter than before and hoping it told him how impressed with him she was.

"Anyway," Oskar said, oblivious to Helen's rising affront, "when mum was over there towards the end, things were terrible back here," he made a loose, circular gesture, phone in hand, "dad had an affair with someone at work."

"You've got to be fucking kidding me." Helen twisted all the way around as she spoke, staring at Oskar, her eyes wide, and now understanding why he had been so tortured. This new, sordid revelation served only to aggravate the previous ones and she felt her low opinion of Ingrid's husband sliding further down towards the pits of Hell.

"I'm afraid it's true," said Oskar, his anger now obvious, "he denied it was an affair and promised it was only sex, can you believe that? I mean, what's the bloody difference?"

Helen's face went blank as she thought about what to say but she found herself floundering, caught halfway between wanting to offer benign commiserations that would calm things down, and loud, vociferous condemnations of his philandering dick of a father. In the end, she did neither, preferring to encourage Oskar to unburden himself completely. "Keep going kid, you'll feel better when you get it all out, take it from one who knows."

Oskar gave a rueful smile. "That's the part I'm not supposed to know about, because it was all hush, hush," he put his finger against his lips and smirked, "but I heard dad say it when he was arguing with mum." He pursed his lips and looked round at Helen, "I was supposed to be staying at Kieran's, he's my best friend by the way, but I came home because I knew something was up and nobody heard me come in so..."

"Eavesdropping?" Helen already knew the answer so it came as no surprise when

Oskar nodded a yes.

"Mum found out about the affair, I'm not sure how, but it must have been before I heard them arguing the night I came home from Kieran's. I thought she would leave him and I packed my case to go with her but as the weeks passed, it was obvious they were just going to pretend everything was normal." He shook his head at this, the look broadcast by his face being a combination of incredulity and disappointment. "How could anything be normal?"

"Well," said Helen, starting an explanation but then stopping, because, unlike Oskar, she understood why relationships could sometimes continue after one or other of a couple indulged in a bit of extra-marital sex. Sometimes it was just about sex and it didn't mean things couldn't rekindle which she supposed was what happened between Ingrid and her husband. "What happened next?"

"Nothing, everything was fantastic and we were one big, happy family except we weren't, because it was all fake, and that's when mum got worse." Oskar was still angry. "I wondered if you'd spotted she's a bit reserved, that's why I asked you earlier what you thought of her personality. She's always been like that for as long as I can remember but it worsened after the thing with dad."

"In what way?" Helen wasn't sure she wanted to hear more about the adulterous dad but she said nothing, instead, stretching her legs and shifting position, trying to ease the numbness that had crept into her lower body.

"Before, she struggled with new people, strangers, but it never took long until she got to know them enough to be comfortable. Now she can't cope. You, for example," Oskar gestured to Helen, "you're her worst nightmare because you're staying here and she can't escape you plus you also talk a lot which isn't good either." He gave a shrug of apology, "From mum's point of view anyway."

"I see." Helen fell silent, considering the implications of Oskar's revelation. "Tell me something," she said, gesturing behind her, "does Sophie know all this, about your mom's problem I mean?"

"Yes, of course she does, it's a longstanding thing so it's hardly a secret."

"And yet, she still invited me here to stay, I'm presuming at short notice and, knowing Sophie, causing great inconvenience to everyone except herself." Helen closed her eyes and, in her head, added another grievance to the list of topics she would discuss with Sophie. "What a selfish fuck she is."

They both exchanged glances, before looking up the stairs towards Sophie's bedroom.

"Come on kid," Helen stood and stretched, "let's treat ourselves to lunch. I had a half-made chicken salad on the go

40

before I disgraced myself earlier and I can hear it calling me home." She winked at him and then, without warning, bolted down the stairs, shouting over her shoulder. "Hurry up, last one in is ..." She disappeared, the remainder of the challenge vanishing in her slipstream, leaving Oskar sitting alone and open-mouthed for a few seconds before he grinned, then unfolded himself and clattered down the stairs after her.

***

The salad was exactly where Helen left it when she had disentangled herself from Sophie and tried to talk her way out of trouble with Ingrid, and she judged now, that the chicken hadn't been on the counter top long enough to poison them. "You find the plates," she said, "and I'll pull the rest of this together." Grabbing a knife from the block over at the sink, she began slicing the chicken into long strips, eyeing Oskar as he crashed around in the cupboards to find plates and rattled his way through the fridge, before he headed over to the table with mayonnaise and two bottles of Budweiser. Helen looked at the bottles and frowned. "We're having beer? Where did you get them from, I mean, does your mother know?"

"I'm eighteen," Oskar wiggled his eyebrows, "and I'm entitled to drink beer, wines and spirits in accordance with the law of the land." He grinned, looking very pleased with himself.

"Yeah, but I'm more concerned with the law in this house, and I'm referring to your mom, okay, I don't need more drama with her today." Helen squinted at him, watching in semi-amusement as he popped the tops from the bottles with a small hook-like bottle opener he removed from his back pocket. "Come on Oskar, is the beer yours or have you found something that wasn't lost?" She put the knife down and folded her arms, trying her best to look stern.

He shook his head but the grin remained locked on his face. "It's Sophie's beer but when she arrived I was promised a share, before we had a little confrontation that is, but she didn't pull out of the deal officially so, in technical terms, I consider this pair to be mine."

"You're bullshit almost matches mine, do you know that?" Helen laughed and snared one of the bottles, reluctant to offer him further encouragement but so engaged by him she couldn't

41

help but participate in his gentle larceny. "However, I'm happy to accept this beer as compensation for all the crap your sister throws out so I'll raise a toast to us, partners in crime." At this, they both swung their respective bottles in an arc, nodding to each other in pleasure when they clinked together.

Oskar tilted his head back before slurping down half the beer in one breath, then he burped and smacked his lips before thrusting his bottle in the air again. "I'll raise a toast to Sophie, for her generosity in providing us with such fine ale."

"Hey, steady tiger." They clashed bottles again but Helen was already thinking ahead to the reaction if Oskar got drunk, knowing that no matter what, she would get the blame. "Come on kid, cool it a bit or you'll get loaded and yours truly here'll be back in the shit." She raised one eyebrow as she watched him hold his bottle up again, and he flashed her a smile which reminded her of the kid in the Home Alone movies when he'd just set somebody's groin ablaze. "You little fucker, Oskar, you know damn well what the score is here." Despite her admonishment of him she laughed, she couldn't help herself, such was the look on his face, and she clinked bottles with him again then downed half the contents of her own, resigned to her fate. "Right, time to chow down and soak up some of that beer and maybe I'll come out of this unscathed after all." She pulled out a chair and plonked herself onto it before gesturing for Oskar to do likewise, then she pushed the chicken salad in his direction. "Eat now," she said, "and perhaps one more beer after that."

"Ok *mum*." Oskar grinned, resting his near-empty bottle in front of him on the table and filling his plate from the bowl, picking up any spillage and throwing it straight into his mouth.

They sat for a few minutes without speaking, crunching through the chicken salad and enjoying the beer and being in each other's company. Helen couldn't help but think they made a very strange pair, but a pair they certainly were, partners in crime now, since they had misappropriated Sophie's beer. Oskar was a bright spot of hope in what felt like a bear market of a day, but his luminosity alone couldn't illuminate the tricky path lying ahead, where an assault from all sides followed by banishment, was the most likely outcome. She knew there was no other option, she would have to face Ingrid again.

"More beer?" Oskar was already halfway to his feet before he finished the question, his face betraying the answer he hoped for and flushing with delight when Helen nodded and gave a thumbs-up. In jig time he was back at the table with two more bottles of Sophie's finest and once again they rattled them together before raising another toast, this time to world peace. They considered downgrading it to peace in the Martin household but decided world peace would be more likely.

"Where do you think she is?" said Helen, savouring the bitterness of the beer as she took another swallow and closed her eyes for a few seconds.

Oskar lifted his bottle and took a swig, rattling the glass against his teeth in the process and rubbing over them with his finger as though checking they were all in one place. "Do you mean where's mum now?"

"Well I don't mean Britney Spears, do I?" Helen threw him a quasi-condescending look then rolled her eyes before downing another mouthful of beer, a smile playing on her lips.

"Who's Britney Spears?" Oskar looked puzzled for a moment, his eyes narrowing as though trying to bring a face to mind, then he reached for his phone and hit the browser app which opened at the arbiter of all things unknown, Mr Google.

"What do you mean, who's Britney Spears?" The question, in an instant, made Helen feel ancient and she rebuked her companion with a playful wave of her hand. "Put the phone down and forget Britney, where will your mom have hidden herself?'

"Probably in her room or maybe in the conservatory," Oskar gave Helen a nervous glance, "why do you want to know?"

Helen sank the rest of the beer and swung the empty bottle by its neck, considering her options and realising they sat somewhere between limited and non-existent "I feel dreadful about earlier and I want to try to make things better. I just need to figure out how to get her to talk to me."

"Do you think that's a good idea?" said Oskar, not looking convinced, and finishing the remainder of his beer in one gulp.

"Probably not," replied Helen, hearing an inner voice telling her to leave well enough alone until she was beer free, but chiding it for being so fucking pusillanimous. "I can't just leave things blowing in the breeze though, fortune favours the brave and all that." She glanced at the empty bottle, then at the fridge behind her, and then at Oskar. "Should we liberate another one of Sophie's excellent beverages?"

Oskar grinned in agreement and retrieved two more beers in a flash. "It's strange," he said, running his thumb around the neck of the bottle and licking his lips, "mum looked relaxed when you were teaming up together against Sophie and forcing her to make lunch," he smirked and took a large mouthful of beer, "but before you say anything, I overheard you all talking so it's not my fault."

"You overheard?" Helen shifted in her seat and threw her hands up to her face, the extravagant manoeuvre deliberate, and intended to conceal how entertaining she found his snooping. "You really shouldn't do that." She removed her hands and shook her head for emphasis, noting he was still smiling at her, and realising he wasn't buying the amateur dramatics. "I'm serious, it's wrong. Next you'll be telling me you climb trees and look in people's bedroom windows as well," she shuddered, serious for a moment, "please tell me you don't."

Oskar's eyes widened and he placed a hand over his heart as his mouth fell open. "Of course I don't," he said, "well, not since they all got blinds. Anyway, we have a small house with lots of people in it so I had no alternative but to listen."

Helen tried not to laugh but it overtook her and she was unable to contain it, knowing it would encourage him, but so tickled that she couldn't help herself. When it finally subsided, she gazed at a thrilled looking Oskar. "Tell me what I need to do to help your mom and encourage her to talk to me again."

Oskar shrugged his shoulders and rubbed a hand across the stubble on his chin, looking perturbed as he gave it some thought. "To be honest, I don't think you'll be able to do that now," he said, "not after what happened earlier."

Helen sat for a while and said nothing, accepting he was probably right; after today's disaster, Ingrid wouldn't come within a hundred miles of her, never mind engage in a rational discussion. It might help if Sophie told the truth about why she left Michael but that was a weak peg on which to hang your hopes. This left only the nuclear option, the one option Helen didn't want to exercise.

"Any ideas yet?" Oskar began swirling the remaining beer

around the bottle, eyes fixed on Helen.

"Yeah, I do," she replied, draining the last of her beer before banging the bottle on the table, "I can't fix your mom, but I can retore normality in the short term by packing my bags and relocating my ass to a hotel."

Oskar's nose wrinkled and he pulled back in his seat, mouth agape. "If that's your only suggestion then it's hopeless, I thought you had a cunning plan and all you've got in your game-plan is a retreat."

"Oh please," said Helen, looking him in the eye, "I'm your mom's worst nightmare, and I'm quoting you here, so if I pack my bags it's one thing she doesn't have to consider. As for Sophie, she's not my problem to solve." She rose, and picked up the empty bottles, intent on binning them, but hesitating at the sight of the forlorn look on Oskar's face. "I'm sorry, but it's the way I see things and unless you can come up with something better in the next five minutes, that's the plan."

"You're running away," said Oskar, dropping his eyes and letting a pout form on his lips, "is that what you do, run away from things?"

Helen flinched at the barbed comment thrown from her friend on the other side of the table and she put the empty bottles back down. "I'm no coward and this isn't a cut and run, but it's not my fight." She stared down at him, nostrils flaring and her lips pressed together and colourless. She could hunt Ingrid down, of course she could, but the aftermath of another fruitless discussion would without doubt only expedite her own eviction from the premises, leaving her alone, and Ingrid worse than ever. It was a hopeless situation and she fell silent, dismayed at Oskar's defeated demeanour which almost broke her heart, but as her dad used to say, a desperate soul only needs good music and Oskar's look of abject misery was like a symphony to her. Somehow, it seeded the germ of an idea in her mind, an idea for which she would thank him much later in life, but which for now, sparked her back into life. "Oskar," she said, sauntering around to his side of the table, "I'm promising nothing but if you come with me right now, I believe I have something in the bag after all, something to bring your mom back to the negotiating table if you like."

Oskar scratched at his neck, then stood and reached for Helen's hand, his face pensive but to a lesser degree than before. "I'll do whatever needs done, I promise?"

Helen shook her head, warming to her idea although it had no certainty attached to it and was based for the most part on blind hope. "Do nothing at all, sit beside me and let me do the talking and with luck, and a following wind, we're back in the game." She squeezed his hand and gave a tug to start him moving, not waiting for any response, and they both headed out of the kitchen, Oskar acting as an unwitting human shield. They were partners in crime again.

Chapter Four

The Party Trick

They found Ingrid in the conservatory after a fruitless search upstairs, Oskar leading the hunt because Helen was anxious to avoid coming face-to-face with his mother too soon and lose the war before the battle had begun. As it was, her bedroom was empty and Oskar was certain there was only one more place where she could be, which is where they now stood, looking at her through the glass in the door. "Ready?" She looked at the boy beside her and saw he looked anything but ready, despite the support of a few beers, so it wasn't a surprise when he shook his head in reply although he threw in a nervous smile and drew his shoulders back as if to convince Helen, or maybe himself, that he was combat ready. Sucking in a deep breath, and hoping he would still trust her after she did what she was about to do, Helen grabbed Oskar's hand and squeezed it tight. "Okay, this is it." She pushed the conservatory door open with her free hand and they rushed in, heads up, with all eyes fixed on Ingrid.

"Hey mum." They had barely crossed the threshold when Oskar did the opposite of what they had agreed, revealing their position and relinquishing the element of surprise.

"Oskar?" Ingrid swivelled in her seat, a burgeoning smile dying on her lips when she saw Helen, a sight which seemed to counteract any pleasure Oskar's arrival might have produced and which at once, caused her face to tighten as she stood to attention, her back rigid and with a demeanour suggesting she was in no mood to take prisoners.

Helen broke the silence. "Ingrid, there's something we need to discuss although I'm aware you've probably heard enough from me already today, but this can't wait so, can you suffer me a few minutes more?" Her pulse quickened as she waited for the inevitable rejection but in the journey from the kitchen to the conservatory she had prepared herself for it and conjured up a plan to counter it by talking so much that Ingrid submitted, just to make her stop. People usually hated moments of silence but Helen found once she started on one of her polemics, they tended to embrace quietude when it arrived and she hoped Ingrid would be no different.

"I do not believe we have anything worthwhile to say to each other," Ingrid glanced at Oskar and then stared back at Helen, "so I would prefer if you would leave me in peace."

"I disagree," replied Helen, easing a smile onto her face, "we have an abundance of things to discuss but they'll have to wait because I need to talk to you about Oskar." As she said this, she tightened her grip on Oskar's hand, hoping he understood it as a signal to keep quiet and he played along, holding her hand and staring at his feet.

"What is wrong with him?" Ingrid's stony look broke, replaced with growing concern at the sight of Oskar's silent form and she took a step towards him before juddering to a sudden halt when Helen took her own step forwards.

"Would it be all right if we sat down?" Helen asked permission to sit this time, hoping a display of good manners might soften Ingrid's antipathy towards her, although judging by her reaction, it seemed like a forlorn hope.

"I have no desire to sit with *you*," she glared at Helen, "but I would like to know what is the matter with my son." Ingrid turned her face to Oskar again and he, in turn, glanced at Helen, his eyes pleading for similar enlightenment.

Helen blinked a few times and swallowed, realising the moment was at hand and saying a silent prayer that what she was about to say would be enough to grab Ingrid's attention and make her forget her hostility. "Well, it's rather embarrassing," she squeezed Oskar's hand harder than before in what felt to her like an advance apology, "but I walked in on him when he was watching porn on the internet, and he was masturbating." She saw Ingrid's eyes widen as she gasped, but one glance at Oskar told Helen his mother's reaction was mild; his eyes were the size of saucers and although he opened his mouth to speak, nothing came out. "I know it's embarrassing for you kid," she kept her eyes fixed on him, "but we need to get everything out in the open." Facing Ingrid to make her final plea, she saw her hands twisting and turning against one another like two snakes fighting in a bag and so she pushed on, desperate to finish the first sortie for everyone's sake. "I had a conversation with him and he admitted he's worried about you so can we try not to antagonise each other and sit down for an adult discussion?" Helen held her breath, the next few seconds determining her near future and whether she would remain in the bosom of the family, or adopt a new role as queen of the nearest Travelodge. She mentally crossed her fingers, hoping for the former, however fleeting the stay of execution may be.

Although Ingrid's face remained blank, she nodded to Helen who, saying nothing more, walked around her, Oskar in tow like a crippled battleship dragged into dock. They all manoeuvred around each other until Oskar and Ingrid sat berthed together on the sofa and Helen then perched in front of them on a small, wooden footstool, shifting in discomfort but still silent. Ingrid reached out and laid a hand on Oskar's arm. "Why are you worried about me, tell me what is going on?"

Oskar said nothing, but directed a disconsolate glance towards Helen, his cheeks still burning and his eyes panicked.

"May I?" said Helen, keen to keep things moving, "he told me what the problem is so I'm happy to talk, if he can't." She was surprised at how well things were working and she thought Oskar's acting was worthy of an award, although it crossed her mind the story about the internet porn might be quite close to the truth.

"Of course, you can talk," Ingrid kept her eyes on Oskar, "I would like to know what the problem is to let it be fixed."

"Thank you," said Helen, feeling awful for lying but pleased it had served its purpose as a conduit to the reopening of dialogue. "Oskar told me you've had difficulties," she paused, "he avoided drowning me in details but although I tried to prise it out of him, he held his tongue so please, don't be mad at him." She searched Ingrid's face for signs of anger but saw only concern so she careered on. "What he did divulge," Helen paused again, realising she was getting close to where it could all go tits up, "is you struggle around people you don't know well and although you've always been a bit reserved, now it's worse which he believes might have made you depressed." She added the last bit, thinking it was likely to be correct and hoping it sounded like something an eighteen-year-old boy would say. "That's why he's worried about you." She tilted her head and looked at Oskar with faux concern, simultaneously flicking a covert at glance at Ingrid, attempting to read her face but finding it impossible.

"I am not sure how to respond to this." Ingrid removed her hand from Oskar's arm and closed her eyes, shaking her head as if to wipe everything out. "It is difficult to even think of it." She said this almost to herself, eyes still closed, her face white, having the air of a woman who had reached the end of a very long and trying day.

"You don't have to respond now," said Helen, exchanging glances with a worried looking Oskar who extended an arm and clasped one of Ingrid's hands in his own, the unexpected contact drawing her back to them, as her eyes fluttered open. "If it makes you more comfortable, I can..." Helen stopped short, caught in the sweep of Ingrid's gaze but this time, rather than sensing opprobrium, she detected a shift in mood, Ingrid's eyes appearing softer and signalling, if not the end of the war, then at least a suspension of hostilities. The opportunity to build bridges made Helen's heart soar, a million possibilities for the future tumbling through her mind but she cautioned herself to tread lightly, aware of the fragility of the armistice and choosing her words carefully to preserve it if she could. "Sophie didn't explain your predicament, but if she had, I promise you, I wouldn't have imposed myself on you." She let the words sink in for the briefest of moments before continuing. "I know I can be an acquired taste, but I promised to help Oskar because his concerns for you are genuine, and that's why I'm sitting here now but," she faltered, appreciating the risks inherent in the offer she was about to make, " but, I'm wondering if the only way I can help is by moving on and if that's correct then I'll leave tomorrow morning." She sensed Oskar was about to pile in with objections and held a hand up to stop him, her attention fixed on Ingrid, awaiting her decision.

"You are correct," said Ingrid, almost at once, "you would help me by moving elsewhere." She withdrew her gaze from Helen as she spoke and glanced towards Oskar who had pulled his hand away and whose face displayed a combination of anger and disbelief. "I am sorry Oskar, but I cannot help my feelings."

"Mum, that's not fair, Helen's trying to help you and you're happy to ignore that and throw her out in the street just because..."

Helen interrupted him before he could say more. "Hey it's not a problem, I'm pretty used to being unwelcome wherever I go." She froze. The words had spilled out before she could stop them, her shock at misjudging the situation so significantly, somehow loosening her tongue. "What I meant to say, was I'm not always the easiest person to accept." Her shoulders drooped and her eyes began to sting followed by a thickening of the saliva in her mouth, both tell-tale signs it was time for her to disappear so she gave Ingrid a curt nod and began to rise from her perch.

"Wait please." Ingrid's hands flew up and she looked Helen up and down before gesturing for her to sit down. "Explain it to me please, what do you mean?"

"What do you mean, what do I mean?" Helen following Ingrid's eyes as they moved over her and she obeyed the command to park herself again, rubbing her eyes and fighting an internal battle against rising optimism but unable to prevent it from surging anyway.

"What you said about always being unwelcome," Ingrid said, "I would like to understand what you mean by that."

Helen rubbed her palms across the front of her jeans, wondering how best to answer a question she hadn't expected to hear asked and, in an unusual turn of events, feeling wrong-footed, and surprised to find herself lost for words. "Oh, I see, that part."

Ingrid regarded Helen for a second and then nodded. "Yes, that part please."

Helen turned to Oskar, and, although not expecting him to do anything dramatic to save the day, she realised immediately he would be of no help whatsoever as he appeared dazed, probably as a result of three beers in quick succession. Giving up on her erstwhile partner in crime, she accepted she was on her own. "What I meant," she said, facing Ingrid, "was people make snap judgements and see me in a certain way, not the way I am, and sometimes it means we part company prematurely, like now."

"I think I understand you." Ingrid tilted her head and the corners of her mouth tugged upwards as she bit at her bottom lip, her face thoughtful but also pensive.

"Do you?" Helen failed to keep the derision from her voice, "I doubt that, but go ahead, describe what you see when you look at me and I promise I'll tell you if you're correct." As soon as she spoke the words, she regretted them, and the blazing look from Ingrid heralded a confrontation she knew she couldn't prevent so she did the only thing she could and crossed her arms to await the burn.

"It is easy," Ingrid stopped biting her lip and once again, ran an eye over Helen, "I see someone who is so certain of her own magnificence, she cannot understand it is unattractive." She cleared her throat. "You said I looked so Swedish but here you are, acting so over-confident like a typical American."

"Wow!" Helen laughed and unfolded her arms, not roasted by the blast but instead, invigorated by it, the haughty, confident tone delivering it serving only to make her smile. "My God, you sure don't say much, then you pile it on, it's like you save your words to use all at once or maybe," she laughed again, "maybe you're the evil twin." Even by her own high standards, Helen was pleased with the line but she was happier still with the sighting of a new Ingrid, a confident and rather ballsy version who was, in her eyes, magnificent.

"You have by your own words, just confirmed my thinking," said Ingrid, smiling and then shaking her head in what appeared to be mournful sorrow.

"I beg to differ, your Honour," said Helen, trying, and failing, not to appear smug, "and unlike you, I have evidence which proves my case." She splayed her arms, showman-like, beaming in triumph as she addressed mother and son. "Ladies and gentlemen of the jury, I'm proud to announce I am *not* an American."

"You're not?" Oskar's head jerked as he drew it back and he grabbed his chin with his free hand, letting it rest there, his eyes bright in contrast to the beer-addled dreaminess of his smile.

"Nope," said Helen, keeping Ingrid in her sight, and with no effort whatsoever, switching to her natural accent, the true voice of much of her childhood, "I'm rather Scottish in fact, so *you* have just been caught stereotyping." She pointed to Ingrid as she spoke, savouring the joy she always felt whenever she found a suitable moment to let the Scottish accent out of its cage. People's response to the sudden switch was always amusing and in this instance Helen wasn't disappointed, as the reaction was just as she hoped it would be; Oskar stared at her, crunching up his eyes and licking his lips, and Ingrid's eyes widened and she let out a sharp gasp. "Well, what do you both think?"

"You *are* Scottish," said Oskar, smiling at Ingrid and then back at Helen, realisation beginning to fight its way through his fog-enrobed brain.

"Yes, I am, but I'm still me." She revelled in the accent again, enjoying the sound of it after its prolonged sabbatical and she looked at Ingrid who sat stern faced, any surprise she might have felt now gone, or at least hidden from view. "Can I ask you to do something for me? I know I say stupid things sometimes and I can be a bit full on once I get started," she gave the Scottish accent an extra shove for emphasis before easing back into a soft, mid-Atlantic drawl, "but could you at least try not to judge me on it? I'm not what I seem, I promise."

Ingrid didn't reply at once but instead, pushed herself further back on the sofa, still holding onto Oskar. "It is quite the party trick," she said, eyeing Oskar, "and it seems to impress children very much."

Helen shot a look towards Oskar, watching his face cloud over and his brow crumple and she gestured towards him, feeling hurt on his behalf and defensive of his emotional capabilities. "Aw come on, that's unfair, this big guy's got more maturity in his little finger than Sophie has in her entire body. Give him a break will you."

"I think it's quite nice," said Oskar, appearing bolstered by Helen's support and staring straight at his mother, "don't you think it's interesting?"

"I think it is different," Ingrid turned to Helen, "and a rather unexpected event if I can put it like that."

"Yeah, I can see that." Bitter experience had trained Helen to say nothing more on the subject, prone as she was to letting her mouth run away with itself, but this time, as her little switcheroo seemed to have caused a partial thaw in Ingrid's ice maiden persona, she felt driven to go for broke. "I use this accent in most situations, I have to back home or I'd need an interpreter beside me every time I went out for milk," she laughed, "it's hard going sometimes." She made a typing gesture to Oskar. "Go on YouTube and search for Scottish elevator and you'll get my drift.'

Oskar grinned, then pulled out his phone and began scrolling through his apps as instructed.

"When you're not doing the porn thing of course," Helen said, winking at him and enjoying watching his face turn scarlet as he abandoned his search and stuffed the phone back into his pocket. She risked a glance at Ingrid and saw a slight break in her stony-faced look.

"I think perhaps you did not catch Oskar in his bedroom after all." Ingrid raised her eyebrows at Helen then turned to Oskar, but he looked away, staring at his feet and avoiding his mother's scrutiny.

"You're right," said Helen, "I lied about that because I was trying to figure out how to get you to talk and it just came out so I owe you both an apology." She gave Oskar a brief nod but his head remained bowed and he didn't see it. "He is worried about you though," she focused on Ingrid, "and he asked me to help which I tried to do, but in my usual car crash way. I can't seem to help it, it just happens, I mean, I keep going on and on and on and saying stuff and before I know it," she paused and took a breath, "before I know it, I've fucked everything up and it all goes crazy."

"Like now do you mean?" said Ingrid, her brow furrowing as she studied Helen's face, "you are talking like you are on an express train."

"No...maybe yes, I suppose I do sometimes get a bit verbose, not always though but...have I fucked things up again because you look mad at me?"

"No," said Ingrid, dropping Oskar's hand and giving him a warm smile, "I am not angry, I was thinking about my mother. I know I can sometimes appear to be a little bit unforgiving but she always told me I should judge a person not by the outcome of what they do, but by their intentions."

"Gran was really nice Helen, you would have liked her and I

think she would have liked you too," Ingrid's sudden thaw seemed to bring Oskar back to life and he pushed himself up in his seat, "she would have been impressed by your accents as well."

"Seems like a reasonable woman to me," Helen replied, unsure where things were heading, but, as the tension had undergone a dramatic shift downwards, hopeful it was in the right direction.

"Perhaps, you could try to think before you speak." Ingrid's tone was lighter but her face remained inscrutable.

"I do think before I speak, but it doesn't always make the jump from my brain to my mouth." Helen gave a tentative smile as she replied, desperate to ask the many questions she had but finding it impossible to settle on the right one. She was, in most circumstances, good at judging a person's mood but Ingrid was a different prospect altogether and was for the most part unreadable, which made the choice of question tricky, if not downright dangerous. They had to discuss the Sophie issue and it had to be now, but there was no easy way to bring it up without risking another explosion. "Oskar," she said, "would you do me a favour and make us some coffee?"

"Coffee?" He looked at Helen as though she had spoken to him in a foreign language.

"Yeah, coffee, you know, the drink coffee; it's like tea but instead of tea, it's coffee." She raised her eyebrows and trained her gaze on his face, trying to convey with only her eyes that she meant for him to take the hint and vanish upstairs to his PlayStation.

"I can make coffee," he said, "what about biscuits, will I bring them as well?"

In his eagerness to please he had missed the point by a country mile but his enthusiastic leap into action was endearing and Helen couldn't help but smile at him anyway. "That sounds good to me but maybe you should go out and buy some fresh ones."

"Why?" said Oskar, "the cupboard's full of...oh, I see."

"Here," Helen dug a twenty-pound note from the pocket of her jeans and handed it over, "no hurry and keep the change." She glanced at Ingrid and saw she was watching their transaction, but once again, her face was expressionless.

"Bye mum." Oskar leaned over and kissed Ingrid on the cheek before backing out of the conservatory, the look on his face akin to someone who had lost twenty pounds, but found fifty.

"He's a nice boy," said Helen, turning her attention to Ingrid and feeling a flutter in her midsection that seemed misplaced for the occasion and which prompted her to run a hand over her cheeks to ensure they were still cool.

"He is, thank you."

"Yeah, he's good fun." Helen realised they had arrived in the land of banal small talk and although she could win Olympic medals for chatter, she could never cope with exchanging platitudes for very long so she stood and stretched, then pushed the footstool to the side with her leg. "Do you mind if I have a comfortable seat?" She pointed to the space on the sofa left vacant by Oskar's departure.

"Of course not."

Helen expected Ingrid to move away but instead, she twisted round in her seat and pummelled the rather flat looking cushion behind her before leaning back, looking relaxed. "Too close, or is it all right now we've bonded?" She tried another smile but was ready to push herself further back if required.

Ingrid ran her tongue over her teeth and gestured to Helen to remain in situ. "There is no problem," she said, "tell me about the accents and how you came to have them, I am intrigued by the mix."

"The accents, yes." Helen knew this is where it would go wrong and now relations seemed to be friendlier, she could have kicked herself for not telling the whole truth about what Ingrid had called, a party trick. "Okay," she sat forward with hands planted on her thighs, "I have dual nationality, British and American so, when I said I wasn't American, it was true because I'm only half American." She glanced at Ingrid, waiting for the inevitable angry response but when it didn't happen, she kept talking. "My mom comes from Scotland, from Glasgow, and my dad was from San Francisco. I stayed in both places on and off - they never lived together."

"So, you picked up two accents," Ingrid tilted her head to one side and again, adjusted the cushion at her back.

"Not quite picked up, no," said Helen, turning around to sit face on with Ingrid, leaning an elbow on the back of the sofa. "When I first went to the States all I had was my own accent and I got bullied at school because I sounded different. So, I made myself do an American one, which wasn't perfect, and today it's a little bit generic, but it worked."

"So the bullying stopped," Ingrid shifted in her seat, "when you took on the local accent."

"Pretty much," said Helen, "but you know what kids are like, they always find the little differences between themselves to justify a beating so it didn't stop altogether, but it made it better." She stopped and shook her head to help dispel the memories of bleeding noses and recess fights, thankful she no longer gave them much thought and happy to leave them in the past where they belonged.

"It is sad," said Ingrid, her eyes losing their focus as she stared at the far end of the conservatory, "children can be cruel I think."

Helen laughed, unable to stop herself. "If you think that's sad, I better not tell you more." She caught the faraway look in Ingrid's eyes and realised another sad story might tip her over the edge and into tears, coming as it was on the back of a very trying and charged afternoon. "Are you okay?" She reached out a hand and was about to put it on Ingrid's arm when she realised what she was doing, and stopped, pulling back and then feeling embarrassed about it but unsure if it was because she offered or withdrew a consoling touch.

"I can listen," said Ingrid, turning back to Helen and appearing oblivious to the aborted attempt at consolation, "if you feel you want to tell it to me."

"All right," Helen nodded, "I'll tell you, but remember, you're getting the story from my perspective, from when I was very young." Ingrid didn't respond to her caveat so she leaned back on the sofa and stretched out her legs, crossing them at the ankles, before launching into what she considered to be the sorry tale of her childhood. "I first met my dad when he appeared at the house one day to take me to the States, I was about seven years old and didn't know who the heck this strange looking guy was so you can imagine my reaction. Now, don't make the mistake of thinking this was a transatlantic tug of love, because it wasn't, and I still don't know what my mother said to him to

57

make him do it but, whatever it was, it worked, and I went to America with the man I now knew as dad." She took a breath and glanced at Ingrid, pleased to see she wasn't crying but picking up a definite air of melancholy from her expression which suggested tears weren't far away. "You might be asking yourself why she would hand me over to someone I didn't know." Again, Helen glanced at Ingrid. "Am I ok to go on?"

"Please, yes."

"Ok, why did she hand me over to a stranger?" Helen uncrossed her ankles then answered her own question, "I'll tell you why, it was because she didn't want me to cramp her style with her new boyfriend, and to be clear, those were her words, that's what *she* told me when I was only seven." Helen almost spat the last of the story out and when she fell silent, she rubbed a hand across her mouth as if to cleanse it of something distasteful.

In the brief silence after Helen's rushed conclusion to her tale, Ingrid sat up straighter, her face drawn and white, but her eyes blazing like hot coals. "I do not understand how as a mother she could do such a cruel thing to her daughter, and at such a young age too...why would she..."

Helen interrupted. "She was a lousy mother, that's why, the lousiest mother you could have but," she paused, sucking air through her teeth, "I still loved her because she was my mother and I hated her for making me feel that way." She sighed and shrugged her shoulders, letting a silence fall between them, pleased Ingrid didn't cry although it was surprising because it was a rather sad story, albeit one she no longer found much emotion in after all these years, or so she told herself.

"Are you all right?" Ingrid's voice was quiet and she sounded weary.

"I'm fine," replied Helen, "but I'm confused about something." She leaned her head on the back of the sofa and watched Ingrid as she adjusted the neck of her blouse with long, elegant fingers, noticing that although she looked worn out, her eyes had a spark in them and the expression she wore was softer than before.

"What is confusing you?" said Ingrid, the hint of a smile playing on her lips.

"I'm a bit perplexed about why I'm still sitting here, I mean, one minute you're on the verge of throwing me out and then the next, I'm pouring out the tale of my miserable childhood and everything seems normal. How did we get from there to here?"

"I asked you a question about your accents or have you forgotten about that?"

"No." said Helen, shaking her head and warming to her theme, "that's the biggest part of the mystery, why you asked for an explanation in the first place. Why did you ask?"

"You said you were used to being unwelcome and I wondered what had happened to make you feel that way, so I asked the question. There was nothing mysterious about it."

"Yeah, but then you tagged me as an obnoxious American." Helen smiled when she said this, remembering how pleased she had been seeing a spunkier version of Ingrid who wasn't afraid of straight talking.

"Yes, I did," replied Ingrid, sweeping a strand of hair from her eyes, "but then I discovered you were only half an obnoxious American."

Helen laughed, shocked Ingrid had told a joke but unsure whether it was deliberate because Ingrid herself wasn't laughing, despite the curl on her lips and sparkle in her eyes suggesting she was considering it. "I don't quite know what to make of you," she said, "and I think..."

Ingrid leaned forward, the smile hinted at seconds before now spreading over her face which somehow, had lost any sign of tiredness. "Why did you stop, please, what were you going to say?" She swept her eyes over Helen, top to bottom and then held both hands out, soliciting for an answer.

"I was thinking before I speak, like we agreed." Helen cupped a hand over her chin in an exaggerated show of being deep in thought, all the while held by Ingrid's eyes as they watched her without any apparent discomfort. She waited for a few seconds, gauging the level of risk in what she would like to say and almost throwing caution to the wind and letting it out, but pulling back, uncertain and nervous. With a sigh she dropped her gaze and shook her head. "I think this might be the part when I go and spoil it all by saying something stupid."

Ingrid shrugged. "At least you have thought about it first,

which is a lot of progress in a very short time I think."

Helen smiled at her and took a deep breath. "Okay, here it comes, and remember, don't shoot the messenger, but I still think we need to talk about Sophie."

"We do, yes," Ingrid's smile flattened and her brow furrowed again, "this must be sorted now or I don't believe I will sleep soundly again."

Helen nodded her agreement. "I wasn't lying about my relationship with Sophie, there is one, but I promise you it's friendship only. Yes, I kissed her and that caused problems but we fixed it and I know Sophie didn't leave her husband on my account, I knew nothing about it until you told me today." She held Ingrid's eyes for every word she spoke, hoping her sincerity was visible.

Ingrid sighed and nodded, the hint of a smile creeping back onto her lips. "Thank you for being honest, I am glad to hear at least a small part of it, but I will excuse myself if that is all right because I need to find Sophie now. She can explain the rest to me."

"That's fine by me," said Helen, feeling herself relax, and stretching out her legs again, enjoying the burn from having sat too long in one place. "My sources tell me she's hiding upstairs in her bedroom."

"I am not *hiding* anywhere."

The voice came from the doorway causing Ingrid and Helen to snap their heads round in surprise before exchanging glances at the sight of Sophie leaning against the door frame with her arms folded, her face twisted with anger.

"Well look who it is," said Helen, nudging Ingrid and unable to disguise the disdain in her voice as she pointed at Sophie, "I've been waiting for you."

"Oh, very funny," said Sophie, stomping towards them and coming to a halt in front of where they sat. "This is all very cosy, when did you two become so close?" She emphasised the last word, glancing at Helen, with her eyes wide and eyebrows raised in sharp peaks.

"What do you mean by that?" Helen's face flushed and she launched herself off the couch towards Sophie, "you'll tell me what you mean you self-centred little fuck or God help me I'll..."

"That is enough." Ingrid pulled Helen's arm back then released it before folding her own arms and glaring at Sophie. "You owe an explanation to me and to Helen and you will give it now, please, and be done with these silly games."

Sophie rolled her eyes. "Ok, if you must know, I'll tell you, it's why I came down anyway," she paused and pressed her face into a frown, "I'm pregnant."

"Pregnant?" Ingrid and Helen spoke in unison.

"Yes, pregnant," said Sophie, sniffing and starting to cry, "I left Michael because he doesn't believe he's the baby's father."

Chapter Five

The Talking Bear

Two days had passed since Sophie's tearful confession had confined Helen to quarters, forty-eight hours spent hidden in her bedroom, ostensibly working but mostly brooding and daydreaming. She sat there now, having just returned from her latest expedition downstairs to put together another cheese sandwich and coffee combo which, although insubstantial, would be enough for now, and meant she could miss tonight's dinner without much discomfort. She bit into the sandwich, chewing without enthusiasm and tasting very little of it and she thought again about her reaction to Sophie's announcement and how, as usual, her mouth opened wide enough for her to fill it with both feet.

After the initial shock, which lasted seconds at most, Ingrid had shot out of her seat to embrace a distraught daughter, leaving Helen to sit watching the spectacle unfold. She had kept her eyes fixed on Sophie who was bawling her eyes out whilst wrapped in her mother's loving arms, and for a moment or two, the drama had been believable.

Helen smiled to herself as she took another mouthful of bread and cheese. The performance that day had been just short of perfection, spoiled only by Sophie's inability to resist taking a quick look at Helen whilst in the throes of unbearable pain. It was the merest flick of a glance, but Helen caught it and she had known at once, everything was not as it seemed. Quite how she had resisted the urge to break into applause there and then she would never know but resist she did, and she had sat there in silence as the scene developed.

Helen scowled at the recollection and looked around the small bedroom as she finished the last of what would be her dinner, feeling caged and restless by her self-imposed bout of solitary confinement, but unable to face going back into the general population just yet. She brushed some crumbs off the smooth, grey quilt covering her bed, then stood and walked over to the window. It hadn't turned five yet but darkness was beginning to fold itself around the house which meant there wasn't much of anything to see so she sighed and closed the blinds, then pulled the drapes shut for good measure.

Her choices for evening entertainment didn't amount to much. Option one was to open her MacBook and do some work and option two involved lying on the bed, staring at the ceiling, so, as both would come with a generous side serving of self-pity, she decided on option two, at a stroke giving herself the luxury of feeling sorry for herself in comfort instead of hunched over a tiny screen. She strode over to the bed and jumped on it, landing on her back and bouncing around until the mattress springs settled, then she clasped both hands behind her head and closed her eyes, allowing her mind to drift back again to Sophie's announcement.

Sophie must have known Helen had rumbled her. When the tears stopped, she had walked over, displaying the contrite smile she always brought forth to wriggle out of trouble, and asked Helen if there was anything she wanted to say, fishing for an apology despite knowing none was due. Helen hadn't stopped to think and had pointed to Sophie's stomach, saying how glad she was about the news and how it was a comfort to know the baby couldn't be hers. This had been the cue for Sophie to dissolve into more tears and for a furious Ingrid to launch a verbal tirade which ended only when Helen made a classic Sophie move and stormed upstairs to hide in her bedroom. She had been there ever since, coming out to grab something to eat from the kitchen only if she was certain nobody else was around.

It was time to consider the next move, and Helen was certain now the next move was hers to make, because, despite her sudden departure from the conservatory, nobody had come looking for her since, not even her partner in crime Oskar, and, had she not been raiding the kitchen cupboards, she might have died of starvation for all anyone seemed to care. She knew she was exaggerating of course but the point was valid all the same and the fact nobody cared enough to bother checking on her had made her feel more than a little dejected.

On considering the available options, she knew it was pointless going downstairs and pretending nothing had happened because Sophie, for one, would never allow her to get off so lightly and if she tried that route, it would lead to an unwinnable argument because as an expectant mother, Sophie would be off limits for anything more than comforting words and general adoration. She could go downstairs and apologise but this would involve having to look at Sophie's smug face, knowing she was bullshitting, but being unable to call her out on it. That wasn't going to happen.

Helen lay on the bed for a while longer, trying and failing to plot her way out of the hole she had dug for herself, cursing her inability to keep her mouth shut and wishing she could take back what she said. It was bad enough subsisting on bare rations and becoming more stir crazy by the minute, but the worst thing of all, the greatest disaster, was that as far as Ingrid was concerned she was persona non grata, if not the devil incarnate. Of course, blame was easy to apportion for this thundering catastrophe; it was all Sophie's fault. Despite launching the initial witty one-liner herself, Helen was convinced the second avalanche of tears from the mother-to-be was a strategic move to fracture the nascent bond she had built with Ingrid and in that respect, it had been a stunning success. Now, alone in her cell, she saw no way back from that, and to make matters worse, her stomach wasn't satisfied by the cheese sandwich and began to rumble its disapproval as though telling her to hurry up and get the damn thing sorted. She glanced at her watch; it was 6 o'clock. Downstairs it was dinner time, a feast of culinary excellence to which she, an unwanted creature, had no invitation, banished as she was to the hinterlands, and forced to survive by undertaking clandestine missions for supplies. At this thought, and in concert with another growl from her stomach, she pulled herself upright and swung her legs over the side of the bed. She knew what she had to do.

Although hunger had played a part in the decision, Helen was also angry at herself for allowing things to get to a point where she was sulking like a stroppy teenager. She sat cross-legged on the bed with her MacBook balanced on her knees, flicking through London hotel reviews and wondering how she ever allowed herself to be so pathetic. Here she was, a respected academic, hiding in a bedroom in deepest, darkest Gravesend, flitting between moments of mooning over her colleague's mother, and going full special forces to forage for food whilst avoiding her. It was absurd. Despite her sulk, she smiled to herself at the thought of being in deepest, darkest anywhere because the words conjured up a picture of a wee talking bear wearing a duffle-coat and hat, and who wreaked general havoc and set fire to the drapes. It was the only thing missing from the house and in her mind's eye she pictured Ingrid's reaction to such an event and it tickled her so much she began to laugh out loud, the effect of which was to make it seem funnier which caused her to laugh even more until...in an instant she stopped, as realisation dawned. Although she hadn't set any soft furnishings ablaze or wrecked the bathroom, she had, in a figurative sense, brought the house down, and not in a way that would garner applause. She had to face it, the talking bear wasn't missing at all, it was her. At this thought the clouds in her head cleared and she saw the way forward, closing the lid on the computer and bouncing onto her feet. She decided it was time to go downstairs after all and do what she did best. It was time for her final gambit; she would have to unleash the bear.

***

Once out of her room, Helen descended the stairs Oskar style, just for the fun of it, the clattering thump also serving as advance warning to anyone who might be in the vicinity. She jumped the last two steps and didn't break stride as she crossed the short hallway and breezed into the kitchen. "Hey Oskar." She kept walking as she spoke, noting the downcast eyes from Sophie and the cold stare from Ingrid and that there was no fourth setting at the table, the absence of which confirmed she was not on the guest list for this party.

"Hey Helen." There was no enthusiasm in Oskar's voice and he spoke without lifting his head.

"How's things?" said Helen, walking beyond the table and pulling open the kitchen cupboards, searching each one before letting the doors bang shut. When Oskar didn't reply to her question she abandoned the search and turned around to face the table, a huge smile fixed on her face. "Ingrid, do you have any marmalade?"

Ingrid's cold stare remained in place as she turned her head. "Marmalade?"

"Yeah, marmalade, I fancy a marmalade sandwich, well, two of them, one for now and one for emergencies." Helen held onto her smile but she knew it wouldn't be for long because there was only so much conversation anyone could have about fruit preserves, and Ingrid's icy glare left her chilled and eager to get on with business.

"We have none." Ingrid turned away and went back to her dinner.

"I guess I'll just have to go hungry again," said Helen, hoping her words would tease out some sort of response but none came. Ingrid continued eating and Sophie pushed food around her plate, not looking up, while Oskar sat with his head down, looking like he wanted the floor to open beneath his seat and swallow him. "Is anybody going to speak to me?" The response to the question was silence and Helen's smile evaporated as she took a slow breath to compose herself before walking over to the table and taking the seat beside Ingrid, the very act of doing so feeling defiant and giving an extra twist to the churning of her stomach.

"What are you doing?" Ingrid's face flushed as she placed her cutlery down on her plate, and she turned to Helen, her face mordant and her eyes cold.

"It's obvious," Helen replied, gesturing to the food on the table, "I'm sitting down to dinner."

"You are not welcome at this table," Ingrid's voice shook but she met Helen's gaze with what appeared to be great effort, "please leave us."

"Am I not welcome, period, or not welcome unless I make a heart-felt apology for joking about Saint Sophie's delicate condition?" Helen glanced at Sophie as she spoke and then back to Ingrid. "You know me, I always like to be sure just how unwelcome I am."

"You cannot help yourself, can you? You seem compelled to deepen the hole and cannot stop digging." Ingrid sighed. "What do you want?"

Helen realised she had arrived at the decisive moment where the choices were stark and she could either attempt to joke her way through the awkwardness, hoping for a sudden burst of warmth due to the brilliance of her humour, or, she could make a genuine attempt to pour oil on troubled waters and somehow, despite the odds being against it, say enough to bring Ingrid back onside. Despite harbouring misgivings, mostly regarding her own ability to harness the right words, she decided to try smoothing things over. "I'd like to be honest about how I feel." She leaned back in the chair and looked between Oskar and Sophie. "You two as well, I'm talking to you. Would you like to know how I feel about things?"

Sophie stopped playing with her food and looked up, shrugging her shoulders in a non-committal gesture and flicking a glance sideways at her mother. Oskar nodded, but didn't speak.

"Ingrid?" Helen gestured towards her, waiting on the casting vote and desperate for her to give the green light because she understood that without Ingrid's agreement, her doom was to spend the foreseeable future stuck in a crummy hotel.

"We are eating dinner." Ingrid pointed to the food on the table without turning her head.

"I'm not eating," said Helen, "and since I'll be the one talking, I can't see the problem." She tried to keep her tone even, not wanting to raise the temperature of the conversation before it got going. "Please, I'm only asking to be heard and if what I say isn't good enough, then I'll go, and you'll never see me again." She swallowed to force the lump from her throat and then looked again to Ingrid, trying not to appear as pathetic as she felt and feeling her heart hammering in her chest as several silent seconds passed.

"All right," said Ingrid, keeping her attention fixed on what remained of her dinner, "I will listen to what you have to say so please, speak."

"Thank you." Although Helen felt the first stirrings of hope, she was wary, realising it could be the last conversation she had with any of them if she wasn't careful, and taking a breath to compose herself before stating the case for the defence. "Okay, I feel pretty lousy right now because I don't believe my treatment has been fair." She appreciated it was a bold introduction and so held up a hand to silence dissent, but as none was forthcoming, she dropped the hand and continued, disappointed by the lack of response but somewhat relieved there was no clamour of disagreement. "I came here with Sophie because she told me there were builders at her place; this was a lie." She looked at Sophie who glanced in her direction but said nothing. "Sophie then lied by omission when she failed to tell me you, Ingrid, can't cope with people you don't know. If I'd known, then I wouldn't have come." Again, she looked at Sophie and again the response was nothing more than a quick glance. "Then, having caught Sophie and me in a...friendly embrace, you, Ingrid, accused me of causing Sophie's marriage to break up which brings me back again to Sophie, who failed to mention this to me on the way from the airport."

"Oh wonderful," said Sophie, her eyes filling with tears, "now it's my fault and all because I had the temerity to get pregnant and have a husband who thinks I'm a slut."

"That's bullshit," Helen said, making a gargantuan effort not to raise her voice and give Sophie another excuse to sob her way into Ingrid's good books, "all I did was relay the facts and I didn't blame anyone, least of all you." She turned to Oskar, eager to proceed and get it over with. "You get a free pass because you've been nothing but decent since I arrived and although you didn't seek me out in the last couple of days, I'm guessing you were in a tight spot so it's fine."

"Thanks," said Oskar, dropping his gaze as soon as he finished speaking, his shoulders hunched, and looking for all the world like he would rather be anywhere but where he was.

"You're welcome." Helen paused to gather her thoughts for the final push, hoping she could express herself well enough to make them listen, Ingrid most of all. "So," she said, "to cut to the chase, I've found myself caught in the middle of a shitstorm not of my making but despite that, you all seem to have conspired to pin the blame on me and I'm clueless as to why. Perhaps it's because I'm not family or maybe it's easier because you don't have to confront your own inadequacies, I don't know. However, you've made me feel the most disliked and unwelcome I've ever felt in my life and you better believe you had a high bar to aim at, so well done." She stopped, relieved to finish but with hope diminishing fast because although Ingrid had stopped eating, nobody said a word and the ensuing silence spoke volumes about

68

how her polemic went down. Helen shook her head, knowing it had been a waste of time and she ran the fingers of both hands through her hair and pushed her chair back to stand. "Look, I came down here to tell you I've booked a hotel and I'm leaving tomorrow morning. I didn't intend to say all that crap but I just hoped for a minute you might be willing to listen to me but it seems I was wrong."

"Do you have to go?" said Oskar.

"As improbable as it may appear, I'd love to stay," said Helen, throwing her hands up in despair, "but check it out," she levelled her gaze on Sophie and Ingrid, "do you think I'm staying to confront this every day? Your sister loathes me and your mom thinks I've wrecked the house from the roof down, Jesus, I feel like I've been under attack since I arrived and I'm not staying here to be the talking bear." At this, she jammed her chair back fully and stood, hands on hips. "Ingrid, I'm starved, I really am so would it complicate things if I made myself some dinner before I go up to pack?"

"You will not make anything." Ingrid pushed her own chair back and stood, bringing her eye to eye with Helen. "I will prepare something for you." She twisted around and retrieved her plate and cutlery along with Sophie's then strode over to the sink, calling back over her shoulder. "Please, you will sit down and I will bring it over."

"Are you making me something before I pack," said Helen, "or are you making me something and I don't need to pack?" She fought to keep her voice steady and tucked her hands into her pockets to immobilise them, aware of the rapid thudding of her heart and certain she could see it battering away under her shirt.

"You cannot help but say more," Ingrid swivelled round, "why do you do it?"

Helen wasn't expecting the question. "I don't know, I've never thought about it," she walked over to Ingrid, this time throwing caution to the wind and standing eye to eye with her, "but I guess right now, I need the certainty." There was no immediate response from Ingrid but Helen perceived a gentleness within her, perhaps some kind of recognition or understanding, and although she couldn't define it with any precision, she was happy to accept it regardless.

Ingrid rubbed at her forehead and moved some hair back from her face, her eyes troubled, yet kind. "You can stay if you want to stay but if you do, there are matters we must discuss tonight," she glanced at Sophie, who was regarding them with apparent interest, "and I would prefer to do that alone with you, if that is all right."

"Thank you." Helen rubbed her eyes, hoping they didn't look too frightful, "and yes, alone is fine with me, tell me where and when and I'll be there." She felt herself gushing and on the verge of telling Ingrid she would do anything to be alone with her so she bit her tongue in the literal sense, giving her what appeared to be a gummy smile.

"Then we are settled," said Ingrid, gesturing to the table, "please, sit down and I will make you something to eat. What would you like?"

Helen took a deep breath and thought for a moment, remembering all the things she fantasised about eating when she was in solitary upstairs, unsure what she could ask for that would hit the spot. She was just about to say she would take anything when it came to her. "Is it true you don't have any marmalade, or did you just say that because you thought I wanted some?" She gave a weak smile.

Ingrid closed her eyes for a second and shook her head. "We have no marmalade. I am very sorry."

"That's okay," said Helen, "a sandwich would be wonderful, but whatever you do, please don't make it cheese, I'm begging you here, anything but cheese. It's all I've had for two days and I couldn't face it." She cleared her throat and took a long, slow breath, beginning to feel more like herself again then, beaming at Ingrid, she turned on her heel and walked over to the table, choosing a seat adjacent to Sophie's.

"What's the sudden passion for marmalade all about, I didn't know you liked it," said Sophie, her smile uncertain.

Helen knew the question was the start of a peace offering but before she could answer, Oskar interjected.

"It's Paddington, isn't it?" Oskar grinned at Helen, the truce seeming to have brought him back to life and he nodded towards Sophie and to Ingrid, who had stopped what she was doing to listen to the conversation. "Paddington Bear I mean, you know, the bear who talks and ends up living with a family but he wrecks their house and gets himself into buckets of trouble." He looked at them all, pleased with himself and confused simultaneously. "Doesn't anyone here know Paddington?"

"Is it true?" said Sophie, glancing at Ingrid, who turned her back and made herself busy again, building Helen's sandwich. "Do you picture yourself as a cute little talking bear?"

"Not an actual talking bear, no," Helen found herself unable to look at anyone and stared instead, at her hands, "but as a metaphor, it's not too wide of the mark perhaps. Thanks a lot, Oskar, I appreciate it."

"That's okay," Oskar replied, "I'm glad somebody else understood it and not just me."

Helen's composure had returned, at least in part and she turned to Sophie, running an eye over her and taking the opportunity to steer the conversation away from all things ursine. "How are you doing hun?" As she said the words she realised it was always the same when it came to Sophie, she couldn't stay mad at her for long, no matter what she did and it was no different now.

"I'm ok," said Sophie, patting her stomach several times, "so far, so good anyway."

Helen nodded and held out a hand towards her, pleased when she took it and gave it a squeeze. "I'm sorry," she said, "I was trying to be funny the other day but I was angry and I was mean to you, it wasn't my finest moment."

"It's fine, I wasn't at my best either." Sophie laid her other hand on Helen's arm and smiled at her then they held tight to each other until Ingrid appeared at the table with a huge, layered sandwich that was so massive, it threatened to spill over the edges of the plate.

"It is salad," said Ingrid, "with...I am sorry, I think Oskar must be having another growth spurt because it seems he has cleaned out my fridge again and I do not have much in."

"It's a cheese sandwich, isn't it?" Helen looked up at Ingrid, wide eyed with disbelief that her hard won sustenance was the very last thing she wanted to eat, and she began to panic that her jaws might refuse to chew it, or worse, that they would chew it but her stomach would repel it.

"Yes, it is cheese," Ingrid replied, giving the slightest of smiles, "cheese with salad. Would you like some coffee to accompany it?"

"No, no please," Helen held up her hands to stop Ingrid from bringing coffee too, "it would just transport be back to my time in the penitentiary," she gestured upstairs, "some things are best forgotten."

"I will get you something else if you like," Ingrid reached for the sandwich, "but I will have to cook it and you seem rather hungry to wait for long so..."

"No," Helen pulled the plate towards her, "it's great and I'm happy to have it, believe me, I'm starved." She eyed the giant sandwich for a few moments, considering how best to approach eating it without dislocating her jaw and, after manipulating it to find the best angle, she took a bite, feeling immediate relief she didn't gag or just open her mouth to let it spill out onto the table. When she finished the first mouthful she glanced up, and found herself the centre of attention with all eyes upon her. "Lovely," she said, smiling and nodding, "fabulous." She then looked down at the sandwich and shook her head.

"What is wrong," said Ingrid, her brow drawn down, "is the sandwich not nice?"

Helen put her elbow on the table and dropped her head onto her hand, all at once unable to meet Ingrid's gaze but flicking her eyes up again towards the giant sandwich and digging her fingernails into the palms of her hands to contain the laughter she felt building.

"Are you okay?" said Oskar, leaning over and trying to make eye contact under the hood of Helen's fingers.

Helen held a hand up, her shoulders jiggling in a silent dance as she tried to contain the giggles, and she pointed at the sandwich with her free hand as her battle against hysteria continued.

"I do not understand what is funny about a sandwich," said Ingrid, pulling back the chair opposite and sitting down, placing both hands on the table in front of her.

Helen coughed a few times, managing to subdue herself enough to speak, and she smiled over at Ingrid who stared back at her in bafflement. "It's a *cheese* sandwich though," she felt the

72

laugh stirring again and fought to contain it, "but it's not just a cheese sandwich, it's a *monster* cheese sandwich." The laugh started again and this time, Helen looked from Oskar to Sophie and back again. "Oh come on, it's enormous, have you ever seen anything so colossal?"

Oskar and Sophie exchanged glances and began to laugh themselves despite looking bewildered.

"It's the biggest cheese sandwich I've ever seen," Helen reached over the table and without thinking, took Ingrid's right hand, "but don't be mad at me, I'm not laughing at you or making fun of you, I just find it hysterical and I don't know why." She held fast to Ingrid's hand, her eyes pleading for things to remain calm.

"I cannot pretend to understand why the sandwich is so amusing," said Ingrid, "but I am not angry with you." She squeezed Helen's hand and then withdrew her own, leaning back in the chair, her face painted with pockets of rosy pink.

Helen turned her attention to Sophie and Oskar as she pulled herself upright. "I'm sorry, I think I'm fine now but it's been a long two days and I'm feeling somewhat emotional as you've probably observed."

"Would you like some cutlery for it or maybe an axe?" Oskar's mouth twitched at the corners as he pretended to chop at the slabs of bread on Helen's plate.

"Please," Helen stifled another laugh, "please, enough. If I don't stop, then..." she swallowed and rubbed at her mouth a few times, "please, no more." She looked at Ingrid again. "You said we'd have to talk if I was staying, how about now?"

"Yes, now will be fine," said Ingrid, turning to look at Sophie, "would you help Oskar to tidy up in here please? Helen and I will go to the sitting room."

"No problem," replied Sophie, "come on Oskar, move yourself." She looked at Helen as she stood up. "I'm not all bad you know."

"I know." Helen nodded then caught Ingrid's eye. "Shall we?" She gestured behind herself towards the door and started moving at Ingrid's nod of agreement. There was something else there too but Helen wasn't sure what it was.

"See you later," said Oskar, looking cheerful again.

"You bet you will." Helen waited until he had passed her before following Ingrid on their short walk to the sitting room. She didn't look back because if she did, she would see the monolithic cheese sandwich and then, anything could happen.

Chapter Six

Houston, We Have a Problem

Helen sat in one corner of the sofa propped up by two plump cushions, watching Ingrid close the blinds and pull the drapes shut and wondering why she was so keen to have a conversation now when she had been doing her best to avoid having one since Sophie's crude introductions just three days ago. The look she had given before they headed to the sitting room suggested it would be about Sophie which wouldn't be a surprise, given the big announcement. What she wanted to say about her though, remained a mystery.

"Would you like a drink?" said Ingrid, gesturing to a light-coloured wooden sideboard at the far wall.

"A drink?" The question was unexpected after the tumultuousness of the preceding few days and Helen could only parrot it back, eyeing Ingrid with caution, but also sensing for the first time that hostilities were at an end.

"Yes, would you like one?" A tentative smile accompanied the offer. "I am having one anyway, or perhaps more."

"Well, yeah," said Helen, "that would be fabulous, what do you recommend?" She made a silent wager with herself it would be Sherry, or worse, Advocaat, and braced herself to have one despite detesting both.

"I do not wish to stereotype you again but I thought as you are Scottish you might enjoy whisky," the smallest of smiles escaped, "although as you are only half Scottish perhaps you prefer something milder."

"Whisky is great but please, a small one," Helen winced at the memory of her last Scotch-related escapade, "I like it but it doesn't like me."

"All right, since it is whisky I will have just ice in mine, is that fine for you or do you need me to dilute it?" Ingrid held up a glass and looked at Helen for confirmation, her eyes watchful but sparkling with mischief nonetheless.

"Yeah, that works for me, thanks." Helen smiled and relaxed into the soft cushions, as she closed her eyes and waited for Ingrid's return with ice. As thrilled as she was to have her to herself, and a friendly version at that, everything still seemed surreal and flip-flopped from minute to minute, especially Ingrid's mood or perhaps, it would be fairer to say, her ability to cope with anything out of the norm. Here she was being nice and playing hostess yet, within the last hour, she had acted like the coldest of cold fish, expecting Helen to pack up her troubles and fuck off. Still, it didn't matter when it came right down to it, because if this was the flip in the flip-flop, it was good enough for now.

When she heard the clink of ice meeting glass, Helen opened her eyes and pushed the hair from her face to find a clear line of sight to where Ingrid stood, watching how she carried herself as she sloshed out the whisky, and appreciating her loose-limbed, easy, comportment which was a far cry from the tight, faltering movements the last time they were in the sitting room alone. It was a beautiful sight to behold but as Ingrid turned to head back to the sofa, Helen pulled her eyes away, not looking up until they were almost toe to toe and then, feeling a sinking sensation in the pit of her stomach as she took the large glass of whisky and watched Ingrid sit at the opposite end of the sofa, just as she'd done before. The flip had become flop. "You know, you don't have to sit in a different Zip Code," said Helen, unable to fight the urge to say it, "what I mean, is I can keep my hands to myself." She looked at Ingrid and shook her head before taking a sip of whisky, enjoying the burn as it worked its way over her throat and down as she tried to remain calm.

"I know what you meant," said Ingrid, not moving closer but swinging her legs up on the couch and stretching out, leaving her feet only a few inches away from Helen's thigh.

Helen laughed then took another mouthful of Scotch, pondering her options as they both looked at each other without speaking and in the end, she decided to travel along the easy road. "You wanted to talk about something?"

"Yes," replied Ingrid, sipping her whisky, "I would like to discuss your relationship with Sophie."

"Okay," Helen shrugged her shoulders, "talk, but we've been here before and if you think you can get a different answer by repeating the same question then you're wrong because there's nothing going on."

"I am aware of that," Ingrid took a mouthful of whisky, "but Sophie told me what happened on the night you kissed her and I would be interested to hear your version." She looked away from Helen and down to the glass in her hand.

"I see, what did she tell you about it?" Helen sounded her internal red alert claxon and braced for impact, caught out by Sophie's apparent willingness to confess all about their brief encounter and stung by the fact she had chosen Ingrid as her confessor.

"When you told me you had kissed Sophie I had in my mind a kiss would be something quick and simple," Ingrid took another sip of Scotch, "but you did not tell me you were in her bed at the time."

Helen took another mouthful of Scotch, savouring the combination of bitterness and heat, and she raised one eyebrow before giving a slow, deliberate smile. "Well, if you think a kiss is quick and simple, you've never been kissed properly." She tipped her head back and downed the rest of the whisky, fighting the temptation to offer a personal demonstration just to see the reaction, and pleased at how she had deflected the question.

Ingrid matched Helen's raised eyebrow with one of her own. "If you know Sophie as well as I think you do," she paused and took the rest of her drink in one swallow, "then you will appreciate there is more in what she does not say than in what she does say, so I am relying on you to fill in the gaps."

"Tell me something, why do you need to know?" It was a diversionary tactic Helen often used, answering by means of another question to buy thinking time, although in this case, she didn't believe it would delay the inevitable for much longer as Ingrid appeared determined to hear the whole sorry tale.

"I am worried for my daughter and I am interested in your...motivations, so please, tell me the truth about what happened."

"I can't see how knowing more can make you worry less," Helen regarded her empty glass, "and that goes double for my motivations. Could I have another one of these please?" She shook the empty glass, still clinging to the diminishing hope she could derail the conversation and perhaps live to fight another day.

"Perhaps you will be good enough to also bring me one," Ingrid held her glass aloft and smiled, "to take your mind off having to find a suitable answer for my question of course."

Helen laughed and shook her head, then pulled herself up from the sofa and walked over to Ingrid to collect her glass. "I would've thought you'd be more worried about Sophie's situation now than something we did once." She took the glass and walked over to the sideboard, amused and concerned in equal measure at how easily Ingrid had seen through her procrastination.

"I am concerned about both things," replied Ingrid, "but I would prefer to deal with one at a time, if it is convenient for you."

Helen didn't reply, but refilled both glasses to the brim before walking back over to the sofa and handing Ingrid her drink. She sat down in the middle of the sofa and pulled cushions over from where she had been sitting just moments before, forcing Ingrid to pull her legs up to make room. "Can I presume she told you about the thing with Michael?"

"Yes," said Ingrid, nodding, "she did, at least she told me what she was prepared to tell me which is Sophie at her finest."

"So, what did she say?" Helen tried to keep the topic of discussion fixed on the baby and Sophie.

"It is as she said before you took yourself upstairs to sulk, Michael does not believe the baby belongs to him and therefore she has abandoned him and cannot return. She also claims," Ingrid downed some more Scotch and sighed, "she also claims to have a male friend who Michael believes to be more than a friend."

"No way, that's bullshit," Helen shook her head, "there has to be more to it."

"I agree," Ingrid took another mouthful of whisky, "and as I said, it is more important what Sophie does not say."

Helen nodded, considering the options and weighing up the likelihood of a platonic male friend causing a problem so huge that Sophie's husband would refuse to recognise his own progeny. She concluded it was indeed bullshit, and when you added Sophie's tendency to obfuscate into the mix, the call of bullshit became even more likely. "Do *you* think the baby is Michael's or do you believe there's any credence to the more than a friend thing?"

"Sophie insists Michael is the baby's father." Ingrid played with a strand of her hair, her eyes distant. "She is equally insistent the only thing between her and the male friend is friendship and I believe her."

"Okay, but how can you be so convinced she isn't lying, I mean, it's Sophie we're talking about here?"

Ingrid drained her glass and smiled. "Oh I know my Sophie and she will tell little lies to get herself out of trouble but," she stood up and beckoned towards Helen's empty glass, "she has always been truthful about serious things, even as a child." She motioned again to Helen with her glass.

"I'm still good here." Helen shot a glance towards the whisky bottle on the sideboard and saw they had made a big dent in it already. "In fact, I'm wondering if we should both slow down a bit." She looked at her glass and scrunched up her face. "The last time I went too hard on this stuff I had a bad time," she grimaced at the memory and raised an eyebrow, "it was the night I ended up kissing Sophie."

"I see," said Ingrid, her face flushing, "am I at risk from your attentions or did you mean I should slow down too?" She tilted her head, catching Helen's startled expression and holding it for a second before covering her neck with one hand and looking away.

"Oh I didn't mean...not that I wouldn't...but I wasn't suggesting anything...' Helen fell silent, any remaining words dying before they reached her lips, and both cheeks burning in the silence that followed. Her eyes fell on Ingrid, just as she returned the same embarrassed look and Helen knew she had to say something, anything, if it broke the moment. "I think maybe I would like to see you drunk," she covered her mouth and coughed, "might even pay money to see it too." She knew it was a poor effort, but in the circumstances she was happy to grab it with both hands.

Ingrid stared at Helen for a few moments and then she laughed, her face brightening in the process and her eyes shining. "I do believe you would pay to see that," she half turned away and raised her glass, "anyway, this is your last chance for a refill so speak now."

Helen nodded, ignoring the warmth still lingering on her cheeks, and relieved the awkwardness had passed without major trauma. "One more then, and I mean one because I haven't eaten much tonight and you don't want me drunk on an empty stomach."

"Would you like me to make you another sandwich, it would be no problem?" Ingrid's soft smile broadened as she headed for the cabinet, and the whisky.

Helen laughed but at once tried to draw it back, desperate to prevent the development of a full-blown case of the giggles which, if they appeared, would be uncontrollable. "Oh no, please don't mention the sandwich," she was still laughing as Ingrid walked back towards her with the drinks, "I can't let that picture inside my head or I might die of hysteria." As she took the refilled glass she was delighted to see Ingrid abandon her anchor point at the far end of the couch and sit closer, all without any apparent discomfort and they sat there for a while, enjoying the Scotch and the pleasant silence between them until at length, Ingrid spoke.

"I have a question I would like to ask but it is not about Sophie, it is about you."

"Fire away." Helen reached for her glass in preparation for needing extra fortification, sensing things might be about to become personal and wanting to be ready.

"To begin with I would like to apologise for making you feel unwelcome here," Ingrid paused and took another sip of whisky, "but I would like to know, why did you want to stay, despite this?"

"Thanks for the apology, it means a lot." Helen relaxed again, despite the discussion bulleting towards a point where she would have to choose how much to disclose. "I should warn you before I answer, it'll be difficult for me to explain my reluctance to call it a day, without sounding pathetic," she took another mouthful of Scotch before setting the glass down at her feet, "but you asked the question so I feel duty bound to tell you."

Ingrid nodded but said nothing, instead, settling herself in to listen.

Seeing no way out of the situation, Helen took a deep breath then launched into what she hoped would be an acceptable explanation. "Okay, here goes. I'm very fond of Sophie, even though she is Sophie," she saw a look of understanding on Ingrid's face and continued, "and I'll admit in the past I've been conflicted about my feelings for her but it's not current, I promise."

"So, despite everything that happened, you stayed for Sophie, is that your reason?"

"She was certainly part of it," Helen replied, "but it's not that straightforward and it's embarrassing but, I suppose I also stayed because...I have nothing else." She bent to retrieve her glass from the floor, catching Ingrid's wide-eyed reaction, and smiling. "I see my pathetic confession shocked you."

"Yes, it did, but I am not sure what it means," Ingrid took another sip of whisky, "you will have to explain it further."

"It's not anything complex," Helen shrugged, then downed the rest of her Scotch in one go, "and like I said, Sophie's here and when I arrived, Oskar was great fun and you were very nice to me, so I wanted a bit more of your niceness and it was like being part of a family."

Ingrid drained her glass then licked her lips. "You say you have nothing else, but Sophie describes things in a very different way, like you have a perfect life, full of excitement and interesting events."

Helen laughed but it was only a reflex, a spontaneous reaction to Sophie's shallow interpretation of her lifestyle. "Sophie sees the superficial, you know, the great job, the nice car, the house, all the friends and sunny Californian lifestyle, but she doesn't attempt to scratch the surface and look for anything underneath." She looked at her empty glass and shook her head. "Do you know what happens at the holidays, at Christmas I mean?" She raised her eyebrows and gestured for Ingrid to answer.

"No, what happens?"

"The nice friends go home to their families but I don't, because I can't. Despite all the back and forth between my dad and my mom, when all is said and done, none of them wanted me in the normal way you would with a kid." Helen looked Ingrid in the eye. "I get one card every year at Christmas from an uncle in Glasgow but nothing else," she smiled, "so you see, I sometimes tough things out long after I should call it quits. Here with you, I just hoped for a chance to be part of something for a while."

"I can understand that," said Ingrid in a quiet voice, reaching out and holding Helen's arm, "it is not easy having a broken family and being alone."

"I know, and I'll tell you something else," Helen smiled at the sudden appearance of a new, tactile Ingrid, and laid a hand on hers, "I'm not having any more to drink because my head's soft and I can't feel my face." She pulled her hand free and poked at different sections of her face, all the while relishing how soft Ingrid's hand had felt underneath her own and only risking eye contact after a sideways glance caught an amused expression. "What's going on in that head of yours, what are you thinking?"

"I am thinking you cannot hold your liquor," Ingrid removed her hand from Helen's arm, and smiled, "but I will be having just one more, so, can I tempt you?" There was a twinkle in her eyes as she spoke.

"Oh," Helen blinked in surprise, barely able to conceal her delight at Ingrid's response, "that is indeed, a loaded question, but in terms of a refill I shouldn't because I'll end up drunk if I do, then there's no telling what might happen."

"Are you sure?" Ingrid stood up, swinging her empty glass back and forth in a lazy motion and gazing down at Helen's beaming face, her eyebrows arched in anticipation of a change of heart.

Helen considered matters for a moment, already feeling the effects of the whisky and recognising the dangers inherent in partaking of even another small one. Despite that, she wanted to keep going because she had just enjoyed one of the nicest mini flirting sessions of her life and a few more drinks could make things very interesting indeed. Not that she was certain it had been flirting of course, but if it wasn't, then it was damn close, and with Ingrid of all people which added to the magic. With that thought, she ignored her instincts and held up her glass. "One more, but please, a really small one."

"One small drink coming up soon," said Ingrid, swiping the glass from Helen's hand and headed over to the sideboard again, returning in less than a minute with both glasses full to the brim.

"Thank you." Helen reached up and took the glass, holding it into tight into her body with both hands and determined it would last the remainder of the evening. "I have a question for you now," she paused, realising she was about to take a huge risk, " but I'm not sure how to ask it though."

"It is unlike you to be lost for words, whatever can you want to know that has tied up your tongue?"

"Well, it's personal," said Helen, shaking her head, "and I'm not sure it's appropriate either, so maybe I can have several questions and build up to it."

"Oh please, tell me what you want to know and if it is inappropriate then I will refuse to answer and no harm will be done."

"Okay, when did you come here from Sweden?" It wasn't what Helen wanted to ask at all, but when it came to the moment, she felt herself engaging reverse gear and just asked the first thing that popped into her head. Luckily it was still something she was interested in and she thought it was a good beginning anyway, a solid base for further probing.

"I came over in 1984," Ingrid laid her head on the sofa back, "I was twenty-seven and I came to work in a hospital." She took a sip from her glass, smiled, and looked at Helen, "Do you want to know what I did in the hospital?"

"I sure do," Helen forced herself to sit up straighter in an effort to maintain her focus, "so continue please, I'm all ears."

"I was an emergency nurse, you know, in the accident department. I loved it very much but," her smile faltered for a second, "I stopped when I had my Sophie and never returned."

"Wait," Helen's eyes and nose wrinkled into a picture of confusion, "you stopped for good, just because you had Sophie?"

"Yes, I did," said Ingrid, "it was not so easy to work and have a child back then, it is much better now of course but, not then. I had Anna just a few years later which made it impossible so Gary, my husband, worked, and I stayed at home."

"That seems such a waste," said Helen, at once raising both

hands, "I'm sorry, I didn't mean to denigrate your life choices, it just came out wrong and too fast."

"It is fine," Ingrid sighed and smiled, "I would not change the time I spent with my children and as much as there were few options for me, it was my decision and I was contented." She rubbed her mouth and closed her eyes for a second, the smile weakening as she did so and then reappearing once more as she eyed Helen. "I was happy."

"I'm glad to hear it," said Helen, not believing a word of it such was the juxtaposition between what Ingrid's mouth said and what her eyes said. "So, you came here in '84 and I know Sophie was born in '86," Helen grinned, "was it a whirlwind romance?"

"You could say so," Ingrid smiled, "we were married six months before Sophie was born which is I think, what you wanted to know."

"I see." Helen took a mouthful of whisky, and settled back into the cushions, intrigued as Ingrid peeled away another layer of restraint and revealed a very different version of herself from the one presented before. "Tell me more about Gary and when you got married."

Ingrid took a sip of whisky and leaned back into the sofa again, her eyes staring into the distance. "I met Gary the same year I arrived in England," she looked round at Helen, "he is younger than I am, he was only twenty when we met, very young."

"That's young, yeah," said Helen, nodding and soaking up yet another surprising revelation.

"Well, it was not long at all until I found I was expecting a baby so, we got married, much to the distaste of Gary's parents who very much disapproved of me," she raised an eyebrow as she looked at Helen, "so you are not the only person who has ever felt unwelcome."

"That's not good at all, why did they disapprove, was it the age gap?" Helen had been surprised to hear how young Ingrid's husband had been when they married but, overall, seven years was hardly huge and she was more troubled by the reaction to the gap than by the gap itself.

"Yes, it was the age gap and they tried to talk us out of it, or I should say they tried to talk Gary out of it, but he would not listen to them because we were both head over heels in love then you see."

Helen leaned forward in her seat, absorbed in the story and keen to know what happened next although the little flutter in Ingrid's eye when she mentioned love, suggested there was more to the story than what she was hearing. "So, did you elope to Gretna Green with his family on your tails?"

"We got married as I have already said," Ingrid chewed on her bottom lip for a second before giving Helen a victorious smile, "but we did not need to elope and his parents of course, came to the wedding."

"I would never have had you down for a shotgun wedding," Helen laughed, "I'm impressed."

Ingrid tutted but her eyes betrayed her mood and she smiled as she replied "I did not need a shotgun to get Gary to marry me, I was nice then, and I can show you the photos as proof."

"I don't need a photograph to know you're nice, but all the same, I wouldn't object to seeing a younger version of you, to be sure you've been consistent." Helen made herself smile but Ingrid's revealing comment highlighted her underlying lack of self-worth, and it was troubling. "Come on, you've got me all excited now and sometimes that doesn't end well so let's see the pictures and be damned."

"I have a few but not lots," said Ingrid, laughing at Helen's reaction, "I shall get them." She put her glass on the floor then stood and walked over to the sideboard again and, after a minute or so of rummaging, she returned to the sofa with a silver box. "Photos," she said, sitting close to Helen and removing the lid from the box. "I am not sure what may be in here, so you must let me look first."

"Yeah, sure." A young Ingrid, free from the troubles plaguing her is what Helen expected she would see, but she also wondered whether the photos would divulge anything less appetising, perhaps a hint of the darkness which had stolen her confidence.

Ingrid flicked through the box with nimble fingers and, after hiding some pictures at the back of the box she turned to Helen and pointed to the photograph at the top of the pile. "This was the wedding party but as you can see, it was not big."

Helen picked up the photograph and there she stood, a young

Ingrid who was very blonde, very slim and who had, quite possibly, the biggest hair Helen had ever set eyes on. Her dress was beautiful but it wasn't a traditional wedding dress, instead it was figure hugging and mid-calf in length and looked made of ivory coloured silk or something not far removed. She turned to Ingrid and pointed to the photo. "The hair," was all she said, with a laugh.

Ingrid raised her eyes and nodded. "Yes, the hair was rather big." She pointed to the photograph. "That is Gary of course, those are his parents and the women are my mother and her sister."

Helen looked at the photo again and then back at Ingrid. "You look like your mom, she's nice."

"I know I do," replied Ingrid, "and as every year passes, I look more like her, sometimes I think I am her doppelganger. What about you, is there a resemblance to your mother or are you more like your father?"

"I have my dad's height, for which I'll be eternally grateful but I'm closer in looks to her than to him," Helen shrugged, "we have the same mouth and colour of eyes." She closed her eyes and turned to Ingrid. "What colour are my eyes?"

"Brown," said Ingrid, without hesitation.

Helen smiled but said nothing, instead, flicking through the photographs, comparing the past with the present and enjoying how much, and in some cases how little, Ingrid had changed over the years. In certain photos, whether it was just the angle of the shot or the way Ingrid gazed at the camera, the resemblance to Sophie today was startling, the only difference being hair colour. "It's weird," said Helen, lifting the wedding party photo again and pointing to Ingrid's stomach, "little Sophie's hiding in there."

"Yes, she is," Ingrid swirled the last of her whisky around the glass, "which brings us back to Sophie and her baby and to you."

Helen dropped the photo back into the box and turned, unsure whether arriving back at this point was accidental or if Ingrid had played a long game. "What do you want to know?"

Ingrid downed the last of her whisky and placed the empty glass on the floor. "That night in Sophie's bed, when you were kissing her," she held Helen in her gaze, "I understand you became sick and vomited so I want to know this; had you not been sick, would you moved beyond kissing?"

There was no hint of anger in Ingrid's voice and she appeared to be calm so Helen gave herself dispensation to nod, and although she knew better than to launch into the whole tacky story, she did nonetheless confess the gist of it. "I'm afraid the answer is no, I wouldn't have stopped and neither would Sophie, I can assure you. In fact, by the time I started feeling a little nauseous we had already progressed."

"Progressed?" Ingrid's eyes were wide. "You said it was only kissing."

"I know I said it was kissing," said Helen, her cheeks aglow, "and that's correct, but I didn't tell you what I was kissing?" She shrugged her shoulders and gave a sheepish smile, watching as Ingrid's mouth fell open, and caught between wanting to qualify the statement and knowing she should keep schtum to avoid landing herself in more hot water. A strained silence fell between them and they sat locked in position, eyes averted, and with a hush surrounding them. At length, when she could stand it no more, Helen broke the deadlock, nervous about propelling the conversation forward but unable to exist comfortably in the dead air. "Can I presume I've fucked things up between us again and you're mad at me?"

Ingrid's reaction to the question was immediate but conciliatory. "No, I am not annoyed at you," she shook her head, "but I am in a quandary because I believe we both have a problem on our hands."

"Oh, we have a problem," Helen perked up at the suggestion they would be collaborating on whatever misfortune lay ahead, "is it the sort of problem another small drink would help?"

"Perhaps." Ingrid's face was emotionless, her eyes unfocussed.

"Ingrid."

"What is it?"

"Would you like me to act as bartender and bring us another small drink?"

"Yes," Ingrid bent and picked up her glass then held it out for collection, "that would be very much appreciated."

"Ingrid," Helen whispered it, "I have a question of my own

for you."

"What?" Ingrid's tone was sharp and she tipped her head backwards, eyes closed tight and lips pressed together.

"Tomorrow morning," Helen rose to her feet, "will you still love me?"

"Will I still...what?" Ingrid's eyes flashed open and she sat open mouthed, staring up at Helen who towered over her.

Helen flopped back into her seat, glasses in both hands. "I mean," she maintained the whisper-like tone, "will you still speak to me tomorrow, without any of these?" She waved the glasses around and waited for an answer, gazing into Ingrid's eyes, the fuzziness in her head not yet expansive enough to blind her to Ingrid's apparent lack of horror at what she had asked.

"I think I should be able to manage," said Ingrid, taking a deep, slow breath, "now, you were being the bartender were you not?" She motioned towards the sideboard where the remains of the Black label sat.

"Yeah, I was getting us small drinks." Helen stood again and nodded. "Ingrid."

"For goodness sake, what is it now?" Ingrid's head snapped up, irritation writ large upon her face.

Helen knew she should say nothing and she gave a silent prayer to Satan to get behind her, hardly surprised when he did just that and pushed her back to centre stage where her motor mouth could flourish. "I'm hungry."

Ingrid opened her mouth as if to speak but she hesitated, biting back the words with apparent difficulty and raising her head to glare at Helen. "You know where the kitchen is," she sounded calm and strained simultaneously, "or have a few drinks clouded your memory?"

"I know where it is, but I'm too afraid to go in there again," Helen made a scared face, "*it* might still be waiting for me."

Without warning, Ingrid stood, forcing Helen to take a step backward to avoid a clash of heads, and looking her square in the eye before grabbing the glasses from her hand. "You will sit and say nothing more," she pointed to the sofa, "and I will get the drinks." With that, she marched across the room to refill the glasses, without a backwards glance.

Helen sat down as instructed, struggling to keep the smile

from her face but working hard to do it nonetheless, fearful of bringing Ingrid's wrath down upon her to spoil their détente. She watched her pour the drinks and followed her journey as she returned with full glasses, taking one when offered then sitting in silence, sneaking a look at her drinking partner every so often and trying to judge a good moment to speak. "Ingrid."

Ingrid turned her head, the motion slow and deliberate, resembling a stop motion figure from an old Ray Harryhausen film.

"I was just trying to make you laugh," Helen gave her best smile, "but you didn't, so I guess it wasn't funny." She worked up her best, sad face and caught, just for a moment, the glimmer of a smile in Ingrid's eyes and on her mouth.

"Helen, we both have a problem and," Ingrid stopped speaking for a second and sipped her drink, "we both need to be serious."

"I can be serious," said Helen, again using her best, serious face, "tell me what our problem is."

"It is Sophie, of course," Ingrid replied, "and I think I now understand something of what is behind her being."

"Okay, what's behind it?" Helen shuffled herself in her seat, getting comfortable, and preparing herself to hear the worst.

Ingrid balanced her glass on the arm of the sofa and then turned herself around towards Helen and tucked both legs up on the seat, stretching around to grab her glass before righting herself once more. "When you were hiding in Anna's bedroom, I spoke with Sophie and she told me what I have already told you, that Michael did not believe the baby was his because of some silly male friend she has. No matter how much I tried, it always came back to this and we went around in circles with Sophie changing the subject always to the one thing. Do you want to know what it was?"

Helen said nothing but she nodded, something in Ingrid's voice hinting she might not like what she heard.

"It was you, Helen, always it was you. It was about how funny you are, then it was about how kind you are, then it was about how much you make her laugh and then," Ingrid took a breath, "then it was about how you would never leave her on her own with a baby her husband had rejected."

"No," Helen's mouth was dry and the word croaked out, "it can't possibly mean what you think it means."

"Yes, very much, yes it can." Ingrid's brow furrowed and her lips became a tight line.

"But there's nothing going on with me and Sophie...it's just a game we play, I mean, I don't..."

"It is a game to you but I think for Sophie it is something more consequential than a silly thing you both do for fun. Certainly, if your kiss had just been a silly drunken kiss then perhaps it would be different, but I fear it is more serious."

"But it was just a drunken kiss," said Helen, shaking her head, "it should never have happened and I thought Sophie and I had settled things."

"I do not like being the bearer of unhappy news but things are not as settled as you imagine them to be."

"This can't be happening." Helen dropped her head into both hands and leaned forward in her seat. "Why did it have to be me?" She kept her head down and fell into silence, trying to force her racing mind to rationalise everything. All this time she had thought it was just a game, something to keep it light and to let them both know everything was good between them. But it wasn't a game and she knew in her heart Ingrid had put two and two together and got the right answer. "This can't be happening, this cannot be happening." As she spoke, she felt a light touch on her left shoulder.

"I could be wrong of course, it is possible I have jumped to the wrong conclusion." Ingrid's voice was soft and calm and with her hand resting on Helen's shoulder she gave a cautious smile. "I have been wrong about a lot of things recently."

"You're not wrong about this though," said Helen, pushing herself up, "and Sophie was right."

"Right about what?"

"About how I would never see her struggling on her own with a kid, she knows me too well for my own good." Helen sighed. "What do we do with this? I don't want to raise a kid with Sophie, I'm fond of her but I'm not mom material."

"And I want Sophie to raise her child with her husband. Michael is a good man and he deserves better than she has served him."

"I'm so sorry Ingrid, I don't know how to fix this without somebody getting hurt. I don't know what to do." Helen picked up her glass again and puffed her cheeks out in exhaustion, the events of the last few days finally catching up with her.

Ingrid squeezed Helen's shoulder then slid her hand down onto her lower back, allowing it to rest there. "We will think of something. I do not know how but we will find a solution together, I promise." The words were hardly out when the door to the sitting room crashed open, Oskar barrelling into the room and towards the couch as Ingrid snatched her hand away from Helen's back and held out both arms towards him in welcome.

"I've got great news," Oskar's face cracked in happiness as he came to an abrupt stop in front of the sofa, "wait a minute, have you both been drinking?" He pointed to the glasses in their hands and twisted his head back and forth, looking between then in astonishment.

"Don't be a dumbass," Helen said, giggling, "we're holding these for someone else." She glanced at Ingrid and winked, then smiled back at Oskar. "What's the good news?"

"It's fantastic." Oskar kneeled on the floor in front of them. "Kieran managed to get me two tickets for tomorrow's game at the Bridge," he looked at Helen "would you like to go to the match with me?"

"The match?" Helen reached out and tried to ruffle Oskar's hair but he laughed and dodged her hand. "Who's playing?"

"Chelsea versus Liverpool."

"How can a girl resist such an offer?" Helen laughed and rolled her eyes. "Tell you what, I'll pay for the tickets as my treat and don't give me any arguments about it, okay."

"I won't argue, I'm broke anyway." Oskar looked at Ingrid and grinned. "I was about to ask you for some financial help."

"I have had a lucky escape then," she replied, "thank you, Helen, you are very generous."

"Yeah, thanks Helen," said Oskar, "so, what's happening?" He glanced between them a couple of times until Helen beckoned him over.

"Oskar," she whispered in his ear, covering her mouth with her hand in a conspiratorial fashion, "I'm helping your mom so could you get lost for a little while?" She took her hand away and winked at him.

"Oh, right," he said, "I need to go and tell Kieran I'm in for those tickets." He unravelled himself and got to his feet. "See you both later maybe." He kissed Ingrid goodbye and was gone almost as quickly as he had arrived.

"So," said Ingrid, "you have a Saturday afternoon at the football with Oskar. How nice." Her voice held a sarcastic edge.

"Yeah," Helen replied, nodding, "let's hope he doesn't think it's a fuckin' date though." She put her glass to her mouth and downed the contents in one swallow.

Chapter Seven

Oh! What a Lovely Surprise

The crowd rumbled in discontent and a baleful booing sound rolled around the stands drowning out the cheers of the small number of away fans in the corner. "No way is that offside," said Oskar, sitting down and nudging Helen's arm, "did you see it?"

"Yeah, I saw it but so did VAR and VAR's call is offside." Helen waited for Oskar to react, knowing what was coming and relishing it anyway as she continued to flick through the emails on her phone, not sure what she expected to find there, but checking anyway.

"VAR's ruining the game," Oskar's lips curled and his brow wrinkled, "it slows everything down and then gets it wrong but I expect you like it though, Helen." He sat with his hands on his knees, head turning left to right and right to left as the game continued to ebb and flow.

"Why would I have a specific liking for VAR, pray tell me?" Helen knew what he would say and prepared herself to defend her American heritage but before he could speak, a collective gasp escaped from the crowd and everyone around her stood, straining their necks to see past the people in front of them who had also jumped to their feet. This was a strange ritual she found very funny. They would all pay a fortune for a seat and then at high points in the game everybody would stand, making it impossible for anyone to stay in their expensive seat and still see the pitch. From her perspective it was absurd but everyone around her, Oskar included, appeared to treat it as part and parcel of the matchday experience and nobody complained.

The excitement over, Oskar retook his seat and restarted his denunciation of video-led stoppages in play. "The thing about VAR, is it's making the game like American football, all stoppages and replays and it won't be long until we don't have two halves and it'll be quarters instead." He glanced at Helen.

"Are you not enjoying the game?"

"Yes, I'm loving it," she smiled at him, hoping her little white lie would escape his notice, "what makes you think I'm not?"

"You don't seem very enthusiastic."

"I'm enjoying it fine." Helen closed her email app and slid the phone back into the pocket of her jeans. "I'm sorry, full attention from now on I promise."

"It's into stoppage time now," Oskar shuffled in his seat, the slight tremor in his voice betraying his nervousness, "five minutes for Chelsea to hold on."

"Will they do it?" Helen lowered the pitch of her voice, attempting to sound serious to atone for her earlier lack of passion.

"It could be tight."

"You mean it's squeaky bum time." Helen laughed at the surprise on Oskar's face. "Yeah, I've heard the term so don't be so shocked I know something about football?"

"What would someone who's half American and half Scottish know about football?" Oskar grinned as he began to rise from his seat at the prospect of excitement at the far end of the pitch.

"Any more of your cheek and it's no Happy Meal on the way home," said Helen, kicking at his ankle, "that means no toy."

Oskar grunted and laughed but his eyes remained focused on the pitch.

Helen sat back and watched him, enjoying his absorption in the game as the minutes ticked down, her pretence at enjoying it put to bed. She hoped she hadn't spoiled his fun although she thought the answer was probably not, given the number of times he had been on his feet with the crowd, shouting at the referee. Overall it had been a pleasant day although for all her contemplation over the ninety minutes, she had yet to strike gold in her search for inspiration about how to deal with the Sophie conundrum. Worse still, with all her concentration focussed on Sophie, she hadn't found time to consider what to do about Ingrid, despite feeling she was hurtling towards the point where she would have to weigh up the risks and decide to act or not. It would be fatal to make the wrong decision and there would be no time added on for stoppages back at the house; getting it wrong would mean a straight red card.

"*Yes!*" Oskar stood, hands in the air, applauding with the rest of the crowd as the whistle blew for full time. "That was brilliant," he slapped Helen on the back, "thanks for coughing up for this, you're a champion, even though you don't understand anything about it."

"You're welcome." Helen smiled followed Oskar as they started shuffling out of their row and towards the exits. "Anyway, I felt I owed you one for the masturbation thing." She watched his face but there was no blush this time.

"I still can't believe you said it in front of mum, I nearly had convulsions."

"I can hardly believe I said it, but it was an emergency so I had no option."

They reached the end of the row and started to climb up the stairs behind the dispersing crowd, their progress slow to begin with but speeding up without warning when, without any obvious reason, the way in front cleared in a sudden rush and they were able to reach the first available exit before too long.

"Bugger," Oskar danced around with a pained expression on his face, "I need to use the gents," he pointed up towards the back of the stand, "are you coming?"

"Yeah I'll come and stand outside the guy's toilets," Helen rubbed her hands together, "that's a good look for me, can't wait."

Oskar laughed. "Heard and understood," he began to ease himself over a seat and into the row above, "back in five minutes."

Helen turned out of the surging crowd, watching Oskar as he ran up towards the back of the stand, weaving in and out of the rows to clamber over seats where needed. Taking her eyes off him, she stood to the side and then, spotting a gap, pushed her way back until she was at the end of a row, tucking herself in there to look out at the almost empty stands, and marvelling at a build designed to ensure they emptied at speed. To her right, about six rows down, a large group of fans had remained seated, no doubt waiting until the rush cleared so they could get out without a struggle. They seemed an eclectic bunch, women and men, young and old, the only thing blending them into a homogenous blob being the blue scarves and shirts they wore.

She was about to turn away to look for any sign of Oskar when someone in the group caught her eye. Right at the back, a man and a much younger woman were having a serious kissing session but nobody other than Helen seemed to be paying them much attention. She could only see part of the woman's face but she could see her man-friend quite clearly when he came up for air. As much as it felt incongruous, she couldn't help feeling she knew him, maybe from back home or from the LSE campus here, and she kept her eyes on him, studying his face whenever it popped back into full view. She considered taking a closer look but decided discretion might be the better part of valour in this instance; one look at the woman was enough to know she was young enough to be his daughter and this signalled trouble in Helen's book. Nevertheless, she was certain she knew the face and had met the man before in some capacity.

"*Helen!*"

At the sound of her name Helen turned around and saw Oskar waving at her from the spot where they had parted company and she started heading in his direction, looking back a couple of times at the kissing couple, all the while trying to place the man's face in context. When she reached her destination she glanced back at the kissers again before turning to Oskar. "Right, are you good to go now?"

"Yep," he peeked over her shoulder, "what's got you so interested, what's happening?"

"It's nothing really, I saw someone I know but I can't place them, come on, let's get out of here." Without further discussion they joined the remainder of the throng and headed out of the stadium.

***

The journey back home was uneventful and although busy on the tube and the train, it was good humoured and free from any trouble. Oskar went on at length about the game, dissecting every nuance and Helen listened without saying much, nodding where she thought it was appropriate and throwing in the odd word of encouragement every so often. He didn't seem to notice her attention was elsewhere.

They got off the train and walked towards the bus stop and although Oskar kept up the conversation as a passionate advocate against VAR, Helen was only half listening, lost in her own thoughts about what to do for the best. She looked at Oskar prattling away with no idea what was going on and all at once, she didn't want to go back to the house to face things just yet. "Oskar," she interrupted his flow, "how about we do McDonalds? It's not far, five minutes' walk I reckon."

"I don't know, we told mum we would be back for dinner."

"Well, we have two options as I see it," Helen held up one finger, "option one, we phone and say we missed the earlier train, so have dinner without us, or option two," she held up a second finger, "we do McDonalds, say nothing and then have another dinner when we get home." She shrugged her shoulders and looked at Oskar for a decision.

"I don't want to lie to mum," he rubbed at his jaw, "but I could manage McDonalds before dinner."

"Happy Meals all round then," Helen clapped him on the shoulder, "come on." They headed off down the road at the pace of Oskar's elongated strides, Helen falling behind him by half a step, happy to trail in his slipstream rather than try to match him.

"I fancy a Big Mac," Oskar licked his lips in a theatrical manner, "with fries and a drink and maybe some ice cream for afters. What about you?"

"I'll just have a milkshake," said Helen, "or dinner will be beyond me," she gave him a nudge as they walked, "then your mom would figure out what we'd done and she'd murder me, which she might enjoy but she would regret it afterwards maybe. What do you think?"

Oskar just laughed and nodded ahead of them towards the next junction, the golden arches of McDonalds now visible a few hundred yards down the street. "I think I'm starving and might need large fries."

"I can stretch to that, come on, let's get in before them." Helen pointed to an approaching group of teenage girls, glad they all looked on the young side for Oskar so she wouldn't have to watch him drool over them rather than his burger.

"Yeah, run," he made a dash for the door, Helen following behind, letting the door swing closed behind her but ensuring it didn't hit anyone.

"You grab a table and I'll do the order," said Helen,

approaching one of the screens and tapping in their order as Oskar bagged a table and spread his large frame over the seat to defend the territory. She stifled a laugh as she watched him and grabbed her receipt as the machine spat it out. Food wouldn't be long as there were only two customers ahead of her, so as she waited, she took the opportunity to grab the usual suspects of napkins, salt and ketchup. It wasn't long before she was at the table with Oskar, dishing out the food.

"Thanks again," said Oskar, piling fries into his mouth and giving Helen a thumbs-up sign when his mouth was too full for speech.

"Don't mention it," Helen replied, "but I need to ask you something, a serious question."

"Okay." Oskar kept chewing.

"I presume you know about Sophie and Michael," she caught his slight nod and went on, "so what I want to know is, whether you think there could be any other reason for her leaving him, setting aside the dubious parentage of her baby." She sucked on her milkshake and snatched another glance at Oskar from the corner of her eye as he wiped his mouth and took a huge slurp of his drink.

"She left him before you know, they had an argument about carpets and she didn't get her own way, so she left." Oskar gave a knowing smile and went after his fries again.

"No way." Helen laughed. "She left him because of an argument about floor coverings, are you kidding me?" She squinted at Oskar, trying to gauge if he was pulling her leg, but he was nodding again, this time with enthusiasm.

"No joke," he said, "she went back a couple of weeks later and they kissed and made up over a new rug or something. I don't like him."

"Why not?"

"He's a dick," Oskar slurped the last of the liquid from his cup, "and he always puts her down in front of people, so he's a dick." He dropped his empty cup onto the table and looked Helen square in the eye. "She can't see it though, Sophie I mean, at least she pretends she can't see it and just laughs it off, but I'm not fooled and I know it hurts her."

"Maybe it's not serious if she laughs it off," said Helen,

shrugging but feeling uncomfortable at the thought of Sophie being subject to any sort of abuse by her husband, despite her own many flaws.

"No way," Oskar was already shaking his head as Helen spoke, "one time they were staying back at the house he had a go at her but I found her in the utility room and she was really upset. I'm telling you, he's a knob."

Helen frowned, wanting to push further but not sure she would like what she heard, her hopes Michael would be a half decent bloke melting away like a Spring frost and leaving her in a tighter jam than she had anticipated. She sat with her head down, picking the paper off an extra straw she had taken. "Tell me something, and be honest, do you think Michael believes the kid isn't his or is this Sophie being Sophie and blowing things way out of proportion?"

"I believe her," Oskar nodded as he spoke, "I know she can be difficult but this time I believe her." He looked puzzled for a moment and then laughed. "You seem so bothered about Sophie's baby but I heard you're glad you can't be blamed for getting her pregnant."

"That," Helen sat up straighter, "was one of my special moments and it nearly caused a lot of trouble."

"Nearly? I thought it did," said Oskar, laughing again.

"I meant terminal trouble, you know, unfixable." Helen began stirring the remnants of her milkshake which had become too thick to remove by sucking alone.

"It's fixed though isn't it," Oskar's face brightened since moving away from the topic of Michael, "you and mum looked like you were having a great time last night and she looked more like her old self."

"Really?

"Well almost," said Oskar, "she did seem rather relaxed and you did too."

Helen said nothing, instead remembering the size of the whiskies Ingrid had poured and how between them, they had killed a full bottle before the evening ended with them bidding each other a very friendly and emotional good night. She closed her eyes for a moment and smiled at the memory.

"Do you like her?" Oskar grabbed his empty cup and began

to tear it into strips, appearing distracted by his endeavour but with half an eye pinned on his partner in crime. "I meant do you like mum?" He stacked all the little strips of paper on top of each other before dropping them into the remains of the cup and he scanned Helen's face as he waited for her answer.

"I'm not sure what you mean," Helen began to blush, "what kind of like are you asking about?"

"Don't be daft," he said, rolling his eyes like Sophie, "I mean ordinary like, not the other one." He smirked and went back to playing with his dismembered cup, still watchful but less so than before.

"Oh that's all right then, yeah, I like her lots in the ordinary sense," Helen released the breath she was holding, "she's nice, but it's early days and she might yet have me deported." She left the joke hanging as she began to button her coat, half convinced her lie was transparent and eager now to leave the conversation at the table and head back to the house.

"Are we heading off then?" Oskar glanced at his watch, "next bus is in six minutes and we need to be on it if we want to get home in time for dinner."

"Yeah come on," replied Helen, relieved to be heading for fresh air, and collecting the debris from their table, ready to drop it into the nearest bin. "Forget the bus though, I'll stop a cab."

Oskar lumbered to his feet and within a few minutes they were in a taxi and on their way back to the house.

***

"Sit here," said Sophie, gesturing to Helen to take the chair next to her own at the kitchen table, "you can tell me about your day."

Helen pulled the chair out and sat down, already bristling at Sophie's opening gambit which made her feel like she was part of an old married couple, ready to share the day's happenings over a tasty, home cooked meal. "Thanks for keeping me a seat, this place is packed."

"I know." Sophie giggled. "I almost didn't get in myself but I'm a regular customer and I know the chef."

Helen smiled and looked over Sophie's shoulder towards Ingrid who was in the process of removing a large ceramic dish from the oven. "Something smells nice," she said, raising her voice to ensure Ingrid could hear, "what is it?"

"It is lasagne," Ingrid turned around and smiled, "I hope you like it."

"I love it," Helen rose to her feet again, "do you need any help?" She hoped the answer would be yes because the alternative would be an excruciating, stilted conversation with Sophie, topped off by an added dash of pseudo coupledom.

"No, it is fine," said Ingrid, "this has to cool for a few minutes and then dinner is ready."

Helen took her seat again, resigned to her fate but determined to say as little as possible without raising suspicions that something was amiss. "So, little baby Reid," she gave a thin-lipped smile, "is she or he, kicking yet?"

"Oh, thanks for asking after my wellbeing, I'm feeling fine today." Sophie's nose wrinkled and she frowned. "You seem a bit off though, what's wrong?" Her face retained its crumpled indignance, fixed in place by a moody stare.

"Nothing's wrong," Helen tried not to sound defensive, "but I'm not as young as I used to be and I'm a bit tired after a whole afternoon with Oskar." She brightened her smile and turned it towards Ingrid who was now approaching.

"Where is Oskar?" said Ingrid, as she reached the table, a bowl of salad in each hand.

"He'll be down in a minute I'm sure, he went up to wash but he won't be long," Helen flicked her eyes over to the lasagne dish cooling on the counter top, "are you sure you don't need me to do anything?"

"Guess what?" Sophie jumped into the conversation, bubbling with bottled-up excitement, and strangling Ingrid's reply at birth.

"Sophie, don't be so rude," Helen gestured to Ingrid, "your mom was about to say something there."

"Sorry," said Sophie, her contrite smile appearing once more as she looked at Ingrid, "I just wanted to see what Helen thought about it."

"I do not think this is the time," Ingrid shook her head, "we are about to have dinner so perhaps this should be for another day." She placed a hand on Sophie's shoulder but her eyes met Helen's and they exchanged an uneasy look.

Sophie was aghast. "It's only names mamma," she squeezed her mother's hand and then turned to Helen, beaming, "I've been thinking about baby names and I want your opinion on possible choices."

"That's nice of you," said Helen, a sense of dread washing over her at what might come next, "come up with anything interesting?"

Before Sophie could reply, Ingrid grabbed hold of the discussion. "I am attempting to persuade Sophie to be patient and wait before choosing names, it is very early for the baby and sometimes it is better to see it, to find a name to suit." She gave Sophie's shoulder another squeeze before turning away and heading back towards the waiting dish of pasta.

"That's a good point." Helen watched as Ingrid retrieved the lasagne from the hob and carried it over to the table, resting it with care on an iron trivet. Their eyes met for a second time and Helen knew for certain they were thinking the same thing and that it would be in everyone's interests to divert Sophie's attention away from her current whimsy.

"I just want Helen's opinion on a couple of names," said Sophie, her voice clipped and with a pout already well established on her lips, "it's no big deal, mamma."

"I know you do darling, but I think your husband's opinion might be more important than Helen's, given he is the father of the child." Ingrid pulled out a chair and sat beside her daughter, piling salad onto her plate and smiling. "Please Helen, do not be offended by what I said."

"I'm not, and I agree with your summation of the situation, Michael's opinion is the hot one as far as I'm concerned. Could you pass the salad when you're done please?" Helen avoided Sophie's aggrieved look, fixing her eyes on the pasta and hoping its arrival on the plate would signal an end to what was becoming an awkward confrontation.

"I've decided if it's a boy I want to call him Oliver," Sophie ignored their attempts to stop the roll she was on, "and if it's a girl," she turned to Ingrid, "I want to call her Scarlett."

Ingrid's eyebrows shot up, "Scarlett is an unusual name," she looked in puzzlement from Sophie to Helen and then back to Sophie, "why did you choose that one?"

"I just like it," said Sophie, reaching over for the salad, "it's a beautiful name, don't you think so, Helen?"

"It's nothing of the sort," Helen pressed her lips into a tight line and shook her head, "stop it Sophie, you're being ridiculous."

"Well it is all right, I suppose," said Ingrid, glancing at Helen in surprise, "it could have been something worse do you not think?"

Helen caught the look and understood what Ingrid was getting at; it was obvious both had expected Sophie to say she would name the baby, Helen, but this was worse, much worse. "Tell the truth, Sophie," she said, as she lifted over the larger of the salad bowls and tipped some of the contents onto her plate, "go on, tell your mother why you like the name or would you like me to do it for you?" She signalled to Sophie to choose who would speak but Sophie only grinned and picked up the large serving spoon that lay beside the lasagne dish, ready to dig in.

"I would like someone to please tell me," Ingrid's accent thickened and her face darkened as she clasped her hands on the table, "unless this is a guessing game for me of course."

"You don't have to guess," Helen sucked at her teeth in frustration, "it's my middle name but I don't use it because I don't like it and Sophie knows this so she should also know better than to come out with this garbage."

"It's not her middle name," Sophie announced it with a flourish, "it's her first name and Helen is her middle name." She held her plate close to the serving dish and scooped some pasta onto it. "She doesn't tell anyone, but I managed to get it out of her because I'm rather good at finding things out."

Helen eyed Sophie and sighed. "You're a real piece of work."

"I know," said Sophie, reaching across and tapping Helen on the hand in a playful manner, "but it's why you like me so much."

Helen nodded as she reached over and started filling her plate. "Shall we tell your mom what you were doing when you managed to wheedle my name out of me?" A flush spread over Sophie's face, suggesting the answer was a definite no, and Helen was pleased, despite wanting to give the gorgeous little fucker a taste of her own medicine. "Are you sure?" she said, keeping her voice light and pleasant, hoping Sophie didn't have the guts to call her bluff.

"I think that is enough," said Ingrid, "both of you stop, please."

"Yes it's enough, I agree." Helen was about to say why she agreed when the sound of Vivaldi's Four Seasons erupted from the phone lying on the worktop near the sink, interrupting the frivolities and sending Ingrid scurrying over to answer it.

Helen glanced at Sophie, but she was busy eyeing her mother and gesturing to find out who was on the phone.

"Gary, my goodness, Gary, where are you?" Ingrid covered the mouthpiece of the phone and whispered to Sophie, "it is dad," and then to Helen, "it is my husband, I shall go to the sitting room with this."

As Ingrid vanished into the hallway, Helen dropped her knife and fork with a clatter and glared at Sophie, her eyes blazing. "What the fuck do you think you're playing at, naming a child after me, huh, when did this marvellous idea appear?"

"You're so sure that's what I'm doing, aren't you?" said Sophie, her face still holding the last blotches of flush-induced redness, "but I'll call my baby whatever I want to call it, no matter what you think."

"This is nuts, you can't," Helen jerked the chair back and turned all the way around to face her. "What about Michael, doesn't he have any say or did you forget he has an interest in all this?"

Sophie shrugged. "No, he doesn't have a say, not after what he's done, so I plan to choose the name myself and I was hoping you'd be pleased."

Helen laughed, feeling unable to speak, and she clamped her hands behind her head, staring at Sophie, not in disbelief, but in horror, realising Ingrid's perceptiveness regarding Sophie's motivations were bang on the money, and watching her own worst nightmare materialise before her eyes.

"I don't love Michael," Sophie's voice was calm, "I don't love him and I won't be going back so there's nothing to tell him." She shook her head and looked down at her plate. "Anyway, he doesn't believe the baby is his so why should he care about a name?"

"Tell me something," said Helen, ignoring Sophie's attempt

at self-justification, "if you don't love Michael, why did you get pregnant? I'm presuming the baby does belong to him of course." She looked over her shoulder towards the kitchen door, listening for any sound of Ingrid returning. "Come on," she turned back to Sophie, "an explanation would be welcome."

"I'm thirty-four," Sophie shrugged, "and I didn't want to miss my opportunity to have children." She sighed and looked Helen in the eye. "The baby is Michael's, I'm not lying about that, but I don't love him and haven't for a while so the separation is permanent as far as I'm concerned."

"Oh Sophie," Helen blew out a sigh, releasing some of the tension she felt, "what have you done?" It was a rhetorical question because it was now indisputable, Sophie had ditched Michael because of some dumbass notion she'd formed that somehow, a ready-made replacement was waiting in the wings to solve all her problems, and the convenient substitute, was, of course, her.

Sophie leaned forward in her chair and reached across the table, taking Helen's hands in her own and pulling them to her. "I've left an unhappy marriage, that's all," she said, "people do it every day and still the world turns."

Helen shook her head at Sophie's reply but she didn't pull her hands away, wanting to offer some comfort as she prepared to be direct and ask the awkward question. "I need to ask you something, it's a doozy, but you need to promise to be honest with me, no matter what."

"I know what you're going to ask." Sophie's voice faltered and she dipped her head.

"Maybe I'm not going to ask what you think."

Sophie rubbed Helen's hands with her thumbs and smiled. "We both know what you're going to ask so why don't you say it and we can get this finished before my mother comes back and roasts the two of us for being ridiculous."

Helen shook her head, the determination to derail Sophie's nefarious plan, vanishing at the look of dejection in her eyes. "Do you know, I don't think it's important, let's leave it," she shook her head again, "let's forget it and enjoy dinner."

"No way, if you won't say it then I'll have to," said Sophie, "but first I have a question for you and the same rules apply, the truth and nothing but the truth if you don't mind." She smiled at Helen, still holding fast to her hands. "When we were kissing and you threw up, I know we wouldn't have stopped at kissing if you hadn't been sick and I suppose I'm wondering what it meant to you, I mean, was I going to be just a casual fuck," Sophie kept her gaze steady, "or was it something more?"

It was the question Helen dreaded but she knew it was coming although the foresight didn't make it any less difficult to hear. She held Sophie's gaze, not wanting to look away like the coward she knew she was, but a suitable answer took a few moments to find. "No, you never were and you never could be, just a casual fuck but I don't know what you were, just that it wasn't that."

Sophie glanced towards the kitchen door then looked back at Helen and gave her hands another squeeze. "I hope what I'm about to confess puts your mind at ease but I haven't left my husband to shack up with you," she sighed, "I love you, you big idiot, but I'm not in love with you."

"Is that the truth?" Helen didn't want to catch Sophie's eyes and see a different answer so she kept her gaze elsewhere, content to accept the explanation despite not believing a word of it.

"Yes, it is, I'm not soft in the head you know," Sophie gave a warm laugh, "although I hoped you might want to help with the baby sometimes, you know, turn up every so often as a beloved aunt or something similar."

"A beloved aunt," Helen nodded, "I've never pictured myself as one of those before so I would need training and of course, you do know I'll buy the kid a drumkit and a trumpet."

"I would be disappointed if you didn't and I'm sure little Oliver or Scarlett will love them and you."

"You can't be serious about the name," said Helen, "please, for me, don't call the kid Scarlett, it's the worst possible choice." She pulled her hands away and went back to her dinner although her appetite had vanished and the food on her plate was now lukewarm.

"Well if I have a boy it will definitely be Oliver," Sophie picked up her knife and fork and started to eat, "but, if I do have a girl then it won't be Scarlett, I'd like to call her Helen because it's a name I love and it would always remind me of you no matter what happens."

Helen swallowed a mouthful of lasagne and put her cutlery down, trying to find the right combination of words and once again, realising Ingrid's prediction was correct. "I thought I was supposed to be the beloved aunt, you know, the one who buys crazy stuff for the kids and gets them to say rude words. Why the need for a memento if I'm still around?"

"One day you might not be there," Sophie bit at her lip, "you might meet someone special and then I wouldn't see you anymore and..."

"Maybe I've already found someone special," said Helen, interrupting Sophie's flow, "I don't tell you everything you know." She regretted saying the words the moment they fell from her lips, not only because of the immediate sadness that fell across Sophie's face, but also because it felt too close to the truth for comfort and took her down a dangerous and very rocky road.

"Do you have someone?" Sophie swallowed, her face picking up a flash of colour again.

"No, I don't have anyone at the moment, I was trying to make the point that in the future it's something that might be possible."

"So, will you be there to help me with the baby?"

Helen tilted her head and her eyes narrowed as she gazed at Sophie. "You know I'll always help you, but remember, it's the beloved aunt thing I'll be there for, trumpets and drums, nothing more substantial than that."

"I know," said Sophie, looking brighter, "but I'm glad to hear you say it so thank you, Aunt Helen." At last, a smile escaped her lips.

Helen was about to tell Sophie to drop the Aunt Helen thing when the kitchen door swung open and Ingrid returned, looking flustered and ill at ease, her face red and her eyes, filled with apprehension. As she returned to the table and took her seat, it was all Helen could do not to rush over and put a consoling arm around her shoulders, such was the change in her demeanour from when she had headed to the sitting room. In the end, caution overruled her instinct and she settled for making the obvious comment. "You look a little peaky if you don't mind me saying so, is everything all right?"

Ingrid didn't answer but instead, looked at Sophie with

downcast eyes. "Your father is coming home tonight, in fact, he will be here shortly so, let us get dinner over with quickly if we can." She retrieved her cutlery and went back to her pasta without enthusiasm.

"He wasn't supposed to be coming here until next week," Sophie sat bolt upright in her chair, wide-eyed and staring at Ingrid, "what's happened to bring him here now?"

"Nothing is wrong," Ingrid began picking at her salad, "he finished his project earlier than expected so he is coming home tonight."

"That's nice," said Helen, grinning, and wiggling her eyebrows, "although it gives me somebody else to upset, unless you think I won't annoy your husband, in which case..."

"Please Helen," Ingrid ran her fingers through her hair, "I believe you could annoy my husband with very little effort on your part."

"Oh, shall I pack now or would you rather wait to be entertained by the talking bear again?" Helen looked from Ingrid to Sophie and then back again. "I can't help but feel I'm the only one who isn't party to a great big secret, anyone thinking about spilling the beans?"

"It is the baby of course," Ingrid turned to Sophie, "so we will say nothing about it tonight," she flicked her eyes to Helen, "please do not mention the baby."

"Sure." Helen saw Sophie nod agreement without arguing, an indication of how serious things were so she felt she had to seek some clarification about what topics remained on the table. "If I can't mention Sophie's condition, would I be safer on any particular topic?"

"Please try to be uncontroversial, if you can," Ingrid put her head in her hands and sighed, "in fact it would be preferable if you said very little."

Helen looked at Ingrid's downturned head, her eyebrows raised, "Well this sounds like a treat, when's he due to arrive?" She wondered what sort of man Gary was that he had managed to silence Sophie and put his wife on edge just by advertising his imminent arrival and the answers she managed to conjure up let her with a feeling of deep foreboding.

"He will be here soon," replied Ingrid, "he was calling from a taxi so it will not take long."

"Fantastic, I'm looking forward to meeting him." Helen caught the glance between Ingrid and Sophie and realised Sophie had gone very quiet. "Are you ok, hun?" she waved to her over the table.

Sophie only nodded, bringing all conversation at the table to a dead stop and they sat in silence for what felt like an age. The longer the silence lasted, the more Helen wanted to say anything at all, and she was just at the point of throwing in a quip about baby names when she heard a key turning in the front door lock and the sound of someone coming in and then dumping bags.

Ingrid stood and smiled, then walked past Helen towards the hallway but she got no more than half way when the kitchen door swept open.

"Hey, Ingrid, hey Sophie."

"Hi dad," Sophie's smile was lacklustre and she remained in her seat, "how's things with you?"

"Things are fantastic honey, oh, do I smell Bolognese?" Gary gave Ingrid a brief hug and then spoke over her shoulder, "and you must be the famous Helen, I presume."

Helen stood, and turned around towards the sound of the deep voice. "And you must be Gary, I presume," she held out her hand, noting his smart grey business suit and slicked back, red-auburn hair framing a rather slight, pasty face, "pleased to meet you."

"That's me," he said, "the man of the house." He shook her hand and gestured towards Ingrid with his head. "I hope they're treating you well."

"Yes, very well," said Helen, looking around at Sophie and then back to Gary, marvelling at the unmistakable likeness. "You and Sophie, you could be twins."

"Yes, we could I suppose," Gary eyed his daughter, "Anna is like Ingrid though, so is Oskar, have you met them yet?"

"Not Anna, but I've met Oskar," Helen laughed, "he's quite something."

"Oskar's fun." Gary turned to Ingrid, motioning for her to come over and when she did, he slipped his right arm around her waist.

"Yeah, he's cool," said Helen, her jaw tightening as she glanced at Gary's hand pawing Ingrid's waist, "in fact we're both not long back from a day out together."

"See, I told you," Gary threw out a beaming smile, "everybody loves Oskar. What were you up to?"

"Oh, we had a great day at the football," Helen put her hands in the pockets of her jeans, "Chelsea against Liverpool. I paid a fortune for the good seats but it was well worth it for the view. I could see everything, Gary."

Chapter Eight

Burning Down the House

"All you have to do is turn it on and then off," Ingrid pointed to the oven, "can you manage that without hurting yourself?"

"Yes, I think so," Helen rubbed at the back of her neck and squinted at the oven controls from various angles, "but I'll sit in here and keep an eye on it, just to be sure."

"There is no need, just switch it on and off at the correct times and remember, I would not ask you to do something so technical if I thought it would be beyond your abilities."

Helen grinned at the compliment then looked over her shoulder at Gary who was sitting at the kitchen table with his laptop open. She mouthed a question to Ingrid about whether Gary knew about the baby yet, touching her own stomach and flicking her eyes towards him but Ingrid shook her head, signalling a definite no and the look on her face was clear; say nothing about it. "What's in there anyway?" said Helen, pointing to the oven.

"It is lamb," Ingrid licked her lips, "I hope you like it."

"I do," said Helen, "I like pretty much anything except the stuff I hate but I don't cook much though, I prefer takeout."

"I got that impression," Ingrid smiled, "but perhaps I could teach you some things when you are staying here, I mean cooking things."

Helen peeked at Gary again. "I wasn't sure how long I was staying," she lowered her voice, "Sophie told me you said..."

"Yes, that four weeks would be fine," Ingrid interrupted, "so that would be enough time for the basics and if you show promise we could perhaps move on to something more challenging."

"She's quite a good cook you know," Gary's deep bass tone filled the kitchen, "and she keeps us well fed, don't you sweetheart." He flashed a grin across at Ingrid and ran his eyes over Helen before turning his attention back to his laptop.

"Okay, I'll look forward to it but please, start easy, everything is high level to me." She turned her back on Gary, but not before she had thrown him a look of disgust. "So, clothes shopping with Sophie, I did that once and regretted it because it took all day, when'll you be back?"

"Around one I think," said Ingrid, glancing at Gary, "please, try not to burn my house down when I am out."

Helen didn't answer as she wasn't certain what Ingrid meant by the comment but her expression suggested it had nothing to do with the Sunday roast.

"Do not burn it down, Helen, please."

"Don't worry, I won't," Helen kept her smile fixed in place, "I promise it'll all still be here when you get back."

"Sophie will be waiting," said Ingrid, "and I have to go," she smiled at Helen before walking over to Gary and kissing him on the cheek, "I will be back at one." With that she breezed from the kitchen and was gone.

Helen watched Ingrid leave then her eyes fell on Gary, who stared back at her, unsmiling, much like the previous evening when she had thrown the comment at him about the football. When he introduced himself in the kitchen she knew at once it had been him in the stadium and she understood why she thought she recognised him because it wasn't his face she had seen before, it was Sophie's. As they had agreed, they could be twins.

"You look like you want to say something," Gary leaned back on his chair and put his hands behind his head, fingers interlaced, "so go on, spit it out."

"Do I?" said Helen, picturing the worried look on Ingrid's face before she left, "what on earth makes you think I'd want to speak to you?"

"It's obvious you have something you want to say to me, I can tell."

"That's so impressive, you should be on the midway at the county fair," Helen gave a mirthless laugh, "you seem to think you can read minds."

"I can read your mind," Gary smirked and ran his eyes over Helen, "so you might as well come out with it, whatever it is."

Helen began to laugh in earnest and she sauntered over to the table and took a seat, making sure she gave Gary a good look over, but he didn't move an inch and his face gave nothing away. "You look much older than I thought you would."

"Not as old as my wife though."

Helen drew back her head and narrowed her eyes. "Yes, technically she is older than you but she's pretty hot," she shrugged her shoulders, "maybe Swedish women age better than English men." She saw him swallow and lick his lips and knew she had scored straight from kick-off.

"Tell me," Gary cracked his knuckles, "has she been her usual, pleasant self?"

"Could you be more specific?" said Helen, playing it carefully to be sure she didn't jump to answer any vague questions.

"Let me think, oh yes," he said, "cold, uncaring, joyless," he paused as though thinking harder, "not forgetting, frigid."

"You can't be serious, frigid?" Helen made sure her face registered surprise, determined she wasn't giving Gary an inch if she could help it.

"Yes, do you know what it's like to have a frigid wife?"

Helen laughed. "I've never had a wife, but when I do have one, I can assure you, she won't be frigid," she gave her biggest grin, "you must not be doin' it right." She bent forward, mirroring his posture and her eye caught a movement in his right hand as it balled into a fist, signalling it was two-nil to the away team.

"So, you're the type to have a wife," Gary's lip drew back in a sneer, "I'm not sure I feel safe leaving my girls alone with your sort." He tilted his head to one side as he raised his eyebrows, and his tongue flicked snakelike, over his lips.

"Gary, I can keep my hands to myself," Helen chuckled and shook her head at him in admonishment, "don't judge people by your own dirty old man standards." She held the eye contact they had made, seeing him blink a few times in succession and knowing she had her hat trick and it was only the first half too.

"My wife won't like it when she finds out what you are," Gary sniffed and shifted his weight onto one hand, elbow on the table, "she'll throw you out."

"Ingrid and I get along...very well." Helen winked, knowing she was pushing her luck but desperate nonetheless to give him something to ponder on which would perhaps wipe the smirk from his face.

"No way, you would never be her type, she doesn't even have a type now, she's too far gone." Gary tapped two fingers on the side of his head to make the point, his smirk wider than ever.

Helen kept smiling, determined she wouldn't let Gary in for a consolation goal but in her head, she was reaching for her nightstand and pulling out her .38 Smith & Wesson. "Tell me something Gary," she said, "why do you stay?" It was weak and she knew it, but it was all she had so she threw it in to give herself time to wind up her next verbal right hook.

"She keeps the house well," he said, "and very occasionally, I get to fuck her." He began tapping on the lid of the laptop. "There are two sides to this story you know."

"Yeah, and I'm betting you're a prick in both of them," said Helen, her smile still intact despite being inches away from losing her cool.

Gary licked his lips and jabbed a finger towards Helen's face. "You have an attitude problem, and I think you might be forgetting you're staying in my fucking house, lady."

"I don't have an attitude problem," Helen replied, "you have a problem with my attitude and that's not my problem at all." She knew she could ignore the comment about staying in his house as there was no way he could risk throwing her out so she decided it was time to talk about his sordid little secret. "How old is she?"

"Who, Ingrid?" The smirk was back.

"You don't know," Helen feigned shock, "or did you just talk about prices?" She laughed at this and looked Gary up and down. "Come, on, you must have been payin' her."

"You shut your mouth about her." Gary stormed to his feet, knocking his chair over in the rush. "I'm warning you, keep it shut." He bent over and yanked the chair upright, slamming it back in its place before grabbing the laptop from the table.

"Leaving so soon?" Helen ran her eye over him again, revelling in his extreme display of petulant anger, and readying herself for one final insult with which to send him packing, revenge not for her, but for Ingrid.

"I've got better things to do than listen to a stupid, American fuck like you." He turned on his heel and headed for the door.

"Gary," she shouted after him, "I just remembered it's trash collection day tomorrow, remember to make sure you're ready to go." As he stormed out of the kitchen and slammed the door behind him, the smile fell from Helen's face and she closed her eyes.

***

As she checked her watch to ensure she didn't miss the cue to switch on the oven, Helen replayed in her head the last conversation with Ingrid, picturing the expression on her face when she asked her not to burn the house down, words which now, left her locked in the horns of a dilemma and trying to decide between exposing Gary for the cheating fucker he was, and buttoning her lip, just for once, and watching the slimy bastard play at being the good husband. There was no easy answer.

Another glance at her watch confirmed it was time to get the lunch started and Helen put her ruminations to one side to consider the technical challenge lying ahead. Reciting Ingrid's instructions in her head, she approached the oven and stood to attention before its control panel, then she pressed the start button before taking a step back to admire her work. As the oven light came on and the fan whirred into action, she saw Ingrid in her mind's eye, nodding her head in silent admiration, cheering her on towards the point where she switched it off as instructed, completing her assignment and first ever Sunday lunch.

With another ninety minutes to pass before she had to attend to the lamb again, Helen made some coffee and took it back to the table with her, letting her thoughts settle on Gary, disconcerted that quite apart from being a cheating slime-ball, he had another side to him as well, and one that was no less unpleasant. On the night he'd arrived home, she hadn't received any explanation from Sophie or Ingrid about why the pregnancy and separation from Michael was a huge secret but it had been clear, Gary must not know. Sophie's silence when she first heard about her father's return, and her instant agreement to Ingrid's plan for omerta, had been the loudest alarm bell of all although the hardest part to watch, had been Ingrid's reaction to his arrival and the way she walked on eggshells in his presence. Her timidity was the reason why Helen had headed upstairs for what she said was an early night, because she couldn't bear to watch any longer. She stared into her drink, watching a few rogue coffee grounds circling around the dark, brown liquid and she gave the cup a nudge to keep them moving. She thought Oskar's reaction to Gary was very telling as he hadn't come down for any dinner on the Saturday night and then, first thing today, he was up and out of the house and off to Kieran's place for a few days, a vote with his feet if ever there was one. The most curious thing however, was Gary's apparent lack of intent to seek him out, content it seemed, to sit with his girls, as he called them, and pleased to have Ingrid dangling on the end of a string which he would jerk every so often. Helen could only wonder what he was like when there were no witnesses.

One positive bit of intel she had gleaned on the previous night was Gary would be heading to Berlin on Wednesday morning for a business trip which would keep him away for a week at least. Until then, this afternoon's spat aside, her Great Plan was to have as little to do with him as possible. The last thing she wanted was a full-blown argument and she knew if she spent much time around him, then a huge bust-up was inevitable. She would have to get through Sunday lunch but after that she planned to decant once again to her bedroom on the pretence of having work to do and on Monday and Tuesday, she and Sophie would be on campus so it would be easy to work late and eat out. Helen sat for a while mulling over her plan of attack and she had almost convinced herself it was workable when all at once she felt guilty. She knew it would be easy to remove herself from the picture for a few days, certain Sophie would hang around with her to keep her company but this would leave Ingrid alone with Gary. In her head she replayed his comments about why he stayed in an unhappy marriage and her feeling of guilt melted away, replaced by one of disquiet. Helen understood she would not be enacting the Great Plan after all and, deep in thought, she sat at the table, alternately looking at her watch and swirling cold coffee around her cup until it was time to see to the lunch again.

After dealing with the oven, Helen washed her cup then sat down at the table, browsing the internet on her phone whilst trying not to think too much about the events of the last few days. She didn't want to go upstairs just yet and she didn't want to go elsewhere in the house as it would risk another meeting with Gary, so she stayed where she was until she heard Sophie and Ingrid arriving home. At the sound of their voices her mood lifted.

"Hey Helen," Sophie bounced into the kitchen, dropping several, well stuffed bags onto the floor just inside the door and tossing her head from side to side, "what do you think of the new me?"

"I think you look beautiful," Helen looked Sophie up and down, not hiding her admiration, "but you know that anyway, don't you?"

"Of course I do," Sophie replied, bubbling over with excitement and flicking her hair again, "and you should see mamma, I think you'll be rather surprised."

Helen was delighted with Sophie's display of preening, enjoying her role as the adoring audience for the performance, but it was nothing compared to the prospect of encountering a revamped version of Ingrid, the thought of which caused a tingle of excitement to flutter through her. "Where is she anyway?"

"I am here," Ingrid's voice floated in from the hallway, "someone has to hang up the coats and it would of course never be Sophie."

Helen swung round in her chair and she was about to shout her agreement about Sophie's lack of coat hanging etiquette, when Ingrid came into view and walked into the kitchen.

"By the smell in here I am presuming you managed to follow instructions and the button did not provide too much of a challenge." Ingrid marched over towards the oven and pulled the door open, inspecting the lunch for a few seconds, before entombing it again for later and turning to smile at Helen. "Do you like my new style," Ingrid wore the smallest hint of a smile on her lips, "or do you think I am too old to have it like this?"

"I think it's fantastic and you look amazing," said Helen, smiling from ear to ear. Ingrid's mousy hair was now just above shoulder length and highlighted in a rich shade of blond, much like it was in the wedding photos they had looked at, and taken together, it was a stunning transformation.

"Thank you," said Ingrid, looking bashful, but pleased, as she tucked a loose strand of hair behind her ear, "it was long overdue but it was Sophie's idea."

"Well done that woman," said Helen, nodding approval at Sophie and delighted her encouragement had brought some life back to Ingrid and that she seemed to be enjoying it.

"Where is Gary?" Ingrid's delivery of the question was guarded, her eyes examining Helen as though trying to extract an answer just by looking.

"Sorry, I have no idea," Helen forced herself to keep the smile on her face, "maybe you should make him wear a tag in future."

"I see," said Ingrid, folding her arms, "and yet I distinctly remember asking you not to burn my house down."

Helen nodded towards the oven, pretending it was what they were talking about. "No, it's all fine, nothing was burnt and lunch looks edible enough to me although I'm no expert and it was the first time I've cooked lamb." She heard the desperation in her own voice and stifled a sigh of relief when, before she had the opportunity to dig herself into a deeper hole, Sophie stopped rifling through the bags, and interrupted.

"Mamma, Helen, I'm going upstairs to try on my new clothes," she had two bags in her hands and held them aloft, shaking them for emphasis, 'but I'll come back down and model them for you." Then, she was gone, leaving Helen and Ingrid alone.

"She gets so excited about new clothes," Helen said, laughing, "when she was staying with me, we went to one of those outlet places and..."

"Helen," Ingrid cut into her attempt at a story, "tell me what has been happening here."

Helen peeked through half closed eyes and saw Ingrid hadn't moved but remained rooted to where she had been before, her arms folded and her expression stern. "I already told you, I have no idea where he went." She knew it wasn't going to end well but in the eye of the storm, she couldn't think of a way to explain it all without spilling her guts about the one thing she couldn't mention and it wouldn't make any sense to say she had been sparring with Gary because, in the absence of any awareness of his cheating scumbag tendencies, it would sound crazy. "He took the laptop and went somewhere and I stayed to make the lunch."

"What did you say to him?" Ingrid wasn't capitulating.

"What do you mean, what did I say to him?"

Ingrid unfolded her arms then pulled out a chair and sat down, looking at Helen without speaking.

"Why are you looking at me like that?" said Helen, dropping her eyes and distracting herself by playing with one of the chunky, silver rings on her right hand whilst gaining an unwelcome insight into how uncomfortable Ingrid must have felt during their first awkward encounters.

"I think you are hiding something from me and it is very obvious," said Ingrid.

"Obvious?" Helen didn't look up, "what do you mean obvious?"

"You are confusing me," said Ingrid, with a sigh, "I am the one with English as a second language yet you do not seem to know the meaning of anything I say."

"Well, technically," Helen lifted her head and gave a hesitant smile, "I could say it's a second language for me too," she pushed the smile a bit further, "but your English is perfect although sometimes, when you get annoyed at me, which is quite a lot I think, then your accent comes out and it's quite funny."

"Is it?" Ingrid bit at her bottom lip.

"Yeah, what I mean is it's funny, but not in a bad way or maybe I mean it's...something else, like if you weren't always annoyed at me then I might be tempted to do stuff to get you annoyed, not big stuff though," Helen shook her head, "little things, just to get to hear the accent." She stopped fiddling with her ring and instead, started playing with her hair as she looked at Ingrid and waited for the onslaught, preferring anything than having to explain further.

Ingrid shook her head. "I want to know what happened, so please tell me."

Helen felt her stomach lurch the way it did on a roller coaster when you dropped over the first big dip of the ride, realising Ingrid wasn't giving up and that she was going to have to confess. "Okay, do you remember I asked whether I would be able to annoy your husband and you said you thought I could?" She looked at Ingrid and saw her nodding. "Well, it turns out you were right and I don't believe Gary and I will be sending each other Christmas cards this year."

"I see."

"That's why I don't know where he is." Helen smiled, hoping she appeared confident and nonchalant, but feeling neither.

"I see."

"He kind of stormed out and there's no way I was following." Helen looked back down at her ring and started twisting it again.

"I am many things but I am not a stupid woman," said Ingrid, leaning over and tapping Helen's arm to get her attention.

"I don't think you're stupid at all," Helen looked up in surprise, her eyes flicking for a second to where Ingrid's hand had rested moments before, 'why would you say that?"

"Just tell me what you said to Gary to make him go off like he did?"

"I don't want to get into it, please, it's pretty dreadful."

Ingrid sighed. "This is becoming silly, tell me what you said to make him leave."

"Okay, I'll tell you but I don't want things to kick off again so please don't be mad, because he just got to me and I couldn't shut my mouth and told him the trash collection was due tomorrow and he should make sure he was ready to go with it."

"I am not surprised he left," Ingrid's cheeks puffed out, "I would also leave if you said it to me."

"You don't understand," said Helen, pushing herself up in the seat, feeling her frustration start to boil over, "he said some things, I won't repeat them, but he said vile things and I tried to hold back and believe me, I did hold back, but I couldn't sit there and say nothing at all." The urge to keep going, to spill the lot and get it over with, was almost unbearable and Helen felt close to letting it all out, sitting there under interrogation whilst the cheating fuck was hiding away God knows where, ready to come out at a moment's notice with a big happy, dad smile on his face. "Ingrid, he's awful..."

Ingrid raised a hand to stop Helen's burgeoning polemic in its tracks. "You are so angry and outraged on my behalf but it is not necessary I can assure you."

"I don't understand," said Helen, caught off balance by Ingrid's demeanour, one showing no signs of anger, "what do you mean?"

"I have been married to Gary for a long time," said Ingrid, "and I know him very well, better than anyone else could ever do so I know what he is like." She leaned over and took hold of Helen's hands. "You can tell me nothing new about what he says because I already know, and there is nothing I also do not know about what Gary does, nothing at all."

Helen stared and said nothing, certain Ingrid's phrasing had been a deliberate attempt to make it clear she knew all about Gary's disgusting behaviour.

"As I said, I am not a stupid woman," Ingrid was still smiling, "and I have eyes and I have ears so you must let this rest and promise you will do this for my sake and not for Gary's."

Helen couldn't speak, and she sat motionless, her eyes wide, any doubts she might have harboured about Ingrid's knowledge of her husband's philandering tendencies, swept away.

"Helen," Ingrid's tone had become urgent, "please promise you will let this rest."

"Okay," Helen nodded, "I promise and I'm sorry." She teetered on the brink of saying more but nothing came and for once she was glad of it.

"Come now, there is no need for sorry, not this time." Ingrid reached over and took Helen's hands in her own, running her eyes over her as though studying an exotic creature. "I think you are a dangerous woman though."

"Do you?" Helen blinked and leaned back in the chair, her brow crinkling, "I'm not sure what to think about why you're saying that." She followed Ingrid's gaze as it examined her and they both sat, hands locked together, saying nothing.

"Yes, very dangerous," said Ingrid, easing her hands away and standing, before walking over to the hob to start preparing the rest of the lunch.

Helen tilted her head back and watched but she said nothing more, instead, allowing her mind to focus on what felt like a thousand possible outcomes of the conversation they had shared, and jolted by the realisation she wasn't the only dangerous woman in the house.

Chapter Nine

Hickory, Dickory Dock

The next few days passed in relative peace. Helen spent a considerable amount of time on campus and although this meant she couldn't be sure what Gary had been up to, Ingrid seemed bright enough so she presumed things must have been to some degree, reasonable. Mealtimes were polite affairs but as the days progressed, Helen's tolerance of meaningless small talk grew thin and there had been one or two tense moments when things almost boiled over. Overall, though, it was bearable and relief arrived at last in the form of Wednesday evening when Gary departed in a taxi for the airport and Oskar, with impeccable timing, arrived back from Kieran's house.

Oskar was on good form when he returned, fresh from a marathon gaming session of Half Life and what he had called serious college time. Helen wasn't averse to some game time herself but she was happy to admit to him she wasn't anywhere near his level. Sensing a willing victim, Oskar issued a gaming challenge and she agreed to a few games of FIFA at the weekend but forgot to tell him she had a skill level of insanely good when it came to soccer games. He would find out soon enough.

With Gary gone, both Sophie and Ingrid had returned to what Helen now thought of as normal and by the time Friday night arrived, they had all settled back into a cosy domestic routine, topped off with take-out food, some beers, and a few games of Jenga. Ingrid won every game which prompted accusations of cheating and although she denied this, her passion when doing so persuaded everyone to agree she must have been cheating. Before heading to bed, Helen had mentioned her first cookery lesson the following day and she had been feeling pretty good about it until she discovered it would involve deconstructing a whole salmon. Her reaction, when Ingrid revealed she expected her to cut the head off a dead fish, prompted peals of laughter from Sophie and caused Oskar to lie his huge frame flat on the floor as he pretended to be the dead fish. Why Ingrid chose a fish autopsy as the first lesson was a mystery but Helen thought she had guessed what the reaction would be and that it would be amusing. She certainly seemed to find it very funny and in turn, Helen had found Ingrid's reaction very funny and the night had ended on a rather upbeat note.

Of course, now, standing half-dressed in her bedroom on a Saturday morning and preparing to confront Moby Dick in the kitchen, Helen didn't find the situation quite so comical. Despite facing the prospect of blood and guts, she took a plain white T-shirt from the wardrobe and matched it up with faded, black jeans and a battered pair of Converse sneakers. A quick blow dry of her hair was the last touch, after which it was all systems go. She glanced at her watch again, noting it was five minutes later than when she had last checked and a bit earlier than they had agreed upon, but she decided to venture down anyway to grab a cup of coffee before battle commenced. She hoped it would settle her nerves.

When she left her bedroom, she took extra care to be quiet, pulling the door over until not quite closed and heading down the hallway almost on tiptoe. She reached the stairs and had taken one step down when she saw Ingrid was already there, standing at the bottom of the staircase, back against the wall. "Hey, Ingrid, you're early." She kept her voice hushed, just above a whisper, and headed down, ready for action despite the certain trauma waiting for her in the kitchen.

"We cannot go in," Ingrid pointed towards the kitchen, her voice trembling and her eyes wide, "it is awful."

"Okay, we can't go in," Helen glanced at the kitchen door and then back again, "but, why not, what's in there?"

"We cannot go in," Ingrid shook her head again, "it is horrible."

"What's happened in there?" Helen's imagination was fertile at the best of times but the horrified look on Ingrid's face sent it into overdrive and she half imagined entering the kitchen and finding a blood soaked, mangled corpse on the kitchen table, dumped there by a maniac who was *still in the house*. She held Ingrid by both shoulders and gave her a gentle shake. "Tell me what it is, come on hun, try to be calm and tell me what's in there."

"It is," Ingrid took several deep breaths, "a mouse." She locked eyes with Helen and nodded as she spoke, confirming the certain, horrific presence, of a rodent.

"A mouse," said Helen, keeping hold of Ingrid's shoulders and looking her in the eye, "are you sure?"

"Yes, I saw it when I went in to set things up for your lesson," Ingrid took a ragged breath, "and it is huge."

"Okay, it's a mouse, a massive mouse, but I need you to show me how big it is?" Helen gave a grim smile, trying to maintain a serious face but struggling.

"It is this big." Ingrid measured out six or seven inches with her forefingers before clasping both hands together in a vice like embrace.

Helen released her grip on Ingrid's shoulders and took hold of her hands, clasping them both together in her own. "I can fix this," she said, using the most soothing voice she could manage, "cos I ain't 'fraid of no mouse." She smiled when she said this but Ingrid didn't respond to the joke. Mice didn't cause Helen any problem and she knew Ingrid's estimate of size was based more on fright than on any accurate measurement but it was possible she might have got the size right, but the rodent wrong, in which case it could be a rat and Helen did have a problem with those.

"What will you do?" said Ingrid, finding her voice again.

"I have a plan," Helen replied, "you sit on the stairs and I'll go in there and deal with it." She gave a gentle tug on Ingrid's hands and steered her towards the stairs, gesturing to where she should sit, before releasing her and making her own way towards the cupboard under the stairs. "I think I'll find what I need in here," she said, opening the door and pulling boxes out, "I helped Oskar put some stuff in here yesterday so I know what I'm looking for."

"Please hurry." Ingrid's voice was tremulous and she sat, hugging her knees but with eyes fixed on the kitchen door.

"Found it." Helen closed the cupboard door and appeared back beside Ingrid, this time, holding a baseball bat. "This should do the trick, what do you think?"

"No," Ingrid's mouth fell open, "you are not going to kill it with a bat, are you?"

"Don't be dumb," Helen shook her head, "I'm going to challenge it to the best of nine innings and the loser has to leave," she laughed, "of course I'm going to kill it." She began to swing the bat in a pendulum like motion, imagining herself walking up to the plate at the bottom of the ninth, needing just one home run to win the game.

"No, it is too horrible," Ingrid, screwed up her face in distaste, "you cannot kill it, can you not chase it out instead?"

"Are you serious?" Helen swung the bat again. "You've been watching too much Tom and Jerry if you think I'm going in there to play chases with it."

"Please, get rid of it but do not squash it," Ingrid pointed to the bat and shook her head in distaste, "not that, please."

Helen looked at the bat in her hand and gave it another swing before setting it down on the floor, against the stairs. "I won't kill it if you don't want me to," she looked at Ingrid's stricken face, "but chances are I'm not going to be able to catch it either, it probably won't come out if I go in there you know."

"Please try anyway or I will never be able to go in there again."

"Okay," said Helen, "I need a couple of heavy towels." She was trying to formulate a plan on the hoof and although she did have the germ of an idea, it wasn't brilliant and was most likely, doomed to ignominious failure.

"I will get them," Ingrid stood, "do you need large or small towels?"

"Bath towels I think," said Helen, "the heavier the better, gloves as well, also, the heavier the better." Helen watched as Ingrid ascended the stairs at speed, all the while doubting the mouse would make an appearance. If it did, her chances of catching it were slim but it wasn't something she would consider attempting without wearing gloves of some kind. She was just easing off her sneakers when Ingrid appeared with the towels and with a pair of heavy black, leather gloves that by the size of them, must have been Oskar's or Gary's.

"These are the heaviest I have," Ingrid handed Helen two thick, white towels, "and these are Gary's gloves."

Helen smiled and took the gloves, slipping them onto her hands and wiggling her fingers in them to test the fit, pleased to find they were too small for her although they would do for now. "Okay, when I go in there, I want you to cover the bottom of the door with this," she handed over one of the towels, "but you'll need to roll it up lengthways first."

"Why do I have to block the door?" Ingrid clutched the towel to her chest like a shield, her eyes popping in distress. "Please tell me it cannot escape from the kitchen."

"Mice have no collarbones," Helen saw Ingrid's eyes widening, "they can flatten out and squeeze through small spaces so best to block the bottom of the door."

"I will." Ingrid's face was pale apart from two tiny spots of red on the top of each cheek. "I will sit up on the stairs after that I think, out of your way."

"Good idea," said Helen, not wanting to remind Ingrid about the ability of mice to climb up stairs, and of course, their tendency to run up clocks. "I'm going in now so be ready to block the door." She gave her fingers a stretch then gripped the bath towel by two corners, wielding it like a matador would a cape. With a final smile at Ingrid she walked over to the kitchen door and opened it with as little noise as possible before slipping into the lair of the beast and closing the door behind her.

Helen's eyes scanned the room for any signs of movement and as she did so, she could hear Ingrid battening down the hatches behind her which made her smile, knowing that if she managed to catch the little varmint then she would be a hero, even if just for one day. So, with Bowie's tune streaming in her head, she crept further into the kitchen, eyes flicking from side to side like a commando and ears pricked to listen for anything rodent-like.

After ten minutes of hunting in stealth mode had produced nothing, Helen was preparing to call off the action and announce the bad news to Ingrid when she heard it, a slight rustling sound, and she froze, trying to pick up its direction. There it was again, a rustling, crinkling sound as though something very small was munching on paper or plastic. Helen cocked her head and continued to listen, in between taking quiet steps in gradual fashion, towards the cupboard nearest the fridge, where she stopped and held her breath as the noise came again, this time louder. Dropping the towel at her feet, her eyes fell on a tall, pink plastic canister sitting on the worktop and she knew it was perfect, far and away a better prospect than the discarded towel had ever been. Even if she had managed to throw it over anything mouse-like, it was very likely to have scuttled out from under it but this was a different proposition and it wasn't at all dissimilar to the jug her dad always used for the same purpose, although he had filled his with water to drown the little critters. Helen reached out and picked up the container, making sure she made no sound as she peeled off its lid, then, counting down from ten in her head, she took a deep breath and at the end of the countdown, yanked the cupboard door open, coming face to whiskers with a tiny, startled field mouse. It hesitated for a split second which was all Helen needed to flick it with the plastic lid and send it tumbling into the container she held below the shelf. As it hit the bottom she pressed the lid on, pushing down hard to seal it before lying the canister lengthways on the counter and blowing out a breath of relief as she bent to gaze at the tiny inmate. After watching it scuttle around in panic or a few moments, she took scissors from a nearby drawer and poked some air holes into the shiny plastic, delighted, and relieved the hunt was over at last.

Helen picked the towel off the floor and threw it over one of the chairs behind her and she removed Gary's gloves, tossing them into the bin, smiling as she did so. As she reached the kitchen door and pulled it open, she was grinning from ear to ear and eager to be the bearer of good news. Stepping into the hallway her eyes caught sight of Ingrid sitting on the stairs and she bounded over towards her and gave a theatrical bow. "Madam, the beast has been captured."

Ingrid stood at once and inched her way down the stairs. "Do you have it?" she said, arriving at the foot of the stairs and glancing over Helen's right shoulder as if to check nothing had followed her from the kitchen.

"Yep, captured and waiting to be relocated as I stand here." Helen stood, hands on hips, the broad grin still plastered on her face as she awaited Ingrid's adulation and undying admiration for her bravery.

"Do you really have it?" Ingrid looked like she wanted to

believe it but couldn't and once more, her eyes flicked beyond where they stood.

"Yes," said Helen, grin still splitting her face, "and it can't escape so you don't have to worry, it's finished and you can safely enter the beast's lair."

Ingrid matched Helen's broad smile then, without warning, threw her arms around her waist and pulled her into a tight hug, burying her head in her shoulder. "Thank you so much."

Helen held onto the hug, sweeping her arms around Ingrid's shoulders and pulling her close, revelling in the soft, golden hair caressing her face as the booming of her own heart hammered in her chest, signalling she should pull back. Not for the first time, she ignored her instincts but as Ingrid seemed as content as she was to remain together, she felt safe to continue and they did so for a few moments before releasing each other and laughing.

"I think," said Ingrid, still laughing, " your heart is battering away and you are perhaps less brave with mice than you want me to believe." She placed a hand on Helen's chest for a second and then took a step back.

"Yeah, the old ticker was going crazy in there with all the excitement," Helen blushed and looked back at the kitchen door, "but we still need to dispose of our little friend in there, although that won't be difficult."

"Do we not just relocate it to the garden?" Ingrid's smile was wavering, the certainty of moments ago, fading away.

"No," Helen shook her head, "I've read if you do, they can find their way back in so we need to take it a few miles down the road I think, to be certain."

"That is okay," said Ingrid, her smile returning, "I will give you my car keys and you can remove it far enough away."

Helen shook her head. "I can't drive a stick shift car, I can only do automatics and you don't have one. Sorry."

"What will we do?" panic reappeared on Ingrid's face, "I cannot drive if that thing is in the car with me."

"You can drive us," Helen gave a reassuring grin, hoping Ingrid would agree, "and I can hold onto little Sven while you're doing it."

"Little Sven?" Ingrid's brow furrowed.

"Yeah," Helen gestured in the direction of the kitchen, "I've decided we should name him and I thought Sven would be good so what do you think?"

"I do not dislike it I suppose," Ingrid drew back and didn't sound enthusiastic, "but why are we naming it?"

"Well, now I haven't smashed his tiny head in," said Helen, "I feel a bond with the little guy, and it seems right he should have a name."

"I see," Ingrid nodded, "are we taking it...Sven, away right now?"

"Yeah we should, before he figures out how to stage a jailbreak and comes looking for me." Helen winked. "Right, I'll go up and change into something more comfortable and then we're off."

"I will get my things too," Ingrid cast a nervous glance back towards the kitchen, "are you sure he will not get out?"

"I promise he won't escape, " Helen grinned, "come on, let's get ready and we'll meet here again in five minutes."

"Okay, five minutes." Ingrid stood back to let Helen go upstairs first then took a final look over her shoulder towards the kitchen before following her in her wake.

***

Once in her bedroom, Helen grabbed a plain, black sweater from the wardrobe, along with her boots and coat and she threw them on before running back downstairs to collect little Sven, arriving at the rendezvous point just as Ingrid walked towards her from the direction of the sitting room.

"Is it...is Sven in there?" Ingrid gestured to the pink container but drew back even as she walked over to where Helen stood.

"Yeah, he's here, would you like to see him?" Helen considered holding the little creature up for inspection but decided it could ruin the moment so instead, she allowed herself to indulge in an inner smile at the way Ingrid was now using his name.

"No," Ingrid raised her hands, "I do not wish to look, please, let us go." She walked past Helen, her eyes fixed on the front door, and headed out to the car, Helen following behind her, holding onto little Sven like a proud parent.

***

They drove for a while, searching for an ideal spot to release the captive and they settled at last on a small patch of derelict land near to the main railway station. Ingrid refused to come out of the car to participate in the actual release so Helen conducted the operation herself, returning to the car with the empty canister and then leaving again to find a bin, when Ingrid made it clear she would not be taking the container back home.

"All done," said Helen sliding back into the passenger seat of the car for the second time, "but I feel quite emotional." She sniffed and then glanced at Ingrid, putting on her best version of a petted lip, and lowering her eyes.

"It was a mouse," Ingrid shook her head and tutted, "for goodness sake, why are you emotional?" She stared back at Helen, her expression one of relief rather than concern for the tiny creature.

"I know he was a mouse," said Helen, "but, he was our mouse and he wasn't an ordinary mouse, his name was Sven."

"Yes, I suppose he did have a name and it is very lovely," Ingrid raised her eyebrows, "but now he is gone, which is for the best I think."

Helen turned away and stared out of the windscreen, saying nothing, but sniffing again, doing her best to draw Ingrid into the game with her.

"Please tell me you are not really upset." Ingrid turned around in her seat, facing Helen and eyeing her with disbelief.

Helen shrugged and presented Ingrid with a sad smile. "I've never had a mouse with anyone before and now our only child has left home and you don't seem to care," she sniffed again for added effect, "so yes, I'm upset." She tried to keep a straight face as she spoke but the smile growing on Ingrid's face made it impossible to hold and she laughed and raised her eyebrows. "I know a way you could help me be less upset though."

"What would that be?" Ingrid took a sharp breath.

"Well," said Helen, turning to point out of the windscreen, "that's a train station and you get trains there," she licked her lips, "we could park the car and get on a train."

"Why would we get on a train and where would we go?"

"London of course, we could park the car and go to London for the day because that's the only thing that would soothe me."

"I don't think we can go to London right now," Ingrid glanced

130

at her watch, "we have dinner to make."

"Forget dinner," said Helen, her enthusiasm for the idea growing, "it's my treat and I'll buy us lunch and I promise not to do anything to get us arrested." She grinned. "Go on, say yes."

"I do not know, it is all quite sudden," Ingrid tapped her fingers on the steering wheel, "and what do we do about Sophie and Oskar?"

"Leave them be," Helen flicked up a hand to dismiss the concern, "they're old enough to fend for themselves." At this, she stopped and put her concerned face on again, forcing a hitch into her voice. "I only hope little Sven can do the same."

This time Ingrid laughed, a warm, rich laugh. "You are not right in the head Helen, I find myself wondering what goes on in there sometimes."

"Oh come on," Helen rubbed her hands together, "our only child has flown the nest and now we're free to do whatever we want, let's do London for the day and cut loose a bit." She paused for a couple of seconds to let Ingrid think about it, bubbling inside at finding an opportunity to steal her away for an entire, uninterrupted day. "You haven't said an outright no, does that mean yes?"

"You are tempting me, but Sophie and Oskar are at home."

"Ingrid," Helen's voice was conspiratorial, "this would be worth doing just to picture the look on Sophie's face never mind to help us get over the trauma of empty nest syndrome." She made a fist and gave Ingrid a gentle bump on the arm. "We can send them both selfies when we get there." The mischievous look spreading over Ingrid's face confirmed to Helen they were going to London and, pulling out her phone, she clicked open the parking app she had downloaded when they were scouting the area for little Sven's release point. Within a minute she had managed to pre-book a space only a few hundred yards away from their current spot and it didn't take long to park up and walk to the station, Helen paying for their tickets when they arrived. They would be in central London in a little more than an hour, barring delays.

* * *

The platform was busy and they settled on a spot towards the front of it but not before Ingrid insisted on buying coffee and

131

muffins because they had missed breakfast. Helen had been watching her since they made the decision to abandon Sophie and Oskar to their fates and for the first time, she saw what she believed was the real Ingrid. She looked relaxed, and she smiled and laughed in a way that made the years fall away from her. Helen thought she looked radiant and as they boarded the train, she gave silent thanks to the little mouse who had made it all possible.

Once onboard, they found two empty seats in the first carriage, airline style seats which Helen preferred, as it meant you didn't have to spend the journey trying to ignore the stranger opposite. With coats stowed above them, they broke out what remained of the coffee and muffins as the train departed.

"I wonder what he's doing right now." Helen tilted her head back as though in deep thought but she flicked her eyes towards Ingrid, checking her reaction.

"What who is doing?" Ingrid swallowed the last of her blueberry muffin and washed it down with a mouthful of coffee.

"Little Sven of course," said Helen, putting on a sad face, "aren't you worried about him?"

"He will be fine," Ingrid smiled and shook her head, "and unless I am mistaken, he will probably have found himself a nice little mouse girlfriend by now."

"What makes you think so?" Helen took a bite of her muffin and a slurp of coffee, intrigued by the turn in the conversation but reluctant to read too much into it, at least not for the moment.

"I think with you as his mother he will find it easy," said Ingrid, tilting her head as she looked at Helen, "am I right?"

"Maybe," Helen dropped her head but looked up at Ingrid, "although you're forgetting you're his second mom so I'm not sure."

Ingrid laughed. "We would make a strange couple do you not think?"

"We already are a strange couple," Helen replied, smiling, "our only son is a little Swedish mouse."

"Yes, he is," replied Ingrid, rubbing at her chin and smiling at Helen, "we have a little mouse child together."

"We do, and we aren't married," Helen took another sip of coffee and wiggled her eyebrows, "our reputation must be awful." Before Ingrid could reply, Helen nodded towards her empty seat back table. "You've finished your muffin already."

"I have. I was hungry."

Helen broke the remains of her own muffin into two parts and held one half out to Ingrid. "I'd be happy to share mine with you anytime but I think you might know that already."

"Yes, I believe I do know."

"Go on then, take it," Helen nodded towards the cake in her hand, "it's not like it means we'd be engaged or anything."

"I *am* still hungry," said Ingrid, holding Helen's gaze, "and I think I would like to share with you." She reached over and in one movement, took the cake and popped it in her mouth before licking the end of her fingers. "Thank you."

Helen felt the noise of the train working its way through her and heard in the distance, the inspector calling for passengers to get their tickets ready. She fished theirs from her pocket, and smiled.

Chapter Ten

The Art of Eating Spaghetti

Central London buzzed with tourists, most of them well wrapped up with hats and scarves but Helen found it cool rather than cold, although there was a slight breeze blowing which at times made the air feel icy as it nipped at her bare neck. Ingrid had come better prepared, bundled up in a tan coloured, wool coat with contrasting scarf and gloves. Helen glanced at her every so often as they made their way through the throngs of people towards the spot where they planned to take their selfie and she found herself thinking that to anyone bothering to look at them, they would seem an odd match. Ingrid looked elegant yet not overdressed, for a day out in the capital but Helen, dressed head to toe in black, was sporting what she liked to think of as her rock star with a hangover look. She couldn't help but wonder what Ingrid thought about it.

They had agreed to take one photo in front of the huge neon advertisements in Piccadilly Circus and then, after sending it to Sophie and Oskar, they would put their phones on silent, planning to savour the reaction from home on their return journey. Helen spotted a good vantage point just beyond a booth selling the usual tourist tat and they took up their position. "Come on," said Helen, tapping at her phone to get the camera ready and beckoning to Ingrid to stand a bit nearer, "I've told Mr. DeMille we're ready for our close-up."

"I am not very photogenic." Ingrid frowned, but moved closer to Helen nonetheless.

"I am," replied Helen, grinning as she adjusted the angle of her phone, "but you need to come closer or I won't get everything in." She put her left arm around Ingrid's waist as she moved in tight beside her, enjoying the closeness but trying not to let it show. "Ok, give it our best smiles on the count of three. One, two, three." As the countdown ran out, Helen pressed the icon on her phone and held it down, allowing the camera to take multiple shots to ensure at least one of them would be useable. "I think we're done," she said, releasing Ingrid and flicking to the gallery app on her phone, then scrolling through the pictures, with Ingrid leaning in beside her to get a better look.

"This one," Ingrid pointed to the screen, "I do not look too bad I think, at least, I am passable."

"Yeah," said Helen, "I think we both look pretty good there, I'll send it on to the kids back home." A few taps on the screen sent the picture off on its journey and set the phone to silent mode before Helen dropped it back in her coat pocket. "Okay, this is decision time now, we are in London and have at least," she glanced at her watch, "five hours to ourselves so, what would you like to do?"

"I am not sure," Ingrid shrugged and looked around her, "there is so much and I cannot decide so perhaps you could suggest something."

"Okay, my suggestion," Helen smiled and pointed through the crowds and towards Leicester Square, "is we can walk down that way to Trafalgar Square and look at the tree, it's not lit yet but I like Christmas trees so I'd like to see that one. Then we could do the National Gallery which is right beside it, because there's an astonishing picture in there I'd like you to see."

"That sounds lovely," said Ingrid, "and I have never been before so yes, let us go there." She gestured to Helen to lead the way and without further ado, they both headed off through the crowds, down through Leicester Square and round towards Trafalgar Square.

**

The Christmas tree was huge, easily twenty meters high. Helen didn't care they were a week too early to see it lit because it was the sheer size of the thing she loved. Her favourite tree was the one at the Rockefeller Centre in New York, not for its size but for its blow you away loveliness. Ingrid laughed at the level of her passion and said she hoped the one they would have at home wouldn't be a disappointment and Helen assured her it wouldn't be, delighted she would still be there when it was time to put it up. When they had enjoyed the tree enough, they headed indoors to the gallery, depositing a donation in the glass box near the entrance and heading up the stairs to the second level, Helen leading the way.

"It's in here," said Helen, taking Ingrid's arm and guiding her into the room, "but forget historical accuracy and just drink in this beauty." They circumnavigated a large group of selfie-stick wielding, Japanese tourists, then stopped in front of a massive canvas."

"It is magnificent," said Ingrid, eyes sparkling, "and so lifelike that they could almost step out and join us here in the gallery."

"This is the Execution of Lady Jane Grey but it wasn't painted contemporaneously so for accuracy, it gets the thumbs down but for the wow factor, I don't think you can beat it. Tell me, how much do you know about English history?"

"I have had three children educated in England so what I do not know about the Romans, the Vikings and the Tudors is not worth knowing and I am aware of the fate of this poor lady."

"Yeah, it was pretty brutal although understandable from a certain perspective, I suppose." Helen grinned at Ingrid, thrilled at her positive reaction to the painting and bubbling with excitement at having an opportunity to show her around. "Would you like a personal, guided tour of my other favourites?"

"Show me all of them," replied Ingrid.

They spent the next couple of hours wandering in an out of the different rooms, Helen acting as an unofficial guide. She had last been there about eighteen months previously and she was delighted to be back again. Every time she came, it reminded her of Eleanor, her dad's sister, who had brought her to London for the first time when she was just eighteen years old and she thought about her again now, as they stopped in front of the last picture on her list of favourites. It was just a painting of a lady in a straw hat but it had been Eleanor's most loved painting as she claimed the woman looked like her when she was younger. Helen smiled as she looked at it once more.

"What is special about this one?" said Ingrid, "it is rather plain compared to the others."

"My dad's sister brought me here when I was a teenager." Helen studied the picture for a moment. "She loved this one so I come to see it when I'm here because it makes me think about her," she looked around at Ingrid, "she was very kind to me."

"That is lovely," Ingrid placed a hand on Helen's arm, "you have a very soft heart, I think."

"Perhaps, I don't know though," said Helen, savouring Ingrid's casual touch, "but I do know I have an empty stomach, so, how about lunch?"

"Yes, lunch, where shall we go?"

"Well, I hope you like Italian because I've taken a bit of a liberty and booked a table at a nice one in Covent Garden, it's not far." Helen shuffled her feet, waiting to see what the reaction would be and hoping her gambit wouldn't fall flat.

Ingrid smiled and nodded her agreement. "You seem to have thought of everything and if I did not know better, I would believe you had planned all of this today." She looked Helen in the eye then started buttoning up her coat in preparation for the cold outside.

"Including little Sven?"

"I would put nothing past you Helen, but no, little Sven was in the house the day before you came, so, let us go to lunch."

With the lunch venue agreed upon, they headed out of the room and made their way downstairs and out of the gallery, Helen pulling her coat around herself and buttoning it as high as it would go in a futile attempt to combat the definite chill in the air now, all the while regretting not grabbing her scarf when they had left the house. She glanced again at Ingrid who was walking at her side as the crowds had thinned, and she couldn't help but smile.

"What is the smile for?" said Ingrid, catching her look.

"I was just thinking, this restaurant does a fantastic spaghetti Bolognese and I might go for that."

"I might consider it myself," said Ingrid, "if it is as delicious as you say."

"It's fabulous," Helen sucked the cold air in through her teeth, "do you like Disney cartoons, you know, the full-length features?"

Ingrid juddered to a halt and regarded Helen with puzzlement. "Disney cartoons, where did that come from when we were discussing pasta?"

"Spaghetti of course," Helen stepped sideways to allow

people to pass them without having to step onto the road, "haven't you seen Lady and the Tramp? They share a bowl of spaghetti and they're eating it and then their lips get closer and closer and it's like they're kissing."

"Of course I have seen the film and I know what they do, but I might order pizza."

"Oh, that's okay," Helen put her hands in her coat pockets as they moved off again, "they do a cracking pizza as well."

"That is good to know," replied Ingrid, flicking a glance to her left, "but I still might order spaghetti."

***

The restaurant was busy but their booking ensured they had a nice table at the window, well back from the door and the cold draught that crept in every time it opened. As they perused the selection of menus, Helen ordered an Italian beer and Ingrid asked for water. They decided to skip any starter and go straight to the main course, leaving room for dessert if they still fancied it and after much discussion, they both opted for pizza after seeing a glorious one delivered to a couple at the next table. It wasn't long before a pleasant waiter arrived to take their order.

"Are you disappointed?" said Ingrid, glancing up at Helen and adjusting the cutlery on her side of the table after the waiter had returned to swap over their knives. "I mean about the spaghetti."

Helen leaned back in her chair, holding Ingrid's gaze and lifting her beer to take a sip. "I might be," she said, placing the bottle back on the table and leaning forward, "but I'd be interested to know if you're disappointed." Her stomach rippled its response to the unexpected exchange, dancing butterflies confirming her instinctive understanding that the conversation on the train that morning, did indeed have a subtext.

"Perhaps," said Ingrid, looking around at the other customers in the restaurant, "but it is such a public place to eat a dish like that and it can be very messy."

Helen took a deep breath, preparing herself to push back and keep the discussion going, hopeful it would remove any lingering doubt that something hitherto inconceivable, was on the verge of happening. "Would you consider eating it at home instead of here?"

"That is a difficult question to answer," Ingrid paused and

poured some water into her glass, "and I am wondering why you want to know?"

"Well, I was thinking it could perhaps be something you teach me to cook and then we could try it together to see if you like my cooking." Ingrid smiled at the comment but said nothing, so Helen pressed on, her previous cautious approach falling away. "I have so many questions I want to ask you but I don't know where to start." She glanced around for any sign of lunch but all the action was on the other side of the restaurant. "I keep trying to understand what you're all about but every time I think I'm almost there you change, and I feel lost in the middle of it."

"Go ahead, ask your questions," Ingrid sat forward, clasping her hands on the table, "and I will try to answer."

Helen shifted in her seat and leaned forward, keeping her voice low despite the busy murmur surrounding them. "Okay, you have a problem which makes social contact difficult for you and I understand, but you seem all over the place and one minute you're cold and the next you're like this, and you confuse me in so many ways."

Ingrid pursed her lips and frowned. "If it makes you feel better, it confuses me also," she took a sip of water, "because I have times when I feel overwhelmed but other times when I can cope. You arrived at a time when I am finding it a little easier to weather the storm, if I can put it that way."

"It sometimes doesn't seem that way," said Helen, reflecting on the yin and yang of Ingrid's emotional state during their initial encounters, trying and failing to see the correlation between those feverish first few days, and Ingrid's subjective experience of them.

Ingrid nodded. "I understand how it must have seemed to you, but believe me, at most other times it would have been much worse, and that is taking no account of your excitable personality."

"Yeah, my personality is quite something," replied Helen with a laugh, "but that's for another time because lunch is served." She nodded towards the approaching waiter who weaved his way towards them through the narrow alleyways between tables, two large platters balanced on his fingertips. He deposited a pair of delicious looking pizzas then checked if they needed anything else before leaving them to enjoy their food. Helen had ordered a plain cheese pizza and she dived into it with enthusiasm, all the while furrowing her brow at Ingrid's choice, resplendent as it was with a selection of hams and vegetables.

"You look afraid of my lunch," said Ingrid, smiling.

"Mmm," Helen chewed faster so she could answer, "it's got things on it, I don't like things on my pizza, never have done."

Ingrid laughed and shook her head. "I like things as you call them, you should try it to see if you like it." She cut a small slice from her pizza then lifted it with her knife before placing it on the side of Helen's plate.

Helen prodded the added slice of pizza with her knife, almost like she was poking a snake with a stick to see if it was dead. "I'll try it," she said, "but I have another question to ask first," she took a drink of her beer, "it's about Gary."

Ingrid finished her mouthful of pizza and took a drink of water. "What could you possibly want to know about my husband?"

Helen hesitated, appreciating she could be about to light the blue touch paper but possessing only a blunt question because she could think of no gentle way to say it. "Ingrid, are you afraid of him?"

"Afraid of Gary, of course not, why would I fearful?"

"Well, the night he came home, you looked nervous, like you were walking on eggshells," Helen put her knife and fork down and looked Ingrid in the eye, "you looked scared."

"I was being cautious," replied Ingrid, "but not for the reason you think. Gary sometimes says things to me, they are horrible things but most of the time I will pay him no attention, in fact I have ignored most of his utterings for the last twenty years." She smiled at this and then pointed to Helen, her eyes downcast. "What about you though, what would you have done if Gary had started baiting me, or if he had found out about the baby and Sophie's separation from Michael?"

Helen felt herself bristle at the thought of Gary tormenting Ingrid and having a go at Sophie. "Are you saying he would have had had a go at both of you, when someone else was there?"

"Yes, for certain, and Sophie, as always, would have faced him down but it is not good for her with the baby." Ingrid gave a sad smile. "So how would you have reacted then, Helen, would you have kept the talking bear quiet or would you have released him to defend our honour?"

Helen dropped her gaze for a second and shrugged her shoulders, "You already know I couldn't have stayed silent." She looked back up and saw Ingrid nod her head in weary acceptance.

"That is why I was being careful, not through any fear of Gary, but because I was afraid of what you might say in the heat of battle." Ingrid cut into her pizza again, no longer smiling. "You may disapprove, but it was easier to play at appeasing him than to see my house burnt down before my eyes."

Helen wanted to say so much but found herself lost for words. On the night Gary arrived home, she had watched Sophie and Ingrid fussing around him, and had looked on in great discomfort as he made a show of having them both on tenterhooks. It hadn't occurred to her that she had been the root cause of it all and now, faced with that reality, she felt nauseous.

"Do not be upset please," said Ingrid, looking thoughtful for a second, "but tell me this, how old is she?"

"How old is who?"

"The woman you saw with Gary of course, come on, I am not stupid and I know you saw something." Ingrid put her cutlery down again and leaned forward. "It is what he does, I know him very well."

Helen picked up the small slice of pizza Ingrid had given her to try and in three bites, ate it all, before wiping her mouth with a napkin and grimacing. "That was disgusting in a way I can't describe."

"Was she very young?" said Ingrid, observing Helen's obvious discomfort.

"Half his age." Helen turned away and stared out of the window, pretending she had seen something of interest, her appetite for a continuation of the conversation, now blunted.

"It is his usual type and unless things have taken an unexpected turn, she will be a blonde of course," Ingrid pointed to her own hair, "Gary likes blondes you see, only now he prefers them to be twenty-three and not sixty-three."

Helen let out a breath and shook her head in astonishment. "You're right, she was a blonde but you're talking like he does this all the time, you can't be serious."

"Wait," said Ingrid, turning away and catching the attention of a passing waiter from whom she ordered more beer and water and only turning back to Helen when he had gone to fetch the drinks. "There was a time just before Oskar was born when Gary was so prolific, I had to get a test done at the local hospital which, as you can you imagine, was shaming to have to experience."

Helen sat open mouthed and stunned into complete silence, hardly able to believe what she was hearing, despite already knowing Gary was a philanderer extraordinaire.

Ingrid's slight smile betrayed her amusement at Helen's reaction. "From then on," she said, "I would not let him near me and now a long time has passed and I no longer care what he does." She stopped speaking as the waiter had returned with their drinks but she started again as soon as he left the table. "A couple of years back it was a bad time because my mother was very ill and I was traveling between England and Sweden on a regular basis. I came back one day when Gary had not expected me and found him with his latest girlfriend, in my bed." Ingrid took another mouthful of pizza and then put her cutlery on top of the plate and pushed it away. "We had a furious row that night and all he kept saying was it was just sex, which was correct, but he could not understand why I was so angry about it being in my bed."

"I don't understand," said Helen, spreading her palms, "why the fuck are you staying with him?" She looked at Ingrid in puzzlement, wondering why she was choosing to live with a man who had no respect for her at all and realising Oskar had heard the row Ingrid mentioned but had taken it for the discovery of an affair rather than for what it was.

"I stay," Ingrid folded her napkin and put it on the table, "because I do not have anything else and it is easier to live with that than with the alternative."

Helen leaned back in her chair, shocked to hear her own words of a few days ago, echoing back at her. "Explain what you mean," she took a swig of her beer, "there has to be a better alternative surely."

"You and I are very similar you know Helen, far more than you might believe." Ingrid poured some water into her glass. "I have no family in Sweden now, only my family here in England and they are almost all grown and living their own lives. I have also not worked for more than thirty years so it is as I said, I do not have anything else that would be better than my current situation."

"You could have left years ago so I don't get it," Helen felt her agitation rising and she leaned forward, "why did you stay with him all this time?"

"I could have walked away, you are correct, but I had young children for most of that time and it would not have been easy for them so I decided their needs should go before my own and now it is late in the day for changing."

"Can you not go home to Sweden?"

"I have spent more years in England than I have in Sweden so when I go to Sweden, I feel I am more English and when I come back to England, I feel so much more Swedish."

Helen sighed and nodded, still shocked but able to understand the dilemma of the dual national. "Whenever I go to Scotland," she said, "I feel like an alien, it's so weird and I haven't been back for years but last time I was there, I felt so out of place I cut it short and went back to the States. Of course, when I'm in the States, I'll always be the Scottish woman so I don't fit in anywhere."

"We are the same," replied Ingrid, nodding, "more than you know so, shall we both risk having dessert or have I managed to put you off your food?"

"Oh no, nothing puts me off my food," said Helen, "I want ice cream."

"I do too," Ingrid was already looking through the menu, "and it says they have pistachio flavour which is my favourite, so I will have that."

"I want chocolate," said Helen, studying Ingrid as she called a waiter over and made the order, marvelling at how she looked relaxed and happy, despite just confessing her marriage was a sham, and her husband an unapologetic fuck of a lothario. As the waiter moved off, Helen drew her eyes away. "All sorted?"

"Yes, it will not be long," Ingrid bit at her bottom lip and poured the last of the water into her glass, " and I have a question for you now."

143

"Feel free." Helen leaned forward then placed her elbows on the table before resting her chin in both hands, watching as Ingrid took a sip of water and took up a matching position on the other side of the table, neither of them speaking, instead, gazing at each other in a comfortable silence. "You said you had a question for me."

"What are your feelings for Sophie?"

"We've been here before," said Helen, disappointed the question hadn't been the one she wanted, and perhaps, needed, to hear, "there's nothing between me and Sophie."

"I need to know," Ingrid paused, shifting in her seat in apparent discomfort, "I need to know... if you would like there to be."

"The night I kissed Sophie, it only happened because we were both drunk, and even if I hadn't thrown up, it would only ever have been a one-night thing for me." Helen caught sight of the waiter with their desserts and fell silent, waiting until the ice creams were on the table and the waiter gone, before continuing with her answer. "I'm fond of Sophie but I don't get the feeling with *her*," she took a spoonful of ice cream, "so the night Gary came home I tried to tell her I might have found someone special but when I saw the look on her face I backed off and told her I didn't."

"So, do you have someone special?" said Ingrid, her gaze steady.

"I might have," Helen scooped up more ice cream, "but I haven't told her and I don't think I ever will because sometimes I'm not sure she likes me, never mind anything more. I can't tell, and if I presume she feels something for me but I'm wrong then...Jesus, it would be a disaster for everyone."

Ingrid picked at her ice cream without eating it and she smiled. "Perhaps this woman is afraid of her own emotions and is hoping you will tell her how you feel because it would make things easier for her."

Helen gave a half-hearted laugh. "It's not an easy thing to do and maybe get wrong and believe me, in this particular case, getting it wrong would be...it would be beyond terrifying for me." She took a deep breath as she watched Ingrid's reaction, feeling caught in the liminal space between confessing her feelings and retreating to the safety of generalisations, yet not safely tethered to either.

"You always seem so confident, why would it be difficult for you?" said Ingrid, still playing with her ice cream.

"Do you know, I'm a few years off fifty and I've had two proper girlfriends my entire life." Helen broke eye contact and gazed down at her bowl, swirling the melting ice cream around it. "I always seem to fall for the ones who could never like me back that way and it's the same again now so the whole thing is impossible."

"Perhaps you should take a chance that this time will have a different outcome," Ingrid smiled and took a small scoop of ice cream, "if you tell her how you feel."

Helen dropped her spoon into the bowl and she stared over the table, courage deserting her when she needed it most, replaced instead with a certainty she was indulging herself in wishful thinking to believe Ingrid would ever reciprocate her feelings. "I don't think I can...look, if you're done there I am too, we should ask for the check."

"I am finished too," Ingrid's eyes were wide and still fixed on Helen's, "and we should head home I think, before we are reported missing."

Helen nodded her agreement and called the waiter over, settling their bill and making sure to leave a decent tip. Then, they were on their way out into the late afternoon chill, heading for the tube and back to the mainline station. On the way, they stopped at one of the tourist shops to let Ingrid pick up something she needed but Helen waited outside, glad of the cold and glad to get a few minutes alone. Soon enough, Ingrid returned and it wasn't long before they were on the train, heading back to Gravesend.

***

"I had a wonderful day with you," Ingrid pulled the driver's door closed and turned around in her seat, "it was rather unexpected but, very lovely."

"Thank you, I did too." Helen meant it sincerely. She had spent a fantastic day with Ingrid although as they had been eating dessert, things had become awkward due to her own lack of conviction about the electric connection between them which had lasted all the way from their hug after capturing little Sven, to the train journey home where they sat gazing at each other in silence. Now they were alone and locked together in the close confines of the car, the space between them charged with an energy Helen had never experienced before, and it was all she could do to check her phone for messages and missed calls. "I beat you in texts, I think, I have twelve but only four missed calls, all bar one from Sophie." On their silent journey home, they hadn't bothered to check how many frantic or angry texts the abandoned pair had sent them and now she had done it, Helen was sure their reception was going to be a frosty one.

Ingrid raised her eyebrows in response then reached into the back of the car and lifted a small, brown paper bag, bringing it over and holding it out to Helen. "This is for you," she said, "I hope you like it as much as I do."

"For me," Helen smiled, "what is it?" She put her phone back into her pocket.

"Open it and find out."

Helen took the bag and flicked her eyes up to Ingrid's smiling face. "I hope this isn't a Prince Charles tea towel because I have dozens of those and I'm running out of places to store them." She reached into the bag, and gasped as she pulled out a small brown bear, kitted out in a blue coat and red hat ensemble, the sight of him causing Helen to throw back her head back and laugh, beaming back at Ingrid. "I think this is where I'm supposed to say something like you shouldn't have, but I can't, I love him, in fact...I love him more because you bought him for me."

"I am so glad," said Ingrid, looking delighted by the reaction, "I saw him and thought of you at once and it was irresistible."

"He's amazing," Helen held the bear up in front of her, "and I think I could rock his style, what d'you think?" She turned to Ingrid, expectation burning in her eyes.

"I think you could do anything...in fact," Ingrid tapped at the gearstick with the fingers of one hand, "I have never met any woman like you."

Helen sighed and tipped her head to the side. "Yeah, I'm sure you don't meet many women as assured of their own magnificence as I am," she smiled, "I'm just sorry you find it unattractive."

Ingrid moved her hand from the gearstick and reached out, gesturing for Helen to pass the bear over and once she had him, she set about sorting the toggles on his coat and straightening his hat. "I did say those words, but it was only half true." She smiled and handed back the bear.

"So you don't think I'm assured of my own magnificence, is that what you're saying?"

"Oh no, you are assured of that, on a subconscious level perhaps, but you are assured of it somewhere within you," she went back to drumming on the gearstick, "but I was wrong to say it was unattractive."

"I see," said Helen, feeling her stomach flip as she glanced out at the emptiness of the car park, "but the other day, you said I was dangerous," she turned back to Ingrid, "but I'd never do you harm so why am I dangerous?"

"I did not mean you would harm me," Ingrid stopped worrying the gearstick and brought her hand back to her lap, "but I was thinking you could convince people anything was possible for them, even if it might not be right for them or could be dangerous."

"Have I done that to you?" Helen pushed the bear onto the dashboard to jam him against the windscreen, a sudden surge of heat washing over her neck as her heart boomed and thumped in her chest.

"Yes, you have," said Ingrid in a quiet voice, "very much so."

"In what way?" The bright headlights of a van leaving the car park swept over them, illuminating the car interior and allowing Helen to get a clear look at the tension etched on Ingrid's face. "You don't have to answer if you don't want to."

Ingrid shielded her eyes from the glare and then looked around at the almost deserted car park before meeting Helen's gaze. "It is very quiet here," her voice trembled, "so few cars."

"I know, and it's dark too." Helen lifted the bear from the dashboard and put him back into his bag.

"I think...I think this might be a good place for eating spaghetti. Would you like to do that here?"

Helen felt icy needles of adrenaline rushing through her, flashing over her head and down towards her feet, all the tension collapsing under its own weight and bringing matters to a head.

"I wasn't sure you would...well...the thing is, yes, I would love to eat spaghetti here, but only if it was with you." She hesitated for a few seconds before going on, knowing once she said it, there was no going back. "I think you might be my special person, as strange as that might seem." Helen heard the tremor in her voice and she felt her hands tremble as she reached up to move some hair from her eyes.

Ingrid rubbed at her neck and chin but kept her gaze steady. "You make me feel so nice Helen, but also afraid, because it is so nice," she took a deep breath and smiled, "but it is not so afraid I think."

Helen nodded, still shaking, and charmed that after all her years in Gravesend, Ingrid's English still fractured a little because she was nervous. She took a deep breath of her own and reached out to hold one of Ingrid's hands, relieved when she encountered no resistance. They sat that way for several minutes until Helen broke the silence. "If we go beyond talking about this, then you need to know the genie will be out and I'm telling you, he's a big genie and he won't go back into the bottle. This has to be your choice."

Ingrid nodded and gripped Helen's hand. "I am choosing to open the bottle with you."

Helen smiled and leaned over, cupping the side of Ingrid's face with her free hand. "You've no idea how good it is to hear you say that." She leaned in and kissed her on the lips, making sure it was slow and gentle, thrilled by Ingrid's first tentative response which soon became more urgent. Within a minute, they sat locked together in a passionate kissing session, breaking apart every so often to smile and look at each other before starting again.

"We have to stop," Ingrid pulled back and brushed Helen's hair away from her face, "it is too much, and I do not think here is the right place."

Helen laughed and kissed Ingrid's chin and down her neck before pulling back herself. "I know, me too," she glanced around the car park, "any further, and it's past the point of no return."

Ingrid nodded. "We have to go home."

"Yeah, I suppose we do." Helen was just about to lean back

in for another kiss when her phone rang, filling the car with the theme from Scooby Doo. "Fuck, I thought I'd left it on silent." She dug into her pocket and yanked the phone out, glancing at the screen. "That's weird," she looked at Ingrid, "it's my uncle, do you mind if I get this?"

"Of course not." Ingrid sat back, watching.

"Hey uncle Frank, what's happening?" Helen pulled down the passenger visor and gazed into the vanity mirror attached to it, checking her mouth for signs of rogue lipstick. She listened without speaking for a few moments and then reached out to Ingrid to hold her hand. "When did it happen? I see, yeah." She squeezed Ingrid's hand. "Yeah, that's ok, look Frank, I'm not home right now, can I call you back later tonight?... ok, I'll call soon, bye."

"Is something wrong?" Ingrid pulled Helen's hand closer to her and began stroking it with her thumb.

"Yeah, I suppose it is," Helen gave a grim smile, "my mother's dead."

Chapter Eleven

The Little Blue Letters

From the moment they stepped in the door, it was obvious Sophie had used the day to work herself up into a state of high dudgeon. Ingrid had removed her coat and Helen was in the process of doing the same, when she came flouncing from the kitchen to glare at the returning miscreants. Helen had raised a hand to stop her before she could start when Ingrid intervened, stepping forward and taking hold of Sophie's arm before leading her back in the direction from which she had just come. This gave Helen the chance to phone her uncle again for more details, after which she headed to the sitting room, not sure if she fancied company but knowing it was where Ingrid kept the Scotch. She sat there, well into her fourth glass, surrounded by Ingrid, Sophie and Oskar and she looked up from staring into her glass and shrugged her shoulders. "I haven't seen her for twenty years, it's not like we were close or anything." She drained her glass and looked around at Ingrid who was beside her on the sofa. "Would it be all right if I had another drink?"

"No, it would not be all right," said Ingrid, frowning, "you have had more than enough for one evening I believe." She reached out and prised the glass from Helen's grip before placing it on the floor beside her feet.

"You can't be serious," Helen grinned at the other two, soliciting their support, "am I really not allowed another small Scotch?"

"She's had a terrible shock mamma," said Sophie, returning Helen's grin, "maybe one more drink would help."

Ingrid shook her head. "Drinking more will not change anything but it can lead to people saying words they later wish they had not." She looked directly at Helen as she spoke, her eyes flashing a warning.

Helen nodded, catching on at once to what Ingrid meant and

despite having downed four large whiskies in quick succession, she still had enough wits about her to know getting blind drunk would be dangerous. "Well, if I can't have a drink, I want more chocolate."

"You've had two bars already," said Sophie, "and it's not good for you."

This time Helen looked to Ingrid for moral support but none was forthcoming. "I think it's slipped your collective mind I'm half Scottish and maybe you don't realise this, but if we don't ingest a certain amount of sugar every day," she paused and looked at them all in turn, "we die." She raised her eyebrows to emphasise the imminent danger she faced.

"I've got a Dairy Milk in my room if you want it," said Oskar, drawing back from Sophie who had aimed a nudge at his ribs, "will I fetch it for you?"

"Yes please Oskar, my reliable and faithful friend." Helen looked at Ingrid and then Sophie, smiling in triumph despite their disapproving looks and, as Oskar hauled himself to his feet and strode off to get the chocolate, she gestured to the space he had vacated. "He is a remarkable guy, and I want you both to know how much I love him."

"Everybody loves Oskar," said Sophie, a peeved expression building on her face as she pulled her knees up towards her and wrapped her arms around them.

"Oh come on Sophie, I love you too," Helen turned to Ingrid, "and I love you as well, I really do, in fact I love all of you."

"That is nice to know," Ingrid put a hand on Helen's shoulder and gave it a squeeze, "and we all love you too, but, I think you could be doing with some coffee now."

"I'll make some, mamma." Sophie clambered to her feet and walked over to Helen, bending over and brushing her cheek with an outstretched finger. "Black coffee coming your way very soon."

Helen gave her a dopey smile and watched in silence as she left the room then she turned to Ingrid and shook her head. "I don't think I can face going to Scotland, I mean it, I can't do it."

"Yes, you can.," Ingrid reached out and took Helen's hand, giving it a soft kiss, "and I will go with you and it will be fine, I promise."

"I know you will but Ingrid, she'll be in the box, my mother will be in there," Helen shook her head again, "I don't want to have to see the box, it's horrific and I won't be able to cope." She leaned back on the sofa and closed her eyes, still holding fast to Ingrid's hand, her thoughts fixed on the traumatic events yet to come and her conscience troubled by a past she had tried hard to forget. They both sat in silence until Oskar returned with the chocolate bar and Sophie reappeared with the coffee, and as Helen drank hers, she said nothing more, her thoughts returning to her tiny mother lying in front of her, in a coffin. Although the others spoke amongst themselves and glanced towards her every so often, she didn't join the discussion, feeling as she often did, like she was alone in the middle of a crowd.

"Are you all right Helen," said Sophie.

Helen looked up. "I'm fine, I promise, but I was thinking about my mother again, I can't seem to stop."

"When did you see her last?" said Oskar sipping at his coffee.

"I was about twenty-seven I think. I came over to London and decided to take a trip up to Scotland but we had a fight and I never went back so," Helen sighed, "that was that, and she would only have been about the age I am now."

"Is there a strong resemblance between you and her?" said Sophie.

"I think so but she isn't...wasn't, tall, I take the height from my dad, although she had my hair colour and my eyes are the same. She was a great singer too, fantastic voice she had and she loved it, but I didn't get the voice." Helen laughed. "She was also very fond of boyfriends which never made its way to me either." She gazed into her empty cup then looked at Ingrid.

"I will get you another." Ingrid took the empty mug and went over to the sideboard, and the cafetières.

Helen waited until Ingrid brought back her refill before she spoke again. "Every year since I last saw her, uncle Frank has sent me a Christmas card, it's always the first one I get so he must post it extra early to make sure." She slurped her coffee. "Every year, inside the card, there's a little blue envelope with my real name written on it and it's a letter from her, my mother."

"What do the letters say?" said Ingrid.

"I don't know, I don't open them," Helen looked down at her

feet and she felt her throat tighten, "but I have them all in a box in the attic, eighteen of them, and I bet there's another one waiting for me when I go home. I only ever opened one of them and that was last year although I don't know what prompted me to do it."

"What did that one say?" As she spoke, Sophie gestured to Oskar for another coffee and smiled a thank you when he nodded and took her cup.

Helen looked up, tears now flowing. "It said she was sorry about how things worked out between us," she sniffed, and took the tissue Ingrid handed to her, "and that she always loved me and hoped one day I would find a way to forgive what she did, which of course I didn't do and now it's too late and I've fucked everything up again."

"Helen, you are too hard on yourself," Ingrid rested a consoling hand on her arm, "come on now, do not give yourself more punishment for the past."

"No, you don't understand, there's more." Helen wiped at her eyes and coughed. "She told me in the letter she was very sick, that she was dying, and she pleaded with me to come home to see her for the final time but I didn't because I was still angry with her and too fucking selfish." Helen pulled her arm away. "Look at the kind of person I am," she rubbed her eyes, dragging away the tears, and then looked over at Sophie and Oskar, "have a good look kids, and see me for what I am." She rubbed her eyes again and then bent forward, resting her head in her hands, a series of sobs escaping as she did so.

"I will tell you what you are," said Ingrid, moving closer and putting an arm on Helen's back, "you are just like everyone else, you are a person who made a mistake, nothing more."

"She's right," said Sophie, kneeling and then shuffling across to Helen before taking her hands and pulling them away from her face. "You aren't any worse than anyone else, in fact you're a whole lot better than most." She kissed Helen's hands and then took another tissue from Ingrid. "Let me clean you up, your face looks silly when you cry."

Helen nodded and tried to smile, letting Sophie wipe her face, and settling into the sensation of Ingrid's hand stroking her back, as she glanced between both and mouthed a silent thank you, knowing she didn't deserve any kindness but grateful for it nonetheless.

"I'd come over too," said Oskar, "but I can't stand snot." He made a face and then grinned.

Helen laughed despite herself and although she couldn't find any suitable words, she gave him a thumbs-up then closed her eyes.

"Are you feeling any better?" Ingrid slid her hand up to Helen's neck and began to make small, circular motions with her thumb at the top of her spine, flicking glances towards Sophie as she did so.

"Actually, I feel sick." Helen sensed Sophie moving backward away from her and she opened her eyes and gave her a weak smile. "Guess I shouldn't have had the coffee."

"Or it could be the Scotch and three bars of chocolate," Ingrid shook her head and turned to Sophie, "I am no expert but I think there could be a link so I will take Helen up to her bed and give her something to settle her stomach, if you can clear the cups away."

Sophie nodded. "I'm not good with vomit, so washing dishes is preferable, believe me."

"Come on, let me help you up," Ingrid put her arm around Helen's waist, "on the count of three we stand up together and we get you to bed."

Helen nodded, doing what Ingrid asked and, despite thinking she would be able to walk unaided, she held onto her all the way upstairs and into the bedroom, where Ingrid deposited her on the bed and told her to undress. In any other circumstances Helen would have had fun with the comment but all she wanted was for the nausea to pass so she started pulling off her clothes as soon as Ingrid left, and by the time she returned, Helen was sitting on the bed in her pyjamas.

Ingrid approached, holding a small glass containing a chalky, white liquid. "My goodness, what are those?" She pointed to Helen's pyjamas, and laughed.

"Star Wars pyjamas of course, doesn't everyone have a pair?" Helen forced herself to smile.

"No, they do not." Ingrid presented the glass to Helen, watching in amusement as she studied it, "Come on, drink this down and you will feel as good as new, unless you do not like medicine, just as you dislike things on your pizza."

Helen made a face and tipped the contents of the glass into her mouth, swallowing it in one go. "Not a problem, nurse."

"Right, get in." Ingrid smiled and pulled back the duvet, letting Helen climb in and settle herself before covering her up and sitting on the bed beside her. "Sleep now," she said, "you will not feel sick very soon and tomorrow morning things will be better, I promise."

"Thank you." Helen closed her eyes. "I wish you could stay."

"I do too, but I cannot tonight so go to sleep." Ingrid bent over and kissed Helen on the forehead then stood, and switched off the bedside lamp.

Helen opened her eyes and watched as Ingrid's silhouette moved across the room and as she got to the door she called after her. "Nurse, can I have a drink of water?"

Ingrid stopped and looked back over her shoulder. "I will bring you some water, but then you must sleep."

Helen lay in the silence and focused on her stomach, feeling the waves of nausea diminishing, and very soon, Ingrid came back with her glass of water and placed it on the bedside table.

"Good night, Helen."

"Night." Once again, Helen watched Ingrid's journey towards the door and she waited until she had reached for the handle before calling her back. "Nurse."

Ingrid froze, then turned on her heel and walked back towards the bed. "What is it now?"

"I can't sleep if I don't get a bedtime story." Helen produced her best, innocent smile.

Ingrid scratched at her jawline and glanced behind her at the door before she sighed, and knelt beside the bed. "All right, once there was a nurse, a Swedish nurse."

"Oh, I like stories about Swedish nurses," said Helen, gazing into Ingrid's eyes.

"And one night this nurse had to look after a very exasperating patient."

"That sounds terrible," Helen smiled, "what did the nurse do?"

"She lost her patience of course, and murdered the exasperating patient and then she buried the body in the garden beside the roses." Ingrid raised her eyebrows.

Helen's eyes widened and she smiled. "This explains how your children turned out."

Ingrid laughed and leaned over, kissing Helen on the lips. "Go to sleep," she pushed herself off her knees and stood, "I am warning you, no more." With that she turned and walked over to the door and out of the room.

Helen lay in the darkness with a smile on her face, knowing she would be awake for hours yet as her mind was racing. Within ten minutes she was fast asleep.

***

The next few days passed in a blur. After much debate, Helen's uncle agreed to her covering all the costs of the funeral although he would make the arrangements on her behalf. A quick phone call to the undertakers was enough to give them card details for a deposit, which then allowed them to book the cremation slot and the venue for a meal afterwards. Helen had no idea how many people would go for the meal but Frank thought up to a hundred so she went with his suggestion, surprised her mother had been such a popular woman.

Sophie wasn't keen to go, citing her delicate condition and how she didn't want to leave Oskar at home on his own and Helen accepted her reasons without argument, weak though they were, pleased she wouldn't have to battle to have some time alone with Ingrid. As for Ingrid, she maintained a quiet calm, discussing things with Helen when needed and keeping Oskar and Sophie on their toes, ensuring they helped around the house to prepare for her short absence. She was a picture of cool headedness and a million miles away from the woman Helen met when she arrived.

When it came to booking their hotel and travel, Helen hesitated over how many rooms to book as she didn't want to presume too much and book just one but neither did she want to book two and send out a different, wrong message. To complicate things, she was wary of prying eyes and eavesdroppers but after a couple of aborted attempts, she managed at last to grab a few minutes alone with Ingrid in the kitchen, ostensibly to discuss travel times. Her heart had soared when, in answer to her question about rooms, Ingrid had smiled and held up one finger and they had locked eyes for a few seconds but drew back from anything more physical when Oskar appeared in the doorway to announce he was hungry and needed biscuits without delay.

Things rolled along after that, the evenings spent all together in the sitting room watching a movie or marvelling at how well Ingrid could cheat at a variety of different board games. Helen drifted in and out of these games as the mood took her and she had quite often found herself deep in contemplation about the impending trip as well as the complications, new and old, in the house.

Tuesday night brought exciting news about Gary coming home for Ingrid's birthday on the Saturday and Sophie, who had taken the fateful call, announced it in a mournful voice. Helen had flicked a quick glance towards Ingrid as Sophie was speaking but she was surprised to see she didn't seem much affected by it. Other than reminding everyone she would be the one to tell Gary about Sophie's situation, she had carried on drinking her coffee and playing the game. Later that night she had appeared in Helen's room for a stolen five minutes, promising that the trip to Scotland the next day would be fine, and there would be no problem with Gary. She made Helen give a solemn promise she would at least try not to release the bear if she could.

Next morning had been an early rise and, with Sophie acting as taxi driver, Ingrid and Helen had arrived at the station just before eight a.m. The journey into London was quick but uncomfortable, the train being, as usual, overcrowded. From Euston however, seated in First Class, things were very different and they had both enjoyed a gorgeous cooked breakfast served on real crockery. The further North they travelled, the lighter the sky became and they passed the hours talking and gazing at the scenery as the train whizzed past. Arrival in Glasgow was bang on time and as their hotel was located just fifty meters away from the station, they had soon checked in and unpacked.

As Ingrid had never been to Glasgow, they decided to have a wander around the city centre with Helen acting as a local guide, albeit one working with a guidebook twenty years out of date. It was a pleasant afternoon, sunny yet cold and they included in their private tour, a stop off in one of the chain coffee shops, more for a bit of warmth than for anything they were serving. Darkness closed in quickly which pleased Helen because it meant the Christmas lights and tree would be another sight to see and after spending a pleasant half hour admiring them, they took a short stroll to the Merchant City, where they had dinner in a decent Italian restaurant before heading back through the cold night, to the hotel, and to bed.

"I'm not sure if I need my pyjamas," Helen glanced over her shoulder, "I can put them on if you like, I brought my fleecy ones and they button right up to the chin." She stepped away from the window, letting the heavy curtain fall back into place, and then stood with her hands behind her back, watching Ingrid remove her make up.

"You can wear them if you wish," said Ingrid, wiping her closed eyelids with a small towelette, "but if you do, I will lock you out."

"I would rather you locked me in," said Helen, "and if you do, I promise not to make any attempt to escape."

"I have already done it," Ingrid gestured to the door and wiped at her eyes again, "the do not disturb sign is on the outside."

"Have you seen the size of the shower in there?" said Helen, pointing towards the bathroom before walking over to the bed and sitting down, "you could easily get two people in it."

Ingrid nodded, closing the compact mirror with a click and putting it and the used towelette beside her on the bed. "That would be a first for me," she said, smiling at Helen and reaching out to her, "but I would like to talk about some things, if it is all right."

"Of course." Helen took Ingrid's outstretched hand and moved closer, glad of the delay because lurking under the barrage of emotions and pleasant physical sensations, there was a nervousness so unexpected, it had thrown her for the moment. "What are we talking about?"

"Tomorrow, you know it will be all right."

Helen shook her head. "I don't know what feels worse, having to look at the box knowing she's in there or all those people looking at me," she gripped Ingrid's hand tighter, "I guess I want it to be over and before you say it, I know I'm selfish."

"You are not selfish," said Ingrid, sighing, "I was like that with my mother's funeral and it felt so hard and I wished it over for days beforehand, but I coped." She leaned over and kissed Helen on the cheek. "Besides, most people will be lost in their own moments and will not be looking at you, the ones who do will more likely wonder why you have brought an old woman with you."

Helen looked Ingrid in the eye. "You're not old, why would you say something like that?"

"It is true. I am sixty-three on Saturday and not wearing well I think."

"No way," said Helen, "age is only a number you know."

"Yes, it is, and I have a much bigger number than you do," Ingrid gestured to herself, "this is not as firm as it once was, I hope you will not be disappointed."

"I won't be." Helen shifted a little to let her turn all the way around "If it helps, I'm nervous about this too because it's been a while."

"If it has been so long you do not remember what to do, we could Google it if you like."

Jeez no, I think that would make me worse," Helen shook her head and smiled, "it hasn't been as long as *that* so I'll be able to muddle through, it'll come back to me."

"I am sure it will. So, what do we do first?"

"Well, I was thinking a shower after a long day might be good but we couldn't go in there fully dressed, so we'd have to undress." Helen felt the icy tentacles of adrenaline kick in and she saw Ingrid's eyes were shining.

"I am not shy about taking my clothes off you know," Ingrid began to unbutton her blouse, stopping half way down and shrugging her shoulders, "but perhaps you would you like to help me."

"Yes, I would." Helen felt breathless as she moved closer and her hands shook as she popped the remaining buttons, one by one, exposing a black bra and pale, smooth skin. She sat for a few seconds, letting her eyes drink everything in and then she leaned in and kissed Ingrid's neck, pulling her blouse down and off her shoulders before kissing them too. When she looked up,

159

she saw Ingrid had closed her eyes and was smiling, and at once, the nervousness vanished and Helen began unbuttoning her own shirt.

"That was very nice," said Ingrid, opening her eyes before reaching over and pushing Helen's shirt down her shoulders and off, watching it drop on the bed and slide to the floor. She removed her own blouse then unbuttoned her jeans and slid them off, keeping her eyes on Helen, who was pulling off her own jeans. "Shall we lie down for a while?"

"Yeah, I think we should do just that," said Helen, climbing back onto the bed and stretching out, watching as Ingrid slid up to lie alongside, then pulling her closer and pushing a thigh between her legs before kissing her on the mouth, tongue tracing the contours of her lips, no longer holding anything back. She pulled back for a second. "I need to know you're sure about this."

Ingrid smiled and pulled Helen tight against her then ran a hand down her back, all the while, kissing the contours of her chin.

"I'll take that as a yes." Helen buried her lips in Ingrid's neck and began to unfasten her bra, the tensions of the last weeks melting away, and the trials yet to come, all but forgotten.

Chapter Twelve

No Weddings, Just a Funeral

Helen squinted her eyes against the glare of the sun and stifled a yawn, eyeing all the solemn faced people gathering on the far side of the crematorium. She had chosen a bench as far away from the main doors as she could but it was still close enough to let her see the cortege when it arrived. "Do I look all right?" she said, turning to Ingrid who sat, face upturned, soaking in the weak winter rays.

"I have already said you look all right," Ingrid gave Helen an appraising look and nodded, "and nothing has changed, you are still fine."

"Not too much black?"

"Yes, far too much black," Ingrid reached out and rested her hand on Helen's thigh, "one thing not black would have been nice but you still look good."

"Okay, I was just checking." Helen smiled and ran her eyes over Ingrid's elegant figure, drinking in her stylish combination of black dress and long, grey coat, to which she had added a silver-grey scarf, just on the right side of blingy. "People will presume you're my girlfriend you know, just because you're with me."

Ingrid laughed. "Do you think so?"

"Yes I do, and some of them might come right out with the question. My mother had two sisters as well as a brother, and they're quite vocal women from what I remember, so yes, expect the inquisition."

"All right," said Ingrid, turning around on the bench and leaning one arm on the support at the back, "if they interrogate me, how would you like me to answer?"

"Yes" said Helen, rubbing at her mouth and nodding, "I'd very much like you to say yes."

"Then I will say yes." Ingrid gestured just beyond Helen to an approaching hearse. "I think this is it."

Helen sat still and gazed at the long, black car as it approached on its slow trajectory, crunching gravel, and snaking around the long driveway. She dropped her eyes as it passed to avoid looking at the coffin but she glanced up again to take in the other limousines gliding along behind it, and she saw her uncle Frank, looking lost and old.

"Come on." Ingrid stood and gestured to Helen to join her.

"I'd rather sit at the back, can't we wait until they go in?"

"We cannot," said Ingrid, pulling her to her feet, "they will not take the coffin in until everyone is seated, now come on." She took Helen's arm and began to lead her across the gravel road and over towards the other mourners.

As they reached the last car in the large cortege, Helen reached into her inside coat pocket and pulled out a pair of Ray Ban Wayfarers, flicking them open and putting them on almost in one movement. She had taken no more than two steps when Ingrid reached up with her free hand and plucked them from her face, folding them and slipping them into her coat pocket.

"Why did you...?" Helen began a protest but stopped short as Ingrid was already wearing an expression which didn't invite further comment. Instead, she silenced the inner bear as they continued to walk alongside the cars, fixing a neutral look on her face when she became aware of the loud murmurs from people who had started to mingle. She saw several people glance in her direction and nudge the person next to them but if Ingrid saw this, she said nothing, although Helen felt the grip on her arm tighten so she pulled her closer as they proceeded.

"Which one is your uncle Frank?"

They had stopped just short of the hearse which Helen felt wasn't ideal, but to go further without at least acknowledging Frank, seemed wrong. She scanned the men who were milling around, all of them in dark grey or black suits, and all with the same polished look they wore with apparent discomfort. At last, she spotted her uncle, and as she did so, he looked up and gave a short wave before heading over towards her.

"Scarlett hen, you're here."

Helen smiled at him as he approached, wincing at his use of her real name but unwilling to chastise him because he looked old and crumpled, certainly much smaller than she remembered. "Frank," she said, as Ingrid released her arm allowing her to move forward and accept the embrace he offered, "It's been a while."

"Aye, it has been and it's a rotten business this." He looked around him and glanced towards the hearse, "I'm glad you came, hen, she would have been pleased."

Helen nodded and forced a smile then turned to Ingrid. "Ah, Frank, I'd like to introduce you to Ingrid," she took a breath, "Ingrid, this is my uncle Frank, my mom's brother."

Ingrid stepped forward and Frank moved towards her, reaching out a hand in greeting. "I'm pleased to meet you hen," he said, "are you our Scarlett's girlfriend?"

They shook hands and Ingrid smiled. "I am, yes. I am very sorry for your loss."

"Thanks, hen, but we expected it for a while although it was a shock when it happened, these things always are."

Helen dropped her gaze and studied the cracks on the paving, not wanting to discuss the circumstances of her mother's death at all, never mind it being something everyone had expected. She glanced at Frank, wondering if he knew her mother had begged to see her one final time and her eyes flicked to her left and to the hearse where she now lay.

"We have to go in now," said Ingrid, resting a hand on Helen's arm and tugging it to catch her attention.

Helen jerked her head up and she nodded. "Of course. Frank, we'll sit at the back out of the way if it's ok."

"I thought you would sit with the family at the front, hen, I told Enid to make sure there was space," he turned to Ingrid, "Enid's my wife."

Ingrid nodded and linked arms with Helen again. "We shall sit at the front with you Frank, thank you." She pulled Helen forward and they walked in step with Frank and the other mourners in their slow progress inside, stopping only for a second or two as they entered the chapel, to take a hymn sheet from a young man standing at the doorway.

Ingrid's easy agreement to sit at the front took Helen by surprise but she didn't argue, instead, walking arm in arm with her into the main chamber and past the crowded benches towards the front row. As they passed the second row of chairs, Helen glanced at the people filling them and saw her mother's two sisters, Marie and Francine, the former nodding and giving a brief smile, the latter glaring at her as she and Ingrid moved to the front and took their seats beside a welcoming Enid.

"Ingrid." Helen's voice was a hoarse whisper.

"What is it?" Ingrid flicked through the pamphlet she had collected at the door and as she turned towards Helen, she handed it to her. "You look very like her."

"There's a meal booked but I don't want to go." Helen glanced at the pamphlet with its picture of her mother on the front page. She appeared old to her eyes but still looked as decorated as she always had, hair and make-up done, earrings in, and a huge smile on her face.

"You have to go," said Ingrid, her voice quiet and calm as she motioned for Helen to turn the pamphlet over, "you should show some respect for your uncle at the very least."

Helen glanced at Ingrid for a second then flipped the booklet over to look at the back page where she saw a picture of a little girl with long, dark hair, sitting on her mother's knee. The gap-toothed grin suggested she must have been around six or seven years old and Helen smiled, remembering the denim dungarees and purple, striped t-shirt she was wearing in the photograph. They had been her favourites and she had a vague memory of uncle Frank buying them when he had taken her on a day out with his own family but time had clouded the memory and she was no longer sure. As she continued to stare at the picture, a murmur arose and people began to stand, signalling the arrival of the coffin. Helen did likewise, feeling a calming touch on her hand from Ingrid as she prepared to face the part she had been dreading most of all.

There were six pallbearers including Helen's uncle Frank and they walked at a steady pace, flanked by the undertaker, and the celebrant who would conduct the ceremony. Their faces were tense as the undertaker spoke to them in a quiet voice, guiding them as they shifted the weight of the coffin from their shoulders down to hip height, before rolling it onto the plinth at the front. They took their seats as the undertaker covered the coffin with a burgundy coloured pall, bowed his head and then walked towards the back of the room.

As these things went it was pleasant enough although the service was of a type Helen liked to call, The Barnum. The celebrant was nice but it was obvious she had never been acquainted with her mother as she spouted forth platitudes which could describe half the people in the chapel. That aside, it was quick, and Helen was grateful to mouth along to the two hymns that followed before she forced herself to watch as the pall flattened out and the coffin made a silent retreat from view. As it slid away, Helen and Ingrid followed the lead given by Frank and Enid and they stood, before making the slow walk out of the chapel. She saw several mourners had started to laugh and she couldn't fight her own smile as Tammy Wynette belted out her mother's final song, and stood by her man yet again.

Frank and Enid stood at the doors of the chapel to shake hands with the long line of people who followed them out but Helen had walked away after telling Frank she couldn't do it. She was relieved when he nodded and said it was all right and that she should wait for him beside the first limousine and she stood there now, in silence, with Ingrid holding onto her.

"That was not so bad, was it?" Ingrid squeezed Helen's arm.

"No, it was fine I suppose," replied Helen, pointing to Frank, "are you mad at me for not doing that with him?"

"No, there was no point," Ingrid gave a thin smile, "he is allowing people to be considerate of his loss and as you do not feel any loss, it would be wasted on you."

"You are mad at me," Helen pulled her arm away, "how can you say that?"

Ingrid shook her head and pulled Helen's arm back over before linking her own again. "I am not angry at you but I am saying what I see because there is no point in lying about it to make you feel better."

"I do feel a loss," Helen said, locking eyes with Ingrid, "but I'm just used to it because I've felt it longer than anybody else. Remember, I lost her the day she gave me away to a stranger and I'll never forget it."

"I know," Ingrid's voice was soothing and she pulled Helen closer, "but if you could find a way to forgive it, then you might find a peace."

Helen felt her throat tighten. "Despite everything, I know I shouldn't have let her die without saying goodbye," she shook her head again, "I don't think I'll ever forgive myself."

"Perhaps not," said Ingrid, smiling and leaning in to give Helen a soft kiss, "but it is not always about you, and although you made a mistake with your mother, you do not have to do the same with your family."

"They're coming," Helen gestured to Frank and Enid and she straightened up, clearing her throat, "and I promise I'll try hard to do better by them in future."

Ingrid smiled as they both stood back to allow their driver to open the limousine door for everyone to clamber in and within a few minutes, they were on their way to the venue for the meal.

**

"That was lovely," said Frank, wiping his mouth, "will I order us another wee drink?"

"Yeah, please, but I'll have a soft drink this time, Diet Coke or something." Helen pushed her plate away and turned to Ingrid. "What would you like?"

"Scotch again for me, please, I think I shall be able to manage a second one."

Frank headed up to the bar, returning quickly with the drinks, and as he took his seat, he pointed to the pint of lager he had set to the side. "I've got this for our Andrew, he should be here shortly." Enid glanced at him, but said nothing.

Helen was confused for a second but then realisation dawned. "No way," she said, as Frank and Enid both nodded, "little Andrew drinks pints now?"

"You mean big Andrew," said Enid, "he's taller than you Scarlett."

"Andrew is my cousin," said Helen, turning to Ingrid, "last time I saw him he was seven I think, it was the last time I was here." She turned back to her uncle. "I'm sorry I haven't been in touch Frank, I find it all difficult."

"I know you do hen," he said, " but it's all right. Isabell was my sister but I was never blind to her faults," he took a gulp of whisky, "and what she did to you was shameful, so we couldn't let it happen again."

"What do you mean?" Helen and Ingrid exchanged glances

166

and watched as Enid reached out and clasped Frank's hand in her own.

Frank took another gulp of whisky, pursing his lips and sighing. "Well, the thing is hen, your mother had another baby when she was hanging wey that Billy Gilmour, a bad lot he was."

Enid joined in. "The whole family were no good, and the women," she rolled her eyes, "faces so hard you could break sticks off them." She looked at Frank and he nodded for her to continue. "She had a wee boy and then she did her usual, boyfriends in and out the house, Social Work there every week," she paused to squeeze Frank's hand, "in the end she agreed to put him up for adoption and we took him when he was two. Our Andrew isn't your cousin, he's your wee brother."

"A brother?" Helen almost breathed the words out as she leaned back in her seat and looked round to Ingrid in astonishment. "I have a brother, Ingrid, little Andrew isn't my cousin, he's my brother."

"I picked that up for myself." Ingrid took Helen's hand and held it close before looking across at Frank and Enid. "How old is your son?"

"Twenty-seven last month," said Frank, the broad smile on his face being that of a proud father, "he's a fine boy, Ingrid, a fine boy."

Ingrid smiled. "Does he know about this, Helen being his sister I mean?"

Frank and Enid nodded in unison and Enid spoke. "We told him last month when we found out Isabell didn't have much time left." She picked up her glass and took a sip of Scotch. "We thought he should know before she died but in the end, he didn't want to see her and he said we were his mum and dad, so that was that."

"Where is he today?" said Helen, leaning forward, still clutching Ingrid's hand, her eyes scanning the bar area for anyone with the potential to be Andrew.

"Working," said Frank, draining his glass and checking his watch, "he said he would come here for a wee while although he was never keen on his auntie Isabell."

Helen nodded but said nothing. She wanted to say all the right things but as she looked at Frank and Enid and then around the

167

pub to everyone else, she realised there were no right things for her to say because she wasn't part of them and never would be. Andrew would just be another stranger to her, a young man she was related to by blood, but not emotionally, and she hoped he felt the same because otherwise, he would be disappointed.

"So," said Frank, "you two," he gestured across the table, "how long have you been seeing each other?"

"This is quite recent," said Ingrid, glancing at Helen and then smiling over at Frank, "we are taking things one day at a time."

"Ah, right." Frank drained his Scotch and then looked at the unclaimed pint of lager before flashing a wolfish grin and dragging it over. "Bugger it, I'll buy him one when he gets here."

Enid drew him a look and shook her head in a faux disgust. "Where did you meet our Scarlett then?" She peered at Ingrid, her eyebrows raised.

"It is complicated," Ingrid smiled at Helen, "my daughter brought her to my home as a visitor, they are working together."

"I see," said Enid, "you have a daughter." Her eyes were wide and lively, flicking between Helen and Ingrid, as she waited for more.

"I have two daughters and a son," Ingrid swirled the last of the Scotch around her glass and then took it in one mouthful, "and I also have a husband."

"Fuck sake." Frank spluttered over his lager and put the glass down before wiping the froth from his chin and scooping foam from the table. "Sorry about the fuck sake hen, you just caught me there." He looked at Helen and smiled. "That *is* complicated."

"More than you could imagine," said Helen, dropping her gaze as embarrassment made little suns of her cheeks and then, from nowhere, she thought about her brother, Andrew, wondering what he would make of everything.

"Ingrid," said Frank, "does she still let her mouth go like a steam train and get herself into bother?"

Helen sighed and shook her head. "Do we have to do this?" She looked around the table, hoping her pained expression would put a lid on things.

"She does," said Ingrid, laughing and squeezing Helen's hand, "not a day has passed since we met that she does not do it, but I find it part of her charm."

"She was always a right wee chatterbox," Enid let out a high-pitched cackle, "it's a wonder her lips didn't fray at the edges."

Helen groaned and sat forward, placing her head on the table and dreading to think what would come out now. She was considering an attempt at changing the subject when a loud voice from her left startled her and as she pulled her head off the table to see who it was, she heard her uncle curse under his breath.

"You have a brass neck showing up here lady." A small barrel of a woman stood there, arms folded and with her jaw set in determined fashion.

"Francine, good of you to say hello," Helen glanced over her shoulder to Ingrid, "this is one of my mother's sisters, the evil one."

"Helen, stop." Ingrid still had a hold of her hand and she tightened her grip.

Francine gave a loud, fake laugh. "Helen? Get over yourself, you're Scarlett McCracken and you always will be."

Helen pulled her hand away from Ingrid to let her turn all the way around and she ran her eyes over Francine, taking in the glass she had in one hand and the row of gold rings on the other, glistening like an expensive knuckle duster. It was exactly how she remembered her, that and the tiny piggy eyes that glared at her in menacing fashion. "Say what you have to say then get your face out my life."

"You think you're so fuckin' special don't you." Francine's voice got louder and the chatter in the pub faltered and then stopped. "Call yourself a daughter, you're nothin' but a disgrace, a fuckin' disgrace."

"Francine, that's enough," said Frank, leaning over in his seat and trying to grab hold of his sister's arm but she yanked it away, spilling the remainder of her drink in the process.

"Don't touch me!" Francine was screeching now. "Look at her," she turned around to the other tables, jabbing a finger towards Helen as she did so, "look at Miss fuckin' US of A. Thinks she's above everybody but left her poor mother to die without coming to see her one last fuckin' time."

Francine had moved into a more central position to give her audience a better view so Helen stood and took two steps forward, joining the floorshow. "That's enough from you tonight

I think, you're drunk and you need to go cool down somewhere." She breathed slowly to help keep her voice steady and her anger in check, and she held up both hands in a gesture of peace. "I know what I did Francine and I know what I am, but it's done, and nothing can change it." She turned around to Ingrid who mouthed to her to stay calm and she nodded, feeling things were going well and keen to get the situation under control.

"Aye, we all know exactly what you are," Francine looked past Helen and gestured towards Ingrid, glass still in hand, "bringin' your fancy bit here, it's a fuckin' disgrace." She put the glass on a nearby table and teetered forward, jabbing her finger at Helen again. "You need a right good tankin' for that, and I'm the very wummin to do it."

Helen stood stock still, hands in pockets and smiling down at the tiny devil in front of her. "I don't think so," she said, half laughing, "you're not going to hit me. Tell me something Francine," she ignored her uncle's audible groan, "were you planning to punch out my kneecaps because that's about as high as I think you could manage." It was over in a flash, to the sound of a collective gasp from the people at the other tables. Helen offered no defence as both hands were stuck in her pockets, so when the gold clad fist landed, it caught her flush on the left eye and she fell back, hitting the table on her way down. Everything seemed to go quiet and slow for a second before a rush of noise erupted and it was like Bedlam.

"Somebody get her home." Frank was shouting and pointing in frantic fashion towards Francine, who was writhing like a snake in a bag and trying to break loose from the grip of a passing waitress who had been unfortunate enough to be in the right place at the wrong time.

Helen sat on the floor in shock, watching the spectacle unfold like she was a casual observer and although she could hear voices at her side, she couldn't drag her eyes away from the scene in front of her. She saw a few people pull on their overcoats and make for the door and she laughed when one old man stopped as he reached each table, downing the remains of any unguarded drinks.

"Look at me please," said Ingrid, kneeling on the floor at one side of Helen, with Enid doing likewise on the other side, "come on, we need to get you up to your seat and I need to look at your eye to see if that cut has to be stitched."

With help from Enid and Ingrid, Helen managed to get back to her seat without falling over, and she sat there, head bowed, as Enid headed to the bar to ask for a towel and some ice. "I'm sorry you had to witness that," she raised her eyes to look at Ingrid who was now kneeling on the floor in front of her, "and I want to go home."

"We cannot go home until I have proper look at your face," said Ingrid as she examined Helen's cut, "you might need stitching and if you do then we will be going to the hospital."

"Can't you do stitches?"

"Of course I can, and I always keep a full medical kit in my bag for emergencies."

Helen laughed and winced simultaneously as the tight pain around her left eye made its presence felt. "That was a joke, right?"

"Yes, and it is lucky for you because if I was stitching anything it would be your mouth to help you keep it shut." Ingrid shook her head and gave Helen a stern look. "Why do you have to do it?"

"I know you," Helen gasped and opened her eyes wide, despite the pain, "you're the Swedish nurse, the one who murdered the exasperating patient and buried the body in the garden beside the roses." She drew back and started to look around in mock panic. "Help me, somebody help me here, she's trying to kill me."

"Be quiet," Ingrid held her hand to Helen's mouth and laughed. "Stop it now or someone will believe you and call the police."

Helen kissed her fingers and smiled. "I hate it when you get mad at me, it makes me feel all weird and I don't like it."

"I know you hate it but Enid is coming and we need to get your face sorted so please, no more just now."

Enid brought a bucket full of ice and two fresh bar towels and she gave them to Ingrid who started to clean Helen's face. "It's an awful mess hen, is it deep?"

"No," said Ingrid, squinting again at Helen's war wound, "I do not think it will need stitching." She took the second towel and folded it before dropping some ice into it and pressing it against Helen's cheek. "Hold this here, it should help keep the swelling down at least a bit but you will have bruising in a couple of days."

"Thanks." Helen raised her head and out of the corner of her good eye she saw Frank talking to a policeman and pointing over to where she was sitting. "Oh fuck, somebody's called the cops, this is all I need."

Helen and Enid both looked round and then stood in unison as the policeman approached them.

"Are you Scarlett McCracken?" He stared at Helen, one hand gripping his baton and with an expression which demanded an answer, without prevarication from the suspect.

Helen held onto the table with her free hand and pushed herself upright. "Officer, whatever she told you happened, didn't happen," she shook her head, "and my name is Helen Miller."

"Right, is that your alias madam?"

"No, it's my real name and it's the one on my passport and driver's license." Helen sniffed and stared at the floor. "My birth name was the name you said though."

"So, you are Scarlett McCracken." The officer folded his arms and looked at her with a lopsided smile.

Helen looked up again and nodded a yes as she repositioned the towel on her face, wincing as she did so, more at admitting to her real name than in response to the ache coming from her injured eye.

"Right then, Scarlett, you're the reason I'm here."

"You're here to arrest me," Helen's eyebrows shot up and she looked at Ingrid and then back at the policeman, "no way, you have got to be kidding me."

The officer smiled and removed his hat then leaned over to Enid and gave her a hug. "Hi ma, have you had a good day?"

"Och Andrew, it was a bloody funeral, of course it was good." Enid laughed and then looked at Helen and Ingrid. "This is our Andrew."

Helen took the cold compress down from her face and she felt Ingrid take it from her as she stared at the young man before her, for the first time in a long time, lost for words.

"Hi Scarlett, or is it Helen?" Andrew stood before her, now

looking shy and unsure.

"Please, call me Helen," she said, her eyes darting over him, "last time we met you were only waist high."

"I know, but they fed me well." He smiled again, flashing perfect white teeth.

Helen felt herself smiling back at him, her response automatic and coming from somewhere deep within her. "I wish I'd known about this, I really do and things would have been different I promise you." She shuffled her feet, feeling awkward and unsure about what to do next, all thoughts about how she would feel at this moment, gone. "I don't know what do here, I have no reference point for this."

"Me too," Andrew held his arms apart, "but we could maybe start with a hug, what do you think?"

Helen at once felt nervous about embracing this strange, yet familiar, young man but she glanced at Ingrid, remembering her words earlier in the day. "Andrew," she turned to him, "I would like it very much." She reached out and walked towards him and they shared a warm embrace for a few moments before pulling back, Helen giving him another good look over. "I should have known who he was the minute he walked in the door," she said, looking around at everyone, "look at him, he's gorgeous, so he's obviously my brother."

Ingrid laughed and shook her head. "I see it did not take long for the talking bear to reappear."

"What talking bear?" said Frank. He had been watching the scene from a distance but now he sauntered up looking almost relaxed.

"It is a very long story I am afraid to say," Ingrid smiled, "but I am happy to tell it."

"Well, let's all go back to my house," Frank looked at Enid and she nodded her agreement, "we have a lot to talk about."

***

After spending the rest of the evening doing a family catch-up, Ingrid and Helen left Frank's house just after ten o'clock as they had an early rise in the morning to catch the train back to Gravesend. The parting was pleasant, everyone exchanging telephone numbers and addresses, and Andrew arranged to visit Helen in San Francisco sometime in the New Year. It had been a nice ending to a fractious day and, as she undressed back in the hotel room, Helen smiled to herself, thinking about how alike she and Andrew were. They were physically similar, with many of the same mannerisms, and both had the ability to talk non-stop without a breath for at least three minutes. There was something of the bear about him for sure.

"A penny for those thoughts." Ingrid was already in bed, watching Helen undress.

"I was thinking Andrew might be a talking bear too."

Ingrid turned on her side and pulled the quilt back. "Yes, but he is not my little talking bear."

Helen pulled on her vest and then stopped, pyjama bottoms held in her hand. "Do I need these?" She waved the pyjamas in the air.

Ingrid just smiled.

Chapter Thirteen

The Birthday Party

Helen's black eye was a popular attraction back in Gravesend, particularly with Oskar, who was obsessed by the story of how it got there and who insisted on walking about on his knees, acting out the part of Francine. His impersonation was very funny although Helen felt duty bound to point out his Scottish accent needed work and he would need to lose another few inches off his reduced height to be accurate. This made him find it all the funnier and his act became so outrageous, Ingrid made him stop, telling him dinner would soon be here and to go and wash himself or he would be getting nothing. The threat worked and Oskar bolted upstairs just as the doorbell rang, to signal dinner had arrived, and very soon the table was laden with the mishmash of Chinese food they had all agreed to share.

"Mmm, this is lovely," said Helen, licking the hot sauce from her lips, "what is it though?"

"It's a pork and prawn wonton," Oskar said, chewing at one of the crispy treats and speaking with his mouth full, "sauce is chili, by the way."

"I don't like prawns, or any seafood," Helen saw Ingrid and Sophie both roll their eyes and she grinned, "but I do like these little things."

"Have you heard any more from your brother?" said Sophie, smiling now and leaning over to grab another wonton, before tipping some more sauce onto her plate.

"It's been," Helen glanced at her watch, "seventeen hours since we last spoke but despite our natural concern for one another, I think we're handling the gap." She shovelled up another wanton and nodded to Sophie. "I think you would really like him you know, when I'm going up there again you should come with me and say hello."

Sophie wiped her mouth and looked at Ingrid. "Does he look

175

like Helen?"

"That is a difficult question to answer," said Ingrid, the hint of a smile appearing on her lips, "he is very tall and handsome, so I would have to say I am not sure."

"He does look like me," Helen flicked her hair and pointed to herself, "we're almost like twins and beauty runs in my family." She tipped her head and gave Ingrid a disbelieving look, raising her eyebrows for effect. "You're not sure, that must be a joke, I mean, look at me." She glanced around the table for confirmation of her status as good looking but all she got in return was a series of shoulder shrugs and some non-committal pouting from Sophie. "You all need to visit an optician."

"You won't be quite so pretty when your black eye develops," said Oskar, pretending he was a boxer and aiming a flurry of fake punches towards Helen's head, "you might even be scarred for life."

"I don't mind a scar," Helen grinned and handed her plate over to Sophie so she could pile on some sweet and sour chicken, "I think it might make me look even better, as difficult as that may seem to you lesser mortals."

"How can a scar make anyone look better?" said Ingrid, shaking her head and helping herself to prawn crackers, "it would be ugly."

"Think Indiana Jones," Helen reached over and took her plate back from Sophie, "Indy had a scar and look how well he did with the ladies." She grinned in Ingrid's direction and caught a glance from her which suggested she was on dangerous ground, prompting her to avert her eyes and change the subject. "Anyway, I was thinking," she nudged Oskar, "I need to go into town tomorrow morning and I might get myself a tattoo."

"Oh Helen no," Ingrid was about to start spooning some rice onto her plate but she stopped dead, spoon in mid-air, "you are not serious, are you?"

"Mamma it's just a tattoo," said Sophie, looking at her mother and scrunching her face up in surprise, "why are you so bothered anyway?"

Ingrid began spooning rice onto her plate. "I do not like tattoos and I do not understand why someone who is supposed to be intelligent," at this she glared at Helen, "would wish to disfigure herself."

"I might get one too," said Oskar, looking at Ingrid, eyes wide and hopeful.

"You will not," said Ingrid, pointing towards the door, "because if you do, you will leave this house, and you, Helen, will also be leaving for encouraging him."

"Looks like tattoos are out kid but I do need to go shopping tomorrow, fancy coming with me?" Helen went back to her dinner, her plan for the following day in some part dependant on Oskar's acquiescence and his love for Ingrid, and she eyed him in expectation of a positive response to her invitation.

"That would be cool," said Oskar, glancing at Ingrid, "I don't like tattoos either mum so don't worry, I would never get one."

Sophie laughed and pointed at Oskar. "You are such a little mamma's boy, do you know that?"

"That is enough Sophie," said Ingrid, her voice sharp, "do not speak to Oskar like that."

"Why?" said Sophie, laughing, "it's only a bit of fun."

"Because he is your brother, that is why." Ingrid frowned and started to eat.

"You're a wimp Oskar," Helen caught another warning look from Ingrid, "but a sensible wimp, and I still love you for being you." She looked around the table and decided to change the subject again. "So, what's tomorrow's plan for the birthday girl?"

"I wish it could be forgotten," Ingrid's face fell and she continued eating, not looking up, "and do not forget, Gary will be home tomorrow."

Oskar and Sophie joined Ingrid in falling silent although Helen managed a grunt in response to the news, marvelling at how five simple words had turned the mood at the table from one of merriment, into one of silent dread. She wondered why Gary bothered returning for Ingrid's birthday because it was clear he wasn't fooling anyone with his presence, but after mulling things over for a moment, she concluded the fucker probably came home on purpose to spoil anyone's chance of having a nice day and this thought spurred her on to ask the obvious question. "Will we be telling Gary about Sophie's news?"

"Yes," said Ingrid, looking over at Sophie and reaching out to hold her hand, "we will have to tell him the news I think."

"He better not have a go at me, mamma," Sophie's face tightened and she pushed her plate away, "I'm not putting up with it if he starts on me again."

"You're not alone in that," Helen reached across and took Sophie's other hand, "because if he has a go at you, I promise, he'll be speaking with a whistle when I'm done with him."

"That is not the solution," said Ingrid, scowling, "you will both calm down, please. I will tell him the news and I will also be telling him to behave, and if he does not," she squeezed Sophie's hand, "I will deal with him."

"I hate him," said Oskar, his face set in misery as he looked around at the others, "I do and I don't care he's my dad so don't tell me I can't hate him because of that."

Helen released Sophie's hand and turned to give Oskar a nudge. "Look, you and I will avoid him as much as possible tomorrow," she winked at him, "your mom's right, we need to cool it and I'll have to pass that message on to the bear." She looked across to Ingrid and pointed at own mouth. "I promise I'll try to keep this shut for as long as I can and if Oskar and I keep out of the way, then it should be doable."

"Thank you." Ingrid smiled and nodded.

"I said I'll try."

"I know and I would appreciate it if you could try hard."

Sophie sniffed and pulled herself up in her chair. "Come on, let's just forget about dad for now, don't let him spoil a good dinner." She smiled at each of them in turn and then gestured to Oskar. "Throw me the last wonton please, little brother, I'm eating for two and I'm still starving."

Oskar passed over the plate to Sophie and everyone went back to eating, the initial awkward silence soon morphing into relaxed banter which lasted for the rest of the evening. Helen played along and kept them laughing as much as she could, but she was worried; a storm was coming, and she could feel in her bones, it was going to be a bad one.

***

The next morning, Helen coaxed Oskar out of bed just after eleven, hoping she could still get to the shops and back quickly enough to give herself time before the birthday lunch to write

Ingrid's card and wrap her gift. She could have gone herself and been back before anyone noticed her absence, but she needed her partner in crime with her to be able to carry out her plan, and as he stood beside her sniffing the testers in the perfume shop, she knew she had made the right decision.

"How do you know what perfume mum likes?" Oskar's nose wrinkled as it encountered another smell it disliked.

"She wore it the time we went to London and I recognised it, how else would I know?" Helen looked back to the assistant and rolled her eyes, then popped her card into the terminal, all the while remembering two glorious days in Glasgow, enveloped in Ingrid's fragrance. "Tell me something," she looked at Oskar, who now stood, hands in pockets, rocking back and forth on his heels, "what did you buy your mom for her birthday?"

"I got her a card."

"Just a card?"

"I'm broke as usual," Oskar made face and shrugged his shoulders, "wish I could get her something nice but I can't."

Helen finished her purchase, said thanks and headed out of the shop with Oskar on her heels. "I have an idea," she said, winking at him.

"About what?"

"Well," Helen stopped and looked Oskar in the eye, "I guessed you might be a bit short so I was thinking I could give you the money to get a gift and you can pay me back, you know, when you're a famous YouTube star or something."

'Really?" Oskar looked keen, and he licked his lips and rubbed his hands together.

"Of course, I'm happy to do it." Helen smiled. Her plan was working and Oskar was happy, both things that pleased her very much. "How about we visit a jeweller, or do you have something in mind?"

"No that would be brilliant, are you sure you don't mind?"

"I don't mind at all, but remember, you owe me one," she laughed, "and one day I might ask you for a favour, that day might never come but..." She stopped, his confused expression at her Marlon Brando impersonation causing her to sigh. "Come on," she pointed to the top of the street, "there's one up there."

They were inside the shop within a few minutes although

Helen stopped before then to give Oskar a wad of notes so he could do the buying and feel good about himself in the process. It turned out he had good taste in jewellery, choosing a gold bracelet Helen might have picked out herself and after the assistant gift-wrapped it, they left the shop, Oskar beaming from ear to ear.

"Here," Oskar handed Helen the bundle of unspent notes, "thanks for doing this, it's brilliant and mum will love it."

Helen shook her head, refusing to take the money back. "Keep it, and spend it on something that isn't porn or tattoos," she shook her head and made a face, "not tattoos anyway unless you want me deported as an example to others."

Oskar laughed and blushed slightly. "Where will I say I got the money?"

"Easy," said Helen, "say you've been saving up for ages and it's why you've always been broke. Sounds believable to me and nobody needs to know any different."

"Ok, I'll say that, but only if anyone asks of course."

Helen nodded and checked her watch. "Right, time for us to head home, come on." She walked across the road to the bus stop with a grinning Oskar following behind her, swinging his gift bag and looking pleased with himself. They had agreed that when they got in, they would go straight to their rooms to sort the cards and gifts, before meeting again at the top of the stairs, Helen's plan being for them to enter the sitting room together to show a united front to Gary, who would, without doubt, be there before them.

As they stepped onto the bus and paid their fares, Oskar glanced at her, his face betraying what she herself was thinking. "Do you think it will be all right today?"

They spotted a free seat and as they sat down, Helen shrugged her shoulders. "I hope it will, but I've got to be honest, my spider-sense is tingling."

Oskar nodded and gazed out of the window, letting the rest of the journey pass in silence.

***

They stood at the top of the stairs, bags in hand, like two soldiers listening for the whistle signalling it was time to go over the top. Even from there it was possible to hear the murmur of

180

extra voices down below which only served to crank the tension up another notch.

Helen nudged Oskar. "I'm Spartacus."

"No, I'm Spartacus." Oskar grinned and gave a thumbs-up, the sign he was good to go and they headed downstairs towards the arena, hesitating at the door to the sitting room and listening for a few seconds to the voices within, before Helen squeezed Oskar's arm and breezed into the room.

"Hey everyone," Helen put a smile on her face, hoping it looked genuine, "look who I found." She nodded towards Oskar who walked past her and over to Ingrid, and as he did so, Helen threw a glance towards Gary and to the young blonde girl sitting by his side who she presumed must be the mystery sister, Anna. Sophie was on the other couch beside Ingrid.

"Happy birthday mum," said Oskar, kissing her and handing over his gift bag.

"Thank you very much, but you did not have to do this." Ingrid's face glowed with pleasure.

Oskar beamed back at her then turned around and nodded to Gary but he spoke only to the blonde girl. "Hey Anna, how's things?"

"I'm fine, Oskar."

Helen watched the brief exchange and at once sensed something wasn't right. She had been watching Anna closely when she spoke and although she saw her smile at Oskar, the smile never reached her eyes and this at once put Helen on her guard as she sauntered over to Ingrid and handed over her gift bag. "Happy birthday," she said," bending down to kiss Ingrid on the cheek, "I hope you like it."

"Thank you, Helen, but..."

"Oh no buts," Helen interrupted her, "it's only a little thing anyway."

Ingrid smiled at her, a sparkle in her eyes. "You have not been introduced yet," she gestured to Anna, "this is my other daughter Anna and Anna, this is Helen who has been staying with us."

Helen bounded over to shake hands and as she did so, she conjured up her best all-American, dazzling smile. "I'm very pleased to meet you at last, Anna." The girl looked up and smiled at her, but this time, Helen saw what appeared to be fear in her eyes and she drew back, feeling uncomfortable and unsure how to react.

"I'm pleased to meet you too, I've heard a lot about you from Sophie and mum," Anna paused and glanced at Gary, "and from dad of course."

Helen followed her gaze but didn't let it linger on Gary for long. "I hope everything you heard was good and if it was then it's true, if not..." She let the rest hang in the air and nodded to Gary, who was sprawling on the sofa in his grey, Nike sweatpants and matching sweatshirt and who had been watching her with what she felt was undue attention.

"All right," said Ingrid, "I shall open these and then get us some coffee and cake."

"I'd like coffee now," said Gary

"No," said Ingrid, "I am opening my gifts first and coffee will come later."

Helen had already moved over to take the spare armchair and Oskar was on the floor beside her, leaning back against her legs. She had a prime view of all the other players and from her vantage point, and from the expression on Gary's face, she concluded the score was one-nil to Ingrid. Things looked promising.

Ingrid started to open the gift from Oskar, unpeeling the paper with care and putting it aside in a neat pile with the ribbon and bow, stopping for a second when she saw the box and glancing over at Oskar with a puzzled look on her face. As she lifted the box lid, she gasped and held it out for all to see, her mouth open and eyes as wide as her smile.

"My God, how did you manage to pay for that?" said Sophie, looking at Oskar in astonishment, "have you had a lottery win you haven't mentioned?"

"That must have cost a bit," said Gary, and as he spoke, he looked between Oskar and Helen, eyeing them with suspicion.

Helen kept her eyes fixed on the back of Oskar's head, determined not to allow a stray glance to betray them and she was glad when Oskar spoke.

"I've been saving all the way from mum's last birthday, because I felt bad," he turned and looked up at Helen, "all I got her last year was a chocolate orange so this year I think I did quite well." He beamed a smile and then turned back to the others and beamed it to them too.

"Oskar, you did not need to spend all your savings on me," Ingrid looked delighted, "but it is so beautiful, thank you."

"That's okay mum, you deserve it," he replied, looking like the cat who got the cream and the keys to the dairy.

"I'll help you put it on." Sophie leaned over and took the bracelet from the box and although it was a little fiddly to begin with, she managed to get it onto Ingrid's right wrist without too much trouble.

Helen reached down to Oskar's head and ruffled his hair. "You're quite something kid," she smiled over at Ingrid, "he never ceases to amaze me." It was true. Oskar's story about saving for a year was part of their plan, but the extra detail about the chocolate orange was his own invention and it fell so naturally into place that she couldn't help but be impressed.

"So, am I getting my coffee now?" Gary sat with folded arms and he was staring at Ingrid. "Are we done here?"

"Perhaps as it is my birthday," replied Ingrid, "you would like to be the one to make the drinks for a change, you know where the kitchen is so feel free." She ignored his shocked expression and grabbed the bag Helen had given her, loosening the ribbon at the top and reaching inside to pluck out the bottle of perfume. "How did you know this was my favourite?"

"Well, I should probably apologise because I saw the bottle on your dresser when I was sneaking around looking for clues." Helen had done no such thing of course and she could almost taste the memory of wrapping herself around Ingrid on the first night in Glasgow, when she had asked her what perfume she was wearing.

"There is no need for sorry, thank you Helen, it is very nice." Ingrid looked around them all. "Now, who would like coffee and some birthday cake?"

"I would," said Anna, "and I think dad would as well." She looked at Gary and he reached out and touched her arm.

"At least one of my girls knows how to look after me," he said, raising a hand and slicking back his hair before looking over at Helen, "but maybe you could help my wife, she isn't as young as she used to be." He laughed at his own joke and Anna laughed along with him.

Helen had stopped watching Anna for a second to give Gary her full attention but she clocked her again now and saw her gazing at him in what appeared to be adoration but once again, underneath the doe-eyed look, her eyes were wary and fearful. "I can do better than just help," Helen nudged Oskar's back to get him to move, "I'll make the coffee on my own and give the birthday girl a free afternoon."

"Aw, how nice," Gary snorted a laugh and smirked, "love the eye, by the way."

Helen ignored him, preferring to bide her time, and after taking orders from everyone, she told Oskar to come through in ten minutes or so to give her a hand to carry everything back to the sitting room. Oskar duly arrived and they were soon back, laden with drinks and cake, and after dishing up, Helen went back to her seat and waited until Gary had sipped at his drink. "Everything okay?" she said, looking straight at him.

"It's fine," said Gary, taking another mouthful.

"It's funny," said Helen, "making the coffee reminded me of a story my dad told me about his own dad, his Pa, as he called him." She glanced around the assembled group and sat forward in her seat. "Well, he said Pa never, ever, allowed any woman in his household to make him coffee, he always made his own."

Gary snorted again. "Don't tell me he was one of those so-called new men?"

"Oh God no, this is my grandfather we're talking about," said Helen, shaking her head, "it was way before all that stuff." She smiled and continued. "Anyway, Pa was from Wyoming, he worked a big cattle ranch there and he was a huge guy, six-four without his boots and built like a brick shit-house." She glanced around everyone again and was pleased to see she had their full attention. "So one day my dad asked Pa why he always made his own coffee and Pa said to him, son, you can let women make you anything, steak and eggs, a peach cobbler, even a cherry-limeade, but never take a coffee from 'em cos you can put *any* damn thing in coffee and it'll hide the taste. You never know what the bitches are givin' ya."

"I heard that about coffee," said Sophie, her voice no more than a tense whisper.

Helen felt an instant pang of love for Sophie because she had heard this story a few times before and was playing along, unrehearsed, but like an Oscar winning actress. "One day," Helen continued, "Pa was brought back to the ranch, screaming and hollering, saying he'd been bitten by a rattle snake and his leg was all swollen up and deep red. Someone was sent to the get the doctor from the nearest town and Pa was laid out on the couch, waiting." She leaned further forward in her chair and put her coffee cup on the floor. "It must have been the pain that made him do it, but when his wife asked him if he wanted some water, he said no, but he sure wouldn't mind a cup of coffee." She glanced up and looked directly at Gary. "He was dead by the time the doctor got there, forty minutes later." Helen let out a sigh and leaned back in her seat.

"Did his wife poison his coffee?" said Oskar, wide eyed.

"Nobody knows," said Helen, shaking her head, "they put it down to the snake bite but my dad was convinced his mom took her chance and poisoned him because the bite didn't look like one from a rattler." Helen let out a breath and from the corner of her eye she saw Gary glance down at his mug and she knew she had scored a direct hit.

"I think I will have more coffee." Ingrid stood and walked over to the sideboard, a smile spreading over her face.

"Make sure you use the pot on the left," said Helen, "it's...freshest." The slight hesitation in her entreaty had the desired effect and Gary jerked his eyes down towards his coffee again, licking his lips and giving Ingrid a sideways glance as she headed back to her seat. On any other occasion his discomfort would have been something to savour at length but the atmosphere in the room was so thick with tension, Helen couldn't relax enough to enjoy his reaction the way she would have liked and she decided instead to change tack and engage Anna in conversation. She was just about to start the ball rolling and ask Anna what she did for a living when, without warning, Gary banged his mug on the floor and launched himself to his feet, staring at Helen with narrowed eyes, his tongue flicking over his lips, serpentlike.

"I presume you know about Sophie's news, I'm sure my lovely wife has been keeping you informed." Gary made a loose gesture in Helen's direction and then shared his sneer with everyone in the room except Anna who had, in any event, dropped her head and was staring at the carpet.

"Yes, I do know about it," Helen replied, "why do you ask?"

"What a stupid question," Gary rolled his eyes and snorted, "I want to know your opinion, why else would I ask?"

Helen took another sip of coffee and quickly surveyed the room, the fleeting glimpse she caught of Ingrid's ashen face, enough in itself to push her in the direction of appeasement, although Gary's twisted face suggested it was already too late and that the storm was about to arrive. "I think it's lovely news," she said, "and as long as Sophie and the baby are well, nothing else should matter."

"Thank you, Helen, for your support," said Sophie, the expression on her face and the tone of her voice hinting at her father's reaction when the news broke earlier that day.

"Is it only me who isn't impressed she's been tarting herself around and doesn't know who the father of her baby is?" Gary's voice rose as he spoke and he took a step forward, the coffee mug on the floor beside him caught by one foot, its contents spewing over the floor. "Really, is it only me who has a problem with this?"

"Yes, it is only you!" Ingrid rose and raced over to him, stopping when she was toe to toe. "We have already discussed it and your views are known so there is nothing more to say on the subject. Let is rest!"

"I fucking will not." Gary raised his hands and pushed Ingrid back by the shoulders. "You've always let her away with murder and look how she turned out, just like fucking you." He turned his back on her and walked over to the sideboard before leaning against it and folding his arms. "She's a fucking waste of space."

"If you are unhappy then you should leave," Ingrid's voice shook, "why do you not go back to wherever it is you live when you are not here?"

The others in the room froze, caught out by the sudden, explosive change in atmosphere but Helen began struggling to get out of her chair, her legs pinned by the weight of Oskar leaning against them.

"Dad, leave her alone." Sophie got up from her seat then

walked over to Ingrid and took her hand. "Why don't you just go?"

"Because it's my house sweetheart and I don't want to go." He laughed and smiled at Anna who was sitting, open mouthed, then he leaned away from the sideboard and began walking back to Ingrid.

Helen spotted his move. "Oskar, shift yourself now," she pushed him but he was solid and didn't budge, "come on, let me up." The only movement she felt was Oskar pushing himself harder against her, holding her in place and she looked down at him in horror and shoved him again, becoming frantic as she realised she wouldn't be able to get to Ingrid before Gary did.

Whilst Oskar and Helen were tussling, Gary marched up to Ingrid and Sophie and pushed his head forward, his eyes darting between them. "Neither of you will ever tell me what to do in my own house," he said, "do you understand?"

"Gary please," Ingrid's voice was almost a whisper and she dropped her gaze from him, "please leave us."

"You must be deaf," Gary almost screamed it and he threw a glance towards Helen, who was struggling to get out of her seat, "I said, you will not tell me what to do in my own house."

At this, Helen got ready to give Oskar the biggest push she had but before she could lay her hands on him, he lurched to his feet and bounded over towards the affray, taking hold of Sophie's arm and pulling her and Ingrid back. He stepped in front of Gary and stared down into his face. "You will never speak to mum like that again, or you'll be sorry."

"Am I supposed to be scared of you?" Gary laughed and pushed his face up and into Oskar's, a move which only served to make it easier for Oskar's huge hand to come up unseen from underneath, grab his throat, and squeeze.

"If you ever speak like that to mum again," Oskar squeezed Gary's throat harder, ignoring the ineffective clawing of his hands, "I'll make you sorry, I promise, so do what she asked and just fuck off." With one last powerful squeeze he pushed Gary away, turning his back on him as he sank to the floor, and ignoring his coughing and spluttering. "Come on mum, come on Sophe, let's go through to the kitchen until he leaves." He glared at Anna, who had moved from the sofa to kneel beside Gary on the floor, and he shook his head before leading his mum and sister out of the room.

It was so unexpected and fast, Helen had stood rooted to the spot beside her chair, at first unable to move and then realising she didn't need to, as Oskar had handled the situation with aplomb. She watched the aftermath for a few moments, staring at Anna who was now consoling an astonished looking Gary and again, she saw a hint of fear in her eyes. As she headed for the door, resisting the urge to have a kick at Gary as she passed, she looked down at Anna and stopped for a second. "I don't get you," she said, shaking her head, "but if you need someone to talk to, come and find me." She shook her head again and then walked on, leaving the room and heading for the kitchen. As she made her way down the hallway, she felt so proud Oskar had stepped up when it counted and she was also proud of the way Sophie had faced the bullying fuck and stood hand in hand with her mother. Now all she had to do was get the pair of them out of the way because she needed an urgent talk with Ingrid and it wasn't a conversation either of them should hear.

Chapter Fourteen

Cats and Bags

When Helen entered the kitchen, the others were already at the table, Ingrid seated and looking shattered, and Sophie standing directly behind her looking down, both hands placed on her mother's shoulders. Oskar sat in front of them, bent over, staring at the floor and holding Ingrid's hands. The only illumination was coming from the under-cupboard halogens which gave the scene a dark, moody tone, almost making it look staged and as Helen walked over to kneel beside Ingrid, she had a notion it resembled a Renaissance painting come to life. "Are you all right?" she said, resting a hand on Ingrid's arm.

Ingrid nodded, "I will be fine I think." She gave Helen a wan smile, then pulled one hand from Oskar's grasp and placed it on his head, causing him to sit upright.

"Has he gone yet?" said Oskar, glancing at Helen and then over towards the kitchen door as if expecting unwelcome guests at any minute.

"I don't think so," Helen replied, "I left right after you did and he was still sprawled on the floor."

"He might not leave," the pitch of Ingrid's voice rose as she spoke and she looked down at Helen, "and I cannot force him to go because he was correct, it is his house as well as mine."

"Then I'll make him go." Helen pushed herself up from the floor and started to turn towards the door when she felt a hand grab her arm.

"No, you won't," said Oskar, tightening his grip around her wrist and standing himself, "I'll make him leave."

Helen looked at the boy before her, his face set in determination as he readied himself to return to the arena to fight for his mother again. "Ok, Spartacus, how about we both make him go."

Oskar hesitated but then nodded and loosened his grip. "Sorry

189

if that was a bit tight, but I didn't want you going in there on your own because I don't trust him."

"I think maybe you should both wait," said Sophie, removing her hands from Ingrid's shoulders and walking round to sit in what had been Oskar's chair. "Just wait for a bit and see what happens, there's no point provoking him further," she looked at her mother and then at Oskar and Helen, "another fight won't help things."

"I disagree," said Helen, "we need to shift him now when we still have the upper hand because if we wait, and he digs in somewhere, then I don't know how we get rid of him so it's now or never." She looked to Ingrid for support, more in hope than expectation, but to her surprise, she nodded her agreement.

"Helen is right, if he does not leave now then he will not leave at all," Ingrid looked up at Oskar, tears now filling her eyes, "I cannot do this any longer, please, I want him to leave."

"Right, come on kid." Helen beckoned to Oskar to follow her as she turned and strode towards the kitchen door, anger boiling in her at how frightened Ingrid looked and no more caring it was Gary's house than she cared for shit. She almost hoped he would make a scene because then she would get the opportunity to pick the fucker up and throw him out on his ear, something she wished Ingrid had found the courage to do long before now.

"Wait Helen," Oskar came bounding after her, "wait." He reached out and grabbed hold of her trailing arm, jerking her to a halt. "Listen," he spoke in a whisper and then held a finger to his lips to silence her.

Helen stood quietly, watching as Oskar turned to signal the need for hush to Sophie and Ingrid, before turning back to her and pointing towards the door. She nodded and then crept closer to it, cocking her head a little and straining to hear what was happening on the other side. She could hear voices, Gary's and Anna's of course, and she was sure she heard Anna mention something about clothes. Helen took a deep breath and turned, leaning against the door without making a sound, certain Gary was packing up and would leave of his own accord but, just in case he fancied a final round of intimidation, believing it prudent to put another barrier in his way even if only to give herself an extra few seconds to be prepared.

"What's happening?" said Oskar, his voice hushed.

Helen looked beyond him and saw Ingrid and Sophie were standing again, holding hands like they had done in the sitting room and looking almost as strained as they had been then. "I think he's packing his stuff and they're leaving."

Shouldn't we go out there and make sure?" Oskar paced on the spot, balling his fists and stretching out his fingers, like a fighter limbering up before going into the ring.

Helen shook her head and as she did so, the noises from the hall got louder and the voices got closer, prompting her to brace against the door. "Be ready." She mouthed the words at Oskar, who gave a curt nod and then stood, feet apart, poised for action.

The noise level increased just before a loud bang blasted through to the kitchen, the sound of the front door as it slammed against the wall. There was another crash as it thumped shut and then, after a few moments of nothing, the sound of car engines roared before the squeal of spinning tyres grabbed the noise and took it off into the distance.

Helen waited in silence, still tense but after a few moments she felt herself relax. "They've gone I think," she looked at Oskar and gestured behind her, "we better check though."

"I'll go, you stay with mum," said Oskar, and as Helen moved aside, he eased the door open and slipped out into the hallway.

Helen remained at the door just in case things weren't quite what they seemed but when Oskar returned, the expression on his face told her the drama was over, at least for a while. He had checked every room in the house, then rummaged through the wardrobes in Ingrid's room, confirming what they already suspected and that Gary was gone, having cleared out most of his clothes. When he broke the news to Ingrid and Sophie, their relief was palpable.

Back at the table, each of them nursing a fresh cup of coffee courtesy of Oskar, the discussion turned to the best way of ensuring Gary couldn't get back into the house.

It's simple," said Helen, "we phone an emergency locksmith and get the locks changed, I don't see the problem with doing that in the circumstances."

"I think we cannot do so if it is his house," said Ingrid, "it would not be legal." She looked worn out by it all, her face drawn and her eyes, red rimmed.

"Maybe, maybe not." Helen wasn't in the mood to take no for an answer when not acting meant the bastard could sneak back in anytime, perhaps even when they were all in bed. "If it's not legal then I reckon he would need a lawyer and a court order and these take time, which is what we need."

"I agree," said Oskar, "I don't think I'll get much sleep tonight if he can just come wandering in when it suits him."

"Me too," said Sophie, reaching for her phone and rising from her seat, "and I'm calling a locksmith now, mamma, it's the only way we can know we're safe tonight." She walked away from the table to make the call and stood, staring out of the kitchen window.

"It's for the best you know," Helen pulled her seat closer to Ingrid and laid a hand on her arm, "I don't want him creeping in here at three in the morning when we're asleep."

Ingrid closed her eyes and nodded agreement. "I think I would like to go to my room and lie down for a bit if it is all right."

"Of course." Helen turned to Oskar. "If you look after Sophie and tell me when the guy's here to do the locks, I'll take your mom upstairs and make sure she's all right."

"No problem," said Oskar, "and I'll keep an eye out for any invaders as well."

Helen smiled at him and then put an arm around Ingrid's shoulders. "Let's get you upstairs."

***

Helen stood beside the bed, gazing down at Ingrid who lay propped up by pillows and covered by a grey, wool throw. "I'll go back down and wait with them for the lock guy," she tilted her head, "is that all right?"

"No," Ingrid blinked a few times and gazed up at Helen, "please, stay with me." She held up her hand.

Helen took the outstretched hand and sat on the edge of the bed, wondering if she should have locked the door to the bedroom but at once dismissing the notion as beyond fanciful. "How are you doing?"

"I have had better days."

"I bet you have but I'm sure it made a memorable birthday though." Helen forced a smile and felt cheered when Ingrid did

192

the same.

"It is one I will never forget," said Ingrid, meeting Helen's gaze, "but it was not always this bad."

"I'm not so sure that's true." Helen looked away, trying to hide the embarrassment she felt on Ingrid's behalf. "You told me you weren't afraid of that fucker and you damn well are afraid of him, I saw it in your face and I saw it in Sophie's as well. I can't believe you've been living like this."

"Please, Helen," Ingrid's voice cracked, "he has never laid a hand on me, he has never beat me."

"Well he laid two hands on you today," Helen felt her anger growing, "so please, don't make excuses for what he did down there."

"I know what he did," Ingrid squeezed Helen's hand, "but please, do not be angry with me." She began to cry.

"Oh no, I'm not angry with *you*," Helen slid further up the bed and pulled Ingrid over and into her arms, holding her there as she sobbed. "It's ok, come on, have a good cry," she kissed the top of her head and pulled her in tighter, "everything will be all right, I promise you." Even as she said the words, Helen felt a sharp spike of doubt because she had only thirteen more days left in England before it was time for her to go home, less than two weeks to decide if what was happening between them, would be able to survive the distance. At this thought she kissed Ingrid's head again and pulled back a bit to have a look at her tear-streaked face. "You need a tissue, maybe two." Helen smiled as she leaned over to take some tissues from the box on the bedside table and she began to clean Ingrid's face, stopping every so often when Ingrid took a sharp, hitched breath. After she finished, she pulled her close again and they sat there in silence for the next half hour until, at length, Ingrid's composure returned.

"I do not know what to do." Ingrid pulled back and looked up at Helen, her tear stained face, white and etched with fatigue.

"I'm not surprised." Helen sighed. "Can I ask you something?"

"Ask anything."

"Well you might not like it," said Helen, "I might be wrong anyway, and the fact I'm asking isn't because I think it's bad, in fact it would be a good thing but..."

Ingrid reached up and put her finger over Helen's lips, a very faint smile tugging at the corners of her mouth. "What is the question?"

"It was something he said downstairs, you know, him."

"What was it?"

"He was going on about Sophie not knowing who the baby's father is and then he said she had turned out like you."

"He did." Ingrid nodded, raising her eyebrows.

"I was wondering if he meant you'd had the same experience?"

Ingrid pulled back from Helen and steadied herself before leaning against the pillows, staring at the wall opposite with glassy eyes. After a few moment her focus returned and she reached out and took Helen's hand. "Gary is not Oskar's father." She started biting at her bottom lip and paused, as if thinking how to proceed. "Oskar does not know, but Gary does and he has made a lot of it for many years and it is part of the reason I did not leave."

Helen didn't react other than to acknowledge to herself she had been correct in her reading of Gary's comment but although she had a barrow-load of questions she held them in, because Ingrid looked like she needed to purge herself of something held as a painful secret for too many years.

"I have already told you about Gary's indiscretions and my test at the hospital. This is how he knew the baby was not his, I would not let him near me so, it could not be his. Several months after that when I was in Sweden to visit my mother and the girls were at home with Gary, I met an old friend and we went for drinks. He was in Stockholm for business you see. We ended up going to his hotel room and things went too far." Ingrid pulled her knees up and wrapped her arms around them, holding them tight. "I think maybe you will not understand it."

"Why wouldn't I get it?" said Helen, twisting around and throwing her legs up on the bed before drawing them up and sitting cross-legged.

"I meant about why I would do such a thing."

"Okay, tell me then, why did it happen?"

Ingrid frowned and bit at her lip again. "I knew I was in a

dead marriage by then and that my husband did not want me, did not find me attractive. Suddenly I found myself with someone I am fond of, and who made it clear he wanted me very much and he made me feel good about myself." Ingrid smiled and her eyes became distant for a moment before she focused on Helen. "It is a very potent mix, to have someone desire you when you believe nobody could."

"I see. So what happened then?"

"I went back to England and tried to put it out of my mind but a few months later I found out I was pregnant and I had to tell Gary who of course, did not take it well to begin with, despite his own activities. After a while however, it no longer seemed to bother him."

Helen leaned forward and gestured to the door. "Tell me why Oskar doesn't know about this, that's the part I don't understand."

"At first he was too young to know about such things, then, when he was about five years old, things between Gary and I became very bad and I was on the verge of leaving and taking take Oskar to Sweden for us to live with my mother. Gary threatened me and said if I left, he would tell him he was not his father and he would tell the girls I had been unfaithful so they would never want to see me again."

"I wish I had poisoned his fucking coffee," said Helen, entertaining only the briefest of notions that her modest attempt at psychological warfare might have backfired and precipitated Gary's onslaught.

"Yes, the coffee, that was good." Ingrid smiled but it fell away as quickly as it had appeared. "Life went on and Gary made a habit of making the same threat whenever it looked like I would leave, and it was many times. He managed to convince me Oskar would not want to know me if the truth came out and then, my mother became very ill for the first time and I knew I could not leave. I suppose I became lost in myself then, and there was never a good time to tell Oskar the truth after that."

Helen unfolded her legs and swung them off the bed. "I think you have to tell him now because if you don't, then you take the risk Gary tells him and I think it's better it comes from you."

"I agree." Ingrid pushed herself to the edge of the bed and

lowered her legs over the side. "I do not want to be alone tonight," she dropped her head onto Helen's shoulder, "will you stay with me?"

"That's a huge risk." Helen, for the first time, felt nervous.

"I know it is but we will be quiet."

"Yeah," Helen laughed quietly. "but what if one of us is a bit of a screamer and when I say one of us, I mean me, but you already know that."

"Well, one of us will have to scream in silence this time," Ingrid tilted her head up and kissed Helen on the chin before resting it back on her shoulder, "can you do that?"

"Uh-huh." Helen put an arm around Ingrid's waist and pulled her in, feeling the heat from her body seep into her own. "What was his name, the old friend in Sweden, you know, the one who made you feel desired when you thought you weren't?"

Ingrid pulled her head up, bringing them both face-to-face. "His name is Erik and the answer to the question you did not ask is no, you are not like him, you are not just someone who makes me feel good."

Helen smiled. "What am I then?"

"You are something wonderful, but you happened very quickly and I am still getting used to it." Ingrid pulled herself tight into Helen again.

"I fly home in thirteen days." Helen felt a knot in her guts as panic set in at the thought and she fought to keep her voice calm, not wanting to make things any more stressful. "I know this has all been really quick and I'm trying not to look too far ahead, but I can't stand the thought of leaving here in less than two weeks."

"I feel that too" said Ingrid, "and I cannot bear to think ahead to it."

"Thank you," Helen leaned over and placed a gentle kiss on Ingrid's forehead, "it's nice to know you feel the same but I know it's worse for you than it is for me because the situation is new for you."

Ingrid gave a wistful smile and lifted her head from Helen's shoulder. "I have something I would like you to see that I have never shown to anyone before."

"What is it?"

"Wait there and I will get it." Ingrid rose from the bed and walked over to a large chest of drawers, opening the middle one and rummaging through the folded clothing before lifting a small photograph from its tucked-in position at the bottom. As she walked back towards the bed she held the photograph out at arm's length. "I am one of the people in the picture but it was taken before I left Sweden and I was very young."

Helen took the little coloured square and almost at once began to laugh. "That's you on the right, I'd know you anywhere I think, your smile hasn't changed." She studied the photo for a few moments, glancing at Ingrid to compare her to the younger version, then she pointed to the tall man. "Oskar doesn't look like him," she tapped on the photo with a long finger, "Erik I mean, apart from the blonde hair I can't see any resemblance."

Ingrid reached for the photograph and shook her head. "After that picture was taken, we danced, and it was a funny dance, at least for the audience but," she gave a long, tremulous sigh, "it made us both realise we had feelings for one another, romantic feelings that is, and we had a brief affair which caused quite a scandal and eventually it led to me leaving Sweden for London."

"Right, I see," Helen nodded her understanding," but then I suppose you still had feelings and when you met all those years later and went to the hotel room then..."

"No, that is not Erik and I did not dance with him," Ingrid tapped her finger on the dark-haired woman in the picture, "I danced with his wife, Pernille."

"You danced with his wife," Helen repeated Ingrid's admission as she drew her head back in surprise, "so that means you had an affair with...his wife."

"Yes," replied Ingrid, her voice playful, "and in the end my heart was broken but it was a long time ago and from that day I have never felt anything for another woman, until I met you."

In her panic about leaving for home, Helen had tortured herself trying to think of ways to prolong her time in England, believing, with what she thought was good reason, that the biggest barrier to any sort of future with Ingrid, would be Ingrid's longer-term reaction to the nature of their relationship. Now she saw the glimmer of a chance and although her stomach still felt unsettled, it was no longer knotted in fear.

"Helen, are you all right? You have gone very quiet."

"I'm all right," Helen reached over and held Ingrid's hand, "you just surprised me that's all, but in a nice way."

"So, will you stay with me tonight?" Ingrid put the photograph in her trouser pocket.

Helen tightened her grip on Ingrid's hand and leaned over and kissed her nose. "You know I will." She smiled and kissed it again. "When will you speak to Oskar?"

Ingrid nodded. "Yes, Oskar," she looked thoughtful for a moment then nodded again, "I shall go now I think, there is no reason to leave it longer."

"Do you want me to go with you for moral support?"

Ingrid shook her head. "No, thank you for the offer but I think this has to only be me." She kissed Helen on the mouth and gave a tired smile. "Perhaps you could be there for after I tell him, for Oskar I mean. He is a sensitive boy."

Helen nodded. "He hates Gary, you know."

"Yes, it seems he does, but do not forget, I have lied to him for all of his life. This is my worry." Ingrid pulled back from the embrace. "I shall go now."

Helen stood back. "Okay, I'll come down with you," she hesitated for a second, "do you want me to tell Sophie?"

Ingrid held up a hand. "No, I will speak with her after Oskar knows but perhaps you could talk to her about her husband."

"I'll try my best," said Helen, wishing she could talk about anything except Sophie and her relationship with Michael, although it wasn't because she didn't want them to work things out and get back together; she did. What she didn't want to do was discuss it with Sophie and risk another awkward conversation. "Are we good to go?"

Ingrid nodded and together they made for the door, stopping for a last kiss before making their way downstairs.

***

They found Oskar and Sophie together in the conservatory, Oskar fiddling with his phone and Sophie lying full length on the sofa from where she broke the news the locksmith wouldn't arrive until about nine o'clock at the earliest which suggested they were all in for a late night. Ingrid thanked her for sorting things out and then held out a hand and gestured for Oskar to take it and when he did, she led him from the room.

"What's happening?" Sophie pushed herself up and swivelled round to face Helen, who was standing, looking down at her." Is mamma all right?"

"Oskar needs a debrief," said Helen, "it's been a big day for him." She pulled a large cushion off the couch to make room and then flopped down beside Sophie, gazing at her tousled hair and pale skin and dreading the conversation she was about to begin. "You're mom's okay."

"But you look worried." Sophie pulled her knees up on the couch and turned around to face Helen.

"Do I?" Helen shrugged and tried to look relaxed.

"Come on," said Sophie, "you know I can read you like a book and you're wearing your worried and don't want to talk about it face." She reached out and placed her hand on Helen's thigh, before shuffling along the sofa to get closer. "What's wrong?"

"Am I really so transparent to you?" Helen felt her stomach flip at what this could mean but Sophie shook her head.

"Not usually, but I know the face when I see it, so what's the matter?"

Helen swallowed and licked her lips. "I lied to you, when you asked me the question about the time we were making out, the night I threw up."

Sophie's eyes narrowed and she nodded without speaking.

"Well, I lied to you about something and I feel bad about it, but I need you to know the truth even though I don't want to hurt you." Helen took a breath, aware if she wasn't careful it would all pour out in one garbled, un-edited stream and when she started talking like that, there was no telling where she would stop. "That night, if we had kept going, it would only ever have been a one-night thing for me and I wouldn't have wanted a relationship with you."

"So I would have been a casual fuck after all." Sophie's voice was devoid of any emotion and she kept her eyes fixed on Helen's.

"No, that's not what it would've been, I just...you make it sound cold and I don't feel cold towards you but I don't get the other feeling either." From the corner of her eye she saw Sophie still wore the same, emotionless look. "Believe it or not, you're my best friend and I love you but I could never be in love with you."

Sophie's flat look broke and she smiled. "I'd worked that out actually, but all the same, I'm glad you feel able to tell me now."

Helen hung her head, closing her eyes and wishing none of it had ever happened. "If I'd thought I'd hurt you I would never have started anything."

"But you never think, Helen," Sophie moved her hand to Helen's arm, "it's always the same, don't you understand?" She tugged the arm, prompting Helen to raise her head. "You go from zero to a hundred," she snapped her fingers, "and people get dragged along in your wake then get left floundering when you blast off in another direction."

"I never meant to hurt you," Helen shook her head, feeling the saliva thicken in her mouth, "I just wanted you to have fun, something nice to look back on down the line and I didn't see the harm in it."

"I know you didn't, but you never took a breath to consider what it might be like on the other side of things." Sophie put a hand on Helen's back. "When I stayed with you it was like being in a film and one minute we'd be working, then bang," she snapped her fingers again, "you'd say fuck it, life's too short, and we'd be off to Carmel for ice cream, all because Clint Eastwood said it was allowed."

Helen shrugged. "It was just ice cream."

"Oh, come on, it wasn't just ice cream," Sophie tilted her head, "and what about the time I said I fancied a hot dog from a street cart?"

At this, Helen smiled, remembering the expression on Sophie's face when she found out where they were going.

"Seriously, New York for a hot dog," Sophie raised an eyebrow, "do you think that's normal?"

"It is for me," said Helen.

"That's the problem though," Sophie sighed, "it isn't normal for me. Every day I spent with you was intoxicating, you were intoxicating, all those attentive little things you did for me, a smile here, a touch there, but then I had to come home and leave it all behind. What I came back to was one grey day after another and a husband whose idea of excitement is a trip to IKEA for breakfast on a Sunday morning."

"I know," said Helen, "do you hate me for that?"

Sophie shook her head. "No, but I should do for making me believe I might have been someone special."

Helen sat up and leaned back on the sofa, forcing Sophie to move her arm. "I don't understand why you don't hate me, but I'll take it."

Sophie stretched out her legs and leaned back, resting clasped hands on her stomach. "I won't allow myself to hate you because I've seen what it's done to you."

"What do you mean?" Helen's brow furrowed and she gestured to Sophie to continue.

"I used to think you had a perfect life, I believed you had everything, but now I know I was wrong, because you have nothing at all." Sophie crossed her legs and glanced towards Helen. "What your mother did was awful but you let your hatred of her consume you to the point where you lost your decency and what was left of your family. I'd hate to be a person like you."

"Sophie, don't say that." Helen's voice was faint and she felt tears pricking at her eyes.

"No, you will hear me because you've helped me fuck up my life and despite everything, I don't want you to fuck up the rest of your own." Sophie reached out and took Helen's hand, pulling her around and making her sit face-to-face. "You are such fun to be with you know. Oskar adores you, even my mother seems rather fond of you, but you have no depth, because when you've had enough, you just pack up your bags, make a joke and crash on to the next bit of fun. You're fake, Helen, every bit of you is fake."

Helen turned away, eyes smarting, and stunned by the sudden attack.

Sophie's voice was sharp. "You will look at me Helen." She stopped speaking but Helen didn't turn her head so Sophie pulled herself up and moved in front of her, kneeling, and looking up at her face. "When are you going to stop running, and let someone in to pull down that bloody barricade you've put up to protect yourself?" She reached up and touched Helen's cheek. "If you can't do it, you'll always have nothing and you'll just keep on hurting other people and leaving chaos behind you."

Helen pulled her head back and away from Sophie's hand, then she pushed herself deep into the sofa and drew her legs up until she could wrap her arms around them. She stared down at Sophie, eyes brimming with tears but still unable to speak, so she bent her head forward and buried it in her knees.

Sophie eyes narrowed. "Listen, there's a lot going on in my family just now and I think it would be best if you went elsewhere. I know you don't fly home for another couple of weeks but maybe this would be a good time to go up to Scotland and spend some time there, with your own family."

"No!" Helen raised her head and glared at Sophie.

"Come on, it's rather a good idea," Sophie reached over and gave Helen's legs a nudge, "you would be able to spend time with your brother."

"No," Helen said again, her voice breaking, "I don't want to go, please."

"Why not?" said Sophie, "it would give you a chance to reconnect with your family, I don't understand."

"You're trying to get rid of me and I don't want to go, that's why not." Helen felt the familiar twist in her guts and she released her legs and wrapped her arms around her midriff instead. "I want to stay here."

Sophie pursed her lips. "I don't understand what the problem is, they're your family. For God's sake, why are you crying, you'd think I'd just asked you to give away your first-born child."

Helen brought a hand to her face and began to wipe away the tears coursing down her cheeks. "No, you don't understand, but...I don't want to go to strangers, I want to stay here with everyone." Her voice shook, and as she struggled to get the words out, she lifted her knees up again, hugging them and burying her face in her arms. She felt so wretched, there was no room in her for embarrassment, but in her distress, she couldn't summon up the words to explain further so she sat there, hugging herself and feeling dejected.

"What is this about, why all the tears?" said Sophie, placing a hand on Helen's foot.

Helen didn't look up, she couldn't face it. "I don't want to go and I want to stay here."

"Helen, look at me." Sophie's voice had risen in pitch but it sounded uncertain.

"I don't want to go," Helen repeated, her head still shrouded, "I want to stay here."

"What is going on?" Ingrid's voice came from the door of the conservatory and she marched into the room, Oskar trailing along behind her. "You will tell me what is happening." She glared at Sophie as she pushed past her, then sat down beside Helen on the couch and put an arm around her shoulders. Oskar stood behind Sophie, open mouthed.

"It's nothing," said Sophie, rolling her eyes, "I just suggested she could spend time with her family in Scotland."

Helen's head snapped up and she turned a tear-streaked face to Ingrid. "Please," her voice shook, "don't send me away."

Ingrid shook her head in confusion. "Nobody is sending you away."

Helen sniffed. "Sophie said I should leave but...I don't want to go."

"Oskar," said Ingrid, "get me some tissues please, from the sitting room." She turned on Sophie as Oskar set off on his mission. "What have you done here?"

"Mamma, I've done nothing." Sophie's eyes were blazing and she glared at Helen before facing her mother again.

"You will tell me what you have done," said Ingrid, "do not take me for a fool."

"Please don't fight because of me." Helen wiped at her eyes and nose and shook her head, trying to defuse things. Even through a haze of tears she could see Ingrid was livid.

"Well, are you going to speak?" Ingrid turned to Oskar, who had brought tissues back as ordered and she nodded a thank you to him as she took them. "Sophie, I said are you going to speak? Do not dare sit there and ignore me."

"Okay," Sophie held her hands up," I suggested she should go to let us fix what we need to fix as a family. I don't think it's a big deal."

Ingrid tilted Helen's face towards her and began wiping it with a tissue but she glanced sideways at Sophie. "You do not think this is a big deal?"

"No, I don't," said Sophie, her brow wrinkling. "Mamma, you

know the history of this," she glared at Helen again, "don't you think it's hard for me that she's here?"

"Please don't fight," said Helen, fresh tears falling, and as she spoke, she turned her head to Oskar, "please tell them not to fight."

Sophie raised her voice, her face tight with anger. "You didn't answer me mamma, how do you think I feel because she's here?"

"And how do you think I would feel if she was *not?*" Ingrid shouted the words out and Sophie jerked backward in surprise, her mouth open, but wordless.

Helen and Oskar locked eyes and she saw his widen, before he took a small step backward. He knew.

Chapter Fifteen

Michael and Oskar

Helen didn't ask the taxi driver to wait and as he did a U-turn to head back in the direction from which they had come, she strolled across the road and took a seat inside an empty bus shelter. Across from the shelter was a row of shops, all of them closed bar a newsagent doing brisk Sunday morning trade and Helen considered venturing in to grab a box of chocolates to take as a gift. She sat for a while considering whether to do it or not, mulling over the many possible outcomes her visit could have, almost all of them ending with Michael telling her to go fuck herself, and in the end, she decided sweets were a step too far. Having made the decision, she allowed her thoughts to drift back to the previous Friday night.

The locksmith had arrived as promised, just after nine o'clock, by which time Helen had pulled herself together and tempers had cooled. Sophie's shock at Oskar's news ensured it became the main discussion point for the remainder of the evening but of greater importance, she seemed satisfied with the explanation given for her mother's outburst and although Helen wasn't convinced they were home free, she had to admit Ingrid had recovered well by throwing in a quick comment about how she was invaluable in times of trouble and that she would hate her to leave every bit as much as she would hate anyone to leave. Of course, this still left the unresolved Oskar situation but it appeared he had accepted the same explanation as nothing he said or did suggested he harboured any suspicions. By the time the locksmith left at around ten o'clock, everyone was exhausted and it was quick goodnights all round and then off to bed. Helen had gone to her own room first, waiting until everyone had settled, before sneaking along the hallway to join Ingrid. Once in bed, they had talked about one problem after another without finding any solutions, and it was during these discussions that

Helen hit upon the idea of visiting Michael to convince him to try to reconcile with Sophie. It was a long shot, and one likely to end in disaster, but she felt compelled to try because she could see no other way things could move forward and her own personal clock was ticking, each remaining day precious and brief.

Saturday had been busy. Helen had a lot of catching up to do for work and so had spent most of the day working through emails and spreadsheets, but she also took the opportunity to check how to get to Michael's and had arranged for a cab to pick her up a few streets away from Ingrid's house on the following morning. Oskar had been in a buoyant mood, decamping to Kieran's place to spread the good news and informing everyone he would be late back and not to wait up for him. Sophie and Ingrid meanwhile, had kept themselves busy with grocery shopping late into the afternoon and when they returned laden with bags, it wasn't long before they pulled together a decent dinner of steak and fries with all the fixings. Later, they had all watched a movie on Netflix before heading to bed, rounding off a normal happy, family day which had been anything but normal.

Helen glanced at her watch; it was almost eleven o'clock. She presumed Michael would now be up and about and she yawned and stretched before pulling out her phone to check for messages. Seeing there were none, she cut back across the road and began the walk to Michael's house, the journey taking her less than five minutes. When she arrived, she stood for a few moments just inside the gate, and then, taking several deep breaths, she walked up the path to the door and rang the bell. She didn't have long to wait for the door to be opened and when it was, she saw a tall, dark-haired man she recognised from photos Sophie had on her phone although it was obvious he didn't recognise her.

"What can I do for you?" He smiled at her as he adjusted his bathrobe, tying the belt in a knot at the front.

Helen took another deep breath. "Well," she said, "that remains to be seen I suppose. I'm Sophie's friend, Helen." She eyed him as she spoke and saw his expression change when she said her name.

"Oh, I see." He strained his neck to look behind her and then sighed. "Is Sophie not with you?"

Helen shook her head." I'm sorry, no, she isn't and actually, she doesn't know I'm here."

Michael's face fell at what was clearly, unwelcome news. "Would you like to come in then?" He took a step back and gestured for her to enter.

Helen hesitated and stared at the open door. She had thought about this moment on the journey, mulling over the safety implications of going into a house alone with a man whose wife had left him and, in all probability, had left him for the woman now standing on his doorstep. To make matters worse, nobody knew where she was. She could never have told Sophie for obvious reasons but as she stood there on the doorstep, she felt a sharp stab of regret she hadn't mentioned her plan to Ingrid.

"Helen." Michael gestured again for her to enter.

"Sorry, yes," Helen gave a toothy smile, "that would be good but I can only stay a little while as Ingrid said she would pick me up in thirty minutes." As she spoke, she took out her phone and sent the briefest of text messages to Ingrid, just two words; *at Michael's*.

"That's all right," said Michael, returning the smile, "she could have come in you know."

"Yeah I told her that too but, you know Ingrid." Helen threw the last bit in and when she saw him nod and raise his eyebrows, she stepped over the threshold into the hallway, following him through to the sitting room and focussing on the positives, after all, Ingrid would at least be able tell the cops where to find her battered, broken body.

* * *

The sitting room was stylish, dark wooden floors set off with a plush, teal coloured velvet sofa, laden with an abundance of contrasting cushions and bang on trend, which didn't surprise Helen, having herself been on the receiving end of Sophie's unrelenting passion for makeovers. The walls were dark grey, studded with colourful, large format pictures, along with several photos of Sophie and Michael looking happy and at ease with each other. There was no sign of any rug but Helen felt the room didn't need it as the warmth in the wood and colourful furnishings made it feel cosy. She liked it.

Michael had left the room to make coffee and he returned now

207

with two large mugs, filled to the brim, setting Helen's on a small brass table he pulled over from beneath the window and carrying his to the other end of the sofa before plonking himself down.

"Nice room." Helen started small.

"Yes, Sophie's design of course." Michael took a sip of his coffee and looked around the room, his eyes settling on one of the pictures of Sophie kissing his cheek as he grinned at the camera. "Is she all right?"

"That's a hard one to answer," said Helen, "but, more or less yeah, she's fine." She reached for her coffee and took a sip before putting the mug back on the table and deciding it was now or never. "Look, Michael, I came over to England without knowing you guys had split and Sophie didn't say a word." She saw sadness in his eyes, as he glanced at her before turning his attention back to the photograph. "I only found out when Ingrid told me when I arrived at her house." Helen was hoping this revelation would spur Michael on to say something but he sat there in silence so she felt compelled to go on. "That's when we both found out Sophie was pregnant and why she left."

Michael turned around. "What did she tell you?"

"Just the basics, that you don't think the baby's yours and you think it belongs to some man friend of hers."

"Not quite true I'm afraid." Michael turned to Helen, then sat further back in the couch and took a mouthful of coffee. "Sophie discovered she was pregnant and we were both delighted, things were fine," he shrugged his shoulders, "well I thought they were fine." He pointed towards the photo of him and Sophie. "That's when the photo was taken, I thought we were both happy together but I was wrong."

"So, she was seeing that guy," said Helen.

Michael shook his head. "No, not in the sense you mean, he was just a friend."

"I'm a little confused then," Helen picked up her coffee again, "because Sophie said she left when you refused to believe this baby is yours and now, you're saying she wasn't seeing the other guy. Who's the baby's father if it's not him?"

"I am, of course," Michael smiled, "I've never doubted it for a minute."

"In that case," Helen took a mouthful of coffee, her brow

wrinkling, "what the Hell is going on? Why did she leave?" She stared at Michael, whizzing through all the possible permutations in her head, no longer sure what to believe, or who.

"Isn't it obvious?" said Michael, "she left for you."

Helen leaned forward in her seat and shook her head. "No, no, no, she did not leave for me, I knew nothing about this."

"Doesn't mean it's not why she left though."

Helen turned to look at him. "Sophie said it was because of the baby," she shook her head again, "you can't leave for someone if they don't know about it."

"Yet here we are," said Michael, "more coffee?"

Helen held her hand up to decline. She was bullshitting and she knew it. True, she hadn't realised in the beginning why Sophie had left Michael but it had become obvious over the last week or so, although she felt she deserved the benefit of any doubts as she hadn't been party to Sophie's plan until rather late in the day.

Michael sighed. "Everything had been going well with the pregnancy and we had reached the two-month point when Sophie arrived back from work one night, almost floating, she was so excited," he looked across at Helen, "she had just found out you would be coming to England and the two of you would be working together again. That's when it all began to unravel."

"In what way?" said Helen, leaning back in the couch, discomfort rolling over her.

"When you two worked together before, Sophie came back home and I think it was a big disappointment for her. All she talked about was you and her and all the crazy stuff you did together, and it took months before she seemed all right again." Michael drank the last of his coffee and put the mug on the floor. "So, when she said you were coming over here, I knew what to expect and I wasn't wrong."

"If she told you there was something going on with us she was lying." Helen hoped to set the record straight about her relationship with Sophie although she knew her denial of wrongdoing was based on a fumbled, drunken, vomit spoiled attempt at seduction and as such, was splitting hairs and akin to pleading guilty to second degree murder rather than risking a guilty verdict on a higher charge.

"No, but I'm not stupid, I know something happened," Michael kept his focus on Helen and held both hands up, "but please, spare me the sordid details."

Helen, with some difficulty, said nothing.

"Anyway," Michael sighed, "it wasn't long before Sophie started to pick arguments, just little things to begin with until one day, she threw in a comment about Jason, I think that's his name anyway, and one thing led to another and suddenly we're having a massive fight and she's telling me she isn't sure the baby is mine. It was ridiculous."

"But you said you know it's yours?"

"I know, and I do, but Sophie tried to make me think it wasn't," Michael laughed, "she was trying to goad me into throwing her out but I didn't fall for it although I did tell her to leave at one point, but only if she didn't want me anymore."

"I see," said Helen, "at least I think I do."

Michael sat back and crossed his legs. "Sophie's great at knowing what she wants but she's not good at taking responsibility for wanting it. She should've had the backbone to tell me she wanted to be with you but it's not her style because she always needs someone else to blame."

"Why don't you come to the house with me and speak to her?"

"She doesn't want me, Helen. I think I bore her."

Helen sighed. None of this was what she had expected, not even Michael himself. She had built him up in her head to be another Gary but he seemed like a decent guy, handsome too, and just what she thought of as Sophie's type. "I think she knows she's made a mistake."

"Whatever you did to her over there, you changed her," Michael's voice was heavy with accusation and he frowned, "I don't think she'll ever be the same." He glanced at Helen, shaking his head. "Why did you do it?"

"I didn't do anything other than have a bit of fun with her, take her nice places, that's all," Helen swallowed before continuing, "we didn't have sex, okay, it didn't happen." She folded her arms then turned her head to Michael and when she saw he was watching her, she turned around in her seat to face him full on. "We didn't have sex, that's the truth...but it came

210

close one time which was my fault and I can't tell you how sorry I am."

Michael nodded. "Did you know she was married?"

"Yeah of course, she talked about you all the time." This wasn't a lie and Helen wished she could find a way to make Michael believe it because Sophie had gushed about him almost hourly, at least in the beginning.

"In that case," said Michael, "it was a fucking lousy thing you did and you should have kept your hands off her." He looked at the floor, tapping his hands on his legs.

"I know." Helen turned her face away but kept him in her peripheral vision, readying herself to get to her feet if things got too hot, "I didn't think."

"Do you love her, Helen?"

"As a friend yes, but I'm not in love with her." Helen turned back to face Michael again. "We talked about it a couple of days ago and I told her what I've just told you, that I've never wanted a different kind of relationship with her. She said I'd helped her fuck up her life."

"That's something, I suppose." Michael gave a sad smile. "Did you know Sophie was pregnant before, a few years ago?"

"No." Helen froze.

"She was," Michael said, "it was month three and we lost the baby. The doctors didn't have an explanation, we just lost it."

"I'm so sorry to hear that."

"Sophie found things very hard for a while, we both did, but she struggled for a long time. I did what I could to help but I messed things up and she left me." Michael turned his gaze to the photo on the wall once again. "I was trying to tell her we had to move on, you know, start to live again, and I suggested we could revamp the house, and get new carpets and stuff. She flew into a rage and accused me of giving carpets the same importance as our dead baby."

"Oh Michael, that's awful." Helen realised she had heard this story before but from a different perspective.

Michael shook his head and gave another sad smile. "She came back after a couple of weeks and we worked things out. We even got a nice rug for the bedroom as part of our new start." He fixed his eyes on Helen. "I thought we had another chance to have a family, but then you came into the picture."

"You still have the chance, I promise you," said Helen, "that's why I'm here, to persuade you to talk to her." She stood up and looked down at Michael. "Come on, come with me to the house now and do this."

"I don't know," said Michael, rubbing his hands together and staring up at Helen, "do you think she'll listen?"

Helen nodded, hoping she was right. "She will, I'm sure she will."

"Is that because you've blown her off now? Do you think she'll settle for me instead?"

"No, it's because you're her husband and she knows she's fucked things up. Why would she say something like that if she didn't think she'd made a huge mistake?" Helen stuffed her hands in her coat pockets, waiting for Michael's decision. He was no fool, that much was obvious, and there was something in what he'd said but nevertheless, she believed Sophie had realised her mistake and the marriage was salvageable.

"Tell me something," said Michael as he stood, "is this a genuine attempt to fix things because you know what you did was wrong, or has Sophie become an inconvenience?" He looked Helen in the eye.

"I'm trying to make good on something I shouldn't have done," Helen forced herself to maintain eye contact, desperate not to falter, "it's all I can do now."

"Okay," Michael said, "give me five minutes to change out of this." He gestured to his bathrobe and pyjama ensemble and turned away to leave the room just as the doorbell rang. "I'll get the door first, shouldn't be too long."

Helen hadn't realised she was holding her breath but as Michael left the room her cheeks puffed and she let out a gasp, relieved to be alone for a while with just her conscience for company although it was proving to be a heavy burden. She wandered over to the window, phone in hand, with Michael's words buzzing around her head as she thought about Sophie and the lost baby and the decent family her own ridiculous behaviour had pushed to breaking point, the word *inconvenience* popping into her head despite her best efforts to block it. Just as she was about to send a text message to Ingrid to alert her to Michael's impending visit, she heard the door open behind her and she turned around to face him again, only to see Ingrid walk into the room.

"There you are," said Ingrid, pushing the door closed behind her and walking over to join Helen at the window, "we looked everywhere in the house and we were worried about you until I received your message. You should have told me you were coming here."

Helen nodded. "I know, but I didn't want to say in case you stopped me, then I got here and started thinking about it, and I got worried he might murder me and nobody would find my body because nobody knew I was here, so I sent the message." She took a breath. "I'm sorry."

Ingrid reached up and ran her thumb over Helen's jaw, smiling as she did so. "You say the strangest things, what goes on in your head?"

"At the moment," Helen took hold of Ingrid's other hand, "a lot of things I don't much like. I've screwed up their lives and I thought I was trying to fix it for them but I think I might be trying to fix it for me too and it doesn't feel good."

"Come on now," Ingrid took her hand away and stood back, "fixing both would not be wrong I think."

Helen nodded and took her own step back as she heard the clatter of Michael running down the stairs. "I told him you were outside in the car, you know, in case he tried to kill me. Please don't say anything."

Ingrid didn't reply and turned away from Helen when Michael came back into the room. "How have you been doing?" Her voice was soft and she wore a warm smile.

"Up and down really," he said, "mostly down though." He smiled back at her. "Is Sophie all right?"

"Sophie is Sophie as you can imagine and she is putting on a brave face." Ingrid gestured to Helen. "She does not know we are here and," she paused, "when Helen suggested we did this I was not sure if it was right, but I now think it had to be done. This must be sorted, for everyone."

"The baby is mine," said Michael, "and I've never doubted it for a second. I know why she left but it doesn't matter, I just want her back."

Ingrid nodded. "Let us try then." She turned to Helen. "Come on, the car is outside."

Helen said nothing and instead, followed Ingrid and Michael outside then sat in the back seat of the car and buckled herself in. She listened to their conversation but said nothing herself, spending the rest of the journey ruminating and trying not to think about the future.

***

Michael and Helen stood together in the hallway awaiting Ingrid's return from her search for Sophie, the plan being that once Sophie was located, Ingrid would stay with her and Michael for just long enough to ensure they had started talking, before leaving to find Helen. It seemed simple but was reliant on Sophie playing ball and Helen knew there was no guarantee on that score.

"I meant to ask you," said Michael, gesturing to Helen's bruised eye, "who did that, a jealous husband?"

Helen smiled at him. "No, it was a little woman about five feet tall," she sighed, remembering the look of rage on Francine's face as she swung for her, "turns out she had a short fuse and long arms."

"Oh right, jealous wife then?"

"No," Helen rubbed her face just below the bruising, "it was my aunt. It happened when I went up to Scotland for my mother's funeral."

"Probably happens a lot to you I imagine," said Michael, looking like he was just warming up and appearing to be disappointed when he was cut short by Ingrid's return.

"Michael, come with me please, she is in the sitting room." Ingrid gestured for him to follow her and he did so, taking one last look at Helen before leaving the hallway.

Helen stood, hands in pockets, wondering whether to hang around in case things kicked off or whether it was time to beat a strategic retreat and await further instructions. She decided to wait for the moment, listening for the shouts that would signal Sophie wasn't in reconciliation mode, but after a few minutes she had heard nothing so, satisfied her diplomatic skills were surplus to requirements, she made her way into the kitchen, intent on brewing up some coffee and tracking down something sweet to go along with it.

As the kettle boiled, Helen rummaged around in the cupboards, hunting for something to satisfy her neglected sweet tooth, primed to accept anything resembling a biscuit but stopped in her tracks when her eyes fell upon a new and unopened, jar of marmalade. Knowing Ingrid must have had her in mind when she bought it, she grabbed the jar and bounded over to the bread-bin to liberate two slices of bread, grinning ear to ear. Today, at last, she was going to have her marmalade sandwich. As soon as she pulled everything together, she sat herself at the kitchen table, regarding her golden treasure with greedy eyes. She took one mouthful of coffee and picked up the sandwich but before she could take a bite, Oskar strolled into the kitchen.

"Oh, you're here," said Oskar, "I've been looking for you."

Helen stopped her lunge towards the sticky treat and put it back on the plate. "Well, you've found me," she said, "how's life as a fatherless delinquent? I'm presuming you're sniffing glue and smoking now."

Oskar grinned. "I treated myself to a new game and a six pack of Bud. The glue's arriving on Monday from Amazon."

Helen ran an eye over him, noting his relaxed demeanour and she guessed Ingrid's news didn't have a downside as far as he was concerned. "Will you look up your real father?" she said, taking another mouthful of coffee and grabbing the sandwich again.

Oskar shrugged. "I don't know but probably not, he would be a stranger and I've got mum anyway." At this, Oskar looked embarrassed and he shuffled his feet, not managing to meet Helen's gaze. "There's something I need to ask you."

"Okay," Helen put her sandwich back on the plate for a second time, "ask away." She knew what the question would be as she had been waiting for it since Ingrid's outburst in the conservatory just two nights ago, and now, here it was in all its glory.

"I'm not sure how to say it though."

Helen smiled at him, ignoring the knot in her stomach, and she pointed to one of the chairs next to her own. "Have a seat, my neck hurts looking up at you."

Oskar pulled out a chair and sat down, still not making eye

contact and looking more nervous than ever. "Do you know how sometimes you see something, but don't realise what you've seen at the time, and it's not until something else happens that it becomes obvious?" The words tumbled out at speed, almost falling over each other in their panic to escape.

Helen's heart sank and she pushed the sandwich away, her appetite gone. "Yeah, I know the feeling. I take it you've seen something like this and it's bothering you."

"I can't stop thinking about it," Oskar looked over at Helen, "I hardly slept last night."

"Maybe it isn't what you think." Helen tried deflection first, but apart from outright denial, she had nothing else in her locker. "Sometimes things turn out to be nothing after all."

"I know but it was right there in front of me, it was obvious." Oskar looked away again.

Helen leaned forward and placed her palms on the table. She decided she would deny it, put it down to his over-active imagination, and then play on how unlikely it would be for her to be his mother's lover. "Oskar, say it, it's fine."

"I know," Oskar gave a brief nod, "but it was a bit of a shock and it's the last thing I expected."

Helen appreciated why he was dragging things out as it was a tactic she used often but this time, being on the other side of it was torture and she half considered saying it for him to get it over with. "Come on kid, say it, you're killing me here."

Oskar shifted in his seat and started drumming his fingers on the table. "Okay," he said, "the night of mum's birthday, after it all calmed down and we went to bed, I couldn't sleep." His face turned red and he glanced at Helen, falling silent.

"I see." Helen felt her own face redden and she closed her eyes, unable to look at the boy across the table. On that night, when she had sneaked back to Ingrid's bed, they had talked for a couple of hours, interspersed with a bit of kissing. Naturally, things became more passionate although they were extra quiet which, as it worked out, made the whole thing more intense and pleasurable. Despite this, she realised Oskar must have heard them and although he didn't catch them in flagrante, one glance at her empty bed would be all he needed to know who was next door screwing his mother. What a fucking disaster. "I don't know

216

what to say."

Oskar took a deep breath and shook his head. "I haven't finished yet," he paused, "it was horrible."

"Oh God." Helen put her head in her hands.

"I was sitting playing on my phone when I got a WhatsApp message from Alicia, she's in one of my classes at college and Kieran's always said it was obvious she fancied me but I was never sure." He stopped again and glanced over at Helen, watching as she lifted her head from her hands and looked him in the eye. "Anyway, I opened the message and it had a picture of her...parts," his face flushed a deeper shade of red and he let out a breath, "and she asked if I wanted to go out with her and if I did, to send her a picture of my..." He met Helen's gaze and gestured to his crotch. "No way am I sending anybody a picture of that."

Helen felt a wave of nausea pass over her and she wiped away beads of sweat that had appeared on her brow. She stared at a mortified Oskar. "Let me get this right, this Alicia girl had been giving hints she fancied you, but you missed them until she made it obvious by sending you a picture of her parts and asking you for a dick pic. Am I right?"

Oskar nodded. "I do fancy her but I wish she hadn't sent it. I was going to ask what you think I should do, I mean, should I speak to her about it or just ignore it?"

Helen picked up her coffee and took a swig, swallowing a large mouthful of it despite it being lukewarm, happy to drink anything to help rid her mouth of the thick, bitter taste that had been building as Oskar was speaking. "If you're uneasy with it then delete the picture and tell her you've done it. You might need to write her off as a girlfriend though, if she's made you feel uncomfortable." She gave him a weak smile. "What do you think?"

"I agree," he said, smiling back at her, "you don't think I'm a prude, do you?"

"Not in the slightest," Helen laughed, relaxing now, "I wouldn't appreciate an unsolicited picture like that, and I'm as fond of those parts as you are, so I know how you feel. Nothing wrong with it." She was beginning to feel better, the nausea subsiding and her heart rate slowing to a steady, rhythmic beat.

"Thanks Helen." Oskar looked relieved, his flushed face beginning to regain something of its former gamer-boy pallor.

"Don't thank me, I'm happy to listen." Helen eyed the abandoned sandwich, wondering if she should try it and deciding it would be worth the risk. She reached over and plucked it from the plate then plunged her teeth into the sweet, sticky deliciousness of it, glancing at Oskar and giving him a thumbs-up. "Marmalade sandwich," she felt the need to explain, "your mom bought me marmalade." She took another bite and grinned at him despite her mouth being stuffed.

Oskar nodded. "I looked for you that night, you know, when I got the WhatsApp, but you weren't in your room." He took a sharp breath. "I know you were in bed with mum. You're sleeping together, aren't you."

Chapter Sixteen

The Spectre at the Feast

The instant Oskar said the words, Helen's sandwich felt like thick glue in her mouth, the glorious sweetness of moments ago, rendered tasteless. She stared at him and kept chewing, fighting her gag reflex and trying to swallow the remainder of the bread, but it was a lost cause. Realising she had seconds to spare before her stomach heaved itself onto the table, she ran towards the bin, flicking it open and spitting the mass from her mouth almost in one smooth movement. She then stood bent over, trying to hold on to what she had already eaten, taking deep breaths and letting the remaining thick curds of saliva drop onto her initial deposit.

Oskar said nothing but he rose from the table and walked to the sink, grabbing a glass from the cupboard next to it and filling it from the tap, before joining Helen at the bin and holding out the glass. "You might need this."

Helen wiped at her mouth then reached for the water without meeting Oskar's gaze, feeling him pushing the glass into her hand and holding fast to it for a few minutes as she remained hunched over the bin. After what seemed an interminable wait, she felt the nausea start to ease off and she forced herself to straighten up and take a few sips of water. As the coolness washed away the bitterness in her throat, she glanced at Oskar who had remained at her side. "Thanks."

"It's ok," he said, rubbing his hands on the side of his legs, then scratching at his jaw, going between the two over and over as they stood there not looking at each other.

"I'm going to sit down," said Helen, glancing up and gesturing towards the table she had so recently run from, "I think you should too."

Oskar nodded and watched as Helen went past him before he followed behind and sat down where he had been before. "I didn't mean to make you vomit," he said, "sorry about that."

Helen shook her head. "Not your fault, it's a specialty of mine, just a nervous stomach." She leaned her head on one hand and allowed her eyes to lose their focus as she played out in her head how she would handle the situation. Her plan to lie was a busted flush, that much was certain, as Oskar would never believe it after watching her chuck up the sandwich and it was also obvious he knew the truth anyway so to lie now would be pointless and, she felt, disrespectful. As much as she was desperate to think of an easy solution, she knew deep in her heart she wouldn't be able to talk herself out of trouble and that she had no ace to play in this game, so, her mind made up, she took a breath and pushed herself up in the chair, meeting Oskar's eyes from across the table. "The answer is yes," she said, feeling her gorge rise as she forced out the words, her stomach beginning to knot as the implications of the statement sunk in.

"I don't think there's anything wrong with it you know," Oskar spoke in a quiet, steady voice, his eyes fixed on Helen, "I wish someone would look at me the way you look at her."

Helen closed her eyes and rubbed at her forehead. "I've never met anyone like her before," she opened her eyes and looked across the table, "but everything's been so fast, and so chaotic."

Oskar pushed himself up from the chair and walked over to the freezer, and after he had a quick rummage through the drawers, he returned holding a large tub of chocolate ice cream before going back to get two spoons from the cutlery drawer, one of which he gave to Helen. "Chocolate ice-cream helps everything I think, might even help your stomach." He grinned as he pulled the lid from the tub and dug in with his spoon. "It's lovely, you should try some." He pushed the tub over the table.

The last thing Helen felt like doing was eating as her stomach was still in a delicate place, but she took a spoonful of the ice-cream anyway, for no other reason than to disguise the unpleasant taste lingering in her throat, and when she did, she was pleased to discover Oskar was right and that it was rather nice. Feeling more confident, she took another spoonful, wagering if she was to throw up now, at least she would get good value for all the heaves to come. As she went in for the third scoop, Oskar plunged his spoon in too and they clashed cutlery, causing them both to laugh.

"Spoon wrestling should be in the Olympics," said Oskar, continuing to push Helen's spoon backward out of the tub as she resisted with vigour, "we could play doubles."

"We could, but you're too good for me." Helen conceded defeat by planting her spoon in the ice-cream and leaving it there. "Thank you," she said, smiling at her giant friend opposite, appreciating he was a friend, as unlikely as it might seem to anyone else.

"For what?" Oskar began making small curls of ice-cream before scooping it into his mouth.

"For not having the screams about me and your mom," Helen shrugged one shoulder, "I didn't know how you would react but maybe I should have known you'd be good."

"I love mum," he said, "and I really like you so if you like each other that way then it's cool because you can both be happy together." He put his spoon down. "You told me you didn't like her that way though, do you remember?"

Helen nodded. "Yes, I lied." She knew there was no point in beating around the bush because the lie she had told was deliberate and she didn't feel bad for telling it at the time because it was necessary. "I liked her from day one. When I arrived and Sophie introduced us, it was unbelievable and I swear my stomach flipped all the way over." She smiled at the memory. "God knows what she thought when I looked at her, I mean, I don't have a poker face."

"What do we do now?" said Oskar, playing with the ice cream and making little swirls which he then knocked down.

"I've had a couple of relationships in the past," said Helen, "and they were nice, but I've never met anyone who I thought could be my special person," she watched him as he brought his eyes up to meet hers, "I think your mom could be my special person." She sighed, a sense of sadness sliding over her and she felt tears pricking at her eyes. "I also think I'll lose her and we've only just begun."

"Why would you lose her?" Oskar's nose wrinkled as he spoke and he let the spoon drop into the half-empty tub.

"It's too soon for her," Helen said, giving a sad smile at her own words and reaching across to take Oskar's hand, "we spoke about it but she needs time which we don't have, especially now you know about us. When she finds that out then I think it'll be over."

"We don't have to say anything about me knowing," Oskar's expression looked half-desperate and he pulled one foot up onto the chair before leaning over and hugging his knee, "I'm being serious, we can pretend we didn't discuss it."

Even as he was formulating his desperate plan, Helen was shaking her head. "I know you mean well but I can't do that to her Oskar, I just can't, come on, how would she feel when she does find out? Can you imagine how awful it would be for her?"

"But you think you'll lose her if we do tell her and I know you don't want that to happen, so why would you tell her?"

"Because," said Helen, "it's not all about me and what I might want." She pulled the tub of ice-cream to her side of the table and plunged her spoon into it again, catching a large blob as she looked Oskar in the eye. "It's horrific, but I have no choice in the matter, I have to tell her." She dropped the cold, chocolatey ball into her mouth, savouring it as it slid down into the depths and hoping it wouldn't attempt to climb back up any time soon.

"Where is mum anyway," said Oskar, "did she go out?" He glanced over at the kitchen door.

"No," said Helen, making a vague gesture, "she's in the sitting room with Sophie. Michael's here."

Oskar let go of his knee and his foot thudded to the floor. "What's he doing here?"

Helen put her spoon down. "Your mom and I brought him here to talk to Sophie because there's a chance they might fix things."

"Why would you want her to go back to him?" said Oskar, leaning back in his chair and folding his arms, in the process looking like the world's biggest sulking child.

Helen wagged a finger at him. "I know you're not fond of him but things have happened you don't know about," she saw his eyebrows rise, and shook her head, "it's not my place to tell you but you should talk to your mom and ask her because I think it would help." She wondered if she should tell him about her own interest in a reconciliation between Sophie and Michael and for a second, she almost did, but she stopped in time, keeping her selfishness tucked out of sight.

Oskar shrugged his shoulders. "I will ask her but I still think he's a knob."

"Give him a chance," said Helen, "please, there's more riding on this than you know." She shifted her gaze and stared at the ice cream tub, realising how close she strayed to the truth, but before she did so, she saw a look pass across Oskar's face which suggested he had perhaps picked up on what she meant.

"Do you think I should find mum so we can talk to her?"

Helen's stomach lurched and she jerked upright. As bad as it felt to be sitting at the edge of the inevitable, doing anything to bring it forward was worse and she knew she had to stop him. "She said she'd find me when it was all right to leave Sophie on her own so I'm sure she'll be here soon enough."

"I think I should go and check," said Oskar, unfolding his arms and scraping his chair back, "will you be all right?"

"No." Helen pushed her own chair back and clutched at her stomach, feeling the ominous churn that signalled only one thing. "I need to go." She stood and half ran to the door, pulling it open so hard that it swung back and rebounded against the cupboard as she lurched into the hallway. There was no chance she would make it upstairs to the bathroom so she ran along the hall towards the small downstairs toilet, praying it was unoccupied and almost throwing herself into in in relief when she saw it was free. She fell to her knees facing the toilet bowl, barely having time to pull the hair away from her face before her stomach chucked back its load, starting with the delicious chocolate ice-cream.

The vomiting subsided after a minute or so although Helen continued to retch into the bowl until she was bringing up nothing but air. After what appeared to be the final dry heave, she pushed herself off her knees and sat, eyes closed, with her back against the cool tiles, having already flushed the toilet towards the end of the last productive spew, and all too aware she would have to sit for a bit longer before cleaning the bowl. A few silent minutes passed before she felt able to move again and when she finally stood, she had to hold the small small sink for support as she bent over to drink straight from the tap, sluicing the water around her mouth to help her spit out the last remnants of regurgitated slime. After drying her mouth with her hand, she grabbed the small bottle of pine disinfectant peeking at her from behind the toilet pan and she splashed some of it into the bowl before closing the lid. She stared for a moment at her reflection in the small mirror that hung above the sink but all she saw there was defeat so she turned away and made her way out of the small closet, heading at last for the sanctuary of her bedroom, to wait alone for her final reckoning.

***

"Helen," the voice seemed distant, "come on, wake up." It came again but this time it was louder. "Helen, wake up, come on now."

The room shook and Helen jerked awake, grabbing the hand pressing down on her shoulder. "What is it, what's wrong?" She tried to sit up but the hand held her down and she began to panic. "Get off me, what's happening?"

"It is all right, come on, it is me," Ingrid was on the bed, one hand on Helen's shoulder and the other resting on her waist, "nothing is wrong but I need you to wake up now."

Helen blinked several times to help her eyes focus, then she shook her head, realising where she was and remembering how she got there. She released her grip on Ingrid's hand and stared up at her in silence.

Ingrid smiled and pushed some hair away from Helen's face. "Oskar told me you had too much ice-cream and you were sick."

"I don't think it was just the ice-cream," said Helen, gazing at Ingrid's pale face, and knowing at first glance Oskar had told her about more than she said which meant the moment she dreaded had arrived. She had no choice but to ask the question. "What else did he tell you."

"Everything," Ingrid didn't look away, "and he is upset and worried because he believes I will now throw you out and it will be his fault because he knows about our relationship." As she said this, she moved her hand further around Helen's waist to her back. "He gave me a lecture on love being love and said there should be no shame in it. I am so proud of him you know," she smiled again, "I forget sometimes he is almost a man and then he does something to remind me."

"I thought we would be over too," said Helen, feeling her hopes rise, "and I know it's all been a little bit fast for you, previous experiences aside."

224

"Yes it has been a little bit fast," Ingrid gave a quiet laugh, "it has been like a hurricane, you have been like a hurricane," she began to rub Helen's back, "and you have turned my life on its head and nothing in it is normal anymore, even I am not normal now."

"Normal?" Helen bristled at the word and slid Ingrid's hand off her back before sitting up and pushing herself against the headboard. "What do you mean by normal?"

Ingrid sighed and reached out, taking Helen's hand. "Do not do this."

Helen pulled her hand away, shaking her head. "No, I want to know what you mean by that."

"Stop it, please Helen."

"No, I won't stop, because you think I'm not normal and now you think you're not normal either, I don't believe I'm hearing this." Helen felt her heart pounding in her chest and her eyes began to sting. "How can you say that about us?"

Ingrid shuffled herself further up the bed then leaned over, resting her weight on one arm and positioning herself face-to-face with Helen. She tilted her head, then smiled. "Do you remember when we met on the first day and I stormed off to the sitting room after finding Sophie draped over you?" She raised her eyebrows. "Do you remember?" She brushed Helen's face with her free hand.

"I'll never forget it," said Helen, folding her arms and setting her face in a scowl, "and by the way, I don't want to be touched right now."

Ingrid trailed her hand down from Helen's face and onto her neck. "Do you remember what I said then?"

With arms still folded, Helen shrugged. "You said quite a lot, be specific."

Ingrid began stroking Helen's neck. "On that day I said you should not tell me what I think," she looked Helen in the eye, "and yet today, you have done just that."

"And I said I didn't want to be touched," Helen held the eye contact, "and yet, you're touching bits of me."

"Yes, I know I am," Ingrid replied, "and it is nice." She shook her head and took her hand away. "What I meant when I said not normal is things are not what they are usually. My husband has,

225

I think, left me, I have two daughters in turmoil and a son who thinks he has ruined my life. That is not how I normally live."

"Why aren't you touching bits of me?" Helen unfolded her arms.

Ingrid laughed. "I plan to touch a lot more of you in a moment but first you need to listen and not speak, is that possible?"

"Of course it's possible," Helen conjured up her best hurt expression, "I'm listening, go ahead."

"I had an impression of what you would be like before we met and I dreaded the thought of you coming here," Ingrid took Helen's hand, "but, although you were almost exactly as I expected, my feelings for you were not at all what I expected and I felt drawn to you from the beginning. It frightened me then but I am no longer afraid. My life may be in turmoil and things upended but I feel able to deal with my emotions and every day it is easier. That is not normal for me."

Helen shrugged. "That's different from what I thought you meant."

"Yes, it is," said Ingrid.

"I'm sorry," Helen offered a half smile, "I spoke without thinking again. Next time I'll try to mind the gap." She gestured between the top of her head and her mouth.

"It is all right, you know it is." Ingrid squeezed her hand. "Things feel better for me just now but I need time because a lot is happening."

Helen nodded. "I understand." She took a long, deep breath, wondering how much to say but fearful of pushing too hard, too soon. In the end she decided to be truthful and to give a voice to her greatest fear. "I'm scared I'll lose you before we really get going."

"I know you are."

Helen wiped away a stray tear as it tried to escape, and she smiled. "It's fine though, I'll be fine, I promise."

Ingrid leaned over and kissed her on the chin. "That is good, because I need more than anything for you to be all right." She kissed her on the chin again. "Michael is staying over tonight, and he and Sophie are working things out which you will see for yourself when we go downstairs for dinner. We have ordered Chinese food."

226

Helen shook her head. "I don't know if I can manage any dinner, I've been sick and I was all alone and it was terrible."

"Then you are lucky I am a nurse," Ingrid raised an eyebrow, "I can do things to make you feel better."

Helen glanced over towards the bedroom door and then back. "Are you saying you want to make me feel better right now?"

"I locked the door when I came in here," Ingrid bit at her bottom lip then glanced at her watch, "and dinner will not arrive for at least another hour."

Helen grinned and closed her eyes. "Nurse, I'm all hot, I think my temperature might be high."

"That is awful," said Ingrid, smiling, "let me feel if you are hot to the touch."

Helen gasped and opened her eyes wide. "Is that where you'd put your hand to take a temperature? What kind of nurse are you?"

"The type of nurse who now has fifty-nine minutes to help you, but if you want to talk instead then..." Ingrid gave a non-committal shrug.

"No, no, silence is golden." Helen grinned as she pushed herself across the bed, making space and feeling blessed by the Gods as Ingrid slid alongside her.

"Remember now," said Ingrid, "you must be quiet."

"Yes, nurse." Helen smiled and closed her eyes.

***

Helen took a rushed, last-minute shower to expunge any trace of Ingrid's perfume from her skin and as a result, she was the last person to arrive for dinner. She didn't envisage eating much but felt reasonably positive that a few crispy wontons wouldn't kill her, although having to creep through a minefield of small talk with Sophie and Michael, very well might. It would be awkward she knew, perhaps even painful, but, buoyed by Ingrid's reassurances, she felt strong enough to battle through it.

"Hey Helen." Oskar smiled as she approached the table and he moved from the seat next to Ingrid to an empty one at the top of the table. "You sit beside mum."

"Thanks," said Helen, smiling back at him, worried he was making things obvious but conceding he might be protecting her from herself by making it impossible for her to moon at Ingrid over the table. She glanced at him as she sat down, wondering if his thinking was so sophisticated as to have thought things through in terms of seating positions. It was possible she supposed, given how he picked up on the way she looked at his mother despite her own belief she was being discreet. She decided to ask him later.

"I heard you've been sick again," said Sophie, her voice dripping with scorn.

"Yeah," said Helen, "I ate too much ice-cream and you know me, can't handle my desserts." She forced a smile. "How are you both doing?"

"We're going to be fine and I'll be going home," Sophie replied, "we were talking about it before you came down." She glanced at Michael and he nodded. "We have some other news too."

"Is it good news?" Ingrid gestured to Helen to help herself to the food in the opened containers, "I would like some good news I think."

"It's about the baby," said Michael as he took Sophie's hand, "we know what sex it is."

"Can they tell so soon?" Oskar looked at Sophie, his eyes widening "I thought it would be ages before you would know."

"I'm almost at sixteen weeks" said Sophie, "so yes, they can tell." She looked at everyone around the table. "Do you all want to know?"

"Yes, I would love to know," said Ingrid, a huge smile on her face, "this will be my first grandchild and it would be nice to be able to pick up little things knowing who I am buying for."

Sophie put her fork down and looked at Oskar, who nodded his agreement. "Okay then, we're having a little...girl," she beamed a huge smile at everyone and squeezed Michael's hand, "we've decided what her name's going to be too."

"Oh Sophie." Ingrid got up and hurried around the table, giving Sophie a tight hug when she arrived beside her. "I am so pleased," she looked at Michael, "for both of you."

Oskar leaned over and patted Sophie's arm. "Congratulations sis, if you're lucky she'll have my good looks." He winked at her and then gave Michael the hint of a smile.

"So, are you going to tell us what her name will be?" said

Ingrid, putting a hand on Michael's shoulder, "you do not have to if you do not want to of course."

"It's fine," said Sophie, "we want you to know." She glanced at Oskar and then up at Ingrid. "We want to call her Freya, after gran."

Ingrid at once took a deep breath and tears filled her eyes. "That is lovely, it is a beautiful name." She bent and gave Sophie another, much longer, hug, and when she stood up, they both gazed at each other, their bond solid once more.

"Good choice of name," said Oskar, looking at Michael.

"Yes," Michael nodded and smiled at him although the smile was cautious, "I think it's beautiful. Sophie told me about your grandmother and it seemed right."

"Mamma would have been pleased you chose her name," said Ingrid, a hand now on Sophie's shoulder as well as Michael's. "Come on, let us have dinner now we have had such good news." She gave their shoulders a final squeeze before returning to her seat and exhorting everyone to eat.

"I'm starving," said Oskar, picking up one of the trays, "who's for wontons?"

"Me please," said Sophie with a grin.

"Me too," said Michael, "thanks Oskar."

"I will have some too," said Ingrid, "pass them around please."

When the tray of wontons reached her, Helen scooped just one onto her plate and then poured herself some of the chili sauce but her appetite, such as it was, had vanished.

"These are lush." Sophie reached over and plucked the last wonton from the tray. "Mamma, Michael and I were talking and we want you to know you can come and stay with us, you too Oskar," she glanced at him and then back to Ingrid. "I mean if you have to sell the house, I presume you will."

"Yes," Ingrid nodded, looking thoughtful, "I presume that will happen so thank you, it is good to know we will both have somewhere to go. I will be visiting my solicitor early next week so I will find out more then."

"Will you have room for us and a baby?" said Oskar, looking concerned, "I don't want to have to share a room with mum, she snores you know."

"I do *not!*" Ingrid looked affronted and reached over, trying to slap Oskar's hand but he was too quick and her hand only skimmed him.

"We have four bedrooms so don't worry," said Sophie, laughing, "in fact why don't both of you come and stay over Christmas and try it out?" She looked around to Michael and he nodded.

"That would be lovely," said Ingrid, laughing, "although it will only be me who comes to stay as I will have murdered your brother by then." She looked at Oskar and raised her eyebrows. "Snoring. You will pay for that one."

Helen sat quietly, gnawing at her thumb as she watched the others enjoy themselves as though she wasn't there. She looked at Sophie and Michael who now seemed at ease together and she knew she would always be their spectre at the feast and that for both to be able to move on, she would have to leave. Just at that moment, Oskar's loud guffaw caught her attention and she turned to watch him laughing, and smiled to herself, wondering, what scrapes they would have found themselves in and hoping he would find a way to evolve from his current incarnation as a half-finished man. Then, of course, there was Ingrid, and Helen risked a sideways glance in her direction but didn't hold it beyond a second or two. If anyone other than Oskar discovered what had gone on between them, then it was likely Ingrid would would lose her daughter and her only grandchild because Sophie would without doubt, see it as the ultimate betrayal. No matter how painful it would be to walk away and leave Ingrid behind, Helen now knew that to be her fate. It was over and she would be going home.

"What will you be doing at Christmas, Helen?" It was Sophie, and the sound of her voice brought Helen back from her thoughts.

"I'm not sure yet."

"Could Helen not come here at Christmas?" said Oskar, "I mean to your place Sophe."

Helen glanced up and over to Oskar and gave him a thin smile. He was still fighting for her, not realising the battle was over, and she loved him for it.

Sophie's voice was sharp. "She won't be here at Christmas, so no."

Helen realised the moment was at hand and she took a breath, then lifted her head to look at everyone around the table. "Actually, Helen won't be here after tonight," she licked her lips, "I'm going home." Turning to Ingrid, she held her gaze for a moment.

"You are going home tomorrow?" Ingrid's voice was steady and gave nothing away.

"Yes, I am. I'll be able to pick up a seat on the early flight or if not, I'll go next day." She rubbed at her mouth. "If it's next day I'll book into a hotel at the airport, I won't stay here another night."

"Why are you going?" said Oskar, his voice breaking up.

Helen smiled as she summoned the bear for one final curtain call. "I've outstayed my welcome, and I've realised nobody wants me here because I'm a problem for all sorts of reasons." She looked at each of them in turn, giving them an opportunity to say it wasn't so but nobody spoke. "For what it's worth, I don't think I'm the same person I was when I arrived ,which will be good for me in the future, but for now, I'm dying inside because for the first time in my life I'm about to lose something very special, something I never imagined I would ever find."

"Don't go then." Oskar's eyes were wide he was close to tears.

Helen knew she wasn't going to last much longer herself without losing her composure so she pushed on. "I have to go Oskar, but I'll never forget you, or anyone here, and I'll miss all of you very much."

"I will be very sorry to see you leave," said Ingrid, her voice cracking and her face drawn.

Helen smiled at her. "But you understand why I have to go, don't you?"

"I do, but I will miss you very much." A single tear rolled down and over Ingrid's cheek.

"You need to all promise me something." Helen pushed her chair back and stood. "Tomorrow morning I'll be leaving early, but please, don't be there, because if you are then I won't be able to cope." She turned her back on Michael and Sophie, meeting Ingrid's eyes for the last time. "I love you." She mouthed the words silently and for a second she thought it was going to be all right when Ingrid reached out as if to stop her leaving, but she pulled it back, and it was over. Helen dropped her gaze and walked around the table, leaving thre kitchen without looking back.

***

It was cold and still pitch black when the taxi pulled up at the house and Helen shivered as she helped the driver load the bags. She wasn't sure if it was the cold making her shudder, she suspected it wasn't, but the December chill wasn't helping.

"Just you darlin'?" The taxi driver looked at her and smiled.

Helen nodded. "Yeah, just me." She stepped around him and settled into the back seat of the car, locking the seatbelt in place then leaning back with her eyes closed. She felt the car shift as the driver got in, then the engine started and she knew it was time. As they started off down the street, Helen turned to look back at the house, smiling to herself through the tears. She never saw it again.

Chapter Seventeen

Happy Frank's Day

She lay on the couch with her eyes closed, enjoying the coolness of the room and the metronomic ticking of the large, brass clock on the wall to her left, soothed by the sound it made, a regular and solid, tick, tick, tick like the echo of her heartbeat.

"They gave me a hundred bucks for the gun," Helen opened her eyes and looked over to the woman sitting in the brown, leather chair, "but to be honest, I would have paid them double to take it."

"How did it make you feel?" The woman looked up from what she was writing.

"Safe, it made me feel safe not having it the house anymore but maybe a little bit sad too because it was my dad's."

"Since then, have you had the dream?"

Helen closed her eyes again and clenched her hands. "Yeah," she said, "twice this week, so far."

"Is it the same or has anything changed?" The woman's voice was steady and clear.

"Maybe a fraction different but more or less the same."

The woman stopped writing and leaned forward in the chair. "Tell me it again and tell me what's different now."

"Okay," said Helen, "I'm in the bedroom, not my own, the one in the house, Ingrid's house." She stopped and took several slow, deep breaths, forcing herself to unclench her hands. "I'm lying down but I hear a noise outside so I get up and look out the window and he's there, the guy in the coat, and the wind's blowing his coat back and it's flapping like crazy but I see it's not a man at all, it's me but my face is different, it's all twisted and rotten." She fell silent, trying to pick up the ticking of the clock over the sound of her own hammering heart.

"What happens next?" said the woman.

Helen opened her eyes again and looked over at the woman.

"I don't think I can."

"Try, please, I think we're making progress here."

"All right. I'm looking down at me, at this thing, and then it starts to move towards the house and I know it's coming inside and if it gets in..." Helen felt her voice getting higher and she paused, letting herself settle before going on. "I know I can't let it in, so I run to the nightstand and take the gun from the top drawer and then I run to the door, but it's locked. I'm stuck in the room."

The woman nodded. "Keep going, you're doing well."

"This time it's different at the door because I see a key in the lock although I know there can't be because it's not the type of lock the door had, but there it is, so I make a grab for it because I know I can get down there and I can save them."

"What happens when you open the door?"

"I don't." Helen clasped her hands and rested them on her forehead. "I drop the key. I'm trying so hard to get it and open the door, that I drop the fucking key and it slips under the door."

The woman shuffled her papers and bundled them together before placing them on the adjacent desk. "What happens then?"

"I can hear screaming, and that thing, it's laughing but it's not a normal laugh, it's all gurgling and wet sounding and that's when I do it," Helen made the shape of a gun with her right hand and placed it in her mouth, mimicking a trigger pull, "that's when I always do it."

"And then you wake up?"

"Then I wake up." Helen released a slow breath. "My dad was a sleepwalker you know," she smiled, "I always thought it was funny because he would be rummaging in the fridge at one in the morning, and he would make weird sandwiches then eat them and go back to bed and he never remembered doing it."

"Have you ever had an episode of sleepwalking?

Helen pushed herself up on the couch and shrugged her shoulders. "I don't think so but I live alone, so I wouldn't know. I didn't want to take a chance though."

"Why are you crying?" the woman gestured to a box of tissues sitting on the table directly to Helen's right, "are you thinking about your dad?"

Helen shook her head and took a tissue from the box before

wiping her face and blowing her nose. "It's not dad," she sniffed then took another tissue, "it's his sandwich, it reminded me of another sandwich and..."

The woman reached over to the desk, picking up a pen and writing something in her notes. "This other sandwich has some significance for you so we can pick up on it next week but I'll book you in for a double session as it's something you haven't talked about yet." She looked at the clock. "How do you feel?"

Helen started dabbing her eyes and cheeks with the second tissue. "Like I'm dead, same as I've felt every day for the last year." She smiled at the woman, "well, maybe not quite so bad but I think I should have come here a lot sooner than I did." She stood up and the woman opposite did the same before they met in the middle and shook hands. "Thanks doc, I'll see you next week." Helen turned and walked to the door but she stopped before she opened it, and looked back. "It's today, you know, Ingrid's birthday, she's sixty-four."

"Is this something you want to discuss next week?" The woman reached for her pen again.

"No," said Helen, shaking her head, "I just wanted to tell someone, that's all." She nodded a goodbye and left the room and within a few minutes she was back in her car and heading home.

***

Helen sat on her porch sipping peppermint tea, feeling nauseous and exhausted, her usual condition after one of her sessions. The only thing that helped to settle the nausea was peppermint tea, a suggestion from a security guy on campus who she'd got talking to one day when the fire alarm went off by mistake and they had evacuated her building. She reminded herself to say thanks next time she saw him. After finishing the tea, she would go upstairs to her bedroom, making sure she wedged the door open, then she would lie down and sleep for a couple of hours. With luck it would be a dreamless sleep and when she woke, and if her nausea had abated, she would have a late lunch. That was her routine for one day every week, and it had been like that now for almost six months.

Progress had been slow in the beginning and it took three sessions before Helen had managed to say anything at all, but only a few weeks later, she had been able to talk about the dream for the first time. From then on, she hadn't been able to shut up and next week's double session wasn't the first time she'd needed extra time. That, however, was the only progress there had been. She could talk about it, most of it, but there was no resolution, no chink of light to give rise to optimism for any sort of normal future.

Most of her friends had drifted off and she didn't blame them as they didn't know how to cope with the person who returned from England. She knew they did their best to help, but, one by one they gave up, writing her off as a lost cause. Work wasn't much better and after four miserable months, during which she was irritable and angry with almost everyone, the staff counsellor suggested a sabbatical and she agreed. She now had until the end of the academic year to sort herself out.

Helen drank the dregs of her tea and put the cup on the table at her side. It was time for a sleep. She had just reached the door, when the sound of a car horn prompted her to turn around, and, despite her weariness, she couldn't help but smile. It was Sonny, the only one who hadn't deserted her, and as he was laden with cookies and beer, she knew her nap would have to wait.

Sonny stopped at the mailbox, collected a handful of letters and then darted up the path. "Hello my angel, how are we today?"

Helen looked him up and down, taking in the incongruity of his outdoor clothing, which included flip flops and denim shorts, with the fact it was December. "Flip flops and shorts, are you crazy?"

"Darling, it's fifty-six degrees out here, anything over fifty and this body is on display," he gave her a dazzling smile, "anyway, do you know what day it is?"

Helen at once thought of Ingrid but she knew it wasn't what he meant. "I'm not standing here all day guessing, just tell me."

"I've just been in your mailbox, so that means...it's Frank's Day!"

Helen laughed, she couldn't help herself. Frank's Day was what they called the day each year when uncle Frank's Christmas card arrived and they always made it a bit special with takeout and beer and, depending on the date, the erection of the Christmas tree. "He's getting earlier every damn year," she said, "he must have posted this in August."

"The man is organized," said Sonny, don't fault him for it and he's super organized this year too," he skipped up the stairs, "you've got two cards."

Helen held the door open and let Sonny enter first. "I bet it's Andrew, he'll have got him to do a separate one, the man's crazy."

"Where will I put these," said Sonny?"

"Mail on the sofa, beer in the fridge and leave the cookies," Helen winked at him, "they'll work with the coffee you're making."

Sonny appeared shocked. "So, we're not having beer? On Frank's Day?"

Helen looked at her watch. "It's ten-thirty in the morning and I'm not long back from having my head shredded, it's not beer time."

"Party pooper." Sonny looked at Helen and sucked at his teeth. "You know what'll happen if you eat cookies after a session."

"I know," Helen said, "but I'll risk it, and I promise, I'll try to hold on to them until after you leave."

Sonny was already heading towards the kitchen and he shouted back. "Make sure you do, these flip flops cost me a hundred bucks and I don't want them ruined."

Helen shook her head and glanced down at the sofa where Sonny had dropped the mail, spotting two coloured envelopes amongst the bills and credit card offers. She had to hand it to Frank, he always delivered although you could never be sure of the actual delivery date which meant Frank's Day was a lot like Easter; it moved around.

Sonny came back with two mugs of coffee and they both flopped on the other sofa with the box of cookies the only thing separating them.

"How was it today?" Sonny took his first cookie and dunked it into the coffee before cramming it into his mouth.

Helen watched him in fascination. He had the figure of a gymnast but put cookies away at a rate capable of shaming the Cookie Monster. "Awful is what it was." She picked up a cookie and took a bite, following it up with a mouthful of coffee.

Sonny raised his eyebrows. "Did you talk about the night in question?"

"No, I did not."

"Will you be talking about it next week?" Sonny lifted another cookie and repeated his dunk and inhale manoeuvre from before.

"No, next week I'll be talking about the sandwich."

Sonny stopped in mid chew and nodded his approval. After he swallowed, he nodded again. "Yes, you need to talk about that, it's important," he wiped his mouth, "did you cry about the sandwich?"

"No, but I cried about the word sandwich, if that helps."

"It does," said Sonny, but not in a good way." He put his coffee down and turned to Helen. "Are you still talking about that fucking dream? I bet you are." He pursed his lips and waited for the official answer.

Helen looked down at her feet and nodded. "You're obsessed," she said, "you know that, don't you?"

"Not as obsessed as your so-called therapist is, she's stiffing you honey."

"She is not stiffing me. I'm just slow."

Sonny slapped is hands together in frustration. "Tell me, what progress have you made?"

Helen looked up and nodded. "Okay," she said, "how about I no longer want to die, is that progress enough for you or do you want more?"

"No, it's great," Sonny threw his hands in the air, "if you die it'll be a waste of your time anyway because you'll be back in this house before you know it, only you'll be haunting it instead of living in it." He reached over and grabbed one of Helen's hands. "Honey, you have unfinished business and you know that's why you can't move on."

Helen waved a hand at him. "I wish you'd brought your counselling skills here earlier, you would've saved me a hundred and fifty bucks."

Sonny gasped and flicked his hair with his free hand before looking away, pouting, and Helen did the same, matching his pose. They sat that way for a few seconds before looking back at each other, both struggling not to laugh. Helen couldn't hold it and was the first to go.

"Fuck you, Sonny." She laughed and gave him the finger.

"You do know we wouldn't, not with each other," he wore a winner's smile, "something would get in the way and believe me, it's a big something." He squeezed Helen's hand and winked at her but his smile faded. "Honey I'm being serious, the woman's shilling you big time," he shook his head and pursed his lips again, "we need to find a way you can finish your business, it's the only thing that'll help you."

"Oh Sonny, no," Helen shook her head, "I'm hardly coping as it is, I couldn't go back into that blind, I just couldn't."

"You think I don't know that? Honey, I see you every week and every week it's the same. You don't eat right and you're still not sleeping. It's hard to watch." Sonny shook his head.

"Sleeping's the worst," said Helen, shuddering, "it's terrible and I sometimes think I'd be ok if it wasn't for the nights. They're the worst."

"You know you need to face this down," Sonny paused, "I know you don't want to, but that's a different thing, isn't it?" He released her hand and picked up his coffee again before liberating another cookie from the box. "Question, how many times have you done it today?" he raised an eyebrow and nibbled at the edge of his cookie, "and don't hit me with any crap, you know what I'm asking."

"Three times. I was planning to do it again when you arrived." Helen put her cup on the floor and folded her arms. "You know I don't like talking about it."

"Uh-huh. How many times would you do it in an entire day?" Sonny cupped his own face with a hand and waited for the answer.

Helen shrugged her shoulders. "I'm not sure, I think I might have it down to ten times. Every day."

"You have to go cold turkey."

"No way," said Helen. This was her line in the sand and nobody, not even Sonny, was crossing it. One thing kept her going and she wasn't letting anyone take it from her.

"It would help you to move on." Sonny smiled. "How many do you have?"

"Twenty-one and don't ask me to delete any, I'm keeping

them all." Helen flicked a glance at her friend and she sighed. "If I delete them, I'm scared I'll forget what she looks like and yes, I do look at them a lot but I've cut it back, so that's progress."

Sonny looked at his watch. "We need to talk more but right now I need to be in the salon, I skipped out to come and see you but I have a colour arriving in twenty, so it's ciao for now I'm afraid." He picked up another cookie to go. "I'll be back tonight and we'll crack some beers for Frank's day and talk the ass out of this, I promise." He leaned over and kissed Helen on both cheeks.

"Do me a favour," Helen pointed to the other sofa, "throw the mail over before you go."

Sonny shuffled over and grabbed the mail, sorting his feet back into his flip flops as he did so, and dropping the bundle down beside Helen. "See you later, babe."

As Sonny headed for the door, Helen shouted after him and he stopped. "Tell me something," she pointed at his feet, "did you really pay a hundred bucks for those? I think I saw similar in Walmart for five."

Sonny held both hands up. "I am now leaving. I will not stay here to be insulted." With that he skipped out of view.

As she heard the outside door close, Helen looked down at the bundle of mail, wondering whether to open it now or leave it until after she'd slept. The thought of a warm bed was tempting but so was opening Frank's card which might, or might not, contain a final letter from her mother. She had prepared herself for there being a letter although she had no plans to read it if it was there, not yet. For the time being it would go in the box with the others until the time was right. She looked down at the mail again and yawned, but as tired as she was, she couldn't resist it, so she plucked the red envelope from the bundle, pulling it open and retrieving the contents. It was the usual Frank-style card, traditional and cheerful, a little robin sitting on a post-box which made Helen smile as she opened it to read the greeting. At the same time, she glanced inside the envelope and saw there was no letter from her mother, which didn't come as much of a surprise although it left her feeling a little bit sadder than she had imagined it would. She supposed it was just another thing at an end.

Helen laid the card on her lap and rummaged in the cookie box until she found what she was looking for; pecan and maple with white chocolate chips. She broke off half and popped it in her mouth, savouring the sweet, nutty taste, and she picked up Frank's card again to check the greeting. When she had glanced at it the first time, something caught her eye and now she looked again, she realised the card was from Frank, Enid *and* her brother. Helen looked down at the mail again, focusing on the large blue envelope with the colourful stamps, which now, couldn't be from Andrew. Puzzled, she reached over and excised it from the bundle, pulling it over for closer inspection and as she did so, she felt her stomach lurch and a cold, tingling sensation sweep over her head, all the way down to her feet. The stamps showed the country of origin as Sweden.

When Helen got back from cleaning herself up and rinsing out her mouth, the envelope was still lying on the floor. She had dropped it when making her run for the bathroom and now she picked it up and walked over to the table next to the window, dragging out a chair and sitting down. Turning it over in her hands and holding it up to her face, Helen sighed as she inhaled the faint smell of Ingrid's perfume. The aroma wasn't overpowering but the effect of it was and after a few seconds, she put envelope down, knowing from the weight, that it didn't contain only a card.

There was no dubiety, and Helen knew she would open the card and any letter it might contain, but right there in the moment, she hesitated, recognising her future lay in the balance. With one final deep breath, she took the envelope from the table and tore it open, pulling out a card and with it, a smaller envelope. She flicked beyond the picture on the front of the card without looking at it, eager to see the greeting inside and at the sight of what was written, she began to cry.

After she stopped sobbing, Helen went to the fridge and came back to the table with a bottle of the beer Sonny had brought, not caring it was still morning and not caring if she had to go back for second helpings, because this was a special day. She picked up the card again and read the greeting once more, this time without tears. It was just one line: *to Helen, the little bear, lots of love from Ingrid and Oskar.* The words had overwhelmed her and even looking at them again now, they had lost none of their potency. Eager to proceed, she took a swig from her bottle then picked up the smaller envelope, opening it with care and removing the letter it contained. She counted the pages, ten in all and she noticed at the top of the first page there was a label with a Swedish address and phone number. She took another drink of beer, her heart pounding, and then she began to read.

My dearest Helen

I hope this letter finds you well or perhaps I should say, I hope you find it, and the generosity of spirit to wish to read it. I would understand if you did not want to hear from me but in my heart, there remains hope you will grant me one opportunity to make good what I did.

This is the fourth time I have written the letter. For the first three, I made a list of all I wanted to tell you but the result was clinical and Oskar made me discard them and begin again. So, for this letter, hopefully the final version, I have attempted to set free my inner bear and do as you would do, and just talk.

There is so much to tell you but before I do so, I need to explain why I did not stop you leaving me that night. I think of it always, over and over and believe me, I have cried an ocean over you. No matter what may happen, I will never be able to erase the stain I feel on my soul for my lack of courage that evening and it is something I will carry with me always. I have thought for a long time about how to explain it to you, but it is in fact a simple thing; I was afraid. I was so afraid to reach out and tell you to stay because I believed it would mean the loss of everything I had left. Looking back now I think my ability to cope failed me at a vital time, and all that had gone before, overwhelmed me. My husband had left me (I am imagining your reaction to those words and when I do, I can almost hear your voice!) I had no income and no idea what would happen. Worst of all, I seemed to have lost one daughter and if I had stopped you, I knew I would have lost my Sophie and any chance to see my granddaughter. No matter what Sophie chooses to admit to herself, I believe she loved you very much. So, I made a choice and I let you go. It was a grievous mistake for which I hope you can find forgiveness but you looked broken that night so I know I am asking a lot of you. However, before you left, you told me you loved me and it is on this I have pinned all my hopes. Do you still feel the same?

I have read back what I have written and I think it is enough for you to understand how I felt then and how I feel today. I cannot wish hard enough for you to you read this and that I hear from you soon.

Helen cried over every word, even at the third reading, and she sat rubbing at her eyes, the remainder of the letter held tight in a trembling hand. It was such an explosive release from the wretchedness within her that she felt compelled to read the words again and then for a third time, panic stricken she might have misread it and her nightmare would continue. After pouring over the text for the third time, re-reading some sections, she accepted it for what it was; a chance to live again. She considered getting another beer to help her through the rest of the letter but didn't want to waste as much as a minute and so, she continued to read.

I have mentioned Sophie and of course there is news of her and the baby. Little Freya was born in May and is now six-months old. As her grandmother of course I think she is beautiful but I am sure you would think so too. She looks very like Sophie and Michael too, (they remain together) but Oskar has asked me to tell you not to worry about that, as she has inherited her good looks from him. Quite how he thinks this is possible I have not dared to ask. I did not tell Sophie about our relationship until some weeks after Freya was born. She was angry of course and very hurt. I did not see her or the baby for over a month, but she came back to me in the end and we are fine. You will be interested to know it was Sophie who encouraged me to contact you and I hope this gives you the same comfort it does me. Of course, there is a lot more to this part of the story but that is for telling face-to-face when I see you. I will see you again, I hope.

As for Gary, I have not seen him since the night of my last birthday. I petitioned for divorce this summer on the grounds of adultery (I refuse to feel guilty) and he has not contested it. My solicitor has managed to get me a generous settlement and along with the proceeds from the sale of the house, I will be solvent. My final decree is next month now everything has settled.

This of course leads me on to where I am living now, with Oskar. I decided I would return to Sweden and live in my mother's house. The house became mine when she died and it had been vacant since then. There are many reasons why I did not sell it at the time but sometimes I wonder if I knew one day I would need somewhere to go. It is a nice house, in need of attention of course, but we are getting there one day at a time and Oskar has been a great help along with his new friend Theo.

As for Oskar, what can I say? He has a new friend, Theo, in fact he has many new friends, and he spends far more time outside his bedroom than he ever did in England. His Swedish is improving and he has started working in a local firm and is learning to be a carpenter. So far, he has made me four chopping boards; it is early days. I am to tell you he has found himself a nice girlfriend and she did not ask him for any photographs. He tells me you will know what this means and I must not to ask you about it. Of course, I will ask you about it when I see you, if you want to see me, of course. I hope you do, more than I can tell you.

So, this is my news, it is a lot of course but it is all the bigger things to have happened. I will tell you more when you come over. Would you like to come over, for Christmas perhaps? We are planning to put up our Christmas tree on 10th December and I have sent this letter in time to reach you before then, I hope. Sophie and Michael will be here with Freya but the house has room for a little bear. I will always have room for a little bear. I have put my telephone number at the top of this letter. If you phone, please do not worry about the time difference. Think about it, but do not worry about it. I would be so happy to hear your voice at any time.

I will leave it there and maybe, if you want to, I will see you soon again. Until then I will be yours, always.

With all my love
Ingrid

Before she had put the last sheet of paper on the table, Helen had taken out her phone and punched in the number written at the top of the letter, taking three attempts to get it right as she was shaking all over. As it was almost noon in San Francisco it would be mid evening in Stockholm and not only that, it would still be Ingrid's birthday. She had no idea what she would say, in fact she had no idea if she would be able to speak at all, but she knew she had to call, even if it was just to let Ingrid know she hadn't put her letter in a box in the attic. Her finger hovered over the green button, still shaking, like the rest of her body. She stood up and took a deep breath, then pressed call.

At the fourth ring, Helen was becoming worried, but Ingrid answered on the fifth ring.

"Ingrid, it's me, Helen."

"It is *you*. You read my letter."

Helen's voice shook. "I did and I'm coming over, so don't you dare put that tree up without me."

"I am so sorry for that night, so sorry. I cannot believe this, oh Helen, I cannot wait to see you."

"Ingrid."

"What is it?"

"Happy birthday." Helen smiled. At last, she was going home for Christmas.

Printed in Great Britain
by Amazon